DARK
FAE

AURORA ACADEMY

DARK FAE

CAROLINE PECKHAM & SUSANNE VALENTI

WELCOME TO AURORA ACADEMY

Please take note of where The Lunar Brotherhood and Oscura Clan have claimed turf to ensure you don't cross into their territory unintentionally. Faculty will not be held responsible for gang maiming or disembowelment.

Have a great term!

Lake Tempest

Lunar Pit

The Capella Observatory

The Dead Shed

The Weeping Well

Rige

The Cafaeteria

Kipling Emporium

The Acrux Courtyard

Altair Halls

Aurora Academy

ELISE

CHAPTER ONE

*D*amn, I love the sound of screaming in the moonlight.

    I stalked a slow circle around my prey, adrenaline coursing through my limbs. My fangs were lengthening with it, demanding I take a taste of him, but I didn't. And I wouldn't. Not while he had that poison coursing through his veins. A piece of shit like him would likely taste like piss on a day when he wasn't off his face on Killblaze anyway. The damn drug was making him delirious though. The pain I was dishing out was resulting in laughter as often as screams.

    Just gotta push harder then, Elise. For Gareth.

    I ran my tongue over my fangs, savouring the sound of his heartbeat as it pounded a panicked tune on the breeze. Yeah he was high as fuck, but he was also terrified of the psycho bitch who had hauled him out of his car, wrapped him in a bubble of air magic and transported him to this backwater alley behind the closed down burger shack on the outskirts of town. I hadn't been sure if I'd have enough magic to get him the whole way here, but I'd done it. It was a damn shame I couldn't drink from him though; I really could have used the magical top up I'd gain by draining his power while I took a drink of sweet, sweet blood.

I guessed I'd just have to find some unsuspecting asshole to drain on my way home to get my fix. For now, I needed to focus on dragging the answers I needed from this pathetic excuse for a man who was currently trying to crawl away across the darkened sidewalk.

I shot past him with my Vampire speed, coming to a halt right before him so that he gasped in horror, his rancid breath washing over my black boots.

He looked up at me, probably wondering what a skinny girl with white blonde hair down to her ass and freckles spattering her nose was doing dragging him into the dark in the middle of the night. But he was about to find out why he shouldn't judge a book by its cover if he thought I looked weak. Pain and grief had carved anything soft and gentle out of me. This was all I had now. My thirst for vengeance was even sharper than my thirst for blood. And I'd get it no matter the cost.

I didn't bother to contain my sneer as I looked down at the asshole who blinked up at me through red-rimmed eyes.

"Fucking bloodsucker," he snarled but there was no real venom in it.

In all honesty I wasn't sure why he was still in his Fae form. Werewolves were usually quick to shift into their Order form at the slightest hint of trouble, but this guy was scrambling across the piss-stained concrete like a worm trying to escape a blackbird. But I was no blackbird. I was his worst fucking nightmare. I just wished he'd realised it before my brother had to die.

I'd seen the signs, I should have done more. I should have read the cards. I should have...

Back the fuck up, Elise, you're here to get answers from this bottom feeder not wallow in self pity again.

One thing I'd learned for sure in the month since the Solarid Meteor Shower when Gareth's body had been found in the dingy corner of that godforsaken academy, was that no one else was going to get to the bottom of what had happened to him. No one else gave a shit about the truth.

The Fae Investigation Bureau had dismissed his death as an accidental overdose even though I'd told them straight that he'd never touched that shit. And despite the pitying looks the FIB officers had given me in response, like they felt sorry for my ignorant ass believing the best of my brother, I knew I was right about that. Gareth was a lot of things, but he wasn't a goddamn junkie. He was a Pegasus for the stars' sake; he could get a better high flying through a rainbow than he'd get from some drug.

Besides, he'd never waste money like that. Or his life. He knew just as well as I did that there was only one way to claw your way out of the cesspit we'd been born into. And that sure as shit wasn't through snorting the weird ass Fae drugs which were probably being pedalled by the gangs at his school.

Just thinking of how proud Mom had been when he'd gotten in to Aurora Academy, how much it had meant to her that he would be getting a chance to better himself, I knew in my bones he wouldn't have let her down like that. He'd gone there to earn a better life for all of us. He wouldn't have started taking Killblaze. No fucking way.

I hadn't been as lucky as him. I'd spent the last year and a half attending our local high school with no boarding facilities and no fancy ass classes on defining your inner Fae, *whatever the hell that was supposed to mean*. And he'd known exactly what that opportunity was worth. Aurora Academy may have been one of the lowest ranking academies in Solaria, but it was still an honest-to-shit *academy*. And everyone knew that even a piss poor academy education was ten times better than a high school one. He'd have left that place with options people like us could only dream of. He'd even managed to land a full scholarship from the Rising Sun Foundation which was designed to give the best of us gutter kids a shot at an Academy Education. And Gareth really was the best of us.

Of course I was smart enough to take the entrance tests too. Book smart, computer smart, street smart, people smart. But I'd known that Mom couldn't cope with the two of us being away at an academy and leaving her on her own. So I'd never even applied to one, knowing he needed it more than me. That he deserved it more too. He was a better person in his sleep than I ever could have hoped to become. And now all of that was worth nothing. He'd made it to his Junior year and ended up dead. *Accidental overdose.* Fuck that. Someone in that academy had killed him and this mongrel was the first piece in the puzzle for me to find out who.

"I'm not telling you anything, bitch!" Lorenzo shrieked, not for the first time.

Vampire strength sure came in handy in a pinch. I stomped on his hand as it landed on the concrete before me, a savage smile tugging at my lips as he howled in pain.

"Wanna rethink that, dipshit? Or shall I start removing fingers?"

Lorenzo rocked back onto his knees, hacked up a load of phlegm from the back of his throat and spat it at me. I shot aside with my Vampire speed before it could hit me, rounding him and catching him by the throat. He was a lanky fucker, a foot taller than me but just as skinny. I still shouldn't have been able to lift him from his feet like that, but then what was the point in having enhanced strength if I didn't use it?

Damn, I was lucky to have been born a Vampire. Right up until my magic was Awakened last year when I was eighteen, I hadn't been sure what Order I'd turn out to be. Mom was an exotic dancer and a Pegasus. She'd loved Gareth's dad which was why she'd given him his surname of Tempa. But when my dad broke her heart less than a year later, she decided to give me her own surname. She didn't like to talk about my dear departed dad with me, but it turned out he was a pretty powerful Vampire and I was lucky enough to have inherited that much from him. So he'd given me one thing I guessed.

When my powers were Awakened, my fangs snapped out as the Vampire in me awoke too. I half ripped the throat out of the guy standing next to me in a bid to drink him dry of blood and magic. It was fucking fabulous. Aside from the night I had to spend in the cell the faculty called the 'detention area' for losing control of my Order form and almost killing him. But that first taste of blood on my lips had been practically orgasmic so I hadn't complained. Worth it. Totally.

My fangs lengthened at the memory, the damn things always hardwired to my libido, though I had zero desire to take any kind of satisfaction from this mutt before me. He'd pay in blood for his involvement in my brother's death but not a drop of it would pass my lips.

"When my family finds out what you've done, they'll fucking destroy you. They'll mutilate you before you die, you'll be begging for them to end you days before they do!" he yelled before he started laughing so much that I threw him back down to the ground in disgust.

Yeah, that thought had occurred to me too, but in the grand scheme of things I'd decided to take the risk. For Gareth I'd chance it, for his dopey smile and hugs that went on too long. For the phone calls in the middle of the night because he never remembered to call at a reasonable hour before waking up feeling like shit for forgetting about me. For the way he always swore that he'd dig us out of this place and build us a better life somewhere once he graduated. For the fact that one of the assholes in that school had taken him from me and Mom. And now she just lay curled beneath the sheets, too heartbroken to face the world while the bills piled up and the days crawled by.

"I'm not scared of the Oscura Clan," I snarled, the shiver down my spine the only sign that it was a lie but he couldn't see that. "I'm ten times scarier than them."

Lorenzo coughed through a mouthful of blood where his face had impacted with the ground, it stained his teeth a rusty colour in the moonlight and the iron tang of it on the wind called to me.

"Kill me once and I'm all gone, kill me twice that might be nice, kill me three times you're getting close, but Oscura Clan will kill me *most.*" Lorenzo pushed himself to his hands and knees as he continued to babble nonsense and

I stalked forward, aiming a kick at his ribs.

My rage leant strength to my limbs and I heard bones crack beneath the force I used as he rolled away from me. The sound sent a shiver of power racing along my limbs. I shouldn't have liked it. But I did. I was a cruel, twisted creature now. And it felt good.

Before he could rise, I pressed my high heeled boot down on his throat, the stiletto just piercing the skin as he flailed beneath me.

"I hacked his emails," I hissed, leaning close as I continued to press my weight down. "I know you were meeting him that night, I know you were trying to get him to join the Oscura Clan." The bunch of psychopathic Werewolves who this asshole called family ran half of downtown Alestria and were so deep into the criminal underbelly of this city that I doubted there was a crime they weren't connected to somehow. If it wasn't for the Lunar Brotherhood meeting them blow for blow at every turn and keeping them on their toes with gang wars and rivalry, then I had to think the whole of the city and beyond would have been under their rule by now.

Fae claimed whatever power they wanted so long as they were strong enough to do so and the gangs had taken most of the power in this forgotten city of Solaria. Sure, the Celestial Council technically ruled the kingdom and it was them who set the laws which the gangs consistently flouted. But short of Lionel Acrux or any of the other pretentious assholes I saw on the news trekking down here to sort this place out in person, I didn't see it changing any time soon. People with that kind of power just didn't waste time in places like this.

"I meet lots of people. Every knows me...everyone knows my *family,*" Lorenzo growled, a little of the wolf in him showing through at last. Yeah, fucking with an Oscura - even a bottom dwelling amoeba like him - was probably a bad idea, but I was goddamn grieving and I had to get these answers. I needed to know what had happened and who was going to pay the price for it. It was tearing me apart, ripping my soul to shreds and destroying what good I had in me.

Besides, Lorenzo was off his face on Killblaze, chances were he'd think this whole exchange was a figment of his imagination come tomorrow - presuming I let him live that long. I still wasn't sure if he'd been directly involved in Gareth's death yet, but if I realised he had been then vengeance would come on swift wings. I may not have had a huge reserve of power left in me, but my magic was strong enough to steal the oxygen from his lungs until he suffocated if that was required. Although, I might have been tempted to go for something a little more violent.

"Your family aren't here now. But Gareth's is. And I'm not letting you leave here without giving me the answers I want."

Lorenzo cried out as he sprang to his feet, launching himself at me. I almost moaned in relief at the excuse to vent my rage on him.

My knuckles slammed into his face, once, twice, three times. Blood flew, curses spilled from his lips, a solid punch crashed into my gut painfully and a spike of twisted pleasure followed it. Yeah, pain was one of the only things I felt now and I was beginning to get a taste for it - but it wasn't enough.

I slammed my fist into his face again, knuckles splitting deliciously before he fell back but I caught him, keeping him on his feet by holding onto his wrist.

He swung at me again and I shot around behind him using my Vampire speed, kicking out the backs of his knees so that he crashed down onto them as I circled around to face him once more.

Grief almost split me apart as I pictured my brother on the floor, his body horribly cold and his limbs twisted. I bellowed my rage, rearing my head back as I caught him by the collar, driving my forehead down on the bridge of his nose.

I heard it crack as Lorenzo screamed in agony, toppling back to the ground beneath me as I refused to release him. Vampire strength was handy as fuck for my new calling in life.

His blood splattered my face, but I resisted the urge to lick my lips, fisting my hands in his black hoodie as I straddled him.

"Tell me what happened to him!" I snarled, losing my cool and feeling the beast within me flex her muscles as I dug into the reserves of my Order's strength.

Lorenzo started laughing maniacally. "He'd kill me worse than you! He's the King... King of the Academy. You can't begin to compare..."

I slapped him to stop the laughter, baring my fangs as his blood dripped from my face down onto his.

"You think you know nightmares?" I growled, nice and low. "You haven't even met me yet. Five minutes in my company has you bleeding in a puddle of piss, think how bad you'll feel after five hours? I want answers, *dog,* and you'll give them to me one way or another. If you're very lucky you might leave this interrogation with your life, but don't expect to keep all of your limbs."

Lorenzo stopped laughing, staring up at me with bloodshot eyes which wheeled wildly. He started twitching beneath me and I had to wonder just how much of that foul drug he'd taken before this exchange. "You're a walk in the park compared to *him*," he breathed. "And if I tell you anything at all I'll pay in more than blood and flesh."

"You *will* talk," I assured him. "Everyone has a breaking point."

"I know," he replied, a bubble of laughter escaping him again as he pressed a hand down on his chest over his heart. "Which is why I won't let you find mine."

"What?" I snapped.

Lorenzo laughed and laughed, his back arching beneath me as he put a small amount of effort into bucking me off of him. I wasn't going anywhere though.

"If you know what's good for you, you won't tug at this thread," he whispered, his eyes glimmering with a desperate kind of clarity for a moment. "I wish I never had."

"What does that mean?" I demanded.

Lorenzo's smile widened for a heartbeat then his eyes suddenly rolled back into his head and his hand fell away from his chest.

"Shit!" I cursed as I spotted the dagger of ice impaled straight through his heart.

I scrambled upright, looking down at his still body as blood pooled beneath him in a mixture of shock, outrage and simmering disappointment. He'd used his water Elemental magic to create a shard of ice to kill himself rather than risk telling me what I wanted to know.

My mind whirled, my lips parting with horror and disbelief. He'd barely told me anything, I was still just as deep in the dark as I'd been before...except...

He's the King... King of the Academy. You can't begin to compare.

So maybe all I had to do was find this King and I'd be able to get my answers. Lorenzo's fear of this so-called monarch probably should have had me running in the opposite direction. He'd chosen death rather than cross him. But I didn't feel fear anymore. The worst had happened. The only thing left to me now was rage and vengeance. And I wouldn't stop until the man responsible for killing my brother paid with his own life.

I backed up before Lorenzo's blood could stain my shoes. At least I hadn't bitten him. No one would suspect a Vampire took part in his death. It'd probably just be put down to gang violence. Add him to this week's body count.

I turned my back on Lorenzo's corpse and stalked from the shadows, leaving the blood and stench of death behind.

Maybe I hadn't gotten the answers I wanted from him, but he'd made it clear where I'd find them.

Looks like I'm transferring to Aurora Academy.

ELISE

CHAPTER TWO

TWO WEEKS LATER

I stood before the mirror in the bathroom of the crappy apartment I'd called home my entire life. Mom was gone. I'd sold the only thing she'd ever cared about: a ruby engagement ring Gareth's father had given her before he'd found his Elysian Mate and dropped her like a sack of shit. Yeah, that's how things went for Fae sometimes: one minute you're planning your life with the man you love, then the next, the constellations align just right and he finds himself standing under the stars with another woman - his one *true* love. You only get one chance to solidify that connection with them or you end up star crossed forever.

I couldn't really blame him for choosing to take his shot at true love - who wouldn't want that? But it left my mom alone. She was already pregnant with Gareth when it happened but she never told him. She just up and left, moved to this apartment, got a job stripping and...doing other things with her beauty and body for money. Then she went and fell for my dad and he disappeared too. *Poof.* Here one day, gone the next. She claimed someone had kidnapped him but it seemed more likely he didn't want to be landed with a brat and did a runner when he realised she was pregnant with me. Whatever the truth of it was, having her heart broken twice was the end for our mom, she focused on her job and her kids and never fell in love again.

It broke her. We'd always known it growing up. Something was missing from her. But no matter how bad things got, she never sold that ring. Her love for her children was almost enough to make her happy at times. Not anymore. Gareth was dead and the little bit of hope she'd clung to had died with him. She was a shell. She hadn't even noticed when I took the ring from her finger.

I'd used the money from selling it to pay for a year in a wellness centre for her on the east side of the city. Who knew that bit of jewellery had contained a priceless blood ruby rather than a bit of cut glass? But it had. And despite the asshole who bought it from me trying to rip me off, I'd managed to intimidate a decent price out of him for it.

Rule one dickhead: don't try and lie to a Vampire, I can hear your fucking heartbeat.

Maybe he could smell the stench of death on me. Maybe he'd seen the emptiness in my eyes. Or maybe I was just that damn scary now. Who knew? All that mattered was that she was safe and the centre would do what they could to bring her back to herself while I worked on getting vengeance for Gareth.

I pursed my lips as I looked at myself in the mirror. I stood in my black underwear, the tattoo which ran across my ribs reading backwards in the glass. *Even angels fall...* The words had spoken to me in my dreams the nights following Gareth's death and I'd gotten them marked onto my flesh, feeling the truth in them so viscerally it hurt.

I pulled my long, white-blonde hair over my shoulders and scowled as I raised the scissors. I'd never looked anything like Gareth; he was all dark, strong features and hooded eyes. My colouring must have come from my father. White hair, pale skin, freckles spattering my nose and bright, green eyes peering out beneath long lashes. I looked delicate, like a doll and I'd never minded that before. But now I needed to be something tougher. And I needed to be sure no one at Aurora Academy recognised me. It wasn't likely; I'd never been for a visit and Gareth had never brought friends home to meet me. We didn't look alike and we even had different surnames. But there was the chance he'd spoken about me, had pictures of me. Thankfully he always called me Ella. The only person who ever did. My heart ached a little as I realised I'd never hear him call me that again.

Come on, Ella, you need to learn to run with the big boys now.

His voice echoed in my memory, haunting my dreams. He'd never seen me as delicate; he'd always known I was fierce. And now that was *all* I'd be.

Anyway, Ella had long, blonde hair so before I headed to the academy, I'd be rectifying that.

I lifted the scissors and took a deep breath before cutting the long locks off in line with my chin. I was careful but I doubted it looked like a professional job. *Ah well.*

When my hair fell to the ground around my feet I shook my head a little, marvelling in the feeling of air on the back of my neck, the lightness of my head. The cut made my features more striking, drawing attention to my high cheekbones, full lips, wide eyes. I looked different even to me and I wasn't done yet.

I cast an eye over the bottle I'd balanced on the edge of the sink, double checking the instructions before emptying it over my hair. I worked the dye in then headed back into my bedroom to double check the bag of belongings I'd be bringing with me to Aurora Academy. My life looked pretty pathetic packed up in one big backpack like that, but there it was.

Elise Callisto: a handful of clothes, toiletries, a couple of notes from my mom and the only thing I had of real value; a binder filled with Gareth's sketches. I hadn't been able to make myself part with them. And it wasn't like he'd signed his name on them anyway. I could easily claim to have drawn them myself if anyone asked. Not that I had a lick of his talent as far as that was concerned. I'd considered having one of them tattooed onto my skin but in the end I'd decided against it. I just didn't think they'd hold the same meaning on my flesh as those pieces of paper did. He'd drawn them himself, those were his pencil strokes, his passion poured onto the page.

I did a sweep of my room, checking to see if I'd forgotten anything even though I knew I hadn't. I was just counting down the minutes on my hair dye. Counting down the seconds until I left for Aurora Academy.

It had taken a few hours on the computer in Old Sal's back office at the strip club for me to hack into the academy's databases and get them to offer me Gareth's scholarship place at the school. I was a Sophomore and he'd been a Junior but it hadn't been much of a change. No doubt starting off in the middle of the school year was only going to draw more attention to me, but that was fine. I was happy to let the spotlight shine on me when I arrived.

Let the sharks circle, I'm ready to bleed for them.

Aurora Academy loomed before me as I strode up the long, paved road to the iron gates. Why did the towering metal fences ringing this place make it seem more like a prison than a school to me?

I hitched my backpack a little higher, cocked an eyebrow at the glimmering sign which spelled out the academy's name and chewed on my cherry gum a little harder as I strolled towards the gates.

They parted magically as I reached them, no doubt recognising me and knowing I belonged. Even though I didn't. I hadn't passed the entrance exams. I hadn't had my power Awakened here. I wasn't my brother...

But here I was all the same. A fox among the wolves.

I approached the huge, gothic building in front of me, the ancient stone and towering walls casting an ominous shadow across the ground. Wide steps carved with the signs of the zodiac led the way to a set of double doors which were pushed open as I approached.

I stopped at the foot of the steps, my senses tingling as I listened with my Vampire senses to find out what I was about to face.

One steady heartbeat reached me, thumping to a tune that was just too casual to make me think I should be expecting violence. I wasn't a fool though. I tossed a shield of air magic up around me as I waited for the door to open fully, ready to defend myself against whoever was coming my way.

The doors opened and a huge guy with sun kissed skin and long, beach blonde hair stepped out. A smile tugged at the corner of his mouth as I spent a beat too long looking at him. His golden eyes trailed up from the toes of my black boots to the top of my lilac hair. I didn't miss the way his gaze lingered on my chest or the way that casual heartbeat was pounding just a little bit harder at the sight of me. Which in turn sent a zip of energy right through me.

His black blazer seemed to be having a little difficulty making it over his broad shoulders and my gaze caught on the way his biceps strained at the confinement too. His shirt was untucked, tie hanging loose and a general attitude of just-tumbled-out-of-bed hung about him. If that was the case, bed hair looked seriously good on him. Sex hair would probably look even better...

Down girl.

I held my fangs back by pure force of will as I gazed upon the first King of this school and the start of my problems. When Lorenzo had let that little nugget slip to me, I'd thought it was gold. Turned out, Aurora Academy currently held court to four Kings so although my search for answers might have been narrowed down, it was by no means going to be easy to get them from any of the men who might have them. I'd done my research well, stalked social media and found out all I could. Safe to say I recognised him easily enough and he looked even better in the flesh. After all the research I'd done, I'd concluded that the man standing before me was my least likely suspect and though I wasn't quite sure enough to rule him out yet, I didn't really think of him as the one to blame for my brother's death.

"Are you Elise Callisto?" he purred, his eyes slipping to my chest again where my shirt was giving him a fairly easy view of my breasts so I could only really blame myself.

"Who's asking?" I took the steps slowly, still chewing on my gum despite the fact the taste had gone. It calmed me though, helped me keep the fangs in place.

He scrubbed a hand over the golden stubble which lined his jaw as he assessed me. "Leon Night. Principal Greyshine sent me to be your tour guide. He has other things to do this morning, I guess. I promise I'm more fun though." Leon winked at me in that casual way that guys did when they knew just how good looking they were. And *dammit* my stomach squirmed with butterflies in response. "You're late," he added as an afterthought.

"You didn't seem to be waiting for me," I pointed out.

"I'm always late." He shrugged. "I'm a Nemean Lion Shifter, we take life slow most of the time."

I snorted a laugh as I made it to the top step and stood before him.

"Something funny?" he asked, running a hand through his golden hair. Everything about him screamed sun and sand and fire. It was captivating and more than a little alluring, but I maintained the visage of being unaffected.

"Leon the Lion?" I teased, a smirk hooking my lips up. I'd laughed out loud when I'd read it in his file during my research before coming here. His star sign was Leo too, it was too fucking funny. "Is that an unfortunate coincidence or something?"

"I come from a family of Lions actually," he said with a shrug, pushing off of the door so that he was right in my personal space, towering over me. "My mom thought it was cute."

"It is," I agreed, still teasing. "Very cute for a little lion cub."

A rumble sounded in his chest but it was more amused than annoyed; I got the feeling it would take a hell of a lot to shatter his cool facade.

"Yeah that's me alright. *Cute.*" Leon pointed the way into the dark hall and I took the hint to start walking. "Don't spread that around though, my family are supposed to be terrifying."

"Oh?" I asked, blowing a bubble with my gum like that didn't interest me at all. Of course I knew all about his family. The Nights were so powerful that they hadn't even aligned themselves with one of the gangs. They were a power of their own. In Solaria all Fae were supposed to claim their own place, fight for the position they wanted in society, and the Nights took that idea more literally than most. They were thieves. It was said that there wasn't a lock in existence that a Night couldn't pick and if you owned something they wanted, you'd be better off giving it to them than wasting your time trying to hide it. Not that I was going to let Leon know that I knew who he was.

"Yeah," he said, frowning at me like he'd never come across someone who didn't know his name before. And maybe he hadn't, but I wasn't gonna start fawning over him any time soon so he'd just have to get over it. "My mother is Safira Night. My father is Reginald Night, you know…"

I shrugged innocently. "Are they reality TV stars or something?" I asked. "'Cause I don't go in for trash TV much."

Leon chuckled and the sound made me want to smile too. There was something seriously inviting about him and I made a mental note not to get sucked in by his charm.

"No, nothing like that," he replied, not bothering to elaborate.

We started walking down a huge hallway with dark panelled wood lining the walls and burning sconces lighting the way. The smell of parchment and smoke mixed with the underlying tone of wood polish and I looked all around, drinking everything in.

"This is Altair Halls," Leon said, sounding a little bored now. "All of the buildings on campus were named after the Celestial Councillors and the dead Royals. There are statues of the four ruling Councillors too and even one of The Savage King if you like looking at stuff like that. Maybe someone thought it might make them come for a visit."

I snorted a laugh at that. The rulers of Solaria were about as likely to drop in on an academy in the gang controlled city of Alestria as I was to suddenly sprout wings and start reciting a sonnet. People like that didn't bother with people like us. They may have been our rulers but I doubted our existence meant anything at all to them.

"So this is where all the classes are held," Leon explained. "Classrooms to the right and upstairs, faculty offices to the left. Everything book related is in this building. Everything physical is outside. Do you need me to walk you around every hallway or is that clear? I've got a map for you anyway..."

I looked around at the vaulted ceilings, gothic archways and imposing walls which didn't hold a single noticeboard or poster. The quiet hung around us and seemed to echo back to us too. It was almost ten, but I guessed as it was a Sunday no one needed to be here for classes. I wondered vaguely why Leon was in uniform. Did we have to wear them in our free time too?

Leon pulled a scrunched up bit of paper out of his pocket and passed it to me. I cast an eye over the hand drawn map for a moment before folding it more carefully and placing it in my own pocket. It didn't look very detailed but I guessed it was better than nothing.

He led me down several long corridors, pointing out things like *that's a picture of some old Altair dude* and *these are lockers, one of them must be yours* and *that bannister is the best fucker for sliding down in the whole school.* It was super educational and I couldn't help but wonder why he'd been chosen for this task. Maybe he'd just been wandering by the head's office at the wrong moment?

We made it to a set of glass doors at the back of the building and paused as Leon pointed up at a huge chart in the shape of the sun which glimmered with golden light on the wall. It was split into four columns each of which were lined with names numbered from one to two hundred.

"This is the leaderboard," he explained. "Each year has its own column and each student has a rank from most to least powerful. The teachers award and detract points based on your strength, your skill with your Element, how well you perform in classes, how well you keep control of your Order form and that kind of thing."

"So I'm guessing no one wants to be at the bottom?" I asked, my gaze slipping to the foot of the Sophomore column where *Elise Callisto* was marked in silver with a big fat zero beside my name. The guy ranking above me, Eugene Dipper, had four hundred and six points. How the hell was I supposed to catch up after missing half a year?

"Don't worry about that. Principal Greyshine said you'll be given a ranking after a few weeks once the teachers have a grasp on where you should fit. Then you'll be on a level playing field with the rest of us."

A flicker of relief filled me at that thought and I nodded, letting my gaze skim up the column until I found Leon's name at number twelve. He grinned proudly then turned away from the leaderboard towards the glass doors.

We stepped out into the sun which had just broken free of the clouds and Leon groaned in a way that was downright sexual. A shot of excited energy raced through my body in response as it took me by surprise. I looked around at him as he started thumbing open every button on his shirt so that his body was exposed to the golden light. I knew Lion Shifters replenished their magic by bathing in the sun, but this was like walking onto a porn shoot. He'd be asking me if I needed help servicing my pipes any moment. My mouth dried up, my gaze swept over his washboard abs and my lips parted without a sound finding its way free.

"We had a bonfire down by Tempest Lake last night," Leon said as if that was an explanation for him getting half naked. "I used a shit load of my magic," he added in response to my blank look. He quickly shed his blazer and shirt, leaving him standing there topless with his plum tie still on which was weirdly hot. Before I could say anything to stop him, he tossed the shirt and blazer into my arms and I almost dropped them, only managing not to by using my Vampire speed to save the catch.

"What the hell?" I demanded.

I knew I'd have to fight for my position in this school the moment I arrived. Fae fought for their place in the world and I was joining a fully established ranking system. I was bound to get it hard from all corners until people realised I wasn't a pushover, but if this was a power play it was the weirdest fucking one I'd ever engaged in.

Leon raised an eyebrow at me in surprise. "Don't you want to carry that for me?" he asked innocently.

"No, asshole, carry your own shit." I tossed his clothes back at him and he caught them easily, cocking his head in surprise. "What?" I demanded.

"Women just tend to want to do shit for me," he said with a shrug. "It's a Lion thing, you know. King of the pride and all that."

"Well I'm not a Lioness."

"No...you're some other kind of little monster, aren't you? Not many Orders can resist me that easily. What Order are you, anyway?"

I half considered biting him just to put him in his box, but that pleasure had already fallen upon the bus driver who had made me late. I'd probably ruined his day and to make matters worse, his blood had tasted bland. Like a salad that was all lettuce. But I'd gotten enough magic from his veins to fill me up so I didn't need any more. I'd bet Leon tasted pretty damn good though...

I looked up at him and smiled tauntingly, letting my fangs descend so he could see for himself what I was.

"Shit," he said on a laugh. "You really are a little monster. But you can still come join my pride if you like?"

"Vampires prefer to be alone," I responded instantly. A little stab of pain went through my heart at the words, realising that that was more true now than ever. Gareth was dead. Mom was gone. I *was* alone. Until I made this right at least.

I looked away from Leon, not wanting him to see a single glint of the

28

pain writhing within me. Luckily, he didn't seem to.

"Well, the offer's there, little monster." He ran a hand through his long hair in a carefree way before pointing to a large building off to our left. "That's the cafaeteria where you'll eat all your meals."

"Okay."

"Ca – Fae – teria. Get it?" he pressed with a grin.

"I get it," I replied. "It's just not funny."

Leon's smile widened and he strolled off across the open courtyard we'd arrived in.

I looked around at the echoing, concrete area, noticing a set of bleachers to the right beyond the yard and a row of picnic benches on the left. Beyond them was a hill covered in long, green grass.

"This is Acrux Courtyard where everyone hangs out between classes," Leon said. "Oscura Clan," he added lazily, pointing towards the picnic benches. "Lunar Brotherhood." He pointed to the bleachers. "And those of us who don't choose to be branded as either sit on Devil's Hill." He nodded to it.

And just like that, the divides in this place were marked out. Set in stone. The gangs had carved up the territory here just like in the city. It wasn't surprising really, but I'd never felt so in the thick of it before. My old high school was firmly in Oscura Territory within the city and there had been plenty of gang members in class. But they were low ranking and had paid me as little attention as I'd paid them. I'd never even met a member of the Lunar Brotherhood before but their reputation for ruthless brutality preceded them. I wondered what it would be like to live in a war zone.

"That's really the most important thing you need to remember about this academy," Leon added, like I might not know. "Oh and we call the space between the bleachers and the picnic benches no man's land. You can hang out there if you want, just don't wander into either territory unless you're ready to sign up to gang life."

I eyed the two turfs suspiciously, wondering how the hell I was supposed to get close to two members of the rival gangs without getting myself killed in the process.

Tomorrow's problem, Elise, just get through today without pissing yourself first.

My subconscious was a cold bitch but she was right more often than not.

We passed Devil's Hill and took a path through the meadow towards a looming stone tower which dominated the view ahead.

"The physical lessons are held down there." He pointed down the hill to the left of us where I could make out more buildings in the distance. "What Element are you?" Leon asked casually, almost like he wasn't interested but as his golden eyes swept over me again I caught a spark in them that said otherwise.

Every Fae born in Solaria was gifted with power over the Element connected to their star sign, so as a Libra my magic was air. Some of the more powerful Fae were gifted control over multiple Elements because they were linked to constellations too, but I'd never met anyone that strong.

"Air," I replied. "You?" Although I already knew from researching him, but I had to keep up the pretence.

"Fire, little monster. All hot and uncontrollable."

"I thought the point of wielding an Element was to gain control over it?" I mused, though I let my eyes trail over his sun kissed skin long enough for him to notice.

"Is that what you'd like to do with me?" he teased.

I smiled without answering. I needed to get close to the Kings of this school if I wanted to figure them out after all. And there was certainly an appeal to getting close to Leon Night's body - assuming he wasn't a secret murderer of course. I had to admit that my first impression of him certainly didn't strike fear into my heart. Maybe a bit of heat into my core...but I wasn't getting a psycho vibe off of him.

"Is that a yes?" he asked, drifting a little closer to me as we walked.

"Do you always proposition girls you've just met?" I asked, slanting a brow.

"Only the hot ones."

"Lucky me," I replied mockingly, inching away again. He was toying with me and I wasn't going to be won that easily, but I didn't mind letting him chase.

We reached the domineering tower and Leon waited for me to open the door before strolling right through it, almost knocking into me. My mouth fell open in surprise. "*Hey,*" I complained as he glanced back at me in confusion. "I wasn't opening the door for *you.*"

"Oh." Leon ran a hand through his long hair sheepishly. "Sorry, with the whole Lion pride thing...girls usually just..."

"Well I *don't*," I reminded him. "And next time I won't be nice about it." I flashed him my fangs and a glare as I swept past him onto the curving wooden staircase before us which I presumed was our destination.

Leon jogged to catch me as I strained my Vampire hearing, picking up on a lot more sounds in this building. There were people close by, quite a lot of them, conversations flowing, laughter, crying, even a couple having sex.

I withdrew my attention, reining in my senses so that Leon was my focus again.

"This is The Vega Dormitories; all the students are housed here. You're up on the top floor, like me." He winked. "Dunno how you wrangled that, little monster."

I stamped out the sly smile which came looking for my lips. I already knew. Because I'd hacked into the school's system and selected a dorm myself so that I could be close to the other two Kings who were housed there. I'd had to get the former dorm mate expelled from the academy by screwing with a few of her exam results, but a quick look into her record told me she was a nasty piece of work anyway. Multiple reprimands for fighting, bullying and even an accusation that she'd molested a guy which had been dropped under suspicious circumstances. Leon would be just along the corridor too so it had that perk added as well. Plenty of opportunity for me to find out their secrets.

"Is the top floor good then?" I asked innocently.

"We have the best view." Leon shrugged. "I like to see the sunrise in the mornings, so I'd say so. The dorms are all the same though so it doesn't really mean anything. Lunar Brotherhood have the bottom ten floors and Oscura have the top ten but the rest of us are assigned randomly between every level. All co-sexes too, just in case you weren't told in advance. Guys and girls bunking in together - they think that by housing us in groups of four it will prevent sex. Or maybe encourage it. Who the fuck knows?"

"Well I guess it could encourage group sex," I laughed.

Sharing a room with guys actually helped me out in my plans to get closer to the Kings so I had no problem with it. Presuming they didn't realise what I was up to and kill me in my sleep that was...

We reached the twentieth floor and Leon swung left along the corridor. He'd pushed his arms back through his shirt and blazer but hadn't bothered to re-button them.

"This is you. The rooms are magically keyed to only open for their occupants," he announced as we reached a door marked 666. *Ominous.* "You'll find your school books, schedule and Atlas in there alongside your uniforms. That's all you really need."

"So this is the end of my tour?" I asked as I moved to lean back against the door. He hadn't even shown me a quarter of the academy from what I could tell.

Leon stretched languidly, raising his arms above his head and arching his spine in a way that was so feline I couldn't help but stare. His black pants shifted low on his hips revealing the deep V which dove beneath his waistband and sent my imagination down a dirty path. I had to yank her back a little violently.

"The sun's shining," he said with a shrug. "I showed you the important bits. My detention is served."

"This was detention?" I asked.

"Hence the uniform. What can I say? I'm a bad boy," he joked and I snorted in response.

"You're certainly something."

"Wanna come sunbathe with me and find out what that something is, little monster?" he asked, leaning his forearm on the doorway above my head as he peered down into my eyes.

"Thanks for the offer, but I'd better check my schedule and figure out where my classes are for tomorrow. I had a fucking terrible guide show me around and I'll end up lost if I'm not careful," I teased.

Leon laughed, a deep rumble sounding in his chest as he withdrew from my personal space. "Do you want these back?" He held out half a pack of cherry gum, four auras and thirteen cents (which was all the money I had in the world now) the hand drawn map he'd given me and a pair of aviator sunglasses which had been perched on my head. In short, everything I'd had in my pockets and on me that wasn't sewn together.

"How the hell did you get those?" I asked, more impressed than annoyed. I hadn't even noticed a thing as he'd lifted them.

Leon grinned. "Maybe I'm more than just cute," he said, still holding my meagre possessions out for me. "But I'm feeling generous so I decided to let you have them back on account of your hotness."

"Wow, I'm flattered," I deadpanned as I reclaimed my crap.

Leon chuckled again and I twitched a smile in response.

"I guess I'll see you around then, little monster."

"Maybe," I agreed.

He sauntered away from me and I took a steadying breath as I listened for anyone in the dorm before me. I instantly picked out three heartbeats and prepared myself for what was about to follow.

I'd faced my first King already, but the next two were endlessly more terrifying.

I took another deep breath, banishing my fear as best I could. Fae fought for their position. I had to go in strong.

For Gareth. For Mom. For me.

I placed my hand against the door and felt the magic sweep around my body before it clicked open to admit me.

Buckle up bitch. Here goes nothing.

DANTE

CHAPTER THREE

I turned over the solid gold medallion that rested against my bare chest, drawing power from the depths of the metal as I used it to replenish my magic. One side read *Oscura Clan* alongside our symbol of a wolf. They were my gang, my family, my life. The other side read *a morte e ritorno*. Which meant *to death and back* in my native tongue.

I sighed, missing my family. Especially since my cousin had shown up dead. It sounded like he'd been off his face on Killblaze then rammed an ice blade into his own chest. That shit was seriously strong and caused more deaths in the city than the gangs did these days. I knew for a fact it made you go fucking crazy. I'd seen it with my own eyes.

I'd been shunning him since he'd started blazing to try and make him quit the habit. But he hadn't. And now look what had happened. A part of me blamed myself for his death. As the future leader of the Oscura Clan, I was like a damn god to my subordinates. And I knew it would have gutted him to be outcast. So now I had to bear the weight of that decision. We hadn't even been closely related. He was like my third cousin once removed or some shit. But I was responsible for *all* of my family and the rest of my clan too. And I should have done more to get him off of that soul-sucking drug.

I was laying on my bottom bunk, hidden by a sheet I'd hung from the side that didn't press against the grey wall. The sheet fluttered as someone walked past, feathers brushing against it and pulling one end off of it so it fell halfway down.

"Gabriel!" I snapped, yanking the sheet back and finding him all the way on the other side of the room, sitting on his top bunk and gazing off into the distance. His heavily tattooed chest was on display and his huge black wings were folded innocently behind him. I pursed my lips when he didn't meet my eye.

I know it was you.

Guy said a dozen words a month and never when you wanted them. He was a Harpy with a serious attitude problem. He always went around half-shifted with his huge-ass wings flapping about the place. I swear he did it to piss me off.

Our other roommate, Laini, poked her head out from the bunk beneath his, looking between us like she was about to step in. Never actually did, but always had that tight-lipped face slapped on.

I shot out of bed, smoke pluming from my nose as I snatched the end of the sheet and snagged it back around the bunk. "If you come in through the window, put your fucking wings away before dragging them over my stuff, *capisce?*"

Gabriel didn't acknowledge me and he was about the only fucker in the academy who could get away with that. He was the most powerful Fae in this place and had two Elements to his name, more than anyone else in this school.

The shit I have to deal with around here. Papà would be turning in his grave if he hadn't been buried in ten pieces. But I'd bet at least one of them was twitching.

"I could eat you in my Order form," I reminded him but he continued to look at the wall, apparently thinking about something much more important than what I was saying. Muscles wise I beat him, but he was a tall bastardo and with those two Elements humming in his veins I couldn't take him on in Fae form. *I could shift though...*

The door swung open and a hot-ass angel had apparently swooped down from heaven to improve my day. The leggy girl with choppy lilac hair and anime eyes that were as green as the pools of Faelandia stepped into our dorm. Her expression said *back off* but she gave my bare chest a lingering look that said *hell yes.*

My dick saluted her and I almost did too.

"Da fuck is this? A photo op? Close the fucking door and come in." Laini stuck out a foot, wafting it to encourage the new arrival further into the room.

"Are you the new girl?" I asked hopefully. Leon had been tasked with showing her around and fuck me I wished I'd volunteered as tribute on that detention shift.

"Define new," she said, strolling through the room with the air of someone who owned the place.

"Fresh, appearing for the first time, brought into being. You look like a specific kind of new though..."

She eyed the empty top bunk above mine, her eyes falling to the bottom one before she rounded on me. "Oh? What kind of new?"

"Spanking." I grinned. She did not.

Static rose in my chest and filled the room, causing her hair to lift a little along with every other hair on her body. I wasn't just any Dragon. I was a rare ass Storm Dragon. Electricity was my thing and a live wire was shooting off sparks somewhere in my body right now.

"He does that when he's turned on," Gabriel spoke his first words of the day and I could have punched him for them as a smirk danced around his mouth.

"And happy," Laini added.

"And being an asshole, so it never really stops," Gabriel said and the new girl laughed.

I bent down, snatching one of my leather shoes from the floor and throwing it at his head with perfect accuracy. He waved his hand, catching it out of the air with a vine conjured by his earth magic and placed it back where I'd taken it from.

My right eye twitched with rage as I glared at him. The electricity burned hotter in my blood, tempting me to shift and rip his head off. He was the single student in this entire school who outranked me magic wise and I had to share a goddamn room with him.

I snarled at him and Laini retreated back into the shadow of her bunk. She was all talk, but she'd never face off with me. I'd tear her apart for it. She was just a low-powered Sphinx.

I turned back to the petite treasure who'd strolled into my life and found her moving my stuff onto the top bunk – *woah what the fuck?!*

Dominance forced me into action so fast, I thought she wouldn't be prepared for it. But as I snatched her hair, yanking her away from my things, she spun around sharply, baring fangs to try and sink into my flesh.

"Shit!" I shoved her back with a blast of air magic and she countered it with her own, a storm crashing between us.

Our power was closely matched, but I could sense I had the edge. I smiled with satisfaction, uprooting her with a flick of my fingers so she slammed into the floor on her back. Her skirt slid up those delicious thighs of hers which looked like they needed a visit from my tongue. "You're on the top bunk, carina. Don't test me." I flipped my medallion around so she could see the name of my gang. A warning.

She nodded, not seeming overly surprised, but then again nearly half the school was part of the Oscura Clan. She didn't yet know that I was *the* fucking Oscura. My great great grandpapà had damn well founded the Clan. So if she thought rising against me was a good idea, she was going to meet the full wrath of my ancestors directly through me.

The fight went out of her and I offered her my hand. She took it, her palm sliding into mine as smoothly as butter as I pulled her to her feet. *I wonder what the rest of her feels like.*

She smiled overly falsely, tossing her bag onto the top bunk and climbing up, giving me a perfect view of her bare ass around a black thong. She didn't seem to mind either, turning and batting her lashes at me over those big Bambi eyes. *Is she baiting me or mocking me?*

"Chin up, carina, maybe we'll be sharing the bottom bunk soon anyway." I winked and she tilted her head, seeming to assess me.

"What does carina mean?"

"Cutie." I rested my forearms on her mattress, owning it. Just like I was gonna do with her. The look in her eyes said she knew it too. Okay so maybe I was being hopeful. But she'd get the message soon enough.

"Oh but, *sweetie*, you've got me all wrong," she said mischievously, crawling forward to give me a view down her top and a sniff of her skin which smelt like my new favourite flavour. Elderflower and cherry gum. "I'm not cute, I'm deadly. And I wouldn't share a bunk with you if the only other option was the roof."

She bared her fangs and I almost wouldn't have minded her having a bite just so I could feel how soft those lips were. But it wasn't worth my reputation. A Vampire needed to suck on people's magic to restore their reserves, but the chances of me becoming anyone's Source was laughable. There wasn't a Vampire in this school who could overpower me to get their fangs into my neck, this one included.

I stepped back, trying not to be rattled by her snarky comment. She wanted me. She had to. It was what girls did. They walked into rooms and wanted me. It was practically a law of nature. I was nearly six and a half foot of stacked muscle with skin the colour of honey and eyes that fucked you before you were even undressed. Who wouldn't want that?

Gabriel released a breath of laughter and I turned to glare at him. His wings flexed out, making him look even bigger and as his muscles firmed, the dark ink on his skin seemed to ripple across his body. *Double Elemental bastardo.*

"I'm Laini." She spoke to the new girl who I realised I hadn't gotten a name out of yet.

"Elise," she replied and that name caressed my ear like a hot, wanton lick.

Laini crawled out from the shadows of her bunk again, revealing all four foot of her. Alright, five, but she was still a short ass. Everything about her was lithe and dark. Her hair was cropped short and gave her a warrior look that contrasted with her pathetic height. Her limbs were toned and her face was the sort of pretty that had made me chase her for three weeks straight when she'd been put in my dorm at the start of the year. But fortune hadn't been on my side. Laini was straight up into girls and though I'd promised her one night with me would change her mind, she'd told me that was offensive as shit (I still stood by it). She was older, a Junior. And apparently her last roommates had pissed her off enough to demand a room change. I sometimes wondered if she regretted that move, but then I remembered I didn't give a shit.

A couple of books tumbled out of Laini's nest and I rolled my eyes. Girl was a Sphinx through and through. Reading restored their magic reserves, but that didn't mean she had to do it non-stop. She loved a book more than she loved sex. And I knew that for a fact because I'd witnessed her callously turn down one of the hottest girls in school in favour of burying her nose in some dull Numerology book. Which was entirely selfish because I totally could have watched.

"And what's your name?" Elise addressed Gabriel, but he'd checked out again, looking at the wall beyond her head. The guy had the gift of The Sight, receiving glimpses of the future, past and present. But I knew he just used it as an excuse to ignore other people when he didn't fancy talking. And he rarely fancied talking. So I wondered if he'd decided to ignore Elise or if he really was mid-vision right now. He never showed interest in girls beyond

42

jerking his head once when he was horny and then they came running. It didn't seem like Elise was the sort of girl who could be beckoned, but I was still gonna lock her down before Gabriel decided to take more of an interest in her.

"That's Gabriel," I answered for him. "He thinks a lot. But stop pretending you care, I know you're waiting for *my* name."

"Nope." Elise shrugged, flopping down on the bed and flexing her hips as she got comfortable. I ran my tongue across my teeth, a dangerous energy rising in my veins.

"Dante," I growled. "You know, like the guy who walked through the nine rings of hell."

"Doesn't ring a bell," she said lightly, taking her Atlas from the welcome pack waiting on her bed. The school tablet wasn't top of the range, but it was good enough to message anyone you liked and I suppose it also had a bunch of school shit like timetables and horoscopes that were useful enough too.

I waited for her to pay me attention again, but she didn't and anger crashed through my chest like thunder. "Let me give you the synopsis then. Dante Oscura, great great grandson of the founding member of the Oscura Clan which runs half of Alestria."

"Oh, *that* Dante." Elise snorted and I snatched her Atlas from her hand, my Dragon side dangerously close to bursting free. And if I let it, I'd rip a hole in this entire wing of the academy. The principal would make me work off that debt by spending the rest of the year in detention.

"Listen, vampira," I snarled. "There's two sides in this school, Oscura Clan or Lunar Brotherhood." I spat on the floor to get the taste of that name out of my mouth. "You're either with us or with *them*."

"Or you can be your own person," Gabriel chipped in as he mentally came back to the room.

"Chatty today, aren't we?" I said through my teeth. "Funny how you only hear the things that interest you, isn't Gabriel?"

"Why would I take an interest in things that don't interest me? That's fucking moronic." He turned away to ponder on that and I snapped back to face my prey. Who was...gone. *What?*

I searched around, turning left and right. Laini giggled as she leaned back against her and Gabriel's bunk.

"Where?" I demanded and Laini pointed.

Fury burned a path through my chest as I slowly turned, gazing down to where Elise was stretched out on my bunk, rolling her neck from side to side.

"Your mattress is *way* more comfy," she sighed contentedly. "What have I gotta do to swap?"

"I'm not swapping. Get up or I'll make you." I leaned down into the low space and she bit into her lip, her eyelashes fluttering, her hips wriggling. I found myself disarmed, watching this little creature toying with me, asking me to play her game.

My anger fell away. "Well, carina, there's a few things you can do for me. Most of them only need your mouth." I smirked and the mischief in her eyes fled into the darkness. She wasn't going to be an easy lay, but she was definitely going to be a worthwhile one.

"Move," I said flatly, but she didn't. "Fine." I dropped down beside her, forcing my way up into her space so she had to press herself against me. "I wouldn't sleep there though," I warned. "You're in the direct firing line of my morning glory. So if you do stay there, that's on you."

She huffed, sitting up to get out and waiting for me to move.

"Oh no, carina, I don't move for anyone."

She ran her tongue across her fangs in warning. "Perhaps I'll stop for a drink on the way."

"Perhaps my hands will slide up your skirt on the way," I countered and she pouted.

"No drinking." She held out her pinkie and I snared it with mine.

"No ass grabbing," I confirmed and she smirked, throwing her long leg over me and shimmying across to get out.

When she was gone, I tugged the sheet back into place to gain privacy then cupped one hand behind the back of my head and stuffed the other into my pants. If Elise thought top bunk was bad now, she wasn't going to enjoy the ride when I brought a girl back to bed. But right now, the only one I wanted in it was her.

GARETH

CHAPTER FOUR

EIGHTEEN MONTHS BEFORE THE SOLARID METEOR
SHOWER...

I did another sweep of the strip club, grabbing empty glasses and taking
requests for private dances by grabbing the golden cards the patrons
left out.

I cast an eye over the requests, a little part of me relieved that no one had
asked for my mom, another part concerned because that meant less tips. She'd
been quiet all week and the grocery shopping had been forgotten. Luckily, I'd
snagged a few tips myself this week so I'd kept them back when handing over
my pay packet to her and bought enough food for us to get by.

Ella would have to come by the club tonight for dinner though. Old Sal
was always generous enough with meals for my sister and I even if she didn't
offer up much else in the way of charity.

Every other Thursday, The Sparkling Uranus ran a ladies night and
Sal had offered me triple pay to get up on the stage. I'd been avoiding it all
summer but maybe I'd have to cave. If Mom couldn't even afford to put meals

on the table then I'd need to up my input.

I hooked another empty glass from a table and the guy there reached out to me, brushing his hand across my ass.

"How much for an hour of your time?" he asked in a gruff voice, his other hand shifting to rearrange his junk beneath his potbelly as his eyes swept over my body hungrily.

I'd been getting more of these advances this summer than ever before and I'd learned how to brush them off without causing offence. It wasn't that surprising; a year at Aurora Academy with three square meals a day and the hours I spent at Pitball training coupled with a growth spurt had made a big difference to my appearance. I was over six foot now and my frame had filled out with muscle, not to mention the fact that people were always drawn to Pegasuses.

I offered the guy a lazy smile, letting my skin glitter a little like I was flattered despite the food he had caught in his teeth. "I'm afraid I'm not on the menu," I said, brushing a hand over his and subtly shifting it off of my body, hiding a shudder of disgust. "But if I'm your type then I can find Clark for you, he'd be more than willing to meet your desires and he'd be a lot better at it than me too."

The guy pouted, shifting his hand beneath his waistband as he licked his lips. "Okay then," he agreed, a little disappointed. But if I was gonna start pimping myself out it wouldn't be to some middle aged, unwashed asshole who pooled his spare change for a blowjob once a month.

I shifted through the crowd, which was fairly thin as it was a Wednesday and still early, then slipped behind the bar.

I kept going through the back to put the glasses in the washer and paused as Mom's voice caught my ear.

"Just a little longer," she begged. "I thought it was a sure thing, I didn't imagine for a moment that he'd fall at the last hurdle. If you just give me a little longer, I can-"

"The debt is up to seventeen thousand auras," Old Sal replied in a cold tone and I inhaled sharply. I knew Mom had been gambling again but I had no idea she'd let it get out of hand like that. How the hell was she supposed to clear a debt that big? "And let's face it Tanya, you're not making as much as you used to. You may still be beautiful but you're getting old. And you've done more than a few rounds of all the punters. You don't earn the tips you used to; you don't satisfy the big crowds in the same way-"

I left the tray of glasses on the counter and headed into the corridor towards Sal's office so I could eavesdrop more effectively.

"I can change up my routines," Mom begged.

"Perhaps we can come up with some other way to settle your debts," Sal said thoughtfully.

"Anything," Mom breathed and I stepped closer to Sal's office door with a knot in my gut. It was ajar and a tip of my head let me see my mom's back, her long blonde hair trailing down her spine over the bunny outfit she wore.

Sal let out a breath. "What we need around here is new talent..." she said slowly.

"But I-" Mom began, though she didn't get a chance to continue.

"Elise is about to turn eighteen, isn't she?" Old Sal asked curiously and my heart lurched. It was one thing to watch my mom earn a living like this, but there was no way in hell I'd be letting my little sister live this life.

"Elise?" Mom squeaked. "She's just about to start high school. Her powers will be Awakened next week and then she'll need to focus on her studies and-"

"Elise is growing into a beautiful woman," Sal interrupted. "She's really filling out and there's an allure to her which is drawing attention whenever she comes here. I've had more than a few patrons ask about her even when she's dressed in baggy T-shirts and sweatpants. Imagine what they'd say if she was in costume."

"I...I'm not sure she'd want to do this kind of work," Mom protested weakly but I was beginning to get the impression she was considering it and my jaw clenched tightly at the thought.

Ella and I had made a promise to each other a long time ago. We weren't going to live this life. We were going to do better and get out of this shit hole. I'd sooner sell my own horn than let Old Sal put my little sister up on that stage. This kind of life didn't let go once it got its claws into you. I only had to look at our mom to know that. There was no laughter in her anymore. No spark in her eye. And stripping led to private dances which led to whoring which I absolutely refused to consider for my sister. Ella was better than this place. Better than this life. And I'd do whatever the hell it took to save her from it.

"Why don't we put it to her?" Sal asked slowly and I could feel the pull of her Siren gifts as she pushed them at our mom. She was lacing her voice with warmth and making Mom want to trust her through her emotional sway. Usually she reserved her powers for pumping lust into the patrons. Using them like this must have meant she really wanted Ella. This wasn't some plan she'd just come up with. She'd had her eye on my little sister for a while. Anger licked down my spine at the thought. "Surely Elise would want to help clear your debt? One year working for me and I'd call it quits. She could just dance on Friday and Saturday nights at first, no need to interrupt her studies. We can keep her to the stage too. No lap dancing - at least not until her birthday..."

The stretch of silence that followed went on too damn long. Where was the outright refusal that should have been bursting from Mom's lips? The fact that it was missing made a tremor of fear run through me. I was heading back to the academy next week to start my Sophomore year and I sure as hell wasn't leaving my sister here with this threat hanging over her. Mom still hadn't spoken and I decided that was my cue to interrupt.

I pushed the office door open and it banged against the wall, making Mom flinch as she looked around at me guiltily.

"My sister isn't going to be working here," I snarled.

Petri got to his feet from the chair he'd been occupying in the corner. Old Sal's right hand man and head bouncer was three hundred pounds of muscle and he was so goddamn hairy it almost seemed like he was in his Order form at all times. He was a Minotaur and had a temper which was frayed on a good day, fucking volcanic on a bad. I ignored him, though it was pretty hard to do as he took up half the small room, but my gaze locked on Sal.

The old Siren leaned back on her worn leather chair, puffing slowly on a cigarette as she looked me over. She was small, her back a little hunched and the white hair atop her head coiled into a bun. Sal surveyed me over the rim of her red glasses, taking another long drag as the scent of smoke enveloped me.

"Your momma owes me a debt, boy," she said slowly. "And I've always been good to your family. But I won't be left out of pocket."

"I'll pay the damn debt," I said forcefully. "I just need a bit of time to get the money together."

"It's a lot of money," Sal said. "And as tempting as you are, boys don't sell for as much as the girls do."

"I'm not offering to whore myself out," I growled. "But I go to school with some of the richest fuckers in this district. I'll get you your money and then some."

Sal took another long drag on her cigarette, the cherry glowing brightly as she considered my offer. "The debt is seventeen thousand auras. I'll let you pay it in monthly instalments. Two thousand a month. Every month. For a year."

"That's twenty four thousand," I hissed.

"Interest," Sal said with a shrug. "It's the only deal I'm offering aside from having your sister come work for me."

Mom was looking at me with wide eyes, hoping I was about to save her. I loved that woman, but I really wished she'd grow some damn balls sometimes. Her whole life she'd let people walk all over her. My father, Ella's father, Old Sal and countless punters in between. She was always waiting for a knight in shining armour when she should have been strapping on her own chainmail. But that wasn't going to change and I wouldn't let Elise pay the price for it either.

"Fine," I ground out.

"You miss a payment and your sister will be on stage that very night," Sal added.

"I'm sure I'll be able to help train her up in how to satisfy the clientele," Petri added with a chuckle and I was struck with the urge to punch his damn face until his big nose was flattened into nothing.

"I won't miss a payment," I snapped. I had no fucking idea how I'd get that money, but I'd do it. Whatever it took. I wouldn't let these assholes break my little angel's wings.

"Better make it binding then." Sal stood and offered me a gnarled hand.

I didn't hesitate. I strode straight past my mother who whimpered pitifully as I slapped my palm into Sal's.

Magic flared as the deal was struck and I was bound to the terms we'd agreed.

I'd bought Elise's freedom.

Now I just had to figure out how the hell I was going to pay for it.

ELISE

CHAPTER FIVE

As if sleeping in a room with two guys who I had good reason to believe might be murderers wasn't enough to put me on edge, I was definitely, one hundred percent late for my very first class.

I'd walked up and down the corridors of Altair Halls (the building Leon had wandered through with me yesterday) but I still couldn't find it. The best fucking bannister in the school for sliding down? Oh yeah I knew that bitch well, me and her went back six dashes up and down the stairs with my Vampire speed but room twelve-oh-one? No, that asshole wasn't here.

Fucking Lion Shifter.

The next time I ran into Leon Night I'd be giving him a tour of my fist.

With a groan of frustration, I fell to a halt in the near empty corridor and took a steadying breath, closing my eyes as I focused on my enhanced sense of hearing. I scoured through meaningless conversations, an argument about a Manticore eating someone's lipstick, a girl freaking out because she'd bought the wrong brand of tampons and finally an overly peppy voice. *"Good morning Professor Titan!"*

Jackpot.

That was the name of my professor and the voice had come from somewhere on the floor below mine. Close enough to make me think it was beneath my feet.

I reached the best fucking bannister to slide down in the academy, glanced around, gripped it in my palms and - shot down the steps with my Vampire speed.

Chicken shit.

I tried to convince myself it was about speed not a lack of balls but the gap between my thighs was conspicuously mocking. Next time. Maybe.

I hurtled around the stairs, spotting a door hidden in the shadows behind them and sighing in relief as I found the numbers *1201* in shiny brass hanging on the door.

I opened the door and discovered another stairwell which I quickly descended before reaching the Potions Lab at the bottom.

White tiles shone everywhere; walls, floor, ceiling, making me think this place was set up to be hosed down and I wondered why in Solaria they would need to do that. My high school dabbling in potion brewing had been admittedly tame, but I had to question just what I was letting myself in for in this place as I looked around at the vials, test tubes, fluorescent liquids and jars filled with all kinds of dark and disgusting things.

"Miss Callisto, I presume?" a husky male voice called from the front of the room and I lifted my chin to look over the sea of students in the huge classroom and found Professor Titan looking right at me.

He had a warm smile on his ruggedly handsome face and bushy sideburns flecked with silver running down his cheeks. Blue eyes observed me keenly as he beckoned me forward and I had a sudden vision of one of those lame high school movies where the teacher drags the new kid up in front of the class and gets them to make a speech about who they are and how much their life sucks while everyone looks on and laughs.

Hi everyone, I'm Elise, but you can call me Ella, like my brother did -

you know, the dead one who I'm here to avenge. I'm looking at a few pricks in particular if you wanna stand up and take a bow?

Yeah, I didn't think so.

I tapped two fingers to my forehead and tipped the Professor a salute before shifting through the bodies without really looking at anyone and dropping into the first empty seat I came to.

I spilled my books onto the desk, flicked on my Atlas and pulled a pencil from my pocket, twirling it between my fingers just so that I had something to do.

Everyone was chatting casually, the Professor seeming in no hurry to start the class.

I felt weirdly warm, like embarrassment was crawling up my chest but I had no idea why. I tapped my pencil against the desk impatiently and looked up, needing to know where that sensation was coming from.

My gaze fell directly into the depths of a guy's sitting three rows ahead of me on a desk to the left of mine. I knew him instantly. The fourth King. Ryder Draconis, leader of the Lunar Brotherhood at Aurora Academy.

He was tall and broad, his blazer abandoned and his white shirt sleeves rolled back to reveal bronze forearms thick with muscle. One fisted hand lay facing me on the desk, the word *lust* spelled out in individual letters across his knuckles.

His black hair was shaved down so hard it was barely there at all and his mouth was set in a firm line. As I fell captive to his gaze, my eyes locked with his and I gasped as I realised his pupils had transformed from a sea of cerulean green into reptilian slits with a brighter hue.

I wanted to look away but I was caught, trapped in the net of his gaze and unable to pull myself back.

A shaky breath spilled between my lips and I raised the pencil to my mouth on instinct, biting down gently on the eraser.

A heavy blink curtained my vision and all the sound in the room seemed to fade away.

My heart thumped solidly in my chest and heat built between my thighs, aching for this creature before me to satisfy my desire.

Holding my eye, he stood from his chair, sliding his fingers into the knot of his plum coloured tie as he loosened it off so slowly that it was torture to watch.

My breathing was growing heavier and I could only observe, begging him to hurry with my eyes while my body stayed glued in place as he began to ease open his shirt buttons.

None of the other students seemed to have noticed that Ryder was stripping and he only had eyes for me as he took a purposeful step towards me.

The eraser flexed between my teeth as I exerted a little more pressure on it, my fangs lengthening as desire spun through my veins like an inferno.

Ryder was watching me with dark promises in his gaze, passion and heat and danger wrapped into one. This was the kind of guy nice girls ran from. The type who shattered dreams and stole virginities and left a trail of broken hearts behind without ever feeling a single second of remorse for it.

And I wanted him to break me too. I wanted to worship him on my knees and give my body up to his torture only to be left ruined when he cast me aside.

He continued undoing the buttons on his shirt, the words scrawled across his knuckles taking up all of my attention. *Pain. Lust.*

Fuck, I wanted him to make me feel those things more than anything in the world right now.

The hint of a moan escaped my lips and I pressed my thighs together in a desperate bid to sate some of the need he'd awoken in me.

Ryder released the last of his shirt buttons and my eyes widened as he pushed the fabric aside. The perfect angles of his chest called to me, but almost all of my attention was caught on the huge bulge pressing against the confines of his zipper.

I took in a breath, about to beg him to take off the rest of his clothes just as a hand landed on my thigh beneath the table and something was thrust in front of my face.

I bit down on the eraser between my teeth, breaking it as the hand on my leg tightened its grip. The cool bite of metal rings contrasted to the warm flesh of his palm as he tightened his hold and the need in my body made me tip my leg towards him to allow more access. I blinked at the textbook which was now blocking my view of Ryder, confusion tugging at me.

"Has no one ever warned you not to look into a Basilisk's eyes, carina?" Dante whispered in my ear, his breath against my neck heightening the desire in my flesh. My fangs ached, my back arched. I needed an outlet for all of this energy that had pent up inside of me.

"What?" I murmured, unable to fully grasp what he'd said.

Dante lowered the textbook and I found myself looking at the side of Ryder's head as he sat facing the Professor with the faintest shadow of a smile playing around his mouth. He was fully dressed, still in his seat, like none of it had even happened at all.

What the hell?

"They can hypnotise you into seeing fantasies. You shouldn't hold that stronzo's eye."

I'd never met a Basilisk Shifter before; I knew they were crazy rare but not a whole lot else about them. I guess I'd just imagined a huge snake and not given a lot of thought to whatever powers he might possess. More fool me.

Dante's hand was still very much on my thigh and as I dropped the pencil, spitting out the severed eraser, I turned to look at him, finding him very much in my personal space too.

"Back up," I breathed, trying to shake off the lingering effects of the desire Ryder had made me feel.

Anger was burning a line through my limbs as I started to fully comprehend what he'd done. He'd invaded my mind, my thoughts, my fucking libido. What the hell was wrong with him? We hadn't even said a single word to each other!

"Or what?" Dante asked, all possessive with his Dragon macho bullshit.

But I wasn't in the mood to be used in a pissing contest for some gang war I gave zero shits about. He wanted to know 'or what'? *Okay then dipshit, you asked for it.*

I shot into motion with my Vampire speed, catching his chin in my hand and forcing it aside half a second before my fangs found his neck.

His palm splayed across my stomach, ready to cast magic to fight me off if I'd taken a moment longer, but I wasn't a fool. And the second my venom met with his blood, the fight was won.

My power immobilised his magic and his limbs lost their strength as he fell under my spell. This was the true strength of Vampires. Once our venom was in the blood of our prey, no matter how powerful a Fae they were, they were beat.

I pressed my fangs deeper and his blood spilled over my tongue like the sweetest taste of heaven.

I groaned, drunk on the lusty energy coursing through my body and the elixir of blood and magic I was sampling now.

I'd drunk from powerful Fae before but *fuck* Dante Oscura tasted *good*. His magic poured into me like a tempestuous storm, filling my reserves in a way that made the hairs raise along the back of my neck and my toes curl with wanton desire.

He tasted like thunder and freedom, rage and uncertainty and the brush of his skin against my lips awoke a shudder of pleasure which splashed down my spine.

Dante's hands slid around my waist and I was surprised to find him dragging me closer instead of pushing me back. Sure, everyone knew that once a Vampire got their fangs in you, you couldn't fight them off magically or physically. But a lot of people still tried to push at me when I bit them. Giving just enough indication of how much they hated what I was doing to them to let me know. Of course I'd been pulled closer before too but that was usually by Fae who consented to my bite or desired me for other reasons.

This felt different...almost like he was enjoying it in its own right.

My magic stores filled to the brim and a deep well of power thrummed within my chest.

I drew back, retracting my fangs and releasing my grip on his chin, stubble grazing my palm as I pulled away.

My heart beat a little faster as I found his dark eyes pinned on mine.

Dante turned towards me before I could pull all the way back, pressing a kiss to my cheek, so close to my lips that it brushed the corner of my mouth, leaving a line of electricity on my skin.

"Calm down, carina, save it for our bedroom," he said, loud enough for half the class to hear him.

"Okay, settle down," Professor Titan called, seeming amused as my cheeks flushed red.

I decided to ignore Dante's comment, reaching out to heal away the wound I'd given him. Before I could brush my fingers against his skin, he caught my hand.

"Leave it," he said, loudly again. "Let the whole school see that when the King of the Lunar Brotherhood uses his seduction techniques on a woman, she instantly leaps on me instead. Let everyone see where you'd rather get your satisfaction. From a real man."

My lips parted to protest what he'd just said. I was about to announce to everyone that I'd simply overpowered him instead of it being the lust-filled experience he'd imagined up, but the dark flash of warning in his gaze made me pause.

Dante knew what had happened. He was also one of the most powerful Fae in this academy. More powerful than me. I'd caught him off guard in a moment that was unlikely to repeat itself and he was willing to give me this chance. Instead of punishing me with his magic to prove to everyone that he was the more powerful Fae of the two of us, he was giving me a free pass. All I had to do was let him twist what had happened against his enemy and use it to ridicule him.

I leaned away from him slowly, breaking the last inches of contact between us as I carefully swept a finger across my bottom lip, gathering a final bead of his blood onto it.

I sucked it from my fingertip and Dante watched me with enough desire in his gaze to make my heart beat faster all over again.

Perhaps this was a way for me to win an inch of his trust. Maybe then I could get close enough to find out something about what had happened to my brother. It was worth a shot. I just hoped Ryder wouldn't take my cooperation as a declaration of loyalty to the Oscura Clan.

One look at the Basilisk Shifter told me all I needed to know about that hope though.

He'd turned towards me again but instead of the heat that had sparked in his eyes when he'd used his hypnotic powers to toy with me, I found a cold, hard wall.

His jaw was tight and the other fist was resting on the desk now, the word across his knuckles seeming like a threat and a promise all in one. *Pain.*

Well shit.

"I want everyone's eyes on page eight-thirteen of the textbooks. You should all remember this potion from the end of last term. I'm going to be reassigning lab partners and you will be working with this person for the rest of the term so please try to be friendly," Professor Titan called over the chatter and the students slowly settled down as they began hunting through their textbooks.

"I'm not going to be working with any Oscura trash," a deep voice said darkly. He hadn't shouted it out but somehow every word was heard clearly despite the size of the classroom.

I glanced up from flicking through my textbook to see Ryder looking at Professor Titan in a way that was at once totally laid back and yet somehow entirely threatening too. His arm was resting over the back of the empty seat beside him and he leaned right back in his chair with his legs spread wide like he didn't have a care in the world. And yet despite that, he still seemed to give off the impression of a cobra poised to strike.

"No Oscura would even work *near* you, scum, let alone *with* you," Dante tossed back even though Ryder wasn't looking at him. He threw an arm around my shoulders and I frowned at him slightly as I shrugged him off again.

"No need to worry, I'm well aware of the gang divides within the school," the Professor replied wearily. "There will be no Oscura-Lunar pairings." He went on to start calling out names and rearranging the class as I cast my gaze over the potion we were going to be working on.

Breath of Slumber

The ingredients seemed simple enough, though there were about twice as many as there had been in anything I'd ever attempted to brew before. I was a quick study though, so with a bit of luck and a half decent lab partner I was fairly confident in my ability to at least put in a valiant effort.

Dante was singing a song in his native language under his breath, tapping his fingers against our desk so that little sparks emitted from his fingertips. It didn't sound like a lullaby though, more like a death threat.

I straightened my spine instead of leaning away from him like I was tempted to. The taste of his blood and power still lingered on my tongue and each tap of his electrified fingers on the desk sent a resounding thrill of energy through the magic coiling inside me now. I'd never tasted blood so potent that it retained a flavour of its original owner once I'd consumed it, but that was what this felt like. As if a little of Dante's electric energy was living beneath my flesh now.

Dante reached into his bag, taking out polished gold equipment and laying it on the desk - from a pestle and mortar to a freaking golden ladle. The last item he placed down was a gleaming chalice engraved with the snarling wolf symbol of the Oscura Clan. He opened a bottle of water, pouring it into the fancy ass cup before sipping from it like royalty.

"Seriously?" I gave him a look of complete disbelief and he smirked.

"I don't drink from anything but this, carina. It's enchanted with the strongest anti-poison spells in Solaria so even if some fucking Lunar scum slipped something in my drink, I'd be fine." He shot a look over at Ryder which told me that was a genuine concern.

A shadow fell across my desk and I looked up at the tall girl standing over me. Her long black hair was braided over one shoulder and her full lips were pursed like I was doing something to irritate her. "Professor Titan says I'm with Dante this term," she explained in a lilting southern accent, casting a hopeful eye at the Dragon Shifter beside me.

I made a move to gather my things but Dante's hand came down on my arm, halting me. "No," he said simply, like it was up to him. "Go find someone else, Cindy Lou. Elise is staying right here."

The way he said my name was downright sexual and I looked up at him as he smirked knowingly. I rolled my eyes and started gathering my things but his hand came down hard on top of my books to stop me.

"Move your ass, sugar," Cindy Lou said impatiently and I looked back up at her with an apologetic shrug.

"I'm trying but there's a Dragon paw all over my things."

Dante chuckled darkly and drew closer to me. "Not yet there isn't, bella."

Cindy Lou sucked in a breath and scowled at me like I was stepping on her toes. But if she wanted Dante it didn't seem like the feeling was reciprocated to me.

I remained silent, unsure what to say. Professor Titan beckoned me to join him at the front of the class again.

"I think I'm supposed to-"

"No," Dante repeated simply, his hot hand curling around my wrist possessively.

Cindy's eyes whipped between us, halting on me and narrowing to slits.

"*Now*, Miss Callisto, unless you want to get detention on your first day. Lab Partner assignments are not up for negotiation, Mr Oscura." Professor Titan's face was set in a steely mask which held nothing but impatience.

"Catch you later, roomie," I said sweetly, tugging my arm out of Dante's grip.

Cindy picked up a notepad I'd accidentally left on the table and held it out to me. "Oh here, sugar. You forgot this."

My brows raised and I reached for it seconds before Cindy stumbled forward and it burst into flames. "Oh my! How clumsy of me."

I moved to snatch the oxygen from the flames with a gasp, but she threw it to the floor, stamping her foot on it several times to put out the fire. I scowled down at the charred pad, bending down to pick it up.

Cindy bent down too and her eyes flashed with a wicked light. She caught my wrist, her nails digging in as she whispered in a voice so low only my Vampire hearing could pick it up. "Keep your ugly purple head away from Dante, sweetie. He's mine."

I yanked my hand free with a snarl, rising to my feet with the blackened pad in my grip.

Cindy settled into her seat beside Dante with a sugary smile and I scowled. I dumped the ashy pad on the desk in front of her and she jumped, looking to me in alarm.

"I'm sure you won't mind putting this in the trash for me. Or in your mouth. Same difference really."

Dante frowned at me in surprise and I rolled my eyes at him, unable to believe he really fell for that sweet-as-pie act she was trying to pull off.

I shot away from them with my Vampire speed to the front of the room, hoping Cindy Lou would get the hint that I wasn't to be messed with.

Professor Titan assessed me for a moment as I stood before him and I fiddled with the collar of my shirt beneath his scrutiny.

"You haven't aligned yourself with the Oscuras already, have you?" he asked mildly, like we were discussing the weather rather than the kind of decision which would brand me for life as a gang member.

"No, sir," I replied. "I'm just trying to get to know everyone."

I tried to get a read on him, but the pace of his heart gave away nothing. His eyes were like two blue pools which echoed on endlessly and I couldn't see any reason to trust or mistrust him.

"Principal Greyshine sends his apologies for not finding the time to welcome you to the school personally yet, but he asked me to tell you that I've been assigned as your Liaison. That means we will be having weekly sessions to check on your progress and make sure you're fitting in okay. Once you've had a few weeks to adjust, I'll assign you a leaderboard ranking based on where I think you fit within the class."

"Okay, thanks," I said, not really having anything to add.

"Try not to worry about the other students ribbing on you. Just prove to them that you deserve your place here and they'll back off. You've also been assigned sessions with the school guidance counsellor, Miss Nightshade. She'll see you every other week to make sure you're coping well. The mental health of our students is paramount here at Aurora Academy."

"Great," I said though my gut plummeted. I didn't want to see a counsellor and have them try to pick me apart. The less attention that was paid to my mental health the better. I was grieving, raging, mentally unhinged, prone to violent outbursts... None of which screamed well adjusted to me. But I'd just have to hope that I could fool Miss Nightshade like I was planning on fooling everyone else.

"Do you have any other questions for me?" Professor Titan asked. "Have you settled into your dorm?"

"I'm doing fine, thanks," I said quickly. "Everyone seems really...

welcoming...so..."

Titan smiled knowingly and I shrugged. Okay so maybe the welcoming part had been a bit of an exaggeration, but no one had been outright violent yet so I was taking that as a win.

"I want to give you the best chance to catch up, so I've decided to partner you with the best performing student in the class. I'm aware that Redford High wouldn't have had such a thorough syllabus and I want you to have every opportunity for greatness here."

"Oh," I said, surprised by the gesture. "That's...I mean you didn't have to but...thank you, sir."

"No problem at all. And don't hesitate to come to me if you need any further assistance. I'll assess you in class over the next few weeks and if I feel you need it, I'll offer private sessions to help you catch up too." He smiled and I couldn't help but return it. Not many people in my life had gone out on a limb for me, let alone offered me additional help. "Please take your seat beside Mr Draconis then."

And just like that my stomach plummeted. My lips parted and I turned to look toward the empty seat Professor Titan was pointing out.

Ryder was eyeing me across the room as if he'd heard the whole exchange and a lump formed in my throat.

Shit on a snowflake.

I tipped my chin high, pushing aside my concerns as I began to cut a path towards him. My heart was pounding with fear and trepidation, but I couldn't let it show. This was what I'd wanted anyway. A chance to get close to all the Kings. I needed to figure out which of them had been responsible for my brother's death. And I'd just been gifted the opportunity to spend time in Ryder's company several times a week. It shouldn't have terrified me, it should have pleased me.

Just keep telling yourself that and you may manage not to piss yourself.
No promises though.

RYDER

CHAPTER SIX

New girl strode toward me, her eyes on the chair my arm was currently slung over. But if Titan thought I was gonna let her sit there, he was fucking deluded.

She slowed to a halt and my upper lip curled back. The viper in me was poised, ready to inject venom.

"Speak," I commanded and her brows jumped up toward her sugary lilac hairline. *Hair like that would look good wrapped around my fist and pulled until she screamed.*

"I'm paired with you so…could you remove the meatloaf resting on the back of my chair?" she asked, her voice honeyed and smooth. I wondered how husky I could make it after a night with my hand locked around her slender throat. But I wasn't willing to get Oscura STIs off this bitch.

"I don't pair with Oscura filth," I growled.

"I'm not in their gang," she said earnestly.

I shrugged one shoulder. "You reek of Oscura blood. I smell it on your breath and it's worse than shit." I inhaled deeply, setting off the deep rattle in my chest as the serpent part of me took over. That noise was a warning and no fucker in their right mind ignored it.

New girl frowned like she'd never heard a snake rattle before. Guess that made sense. My Order was rare as hell.

She glanced over at Dante then back to me. "I'm a Vampire, what do you expect? I'll drink from *any* powerful shitbag. You included."

My brows lowered and she didn't recoil from the dark glare I was giving her. I hated to admit it, but she *had* just made a decent point. And if new girl was power hungry, I had a lot of power between my legs she could take the benefit of.

I scrutinised her from head to toe, deciding if she made the cut. Though one look at her when she'd walked into the classroom was all I'd really needed. That was why I'd sent her the vision. She looked fragile, but her eyes said warrior. And that was my kind of female.

I gestured for her to sit, not removing my arm and she pursed her lips before dropping into the seat, falling right into the cage my body made. I leaned in closer and she didn't squirm, flinch or wince. Which was a fucking miracle when it came to me. "If you make an alliance with the Oscuras, I'll break your pretty legs and wear you around my neck for a week."

She gave me a sideways glance which told me she was one percent unsettled by that comment. But then her eyes roamed up my body, taking in the nearly two hundred pounds of muscle that was me and a smile quirked her mouth up at the corner. "I don't make alliances. But I am on the lookout for a permanent blood Source, so I'll be sampling the menu around school until I figure out who suits me best."

I licked my lips seductively, trying to catch her in my gaze again. She was making an effort to avoid my eyes since I'd hypnotised her into a literal mindfuck. I finally snagged her gaze, pushing my power over her and her lips parted into a perfect O.

I sent her a vision of me fucking the life out of her, sprawled across this very desk while she drank deeply from my neck. Maybe a Vampire was just what I needed right now. Biting was one of my favourite forms of pain after all.

I released her from the vision and she pressed her thighs together, heat emanating from her like a furnace.

"Stop fucking doing that," she hissed, turning away sharply as Titan started passing out ingredients to everyone around the room.

"Why? Because you have an audience or because you want the real deal?" I smirked and she shot me a glare which made my dick twitch. *The angrier the better, baby.*

"Those are my only two options?" she snorted and it disarmed me for a second, drawing one rumbling note of laughter from my lips. The students in front of us turned around, completely surprised that that noise had come from me. I was fucking astonished myself.

I leaned in close to her ear, rolling the ball of my tongue piercing between my teeth. "I don't believe you didn't enjoy it. You're quivering, new girl." She tilted her head away but didn't altogether move and the action gave me a view of the goosebumps peppering her flesh.

"My name is Elise. Not new girl. If you insist on calling me that, I'll call you snake boy."

"Nothing about me is a boy."

"Snake *man* then. But that sounds like a pretty shit superhero name so it's up to you."

"You're witty. I like that. Have you ever been hate-fucked against a tree?"

"What?" she gasped and I grinned as I finally shook the foundations of that cocky façade.

"I'm asking for a friend. He's a tall guy, gets even taller when he's happy and he has a piercing you can't miss."

"Please tell me you're not describing your dick right now." She started laying out the ingredients before her, tugging the ceramic bowl closer to make

71

the potion as she read the instructions on her Atlas.

"Bing bong!" the cheery voice of Principal Greyshine sounded over the tannoy and it set my rattle off in irritation. Titan looked exhausted already. "Ahoy team, I hope you're having a dope morning. I'm just swinging by with a few morning announcements...firstly, I'd like you all to be real welcoming to our new homegirl, Elise Callisto, who started at Aurora just yesterday. Make sure to show her how totally fresh our school is."

Everyone in class looked to Elise and she dipped her head so her hair curtained her view of them. I smirked, mildly interested about what she thought of Greyshine's way of talking. The guy was like a fucking throw-back to the 90s.

He went on, "The cafaeteria will now be hosting the Faetography Club after an incident near the Lunar Pit in The Iron Wood resulted in a camera being forcefully inserted into Eugene Dipper's nether regions. FYI, the camera was removed and is still in working order if you would like to come forward and claim it, Mr Dipper."

Eugene shrank into his seat at the front of the class, his neck turning almost as pale as his white hair. *You shouldn't have wandered onto our turf uninvited then, should you, you little asshole?*

I glanced across the room at my gang brother and second in command, Bryce Corvus, who'd done the deed and he grinned at me. He was the image of his prison-bound father with his choppy black hair, almond eyes and skinny frame. He always had a cigarette tucked behind his ear and was known to light up around weaker professors. Titan played nice with his students, but he'd enforce detention on us too, so it wasn't worth his time.

Principal Greyshine's announcement finally ended, "That's all for now. Have a banging day. Catch you on the flip!"

Titan sighed heavily then motioned the class back into action. "Continue."

Elise started reading through the instructions again and I caught that

Dragon asshole glaring over at us.

"Have you fucked Inferno yet?" I jerked my chin at Dante. We called him Inferno amongst the Brotherhood, mostly because he hated it. He was a Storm Dragon, not fire. That was something he was proud of apparently. Fuck knew why.

She followed my gaze to Dante then rolled her eyes at me like that question was outrageous. *Good to know.*

I snatched a jar of lavender from her hand, stopping her from ruining the potion before she even started. "Crush the lavender first, don't just pour in full sprigs or you'll fuck it up." I took one out of the jar, clasping it between my finger and thumb and crushing it to dust, sprinkling it into the bowl.

She watched attentively then repeated the process to meet the required amount. I pocketed what we didn't use for my own use, not caring if Titan saw me or not. He wouldn't dare call me out on it. Elise turned to me when she'd finished stirring in four drops of Faefly elixir.

"You don't exactly strike me as a master of potions," she commented, arching a brow.

"I have plenty of need for potions," I said darkly. Mostly poisons. A little Basilisk venom mixed with nightshade left in the light of the moon was so deadly, you only had to inhale the fumes to bust a lung. Probably best to distract from that particular hobby though. "I know a great one for lube, wanna try it out sometime?"

"That's gonna be a hard no."

"I'll let you suck on my power," I offered with a smirk.

"I'm guessing that's what you call your dick, so no thanks." Her flushed cheeks told me otherwise. Every girl I'd met was curious about what a night with me was like. The danger drew them in. But the fantasy wasn't like the reality. It took a special kind of girl to enjoy what I enjoyed. So I always sent them a few visions first to ensure they really knew what they were getting into. Elise would be no different.

I'd catch her unawares the next time I hypnotised her with one of *those* visions. She'd need her heart restarted after she experienced that.

I loved the sound of breaking bones. I *adored* the snap, snap, snap with every kick or punch or bite. Pain was everything. Their pain, my pain. At some point it melded in the middle until it was one and the same. I dished the blows so hard I received them too. My magic reserves swelled; inflicting pain on this rat restored them, making me feel invincible.

"Oscura scum," I spat on the bloodied Fae at my feet, stepping over him and cracking my neck. Pop. Not pain, but something.

Every Oscura I made bleed was a victory for the Lunar Brotherhood. Another inch of turf claimed. Another enemy crushed. I circled my prey, flexing my arms, making a show for my brothers up on the bleachers.

"This little *Oscum* trailed into our camp, brothers!" I thumped my fist against my sternum and blood sprayed from my knuckles, flecking my skin, coating me in my victory. A roar of fury went up from my gang, and the hollow thump of fists hitting chests resounded in my ears. "Do we let him live?"

A chorus of *no! no! no!* rang out like a death march. I continued circling my victim as he curled in on himself, protecting his head. They always did that. When *I* was down on my knees, I never cowered. Fear didn't exist in me. I lived between two emotions. Pain and lust. Those two feelings were all I needed and both were printed across my knuckles to remind everyone else in the world of that.

Pain across my right because it was the hand which did the most damage to my enemies. I didn't have mercy on them. In fact, I couldn't recall ever having mercy on anyone. If a doctor cut me open they'd find a knife in place of my heart, stashed there as a last resort.

I wouldn't actually kill the Oscura kid. There were some lines drawn at this school, though the teachers tended to stay out of the way of what went on between the gangs. That was our business and anyone messing with *us* messed with our families outside of this place who weren't a slave to any rules. No, we were done here. My magic reserves were full and energy settled in my veins like rain.

As a Basilisk, I was a rare Order form and hell if it gave people the shits around here. Since my Order had emerged, I'd been bound by the needs of my kind. Pain was no longer something to be avoided, it was as essential as breathing. I'd been dealt enough of it in my life to know what it was like to be the one cowering. Now *I* made the rules. And my Order ensured I'd become a master of pain. A fucking god. And what most people were too afraid to learn, was that pain often rode the boundary of pleasure. You only had to push hard enough to get there, expand your mind, overcome your instincts.

As the adrenaline wore off from the high I'd ridden during the fight, my needs flipped like a switch. Pain gave way to lust. But fulfilling my sexual needs was a challenge in itself. I had to compromise. Hard. Half the girls in school were terrified of me, and the other half would fuck me any which way till Sunday. *Except* the way I needed. And the only way I craved.

I dragged the kid up by the scruff of his neck, angling him to face the rest of the Brotherhood. "You won't come back here."

He nodded frantically, dribbling blood.

"You won't run to Inferno either. He's not gonna fight your battles. You want revenge? You come back when you're strong enough to face me yourself." I shoved him away and he stumbled off in the direction of his Clan as fast as he could manage with a broken ankle.

I spat a wad of blood on the ground. He'd gotten a few good punches in at the start. Part of me had let him land the blows. It riled me up, got my blood pounding. I pressed my tongue against a loose tooth at the back of my mouth, the pain the sort of deep heat I liked.

Some called me a masochist. Others a sadist. Frankly, I didn't give two flying fucks what I was so long as I was me. Ryder Draconis. King of this academy.

Despite the name of my gang, there were in fact girls in the Brotherhood. We didn't discriminate for shit. There were only two requirements for joining. One: you were strong. Strong physically, strong of heart, strong of mind. Whatever it was, I didn't care so long as you added some kind of strength to our ranks. Two: you had never been in Oscura Clan, never fucked anyone from Oscura Clan, never had so much as a fucking kind thought in the direction of Oscura Clan. When you entered the Lunar Brotherhood, they were your mortal enemies. Pure and simple.

My gaze raked across the girls on the bleachers as they pushed up their tits or threw seductive looks my way, knowing what I wanted. I'd had my fair share of them already; some came closer to fulfilling my needs than others. But as I looked across them, searching, hunting, I realised who I was really looking for. New girl.

It was lunchtime and I hadn't seen much of her since Potions Class. She wasn't gonna be found here amongst my people, so where? My teeth stamped tightly together as I turned my full attention to the hunt.

If she's with Inferno I'll destroy her.

Why this particular girl worked me up was a mystery, but maybe it was the thought of Dante claiming her first. That conniving piece of shit already had an advantage by sharing a room with her. She didn't seem like an easy nut to crack, but I knew Dante would be readying his nutcracker. So I had to piss on my territory fast if I was going to win her.

"Good fight." Bryce appeared at my side, his eyes following the kid as he limped back into Oscura Clan on the opposite side of no man's land. They banded around him, the wolves drawing him in to heal his injuries. "Orders?"

"Double our eyes on Inferno," I grunted. "He'll want blood for blood."

Bryce nodded, sweeping a hand through his dark locks.

I wiped my face with the back of my hand, smearing the word *pain* in red. I couldn't walk onto Oscura Turf without taking on fifty rabid Werewolves so I hoped new girl wasn't there.

Devil's Hill rose up at the far end of no man's land, thronging with unallied students. And there she was, sitting next to the hot Sphinx who bunked with Inferno and Gabriel Nox. Nox was as absent as the fucking moon right now. I swear he lived in actual shadows that fucker. But if you ever pissed him off, you'd know it like a murderous clown stepping into your living room.

I nodded to Bryce in dismissal and walked toward her.

"New girl." I pointed at her as I strode up the hill, causing students to scatter from the bloody, shirtless monster who roamed between them.

She was halfway through a cheese sandwich, mid-bite, pausing to look up at me with a slightly pissed off expression. Didn't look like interrupting her lunch was a good move. But I didn't do courtesy. Pain and lust. That was it.

"I wanna talk to you," I commanded, curling a finger to beckon her to stand.

The girl beside her threw Elise a fearful look, but new girl got up, finishing her sandwich as she walked toward me. "I don't like being beckoned," she said flatly, brows raised.

"What *do* you like? I'll give it to you right now," I purred, causing her friend to splutter into a coughing fit.

She thought on that for a moment, drawing a crumb from the corner of her lip and sucking it off her finger. My dick felt it all.

"Orange soda," she announced. "Can't seem to find that bliss anywhere in this place."

"Done." I offered her my hand and she eyed it with as much distaste as if I'd just whipped out my junk. "Take it."

"No thanks. You do know you look like you just stepped out of a horror movie, right?"

I glanced down at my bloodied flesh then shrugged, turning away from her. "If you want soda, come the fuck on."

77

I marched back down the hill through no man's land and into the nest of cliques that filled Acrux Courtyard. I felt new girl's presence, the heat of her skin prickling against my back. I was cold blooded through and through. And that wasn't some fucking metaphor. Basilisk blood ran ice-cold. The only way to warm it up was by laying in the sun or rubbing hot flesh against my own. The latter was something I was gonna achieve with new girl once I jumped through the hoops she laid out for me.

Orange soda was easy. It was step one. Step two was mind-fucking her into oblivion to figure out her hard limits. I didn't have hard limits. Unless you counted cuddling, spooning and heaven fucking forbid *canoodling*. Frankly, anything that ended with an *ing* that didn't start with fuck was a solid no from me. I didn't kiss, I tongue-fucked. I didn't caress, I clawed. I didn't go down on girls, I feasted on them.

I led her over to the Kipling brothers, the three of them in varying years at the academy. All of them were Griffins and were clever as shit. They weren't very powerful magically so they'd made themselves invaluable to every student in the school instead. If you needed something you couldn't get yourself, illegal or otherwise, they could get it for you. Mostly, they set themselves up as a snack store to keep the professors from looking too closely when money was exchanged. But I reckoned the Kiplings could get a fucking elephant into the school and no one would be any the wiser.

"Orange soda," I demanded as we arrived under the small marquee they called the Kipling Emporium, holding out my hand. I didn't pay for anything with money, what I gave them was protection. Pretty sure the Oscuras gave it to them too. So essentially, the Kiplings got a free ride in this school. No one messed with them. Ever.

The skinniest one, Kipling Junior, turned to the well of ice his brother had created with his water magic right on the flagstones. He fished out an orange can and handed it over. I passed it straight to Elise and her hand closed around it before I let go. Our fingers skimmed and she shuddered as my frozen skin met her warmth.

"What do you say?" I growled, my eyes falling to the rise and fall of her breasts as she inhaled. Yeah we were definitely gonna fuck. I didn't give orange soda to just anybody. And she knew it.

She took the can, pulling the ring. Click-hiss. She brought it to her lips and took a long swig, her throat bobbing as she swallowed and making me hard as rock. She kept drinking, chugging the whole can before crushing it in her palm and releasing a breath of satisfaction.

"Thank you." She tossed the can at my feet and walked away. And that, ladies and gentleman, was going to cost her big time.

GARETH

CHAPTER SEVEN

EIGHTEEN MONTHS BEFORE THE SOLARID METEOR SHOWER...

*E*verything changed at Aurora Academy the day term started and a new batch of freshmen arrived. The school was ripped apart into two factions more clearly than ever before.

Ryder Draconis was the infamous son of the Lunar Brotherhood founder and his mortal rival Dante Oscura was the Dragon born of Werewolves – also a direct descendant of the founding family of the Oscura Clan. To put it simply, they were at war. And they were determined to drag the entire school onto the battleground with them.

They'd only been attending the school for a few weeks and the atmosphere in Aurora was already more dangerous than it had ever been before. No one wanted to piss off the gangs, but they constantly pressured everyone to pick a side. Barely a day went by without fights breaking out in the halls and the teachers dealt with it by turning a blind eye or bowing to *their whims.*

The dormitory tower was now firmly divided, the top half belonging to Oscura Clan and the bottom to the Lunar Brotherhood. With my room on the ground floor, I was solidly in Lunar territory. Going for a piss in the communal bathroom at the end of the hall had become a genuine fucking threat to my day.

The other three Fae in my dorm had already signed up to the Brotherhood, but I wasn't budging. I didn't want to be part of any gang. And no one would tell me otherwise.

I headed to the bathroom just before midnight, shirtless with a toothbrush and toothpaste clamped in my hand. I didn't leave my stuff lying about anywhere. And I certainly wouldn't be leaving something as precious as my toothbrush about for someone to screw with - I'd learned that lesson the hard way in freshman year.

I pushed through the door and almost stopped in my tracks as I spotted Ryder standing before the mirror, his jaw slathered in shaving foam as he scraped a fucking knife down his face like a savage.

"There's a spell for that you know," I said before I could stop myself.

The muscles of his bare torso flexed and I tried not to lose my nerve. I'd spent my summers working at Old Sal's bar and I knew how to charm my way around the meanest of bastards.

"Did I ask for a fucking fact of the day?" he spat, his cold green eyes scraping down me like he was considering shoving that knife somewhere into my body.

Abort mission.

I mock saluted him in the way my sister and I always did to each other, heading to a sink a few down from him and squirted toothpaste onto the brush, stuffing it in my mouth. Ryder finished his shave, rinsing the knife in the sink and wiping his face on a towel. He tucked the blade into his pocket then just stood there, glaring at me in the mirror. I didn't want to be afraid, but I'd heard the rumours about Ryder Draconis. Backing down wasn't in my nature though. I was Fae.

Pressure was mounting in my chest as that asshole just kept staring at me until I washed out my mouth.

"You chosen yet?" he demanded like that was a perfectly normal question. I knew what he meant though. It was what every unallied student was asked daily.

I gave him my best smile which probably could have made the devil soften to me. But apparently this guy's heart was harder than his.

"I don't do gangs, freshman," I said, reminding him I had a solid year of magical training on him. "So I'd appreciate it if you and your little friends stop asking me that."

I moved to head past him and he lurched forward, throwing his shoulder into mine so hard I stumbled back.

My heart juddered as his eyes flashed, turning to snake-like slits. I knew his Order, but I hadn't witnessed it yet. Something told me I didn't want to either.

I lifted my chin, refusing to bow to the challenge in his eyes.

Ryder cracked his neck, curling his right hand into a fist and I noticed the word pain *tattooed across his knuckles. Was he for real?*

"I'm going to bed." I moved to step around him and he blocked my path, ramming his whole chest against mine. His fist came at me so fast, I almost didn't have time to throw up a shield of air. But I managed it a second before his fist collided with it. He slammed his knuckles into it again and again until they split open on my magic. I watched in shock as he sucked the blood from them then spat it on the floor at my feet.

"You wanna see what this freshman *can do then, you asshole?" he growled and I stepped back on instinct.*

Shit, this guy is crazy.

"I'd rather not." I drew more air around me, ready to knock him on his ass if he tried to attack me again. I had to show a strong front but I could feel

it starting to crack.

He grinned in a way that was anything but friendly then marched out the door, leaving it swinging as he went.

I ran a hand down the back of my neck, my heart pounding a rapid tune. I glanced in the mirror, locking eyes with myself and falling into a mental pep talk.

Forget the scary-ass snake. You've gotta focus on the real issue here. There's only one week left until your first payment is due and you have fuck all to show for it.

The two gangs entering the school had thrown a serious spanner into the works for me. The unallied students were being terrorised, threatened and bullied on a daily basis. I had to watch my own back too so I was pushed for time trying to come up with ways to raise the money I needed. But I couldn't waste another day.

I swallowed thickly, heading out of the bathroom as several more of the Brotherhood came in, glaring at me as I headed past them.

I hurried down the corridor, frowning as I spotted my roommates standing out in the hall.

"I'm not going back in there," Rowanda said, folding her arms with an anxious expression on her face.

"Yeah fuck that, man. He can have it." Carl headed past me, giving me a look that said turn back now *before jogging away.*

Harvey looked my way, seeming relieved as I approached. He was my closest friend in this place, a fellow Pegasus and Pitball player. He scraped a hand through his unruly copper locks as he approached. "Bro, you will not believe who's in our fucking room."

My heart sank like a stone. "Ryder Draconis?" I guessed.

Harvey nodded, his eyes widening. "Did you know he was gonna do this?"

"Do what?" I frowned.

Rowanda pushed the door open with her toe, gesturing for me to go in.

I frowned at their fearful expressions, pressing my shoulders back as I headed through the door. I nearly shifted in alarm as I found the cause of the fucking disturbance. Ryder was in his enormous Basilisk form, thirty feet of snake as thick as a car coiled around our entire dorm. His scales were inky black as they spread across all four bunks. His head lay on my pillow and he lifted it, his tongue flicking out as he bared row upon row of fangs wet with venom.

"By the sun." It took everything I had not to run for my damn life, but I refused to give in to that urge. Refused to cower. "What do you want?" I growled, my skin shimmering as my Order form threatened to come out. He might have been a mean prick but snakes couldn't fly and they couldn't kick either. My main threat was those powerful jaws which looked almost big enough to swallow me whole. Order form or not.

Ryder hissed at me and a deep rattle sounded from within his body. His eyes were two green slits that were void of warmth. A threat. But what the hell for? If he wanted a fight, he would have started it by now. Please don't freaking start one.

A ripple ran across his body then he shifted back into his Fae form, laying butt naked on the bottom bunk to my left. My bunk.

"Get your ass off my bedsheets," I demanded, moving forward just as Ryder hooked up my journal and my gut dropped. He'd found my shit. I kept that journal under my mattress and behind a concealment spell and he'd fucking found it in less than the time it took for me to get back from the bathroom.

"Who's Ella?" Ryder asked, a twisted smile on his lips. I didn't write much in that journal. It was mostly for sketches and a few notes but pressed between the pages had been a card Elise had given me before I'd come to the academy.

I clenched my jaw, refusing to answer and Ryder read out what she'd *written to me.* "Be the man you always wanted to be, Gare Bear. Love always, Ella."

"Give that back," I growled, fury pulsing through my veins.

"She sounds hot," Ryder mused, ignoring me as he twisted the card between his fingers all too close to his dick for my liking. "Does she like it on the top or the bottom? I don't let them on top, I live up to my name."

I lost my patience, his meaty fingers wrapped around that card making me feel like his hands were on my sister. That was my line. And he'd well and truly crossed it.

"Give me it." I stole the air from his lungs and Ryder choked, his jaw locking as I held his life in my grasp.

He glared at me with a dare in his eyes, the seconds ticking by. Tick tick tick.

My pulse started to race and I frowned as he continued to glare, turning goddamn blue. "Shit," I hissed, dropping the cast before I killed the idiot.

He sucked in a breath which turned to a heady laugh like he'd seriously enjoyed that shit and I took a wary step back.

"Here's how things are about to go." Ryder dropped out of my bunk, taking a pair of my folded sweatpants from the shelf beside the bed and pulling them on like he owned them. "You're gonna take your card and whatever else you can before I count to ten. Then you're gonna get the fuck out of my new room before I shift again and give you a bite you won't recover from for a full week."

My heart juddered. I did not wanna give up my room. But I also didn't have a week to sacrifice in the ward. I had a responsibility to my family and okay maybe I was five percent scared of what this guy could do to me if I pushed him.

"One...two..."

I stalked forward with fury in my chest, snatching the card from his outstretched hand before scooping up my journal. He continued counting down and I ground my teeth as I stuffed my things into a bag, slinging it over my shoulder and heading for the door.

He reached zero as I made it there, then called out to me, "I like your attitude, journal guy. You'd thrive in the Brotherhood."

I raised my middle finger in answer, heading out the door and slamming it behind me.

Screw him and his Brotherhood. I was never gonna cave to that bullshit. But I got the feeling that avoiding his gang wasn't going to be possible any longer. Ryder had forced me out on my ass and he wasn't even a trained Fae. He knew how to manipulate the people around him so the next time he came for me, I had to be ready.

Elise

CHAPTER EIGHT

A week at Aurora Academy had me learning a lot of interesting things about my classmates and murder suspects. Namely about their routines. For example, it quickly became apparent that Leon and his two roommates always headed outside when the sun was shining. Considering the fact that the dorm allocations were supposed to be random, it seemed fairly suspicious to me that his two female dorm mates were both of the Nemean Lion Order too. I guessed there were some perks to being the resident rich boy.

Since my brother had died, his bunk in Leon's room had gone unused so that meant there were only three of them sleeping in there and the girls were in Leon's pride. I wasn't sure if he was actually screwing them or if he just used them as weird kinda slaves. I often saw them - and lots of other girls besides - carrying his shit for him or bringing him meals from the cafaeteria. Mostly he just seemed to sit about on his ass and let them wait on him hand and foot. Unless he was at the gym or in Pitball practice of course.

I'd stuck my head into the school gymnasium once, eyeing the racks of weights and smelling the man stench with distaste. There seemed to be some kind of gang schedule which allowed Oscura and Lunar access to it at different times, but there was no handy pamphlet to say when. I didn't want to risk heading in there during a gang allocation and accidentally making it seem like I was interested in joining, so I'd avoided the place since.

So far, I'd been keeping both Dante and Ryder at something of a distance while observing their tics and habits as I tried to figure out the best ways to crack them. The problem with them was that getting close to one would infuriate the other. And it hadn't slipped my attention that the two of them had been entering into a weird tug of war type competition over me since my arrival. I guessed they saw any fresh arrival as a potential member to their gangs but there was no way in hell I'd be joining either.

I released an irritated breath as I banished them from my mind and focused on the task at hand instead.

The weather forecast had said sunny intervals and my horoscope had informed me that dedication would pay off for me today too so it seemed like fate would be on my side.

Gareth had always had a paranoid streak ever since he'd caught one of Mom's boyfriends stealing his stash of chilli chips one night and he'd gotten pretty damn good at hiding things. In my heart, I just knew that he wouldn't have wanted to leave stuff out in a communal space in his dorm which meant that I would almost certainly find whatever he'd valued hidden away somewhere in that room.

I hung out in the corridor, perched in a windowsill as I jotted away at my Cardinal Magic essay so that it wouldn't seem strange that I was here. Students often hung out in weird places like this due to the lack of privacy offered by rooming with four people, so I wasn't drawing much attention in my perch.

It was stiflingly hot in the window ledge though so I'd thrown the window wide and was enjoying the breeze that swept in from it. The dizzying fall a few feet to my right had my morbid imagination working on overdrive as I wondered what it would be like to fall down there...or push someone else.

If I don't watch out I really will end up as a psychopath. Then maybe I'll have to kill myself to get justice. And where's the justice in that?

I couldn't really concentrate on my essay with most of my attention on the door down the hall and occasionally on that fall so I slowly gave up, doodling on the foot of my page instead.

I lost myself to dark thoughts of severing limbs and breaking bones, making the murderer pay in kind for what they'd taken from me. I wanted to give them a physical wound for each emotional scar they'd caused me. But even a hundred years of torture wouldn't come close to the pain that losing Gareth had forced me to endure. Sometimes it felt like two people had died that day. My brother and the girl I'd been when he was alive. I wasn't entirely sure who I even was now. Just a cold, hard shell for vengeance or a lost girl needing answers? Maybe both. Maybe neither.

I blinked against tears which prickled the backs of my eyes as I thought over some of my fondest memories of him. Once he'd emerged in his Order form as a Pegasus, he used to let me ride on his back through the clouds whenever I wanted. I didn't think I'd ever felt freedom like I'd felt between his wings, soaring through the sky. And I guessed I never would again.

I jabbed my pencil down a little harder than I'd intended, accidentally severing the overly large penis I'd drawn onto a little demon representation of Ryder Draconis.

I blinked at the ruined sketch, clearing the unshed tears from my gaze as I tried to focus on the paper and push my grief back into the fortress I'd built within my heart to house it.

"I think you may have lost some of your talent."

I shrieked in alarm as a voice came from outside the window beside me, almost falling from my perch in the windowsill before a strong hand caught mine to save me.

"Try not to fall," Gabriel said irritably as I looked up into his angelic face in alarm. I wasn't sure how the hell I'd missed his arrival; with my

Vampire hearing that shouldn't have been possible.

He was perched on the stone balustrade which ringed the wall outside the window, his body transformed into his Order form. I wasn't sure I'd ever been so close to a Harpy in their shifted state and I found myself staring. Huge black, feathered wings sprouted from his back, spread just a little to help him balanced in the precarious position. Shining silver scales which looked more like armour coated the lower half of his body before giving way to the muscles of his bare chest and letting me look over his tattoos. His skin was scrawled with countless markings but there was something of a theme to them, star signs and constellations curved around each other in a way so beautifully detailed that I couldn't help but drink them in.

"What the hell are you doing out there?" I asked. He hadn't released my fingers and the warmth of his hand on my flesh was drawing a lot of my attention. I'd barely spoken two words to him before and now he was just... holding my hand?

"Do you mean physically or are you asking in the larger sense of the question? What are any of us *really* doing? Is it up to us or have the stars already made all of our decisions for us?" He cocked his head at me and I frowned, wondering if he had a screw loose or if maybe he was just...

"Are you teasing me?" I asked, raising an accusatory eyebrow.

Gabriel's eyes brightened in response to my question but he didn't confirm it. His gaze slid back to my doodles and I retrieved my hand from his grip, folding the page over to stop him from looking. I wondered if he'd recognise the maimed figures of Leon, Dante, Ryder and himself in my scribbles. I'd drawn him as a fly with his wings pulled off as well as a bird on fire and a crucified man complete with tattoos, but I really wasn't much of an artist. The facial features were just crosses for their dead eyes and little O mouths to depict their shock as I killed them. Not exactly professional pieces.

"Are you trying out a new style? I'd have to say I prefer your original designs."

"What do you..." My lips parted as something clicked together in my mind and I pointed a finger at him. "Did you go through my things?"

"Define *yours.*"

"My stuff. The things I brought from home...the, my-" I couldn't quite bring myself to say it. If he hadn't looked at Gareth's drawings then I didn't want to mention them to him. I didn't want anyone else to see them. Especially not one of the men I suspected of killing him. They were all I had left, they were everything to me. They-

"If I'm the most powerful person in the room and there are things in that room, then don't they just belong to me anyway?" Gabriel asked in a low voice which made the hairs raise along the back of my neck. His gaze trailed over me like he could see every scar on my soul shining out through my eyes. "And if those things are mine, it would make sense for me to look at them." For a moment it didn't seem like he was just talking about my stuff, but like he meant me as well.

"What did you do with them?" I demanded, too stunned to even think of anything else to say and absolutely refusing to cower before him no matter how strong he was.

"Nothing. I only looked. You'll know about it if I decide to touch." Gabriel took off before I could respond, his wings throwing a gust of wind into my face and blowing my hair back.

"Asshole!" I shouted after him, shock thundering through me too keenly to give me the clarity to insult him any better than that. "What the hell is wrong with you?!"

Define yours. Who the hell did he think he was? Of course the stuff I'd brought here with me belonged to me, who the hell else's would it be? He was damn lucky he'd flown off when he had or my fingers would have been locked around his neck right about now.

Gabriel flew up into the clouds just as they sailed away from the sun, letting it shine down over the academy. I slumped back against the wall in defeat, fully intending to track down Gabriel and finish our goddamn conversation with my fists. Just as soon as I checked on Gareth's sketches and made sure he hadn't done anything to them.

I got to my feet, meaning to do just that right as the door to Leon's room opened. He stepped out, followed by the two Lioness girls. One of them was carrying his coat while the other offered up a bag of chips as he dipped a hand into it, apparently unable to support the small packet on his own.

They turned away from me without even noticing my presence and I quickly cast a gust of wind towards their door, stopping it from falling closed as they walked away.

My argument with Gabriel would have to wait. I needed to take this opportunity to see if my brother had left any clues behind in his room.

I shot towards the gap in the door with my Vampire speed, slipping inside before letting it fall closed behind me.

Three of the bunks were clearly still in use but the one on the bottom left of the room sat bare and unadorned.

I didn't spare much attention to the various bits of Pitball uniform and men's clothing strewn about the rest of the space. It was almost like the two girls didn't live here at all and I'd wandered directly into Leon's man cave.

I stepped forward until I made it to the stripped bed and slowly lowered myself down onto it.

My breathing hitched as I felt a divot in the springs beneath me. Was this a spot he'd liked to sit in? Was my soul residing in a place that used to house his so often he lost count of the time he'd spent here?

My fragile heart was trembling, but I couldn't let it rule me now. I had to conduct my search. And quickly. Who knew how long the sun would stay out on a cloudy day like this? The Lions wouldn't linger outside if the clouds returned.

I ran my hands back and forth over the mattress, feeling with my flesh and my magic for something unusual but there was nothing there.

I chewed my lip and dropped off of the bed, looking into the dark space beneath it. I shuffled into it, sweeping my hands back and forth as I continued my hunt. Lint and an old sock found me but no secret hiding place.

"C'mon," I growled, my patience thinning as I wore through my time.

I shuffled back out from under the bed and looked around it with a frown. The closet doors were hanging open and I could see that Leon and his roommates had made use of the space which used to be Gareth's already. Plus a closet was an obvious hiding spot and Gareth tended to be smarter than that...

Think, Elise! You knew him better than anyone!

My brow furrowed as I turned in a slow circle. A huge poster hung on the wall at the foot of the bed depicting the Solarian Pitball League slogan. The top corner of it was a bit dogeared, like it had been tugged on more than once.

I shot forward and peeled off the bit of tape holding it to the wall, lowering the poster to reveal...nothing.

I frowned at the blank space, running my hand along the smooth wall before suddenly feeling the faintest prick of magic against my palm. Gareth always did have a knack for concealing spells. Luckily, I knew the kinds of locks he cast and quickly directed my own power into unravelling it.

The seconds ticked by as I picked apart his spell, eventually forcing the vision of a smooth wall away with a surge of will so that a hole about the width of my splayed hand was revealed.

I reached into it, pulling out an Atlas with a jagged crack running through its screen and a well-used journal with a brown leather cover and several pages hanging loose. The final items were three clear test tubes housing a few violent blue crystals in each. I recoiled from the vials of Killblaze, recognising the drug even if I'd never gotten so close to the stuff before. I tossed them back in the hole, not wanting anything to do with them and wondering if that meant Gareth had been dealing. I knew without a doubt he'd never take the shit but dealing...we'd always been hard up for money and he'd sent Mom quite a bit of cash over the last few months leading up to his death, claiming to have a part time job. I guessed drug dealing was part time.

I sighed, trying not to be disappointed in him as I gave my attention to the other things I'd found and my heart pounded with triumph as I shoved the haul into my blazer pocket. I stuck the poster back into place and turned for the exit just as a casually thumping heartbeat drew closer in the corridor outside.

Triple shit with a cherry on top, I've fucked it. What kind of Vampire forgets to keep her senses tuned in to her surroundings when she's breaking and entering?

I glanced at the window half-heartedly but quickly abandoned that idea. We were on the twentieth floor and I'd go splat from that fall if I even attempted to climb out there. I might have been able to control the fall with my air magic but I'd never attempted it from a height like this and I wasn't inclined to do so now.

I cast around in desperation, wondering what the hell I was going to say to cover my ass when he came in here and found me-

The door clicked open and I snatched a Pitball ball into my hands at the last second, slapping an amused look on my face just as Leon came in. Thankfully he was alone. Or maybe not thankfully - I could have just thrown myself at the mercy of a psychopath for all I knew.

"Little monster?" he asked in confusion, coming to a halt on the threshold. "How did you get in here?"

"It was open when I came looking for you. And I'm nosey so..." I shrugged, fronting out the situation.

"Okay...so what are you-"

"I wanna play Pitball," I said quickly, tossing the ball up and down in my hand like it was obvious. He was the team captain so it made sense for me to come to him about it even if I could have just gone to the coach instead.

96

"You do?" he asked, his attention piqued.

"Yeah. I'm a damn good player and I hear you need some of those. So..." Joining the school Pitball team hadn't actually been on my to-do list. That went more like this…

1. Find out who killed Gareth.

2. Kill that motherfucker. Slowly.

3. Figure out the rest of my life (presuming said murderer doesn't kill me first and I don't get caught).

But still, playing Pitball might not have been the worst idea I'd ever had. I'd played a lot in my old high school and I hadn't lied about being good. Gareth had been on the academy team too so it could be an opportunity to get closer to some of his old friends and find out more about the things he'd been up to here. Plus, more than half of Pitball was just about beating the crap out of people and I seemed to be in the mood to do that pretty much all of the time at the moment. Venting some of my rage could be a good thing. It might help me keep a clear head when the darkness tried to swallow me so I could do what I needed to find the killer.

"You'd better be able to back up that claim," Leon said, his gaze trailing over me in an assessing way.

"I can. Do you want me to try out?" I asked, smirking at him. "I can wipe that pretty smile right off your face for a start."

Leon snorted in amusement. "Alright. Come for a tryout tomorrow down at the pitch. We can see if you've got what it takes to make the cut."

"Oh, I do," I promised as I tossed the ball into his stomach. He threw his arms out to catch it and I slipped around his back and out into the corridor.

"You're leaving already? The girls are off finding me some snacks so-"

"Soooo...?" I raised an eyebrow at him, daring him to finish that thought but he only grinned, pushing a hand through his long hair as he leaned back against the wall again.

"So, I'll see you tomorrow after class then," Leon said.

"It's a date," I agreed before shooting away from him.

I needed to check the haul in my pocket and make sure that Gabriel hadn't damaged the sketches while I was at it.

Of course, when I headed to the far end of the corridor and into my dorm I found that I wasn't going to have time alone in there.

Laini looked out from her bed as I arrived and I smiled at her in a way that felt fake even to me. She ducked back into the sheet-made cave which surrounded her bed with a casual *hey* and I hopped up onto my bunk.

The first thing I did was crawl over to the little shelf which sat above the foot of my bed. A collection of textbooks were piled on top of it alongside the envelope filled with the only belongings I really cared about in this world.

I held my breath as I slid the sketches out and leafed through them carefully. I knew them all like they were old friends and I traced my fingers over the broad lines and delicate details as I checked each of them for any signs of damage.

A shuddering sigh escaped my lips as I completed my count. They were all there, all okay. Whatever the hell Gabriel had wanted to prove, he obviously felt it could be done without actually taking them from me.

A tear slid down my cheek and splashed onto the back of my hand. I rubbed it away absentmindedly and decided to take a leaf out of Gareth's book.

I lifted one of my Astrology textbooks into my hands and opened the cover, slipping the sketches inside. It took me a few minutes to construct a glamour into place which would hide them from anyone who came looking. I bound them to the front page so that they wouldn't fall out and made them appear as nothing more than just another blank sheet of paper in the front of the book.

The magic pulsed from my fingertips, drawing from the diminishing well of power within me. My supplies were growing low again. I needed to drink from someone. My mind went to Dante and the way his power had sizzled through my veins. The thrill of it had kept me up at night more than once, making me crave another taste. That wasn't going to happen though. Dante was more powerful than me so claiming him for my Source was pretty much impossible. I might have been able to sneak up on him once or twice but it would only end in him beating the crap out of me with his magic in a public way to reassert his dominance. I sighed, letting that idea go. I'd just have to find easier prey.

I glanced back over my shoulder to make sure Laini was still safely tucked away within the confines of her bed and pulled the broken Atlas from my pocket. I tried switching it on but unsurprisingly, it was out of power. As I eyed the damage I had to wonder if it would even load up with a full charge. It was worth a shot though so I plugged it in, sliding it beneath my pillow as I lay down, putting my back to the room as I took the journal from my pocket.

I leafed through it with interest. There wasn't much written in it – it was mainly just sketches of things and people who had caught Gareth's attention. There were the odd words or notes added here and there and I frowned as I tried to figure out if there was any deeper meaning to any of it. Some of the sketches seemed to have a purpose to them and I had to wonder if there was something here that might help me figure out what he'd been up to before he died. But if there were answers here, they weren't leaping out at me. I'd just have to study this thing front to back again and again until I figured them out.

When I was sure I wasn't going to glean any more information from the journal right away, I surreptitiously moved it into my school bag, sealing it into an inside pocket with magic. After finding out that Gabriel had been snooping through my things, I wasn't going to risk leaving anything important in the dorm while I wasn't here again so I'd just have to keep the journal close at all times.

I looked over at Gabriel's bunk, pursing my lips in annoyance. Who did he think he was, going through my shit?

With a twist of my lips, I ripped a piece of paper from my notebook and scribbled two words onto it before shooting from my bed over to his.

"What are you doing up there?" Laini gasped in alarm from beneath me.

"Making sure this asshole understands my point," I replied as I pulled back his duvet and the smell of earth and cedar assaulted me.

I bet Gabriel's blood tastes like ecstasy.

"He's the most powerful Fae in the school. Are you insane?" Laini demanded but I only scoffed.

He might have been powerful but that didn't give him free rein to be a nosey asshole in my opinion. I was the one doing the snooping around here and I wouldn't take kindly to him taking an interest in me.

I dropped the note onto his sheet, the words winking up at me tauntingly. *Define yours.* I smirked to myself and placed the duvet back down over it. Let's see how he liked having his personal space invaded while he wasn't here.

I scooted back to my own bed once my mission was complete. That should have been enough to make my point without being an out and out threat. Because as much as it angered me to admit it, Laini had a point. Gabriel was much more powerful than me. And although my fantasies about strangling him for going through my stuff were nice, I knew it wasn't going to happen in reality. So I just needed to establish some firm boundaries with him. At least until I figured out if he was a murderer or not. If he *was* I'd figure out a way to kill him somehow.

I lay back on my bed and sighed. This place would probably be the death of me. But not before I ripped it apart first.

LEON

CHAPTER NINE

Someone planted a plastic cup in my hand and I tossed the contents into my mouth.

"Argh!" I spat it out and threw the cup so it bounced off the back of her head. Her. The girl who'd dared bring me that piss water from the tap. The actual motherfucking *tap*. "Mineral water, Mindy!" I roared at her and she flinched around, grabbing the cup from the floor.

Girl was new. Freshmen. Cute ass. I liked her smile too. But right then I was about as mad as I could get. Alright, maybe not *quite* as mad as I could get. But still.

I frowned, sauntering over and slinging an arm around her shoulders. "You know I hate to shout, Mindy."

"It's Lillia-"

"Shhhh Mindy." I called them all Mindy. Made it miles easier to remember. They didn't really mind, not that I asked. I pulled her into my arms and she giggled, running her hands down my chest. "Min..?" I started for her and she said, "-dy."

"No, *min*eral water. Keep up Mindy." I nudged her away, folding my arms as I returned my gaze to the pitch. Where was my damn whistle when I needed it? I had a golden whistle, custom made. A real beautiful thing to behold. But I had to keep an eye on it because Dante was always eyeing it up. I gave him gold no bother because my family threw it at me like it was confetti, but that whistle was mine. I'd designed it top to bottom when I'd made Team Captain. It had the four Elemental symbols engraved on it plus the Solarian Pitball League insignia at the bottom. One day, I was going to get the Fireside of The Skylarks, Alid Kerberos, to burn a mark into it too. It was mine. And when something was mine, I did not let it go.

I wouldn't even have needed a whistle but our coach, Professor Mars, ran detention on Thursdays so I always filled the role for him then.

I sought Dante out on the pitch - if you could call this shitty sandbox with a hole at the centre of it a real pitch – and found him stroking my damn whistle.

"Dante!" I waved my arms to get his attention. "Bad boy!" I mocked then patted my knees. "Bring it back. Come on." I made kissing noises at him and he smirked, promptly placing the whistle around his neck on the chain. "No, Dante," I complained, serious now. I pushed a hand into my shorts pocket, taking out a few gold coins. It was like trading doggie kibble for the TV remote.

He was a damn magpie. And birdie would come flying when he saw these. I pinched them between my fingers and let the sun catch them, shining them in his direction.

His head lifted and he wandered over, his eyes never wavering from the gold. He reached for them immediately and I held them behind my back. "Whistle. Now."

Dante sighed. "But it's so…"

"I know. And it's so mine. Give it or I'll cut you from the team." I meant it. Sort of. Dante was a solid Airsentry and though he was no Lance Orion from *Zodiac Academy*, we still might have had a shot at beating their asses if we were all on top form in our next match against them. Maybe. Okay, probably not. But I was a major optimist. And as Captain, I was determined to enthuse my players as best I could. The team hadn't even made it beyond the qualifiers for years before Dante and I had signed up to play defensive positions. And we'd barely scraped by this year in our first match of the quarterfinals. But if we had another one or two strong players, I reckoned we could actually win the whole tournament one day.

Dante handed it back to me with a terse frown and I tossed him the coins, planting the whistle in my mouth and blowing it so hard he winced.

"*Stronzo*," he snapped, throwing a hard punch into my arm. "My fucking ears."

"You need to *stronzo* back onto that pitch and play ball, Dante." I pointed.

"That is so out of context." He rolled his eyes but did as I asked and moved away across the pitch to the Air Quarter. Not many people outside of the Oscura Clan could claim to call Dante their friend, but we'd built a bond on Pitball and beer which was hard to deny.

"Hey," a soft voice announced the arrival of Elise and I turned to find her in the extra small uniform I'd purposefully given her. I grinned, raking my eyes up her bare legs, taking my sweet time over her nipped in waist, then riding the express train to her rack. Yep, I was happy to disembark there. More than happy. Until her hand caught my chin, yanked it up and pinched so hard I grunted.

I bashed her arm away, rubbing my face. "Be careful. This face is worth a lot."

"Not enough to afford that long of a look at my chest, Leon. Do you also stare at Dante's tits like that, or is it just the female members of the team you perv on?"

"I don't need to look, he lets me fondle them in the locker room." I flashed her my best grin and she choked on a laugh as she tried to keep it in.

My grin widened and I slid my hand down her back, prodding her onto the pitch. "If you can outwork Gladys you can have her spot on the team. She's only a sub filling in for the Airstriker position anyway. The guy who had it before, he..." I pressed my lips together as Gareth's face pushed into my head. I battled the image away, swallowing the lump in my throat along with the knot of guilt in my gut.

Elise had dropped down to tie her shoelace and I managed to recompose myself by the time she stood up again, her jaw set.

"Well he's gone, so just do better than Gladys." I leaned in and whispered, "Anyone's better than Gladys."

"Hey!" Gladys snapped.

"Oh come on Gladys, you only play to impress Harvey." I pointed at Harvey who looked at Gladys like he'd never seen her before, raking a hand through his coppery hair.

"Leon!" Gladys screeched, turning bright red.

"I'm done with the dead weight, kitten," I said, making my decision. "In fact, Harvey, do you want to go out with Gladys?" I cupped my hands around my mouth as I shouted.

Harvey shrugged, then nodded and Gladys lit up like a Christmas tree.

"Perfect. I'll text you her number." I waved Gladys off the pitch. "You're off the team, Gladys. I'll be *gladys* to pass on a recommendation to another school club."

She headed away, not seeming remotely bothered. I could finally understand why we came last in nearly every tournament in the history of the inter-school matches. A third of the team didn't have any skill with a ball.

"Right, out you go. Let's start with the basics. Catch a ball and get it in the Pit." I ushered her onto the pitch, folding my arms as I stuck the whistle in my mouth. Instead of the fancy enchanted holes that some prestigious academies could afford, we had one in each corner of the pitch that worked correctly about sixty three percent of the time. So when the Elemental balls did shoot out of them, that was worth celebrating.

At the centre of the pitch was the Pit where all goals were made. The game was simple. Get the ball in the pit before the other team did. There was only five minutes per round so there was no room for mistakes. If the ball wasn't in the Pit by the time the clock ran down, it exploded. And it fucking hurt when it did.

"Okay." Elise jogged out onto the pitch and I shamelessly pictured her ass bouncing up and down on my lap before she turned back to face me.

I blew the whistle and a fwooomph sounded as an Airball shot out of the hole in the Air Quarter. It reached twenty feet – *Zodiac Academy's* Air Hole shot it fifty, not that I was jealous – and everyone waited for Elise to go for it.

She lazily swatted her hand and a slap of air knocked it right into the Pit.

My jaw fell slack. "You're in. Fucking *in*."

She beamed, twirling around and lifting a pretend skirt as she curtsied. I grinned stupidly then noticed Dante doing the same. I blew my whistle so loud it hurt my own ears and everyone on the pitch flinched. "Right, now do it while everyone else tries to stop you."

"Everyone?" Elise asked, her eyes widening, but this chick clearly wasn't too fazed. She was already planting her feet and twirling a storm in her hands. That not-so-innocent, puckered lip look was sure getting me hard. She'd look so damn good on her knees.

"No Order gifts," I called to Elise and she pouted. *I bet I'm gonna have those lips wrapped around something after this try-out. She definitely wants me.*

I blew the whistle and Dante ran at her, a fucking force of pure muscle. She realised both he and the other nine players were also gunning for her and stumbled back before turning and sprinting across the pitch to escape. The Earth Hole had ejaculated a heavy Earthball half a foot away from itself like it had given up on life and died.

Elise raced for it and I admired the muscles working in her calves, her thighs, her ass. I dunno what it was about her that got me so switched on, but I was a walking boner every time she got too close.

She leapt onto it, snatching up the heavy Earthball with a strength that made my brows lift. She raced back down the pitch, knocking the Waterback, Harvey, to the ground with a powerful blast of her magic.

She charged toward the Pit and Dante outpaced everyone else, his arms powering back and forth. She raised her hands to throw the ball but Dante took her to the ground before she made it, pinning her down with his hips and laughing in her face.

I counted down from five and waited for him to get up. But nope. Their mouths were too close and they were still on the fucking ground.

"You're Out Callisto!" I barked, mostly to get Dante to move. Which he still didn't do. He had her wrists pinned and she was smiling like a cat, her hips writhing as she feigned trying to escape, when in fact I expected his dick was getting more attention than a Solarian Pitball match on prime time TV. I blew my whistle and Dante finally got up, tugging her with him. I did a boner sweep and yep, there it was. That big-ass fucking Dragon was getting a rager all over my pitch *and* all over my girl.

"Play on! Callisto, come here," I demanded. She jogged over and Dante tilted his head as he watched her go. And her ass go. He not-so-subtly rearranged his crotch and I sighed. I loved that guy. Sharing was caring. But also…owning meant boning.

I locked my arm around her the second she was close, guiding her away from the pitch as the fwoomph of another Airball filled my ears. The stampeding sound of feet told me the team were running for it so I tugged Elise behind the bleachers while they were busy.

"Is this where I have to sit while I'm Out?" She wrinkled her nose as she stared at the gum stained floor.

I shoved her back against the wall behind the seats, her top riding up because it was too damn small. I placed my hands on her hips, stepping closer. "No, this is where you go while I try to swallow your tongue. It's a fun game, wanna try it on me first?"

She planted a hand on my chest, but didn't throw me off, her eyes dancing with mischief. "Is this because Dante had his hands all over me?"

"They weren't all over you."

"Yeah they were. You couldn't really see, but he got them *everywhere.*"

"You're baiting me," I purred, moving in to taste her sweet breath and try for that kiss.

She gave me the cheek with a teasing giggle, her hand floating lower onto my stomach. I inhaled, my mouth bone dry. "I taste like candy," I promised, giving her the slanted smile that always worked. Girls fell at my feet like dead flies. Sometimes they went down on me so long I took a nap in the middle. I wanted her to take control and just get her hands all over me, but she wasn't playing ball.

She rested her head back against the bleachers. "I taste like soot," she teased. Her fingers reached my waistband and she hooked a devilish finger into it, almost grazing my junk. I let out a lion's growl and she bit into her lower lip. That fucking lip.

"I want your mouth." I shoved her hand away, done with this game as I caught her hips and crushed my mouth against hers. I bit down where she'd been biting and she gasped. She didn't taste like soot, she tasted like cherries and fucking sunshine. I ground her against my arousal and she moaned. By the stars, that sound needed to be my new ringtone. "Do it again," I begged.

"Make me," she whispered. I opened my eyes, still kissing her just because I needed to see how her face twisted in desire for me. She was totally absorbed in my kiss and I hoisted up her legs, grinding into her until I drew that noise from her again.

"Screw practise, come to my room. You're already on the team." I wanted her frontways, sideways, backways and always. Something in me just needed her. I couldn't explain it even if I tried. I doubted my half a brain cell Numerology teacher could either. She was like a shell without the nut inside. *Speaking of nuts*. Elise was grinding into mine and it felt like pure sin frozen into a popsicle and stuffed in my mouth.

"Let's go. You can do whatever you want to me," I panted and she drew away, her lips puffy from where I'd kissed her so hard.

"*Wow* lucky me," she said dryly then she tapped my nose, unwound her legs from me and straightened her top. "But I'm kinda hungry. See ya Leo."

"Leon," I corrected tersely, knowing she was playing me like a fool.

"Right," she laughed. "Thanks for the candy." She sashayed her hips and I just stood and watched her walk away with my hard-on sinking like the Titanic.

ELISE

CHAPTER TEN

I jogged away from the Pitball pitch, pressing my fingers to my lips where they still tingled from the force of Leon's kiss.

Making out with possible murderers now, are we?

I frowned at that thought. My inner snarky bitch had a point. But something about Leon made it hard for me to consider him as a real suspect. I wasn't a fool, I wouldn't dismiss the idea entirely but the other Kings just seemed so much more likely. They were violence personified. I doubted Dante or Ryder would even deny the fact that they'd killed people. Their gangs certainly did it often enough. And Gabriel...well it was pretty damn hard to figure him out but he had that strong, silent, psycho vibe going for him anyway.

I put on a spurt of Vampire speed and shot toward the dorms, not slowing until I made it to our room and pressed my back against the door inside.

"Laini?" I asked, the sheet was closed around her bed but there was no response. I trained my hearing on the room, searching for a pulse which wasn't there.

I actually had the room to myself for once. I glanced at the open window and pulled it shut to give me an extra second of warning if Gabriel appeared.

Those Harpy wings of his meant he could move in near silence and arrive so suddenly that I barely even heard his heartbeat coming. Not many people could sneak up on me and knowing he could do it so easily was more than a little unsettling. He hadn't mentioned the note I'd left in his bed. In fact, I didn't think I'd heard him utter a word since that interaction at the window. And as far as I could tell, he hadn't been snooping into my stuff since either. So for now we seemed to have come to an understanding about boundaries at least.

I quickly pulled the broken Atlas from my bag and hopped up onto my bunk. I crossed my legs as I frowned down at it. It had come on last night but I hadn't gotten a moment alone to study it until now. The damn thing had a passcode and I'd needed a bit of time to think through the possibilities before I attempted to enter any. I didn't want to lock myself out. I was sure I could hack my way past it if I did, but it would be a pain in the ass. Besides, if this had been Gareth's Atlas then I was pretty sure I'd be able to get into it.

I took a deep breath and tapped in my own birthday.

The screen flashed and I smiled triumphantly as the Atlas unlocked for me.

When we were younger one of Mom's 'friends' had given us an old Atlas. He was the kind of guy who sneezed money so it had clearly been no bother to him, but it had meant a hell of a lot to us. Gareth had chosen my birthday for the passcode to make it easier for me to remember and it seemed he'd decided to keep using it since then too. He'd always said the two of us had no secrets and he never wanted us to, so I guessed he never minded the idea of me knowing his code.

I took a peek at his FaeBook page but it was pretty empty, there were a few photos that he'd been tagged in but he'd never really done the whole social media thing. I shut that down and headed to his emails. At first there didn't seem to be anything of interest there either but then I spotted a mailbox tucked in the bottom corner marked with one word. *King.*

A shiver tracked down my spine as I opened it. There weren't many messages there but I quickly read all there were.

King:

The full moon is tonight, don't be late.

Gareth:

I'm not sure she's ready. Shouldn't we wait?

King:

I don't have another month to spare. You should know that by now. Meet me at midnight as usual or you'll pay in her place.

Gareth:

Okay, I'll be there.

I pursed my lips. *Be where?* King had said to meet him as usual...

I quickly switched to the map on the Atlas, typing away to access the GPS records. A quick search on my own Atlas gave me all the dates of the full moons over the months leading up to Gareth's death and I entered the information into the GPS search alongside the midnight time stamp.

Jackpot.

Six full moons in a row, Gareth had headed out in the middle of the night to Acrux Courtyard where the students hung out in our free time between classes.

Who were you meeting?

My mouth was dry. What if it was more than just him and this King person? He'd mentioned a girl. If several people met at that time then maybe they still did? It was a full moon tonight...

I looked out of the window as my heart started beating faster. If there was even the slightest chance of that being the case then I had to know.

We'll never keep secrets, Ella.

My triumphant smile turned sour as I thought back on that. Because it had been a lie in the end. Gareth had secrets. And I was beginning to think they'd gotten him killed.

A knock came at the door and I frowned, pushing myself up and heading across the room to open it. Cindy stood there, a pout pushing out her painted pink lips as her eyes fell on me. She glanced over my shoulder. "Is Dante here?"

"No." I pressed my shoulder to the doorway and pulled the door over to block her view - and to piss her off.

She huffed, her eyes sliding up me and pausing on my hair. "Purple's not really your colour, sweetie."

"Green's not yours either but you wear it every time I'm anywhere near Dante. It's kind of sad how little you think of yourself, Cindy."

"What's that supposed to mean?" she spat.

"You're clearly threatened by me. But you're welcome to Dante if you want him." My gut twisted in a way that said that wasn't entirely true, but hell if I was ever gonna admit it.

Her lips twisted into a sneer. "What's to be threatened by, sugar? You look like a half price hooker, I bet your mommy was one too-" *Crash.* I threw her into the wall opposite with a blast of air, fury pounding through my veins.

"Don't you ever talk about my mother!" I snapped. I had no issue with being called a hooker. Or even her insinuating my mom was one. Because frankly, sometimes she was. And more power to her. But a cheap one? Oh hell fucking no.

Cindy raised her hands to fight back just as Dante rounded the corner and she quickly dropped them, bursting into tears instead. I growled my irritation as Cindy ran into Dante's arms.

"She's crazy!" she wailed. "She attacked me." Dammit she was a good

116

actor, there were actual real-life tears rolling down her cheeks.

"Did you, carina?" he asked in surprise.

"Yeah but she-"

"I was just coming to look for you and she *flipped*." Cindy backed further into his arms, recoiling from me. It was fucking overkill.

"Oh come on, you can't really believe that shit." I tutted and Cindy buried her face in Dante's blazer with another sob.

"Walk me back to my room," she sniffed. "I don't feel safe around her."

Dante slid an arm around her shoulders with a sigh. "Come on then." He steered her back down the corridor, throwing a glance over his shoulder at me and I rolled my eyes.

Cindy Lou was officially my enemy. And it wasn't like I needed any more of those in this school. But it looked like she was determined to get on my shit list. So that was right where she was gonna go.

I hadn't slept. I'd meant to, but sleep just wouldn't come while I knew where I was going and what I was doing. *I might just be about to catch a murderer.*

Gabriel wasn't back yet. The window was open a crack for whenever he decided to appear but I didn't read into his absence. Maybe he wasn't back because he was the one the messages had been from. But it also wasn't unusual for him to be out this late. He kept his own hours, did his own thing. He was as unpredictable as the wind he spent so much time soaring through.

I slid from my bunk and landed on the floor silently. A soft glow came through the sheet wrapped around Dante's bed letting me know he was still awake and on his Atlas but he didn't have any sound playing on it.

I'd kept a pair of black leggings and a tank top on and I reached out to snag a hoody from the closet too. I stepped towards the door but the sheet beside me was pushed back as Dante sat up in his bed.

"Going somewhere, carina?" he asked me in his lilting accent. A white sheet was draped around his waist but his chest was bare, giving me a look at the hard muscles of his body.

"Hunting," I replied, flashing my fangs at him.

He eyed me with interest.

"You don't usually wait for night to hunt."

"What are you, my mom?" I asked. "Is there some reason I shouldn't be going out in the dark that you want to tell me about? Because I sleep with a monster beneath my bed and I'm not dead yet."

Dante grinned, flexing his fingers so the gold rings he wore caught the light. They should have made him look like a total douchebag but somehow they didn't. He wore gold because as a Dragon Shifter he drew his power from it and the jewellery he wore seemed more like a warning than anything else. Not that anyone needed reminding what he was. He was one of the biggest guys I'd ever met, his emotions sent static energy skittering through the air. I could more easily forget that the sky was blue than forget what his Order form was.

"Well don't stay out too late, it's a school night," he teased.

I rolled my eyes at him and kicked my sneakers on as I headed for the door.

I pulled my hood up over my lilac hair as I made it out into the corridor and jogged down the stairs before pushing my way outside.

It might have been a full moon but with the thick clouds that didn't mean anything. It was pitch black outside and without my enhanced Vampire sight I probably would have struggled to see much of anything.

It was five minutes to midnight. I was cutting it close but that was what I'd wanted. I didn't know what Order of Fae might be out here and the last thing I needed was to be detected hanging around waiting for them. Better I arrive when they did and caught them that way. With my speed I could get away quickly enough if it became necessary.

A huge tree stood on the sloping meadow of Devil's Hill before the courtyard and I headed straight for it in the dark. I used my strength to help me scale its trunk and perched on a thick limb as I looked out towards the bleachers and picnic benches which marked out the gang territories within the school.

I held my breath, my pulse like the frantic beat of hummingbird wings as I waited. And waited. And waited.

All was still in the courtyard. And everywhere else for that matter. Nothing moved, no sounds disturbed the silence. It was just...empty.

At twenty past twelve I sighed and dropped out of the tree. Whoever Gareth had been meeting on the full moon had obviously stopped coming after his death. Maybe there was no point without him. Or maybe they met somewhere else now just in case someone caught on to them. That's what I'd do, I guessed. If they killed him they wouldn't want to keep doing anything that they'd done with him. Cut off all leads. Make it harder to find them. Yeah. This asshole was smart enough for that. I'd just have to keep searching. The full moon was obviously important though so maybe I could figure out where else they might hold clandestine meetings on campus. There couldn't be that many options...

I trailed towards the courtyard as my thoughts spiralled through the various possibilities. It was hard though, without knowing what the meeting was for, how could I figure out how much space they needed? If it was just two people talking then it could be done just about anywhere. A group would be harder to hide, especially if they were casting magic...

I made it into the centre of the courtyard and I glanced about at the abandoned space with a shiver of anticipation running down my spine. This was the only part of the courtyard I'd ever entered. Dead centre. No man's land. All students walked through the middle to Altair Halls for classes and the cafaeteria. But no one aside from the gangs deviated from the path.

My gaze trailed over the picnic benches where the Oscura Clan held court. There was nothing particularly intimidating about them without the pack of Werewolves and their hangers on filling them.

The Lunar Brotherhood bleachers on the other hand were just as ominous in the dark, towering up to my left, silently daring me to step closer.

A shiver danced along my spine.

Since Gareth had died, I'd found it hard to truly feel anything. But fear was always potent. And a little tempting too. It made me feel alive.

I took a step closer, biting my lip at the thrill, the sharpness of the emotion. I just wanted to experience it. To push into it for a moment.

It was so dark that even *my* eyes couldn't pick apart the shadows as I drew closer and closer to the stacks of wooden benches but adrenaline trickled along my limbs like the sweetest warning, seeming to whisper *danger* in my ear.

I made it to the foot of the towering rows of seats and brushed my fingers across the wooden bench where Ryder always sat, glaring at anyone who so much as glanced his way. Violence always seemed to dance around him like a promise and there was something about it that drew me in despite myself. He was a mystery. I wanted to know what made him tick beyond the only two emotions he claimed to feel. Pain and lust. I didn't believe anyone could truly be defined so simply no matter what he thought.

"Are you here to sign up to the Brotherhood?" Ryder's voice came from right behind me and I gasped in fright, whirling around to look at him.

He was shirtless, buttoning his fly and I realised he must have been near by in his Order form before shifting back. A snake's heartbeat wouldn't have drawn my attention; I'd learned to ignore animal sounds within the first few months of my Order Awakening.

He stepped closer to me, glaring as he waited for his answer and I fell straight into the trap of his gaze.

My lips fell open as he pushed his hypnotic powers over me. Now that I knew what was happening, I could tell the difference between the visions he sent me and reality but it didn't stop me from seeing and feeling everything he wanted me to. There was a slightly fuzzy quality to everything outside the two of us, like he hadn't bothered to give it much attention when he created this vision, but I guessed that didn't matter when all of his focus was on me.

Vision Ryder stepped forward and pushed me back so that my ass hit the bleachers, the sting of it seeming so real that a gasp escaped my lips. He caught the backs of my knees and slid me towards him so that he was positioned between my thighs and the ache I felt for him increased as he smiled down at me, the moon slipping out from the clouds to cast him in silver and shadows.

In the blink of an eye both of our clothes were gone as if they'd never been there at all and he pushed me so that I fell back to lie beneath him.

"Ryder," I warned but it came out as a breathy plea instead as he positioned himself to claim me.

"You wanna scream my name a little louder?" he teased, leaning forward and wrapping his huge hand around my neck.

I wanted to fight him off but the Elise in his fantasy just lay there, staring up at him with wide eyes and a thundering heart.

His other hand gripped the hard length of him and he lined himself up to take me, pinning me in his gaze like he wanted to drink in exactly what I was feeling.

My breaths came in urgent pants and I found myself wondering just what he would feel like. Would this fantasy live up to reality or was he being overly generous with his true capabilities?

Ryder didn't waste any time making sure I was ready for him. The feeling of him slamming inside me was so real that an actual moan escaped my lips. It might have been a fantasy, but it felt so good that it hurt.

Ryder's eyes lit with that knowledge as he started moving faster, his hand tightening around my neck enough to cause a flicker of pain but not enough to cut off the moans spilling from my lips.

"More," I breathed and his eyes sparked with excitement as I realised that had come from the real me and not his fantasy version.

In his vision I started clawing at his arm where he pinned me down, drawing blood with my fingernails as he continued to thrust into me harder and harder.

But that wasn't right either. I wasn't some weak, submissive girl who'd just lay beneath him and put up a half assed fight. I was a Vampire with more strength in my limbs than he even knew. If I wanted him off of me he'd be off.

The vision flickered for a moment and I was standing before him again, fully dressed, lips parted, breathing heavy. Then I was beneath him again as he fucked me so hard that I was begging him to release me into an orgasm I could feel building. He wasn't going to make me come with some unrealistic fantasy of us though.

With a snarl that was half lust and half rage, my fangs snapped out and the vision shattered.

Ryder's eyes widened with surprise and I got the feeling that hadn't happened to him very often.

"I think you've got me all wrong, asshole," I growled as I stalked towards him. "I'm not some submissive little Fae just begging for you to fuck me. I'm a monster of my own variety. And I like it better on top."

I leapt at him with bloodlust pumping through my veins and my fangs aimed at his throat. With my speed and strength he didn't stand much chance of fighting me off from this distance but he didn't even try.

I slammed into him, driving my fangs into his throat as my weight collided with his chest and I sent him crashing to the concrete beneath me. A hiss of pain that sounded really damn sexual escaped him but I didn't care. I dug my fingers into his chest and sucked on his neck, not even trying to be gentle with him as I drank deeply from his life force.

His blood rolled over my tongue and I moaned in satisfaction as the raw brutality of his power flowed into me, riding on the coppery taste. I drew more and more of his magic into my body, swallowing greedily like I'd never be able to get enough.

I straddled him on the cold ground, pinning him down with my strength forcefully even though he wasn't making any effort to fight me off. He moved his hands to grip my waist, pushing up my shirt until he was grasping my flesh and a groan of pleasure escaped him.

He pulled me down so he could grind against me, making sure I felt the bulge of his arousal keenly between my thighs and sending an ache of a different kind through me. But I wasn't going to be taking anything from him apart from blood and power.

I shifted, catching his wrists and tugging his hands off of me before slamming them down onto the concrete by his head to stop him from pawing at me.

"Fuck," he breathed on what sounded like a laugh.

I growled at him, driving my fangs deeper as I took my fill of his blood until his energy was coursing through my veins, making my heart pound to a wild, untameable beat.

I finally pulled back and glared at him as I slowly released my hold on his wrists and made a move to stand.

"Wait," he said, snatching my hand into his grasp. "Do it again."

"What?" I cocked a brow at him. I wasn't sure I'd ever bitten anyone quite that violently before aside from when my Order was first Awakened and I'd certainly never had anyone ask me for an encore right after I'd finished.

A bead of blood slipped down my chin and he reached out to touch it, brushing his thumb across my jaw and smearing it over my skin.

"I wanna see your pretty skin painted red with my blood."

"You're so dark," I breathed, wondering why I was lingering here. I'd taken what I wanted from him and made my point clearly enough.

"You have no idea."

And I don't want to. Right?

I rolled my eyes like he didn't intrigue and terrify me in equal measures and got to my feet, pulling out of his grip.

Ryder got up too, towering over me as he took a step closer. The glimmer in his eyes said he wasn't done with me, but I wasn't planning on hanging out in the shadows with him any longer.

"What the hell were you doing out here in the middle of the night anyway?" I asked suspiciously.

"Why? Do you wanna make this rendezvous a regular occurrence?" he asked roughly, his eyes scraping over me in a way that shouldn't have been legal.

"Are you offering to be my Source?" I asked, wondering if I should try and claim him for my own personal blood donor. Not that I had any reason to think he'd agree to that; he was stronger than me so I wouldn't be able to overpower him most of the time but he had claimed to like being bitten so it couldn't hurt to ask. And his blood was amongst the best I'd ever tasted so if I could get more of it then I definitely would.

"How about we make a trade?" Ryder asked, a glimmer in his eye. "I'll let you keep sucking on my neck, so long as you start sucking on some of my other body parts too."

I let my eyes run down the hard muscles of his chest and came to rest on his fly as I licked my lips slowly. That didn't even sound like the worst offer in the world but I wasn't going to be whoring myself out for anything. I'd watched my mom live that life and it had broken her. My body was my own and if I was going to be giving it to anyone then it would be on my own terms, not in payment for anything.

"Never mind then," I said dismissively. "But thanks for the drink, sweetie," I added casually, taking a step back.

"Sweetie? There's nothing sweet about me, new girl," he scoffed.

"Sure there is," I purred, holding my ground as he advanced again. "You taste like rainbow dust on a fresh summer morning dipped in sugar." I licked his blood from my bottom lip to emphasise my point and his brow furrowed.

"I doubt it. Maybe you need another taste." He bared his throat to me and I smiled, no fangs in sight.

"Thanks but no thanks. Wouldn't wanna get diabetes." I winked at him then shot away with my Vampire speed before he could respond, leaving him alone in the dark.

GARETH

CHAPTER ELEVEN

EIGHTEEN MONTHS BEFORE THE SOLARID METEOR SHOWER...

I strolled into Altair Halls with a frown pulling at my brow and my eyes on the tiled floor. I was down to six days and I still hadn't gotten the money I needed to pay Old Sal. I hadn't been lying when I'd said that I went to school with some of the richest fuckers in Alestria but the problem was they all came from criminal families. And people like that weren't easy to rob or con. Especially if I was planning on not getting caught.

But if I didn't do something soon then Ella was going to pay the price and there was no way in hell I'd be letting that happen.

I was running the line of being late for class, but I wasn't too concerned. My Cardinal Magic teacher, Professor Montague, was pretty easy going and I was acing her class so I knew she wouldn't mind if I wasn't quite on time.

"For the love of the stars, where the hell is it!" a girl's voice caught my ear and I looked up as she stomped her foot. Like, actually stomped her foot like a Disney character or a three year old. I wasn't sure why, but it made me smile.

She turned around and caught me looking, my smile widening as I spotted the pout on her full lips. Her dark eyes were shrouded by long lashes and raven hair fell to her waist in a straight sheet like a spill of ink. I hadn't seen her before but I sure as hell wouldn't mind getting to know her better.

"Can I help?" I asked, moving closer to her as her eyes swept over me slowly enough to let me know she hadn't missed an inch of my muscular frame.

"Yes please, sugar," she said, a hint of a southern accent spilling out as she moved towards me. "I'm supposed to have Potions with Professor Titan but I can't find the classroom anywhere. I started school late because there was a mix up with my paperwork so today's only my second day and it's already all going wrong before it's even begun."

"Don't worry about it, no one can ever find the Potions lab without help the first time," I reassured her, moving even closer. "I'm Gareth."

"Cindy Lou." She held out a slender hand and I took it, smiling down at her.

"Come on, I'll walk you to class." I tilted my head in the right direction and she fell into step beside me with a relieved smile.

I asked her about her family as we walked and she told me she was one of six siblings, all girls. She was the first to go to an academy for her education and all of her sisters were jealous enough to spit. I told her about Ella but was vague about my mom and then we were rounding the staircase which concealed the entrance to the Potions lab in the basement.

"Here you go," I said, offering her a smile as I turned to leave.

She caught my hand before I could and I looked at her in surprise as she pushed up onto her toes and pressed a kiss to my cheek.

"Thank you for coming to my rescue, Gareth." She gave me a quick smile, her cheeks heating a little before she darted into her class.

My skin burned with the mark of her lips and I was half tempted to follow her inside and ask her to meet me in the cafaeteria later for a drink. But I couldn't really barge into her class and I imagined if I did the embarrassment *alone would be enough to guarantee she gave me a no.*

I turned away, my smile widening as I thought about her full lips and I made a mental note to seek her out again at some point.

The corridors were almost empty and I really was late now so I broke into a jog as I headed for my class.

I ran up the stairs and rounded a corner suddenly, slamming straight into another student before I could stop myself.

The guy cursed and books fell all around us as I was almost knocked onto my ass from the impact. He was a freshman but he towered over me and his body was lined with hard muscle. I knew his name, though I doubted he knew mine. Gabriel Nox. The only student to attend Aurora Academy while wielding two Elements in ten years. Who knew why a Fae that strong had applied to attend this place. A guy like him might have even gotten into Zodiac Academy – *the best damn school in Solaria - but he'd chosen to come here instead.*

He was untrained but was still the strongest Fae at Aurora. News of his arrival had spread like wildfire after his powers had been Awakened and his picture was splashed all over my FaeBook feed every day. He even had groupies who called themselves the Harpers because he was a Harpy. It was sad but true. And it probably would have served me well not to piss him off the first time he'd even noticed my existence. But shit happened I guessed.

"Watch out," he snapped and I bit my tongue on biting back. It wasn't worth it with someone that powerful.

"Sorry, man," I muttered, moving to help him gather his shit.

His Atlas had skittered right across the hall and I hounded after it, picking it up quickly. He'd been looking at something when he'd dropped it and the page was still open. My eyes fell on the bank statement with more than a little surprise.

Payments received this month:

Falling Star - *10,000*
Falling Star - *10,000*
Falling Star - *10,000*
Falling Star - *10,000*
Falling Star - *10,000*

Account Balance: 834,679.76 Auras.

Before I could tear my gaze from the screen and the insane amount of money this guy had at his disposal, Gabriel snatched it out of my grip and grabbed a handful of my shirt.

He slammed me up against the wall hard enough to drive the breath from my lungs and I stared up at him in shock.

"What the hell?" I snapped, trying to shove him off of me.

"Why were you snooping into my personal shit?" Gabriel snarled in my face, not backing down one bit.

"I wasn't!" I denied even though I fucking had been and we both knew it. "I was just trying to help you pick it up."

"Who asked you to spy on me?" Gabriel demanded, lifting a hand as water started to run between his fingers.

I was a sophomore; I had a year's worth of training on this guy but something about the look in his eyes made me hesitate to fight back. He seemed unhinged, like he was actually considering killing me for looking at his fucking rich boy bank statement.

"No one asked me to do jack shit. Now get off of me," I growled.

Gabriel looked deep into my eyes for a long moment then shoved me away from him so roughly I almost fell.

"Fucking psycho," I muttered as I started to stride away from him.

A torrent of water smashed into me so hard that I was thrown from my feet in an instant. I cried out as I tumbled across the floorboards, rolling and rolling until I hit the wall at the end of the corridor.

Vines sprung up around me, twisting their way all over my body and pinning me in place as I fought to get up.

"You might want to think a little harder before you insult me like that again," Gabriel said as he strode past me, leaving me bound in a puddle in the middle of the corridor. Soaking wet and fucking fuming. "And stay out of my business. If I catch you trying to look at my personal shit again, I'll fill your lungs with water and let you drown."

His footsteps moved away from me and I was left struggling against the vines he'd created with no chance of escaping them without help.

Shame burned through me as I failed to free myself, knowing I'd be stuck like this until someone came along and released me from his magic.

I clenched my fists against my sides and ground my jaw. I hadn't wanted anything to do with that asshole or his fucking stuff. But I had seen his bank account balance. And the one thing I needed was money. Which he seemed to have altogether too much of. Especially for someone who was as big of a dick as him. Which got me thinking. Why was he receiving payments from someone with a code name? Who was Falling Star? And why had he freaked out so much about me seeing it if there was nothing unusual about the transactions?

Growing up the way I had, you got to know how to read people pretty quickly and I'd formed a damn good sense of what made people tic. Normal people didn't react like that if someone caught a glance at their finances. Only someone with something to hide would overreact that way.

Gabriel Nox had a secret.

I was going to find out what it was.

When I did, he'd have to pay to keep me quiet.

And the price would be the cost of my sister's freedom.

DANTE

CHAPTER TWELVE

My dorm was empty so I took the opportunity to call my mamma. The phone rang and rang as I lay on my bunk, twisting my medallion between my fingers. When she answered, a series of howls sounded before she spoke. She was out of breath and jealousy hit me as I realised what she was up to tonight. I could run with my pack at school, but there was nothing like running with my closest famiglia.

"We're on a run, dolce drago, is everything okay?" She called me her 'sweet dragon' and I quietly loved that. But if she ever said it in front of my friends I'd electrocute her.

My family were all Werewolves. I was a rare-ass Dragon born to a family of baying hounds. You should really see the family photo album. There was nothing quite like a twenty foot Dragon at the heart of ten wolf siblings to point out how different you were. And because of my overly tactile, fantastically friendly family, I was more used to physical affection and overt touching than most Fae of my Order. Dragons were known for being standoffish. But nurture made me crave warm hugs and wet licks. I just didn't let that side of me show too often while I was at school.

"It's okay, Mamma. How is Uncle Matteo coping?" My uncle had lost his son Lorenzo to fucking Killblaze a few weeks back. He'd gone insane and skewered himself on a blade of ice while out of his goddamn mind. Looked like he might have run into a wall first too. My family covered it up so fast, you'd barely know Lorenzo even existed once.

The two of us hadn't been close. He was a year older, a bit of a shit if I was being really honest and he'd brought shame on the Clan by getting hooked on Killblaze. My brightest memory of Lorenzo was him forcing my head down a toilet when I was eight years old to try and make my Order Awaken. Wolves tended to Awaken young, but I was the odd one out. Guess I still was.

I'd lost my temper watching a Pitball match when I was thirteen and turned into a huge ass Dragon in the middle of the stands; it had been a shock to everyone involved. But half the Oscura Clan had attended that match and I'd been celebrated for fucking days. A Dragon in their ranks? The Lunar Brotherhood couldn't claim that shit. Dragons were rare as it was. And when they found out I breathed electricity, my mamma cried tears of pride for a week.

"He's been starting fights with the Lunar Brotherhood all over town. It's anger mostly, but it's causing a few more turf wars than we need right now. And your Uncle Felix isn't helping. He's leading the attacks." I ground my teeth. Felix was my father's mentally unstable brother. The last fucking person I wanted holding my position right now. He was too volatile to be making decisions for the entire gang. He'd once caught me stealing from his wallet and hung me from a bridge in downtown Alestria for a full day.

"I could come help?" I offered, sometimes hating that I had to be stuck here while the real gang war went on outside these walls.

"No dolce drago, you focus on your education. You'll be King of our family one day, but you need to be bright. Learn all you can. La conoscenza è potere." Knowledge is power, that was true. We didn't underestimate education amongst the Oscuras. If you wanted to win a war, you had to be *smart* smart, not just street smart.

A creak sounded somewhere close by and I yanked back my sheet to check Gabriel hadn't snuck in like a silent fart. Empty. My mind always played tricks on me when I spoke to mia famiglia. I didn't want any of the Brotherhood lurking in and listening to what I said to them. I had a silencing bubble in place, but a senior could slip past it if they knew the right spell.

"I have to go, Mamma. Have a good run. Maybe we can fly under the moon together next time I come home?"

"I'd like that, bambino. Ti amo." The line went dead and I sighed. As a Dragon I shouldn't have let anyone ride me. It was a law amongst my kind, but I'd broken it a hundred times with my family. I'd never met the Dragon Commander, Lionel Acrux, and I imagined he wouldn't be seen dead in a city like Alestria. So fuck if I was gonna obey his rules.

I'd carried all of my ten brothers and sisters to the top of Mount Fable once. Mamma said I had to stop doing it when I went to school. People would talk. And talking led to rumours. Rumours led to lies. Lies led to cut throats. But I'd never met any other Dragon in Solaria so hell if I respected their opinion. Most of them were born from pure-blooded families who refused to mate with anyone outside of their Order. Seemed pretty boring to me, but I supposed it was the only way to ensure future generations of Dragons considering how rare we were. They probably didn't even realise I existed, so why would any rumours reach their ears about me? I didn't really give a shit either way, but Mamma was adamant so I'd stopped letting anyone on my back.

Needing a piss, I jumped up and closed the distance to the door. I opened it and fate would have it that Elise was walking in. I smiled broadly, planting my shoulder against the doorway. "Look who it is? Amore mio." I clutched my heart as if she truly affected it.

"Move, Dante." She wafted her hand to try and make me move. Yeah, like that was gonna work.

"Has anyone ever told you how bossy you are, carina?" I lifted a brow.

"Multiple people on multiple occasions. Now move." She stepped into my personal space, a threat in her stance, but I wasn't afraid. Turned on maybe, but never afraid. "You won't like what you find in there, I just jerked off into your pillow."

"You're joking," she snarled, fangs on show.

I smirked. "Am I?"

"I swear to the sun, Dante, if you have I'll-"

"You'll give me daily blowies to keep my libido under control? Deal." My grin widened and she slammed her hands against my chest, throwing a blast of air into them that sent me stumbling backwards. I continued to smile as she ran across the room, climbing up to her bunk and inspecting her pillow from a safe distance.

I snorted and she let out a growl.

"Asshole." She threw herself up onto the bunk, laying down on her not so spunky pillow.

"I don't need inanimate cushy objects to get me off, Elise. Besides, your pillow smells like you. Why would I want that all over my dick?" Time to play hard to get.

She didn't bite the juicy worm I was dangling and I pressed my lips together. I moved to exit again, finding Gabriel standing there for who knew how long. He was shirtless, wings pressing against the doorway so my way out was thoroughly blocked. He stared off into the distance, apparently thinking about something.

"Gabriel," I snapped. "Get out of my way."

No response. And I was seriously starting to need a piss now.

I snapped my fingers under his nose and he didn't even fucking blink. "Stronzo!" I barked forcefully in his face, and he wiped a fleck of spittle from his cheek, still lost to his trance.

Elise started giggling and for a second, I could have sworn the two of them were silently ganging up on me.

Fuck this. I'm not gonna stand for it.

Electricity crackled in my veins. My spine pulsed with the urge to shift, but not here. I couldn't. But I *could* cast a storm which would knock bird boy through a wall. I didn't care if he fought back, he was clearly baiting me. And Dante Oscura did not back down from a fight.

"You asked for it, Gabriel." I gathered air in my palms, charging it with sparking electricity as the Dragon part of me came to life. "I am Dante Oscura," I growled, drawing my shoulders back. "A morte e ritorno!"

Gabriel walked past me, his wing brushing right over my face. By the time I turned around to glare at him with a vein about to burst in my temple, he was already perched atop his bunk like a fucking eagle.

"Fuck you, Gabriel. Fuck you so hard."

"No thank you," he said calmly and my lips twisted with rage.

Elise's giggles rose into the air and I scowled as I marched out of the door, nearly knocking Laini over as she headed in too. "Are you all just showing up on cue to piss me off?" I snapped at her as I walked by, making her recoil against the wall for half a second before she hurried into the dorm.

I headed to the bathroom and had the angriest piss of my life. I knew what was really stoking my rage though and it wasn't lilac haired girls or even winged assholes. It was Felix Oscura standing in my damn place back home and making shitty decisions for the gang.

I felt threatened and with Elise's laughter still ringing in my ears, I knew it was time to assert some dominance. To remind the world who the real leader of Oscura Clan was. Since Elise had arrived, that dorm was bringing down my reputation. So I was gonna show her why screwing with me was a bad goddamn idea.

I zipped up my fly, stalking back to the room and kicking the door wide. It smashed against the wall, juddering on its hinges before I threw it shut again. I strode toward Elise, electricity rushing along my skin and making the lights flicker above us. I pulled off my medallion and dropped my rings to the floor with a clang clang clang.

Elise moved so fast, I barely caught her. But I was ready for her Vampire speed and I hazarded a guess at which direction she'd take as she sprang off the bed. I caught her with a grunt of triumph, locking my arms around her so she had no chance of escape. Her back was to my front and I couldn't ignore the feel of her ass against my crotch. But that was the last thing I was going to focus on.

"Get the hell off of me!" she demanded, kicking, scratching, trying to bite. But I didn't let her get near me with those teeth, tightening my grip so she couldn't. I dragged her to the window and she gasped as I elbowed it open. I caught sight of Gabriel watching us with a frown and Laini flapping her arms up and down, shouting something I didn't care to hear.

We were on the top floor. Plenty of time to catch her before she broke her neck. Probably.

I shoved her out and she screamed bloody murder as she plummeted. I was already jumping after her, saying goodbye to my clothes as I burst free of them, my size doubling, tripling, expanding and expanding. My wings tore out of my back and my navy blue scales shimmered like oil under the waning moon. I nose dived toward the ground, tucking in my wings, releasing a roar that made the school walls quake. Everyone would hear that sound and everyone would damn well know who it belonged to.

Elise tumbled toward the ground below and I snatched her out of the air in the clawed talons of my hind legs at the last second before death. *Better not kill the vampirina.*

Her screams were lost to the wind as I flexed my wings and two powerful beats carried us upward. I spiralled higher and higher, my grip on her tightening as Aurora Academy shrank to a sprawling gothic shadow below.

I tilted my head to the sky and released my Order magic, a twisting maelstrom of electricity ripping a hole into the clouds. Even the moon seemed

138

to shy away from my power. I was a beast. A king. A warrior. And I was not going to be laughed at by *anyone*.

A shadow caught my attention below and I spotted Gabriel racing up to meet us, eyes like iron, his mouth in the thinnest line I'd ever seen it.

I angled my head toward him, sending a warning blast of lightning past his head.

What the fuck did he think he was playing at?

His black wings spanned almost eight feet wide, beating hard and driving him up toward me at a ferocious pace. Silver armour glistened on his skin as he called upon it to shield him and I knew what that meant. War.

I let him come to me, whipping my razor sharp, two-pronged tail sideways to try and knock him out of the air. He rode the wind with grace, ducking under the blow and disappearing beneath my belly.

I roared as something slashed my leg and three words sounded from Gabriel, "Trust me, Elise."

He cut me with something again and I bellowed as my grip loosened and Elise wriggled free. She fell. I sensed her go and panic momentarily seized me as I bolted down to catch her. My eyes practically bled when I saw her cradled in Gabriel's arms like he was some angel who'd fallen straight out of heaven to rescue her.

A storm built within me and around me in the clouds as I swooped towards him, fury pulsing under my scales. I stared at Elise in his arms and a growl rumbled through me like thunder. I couldn't fight him while he held her and the smirk on his face said he knew it. I may have wanted to put her in her place, but I never would have really hurt her. Now he'd intervened and he'd had no right.

I turned away from them, my rage too much to bear as I soared into the clouds and flew as far away from them as possible. I brought a storm down on the academy, descending into a mood as I drowned myself in the crashing thunder and endless darkness of my own tempest.

139

ELISE

CHAPTER THIRTEEN

Gabriel's arms were tight around me as I cringed against his chest and the wind whipped through my short hair, throwing it into my eyes. Rain battered against us but with a wave of his hand, he directed it away, his control over the water diverting its path and keeping us dry.

His powerful wings flapped hard as he carried us up towards the silver sphere of the moon for a few eternal seconds before he twisted to the right, flipping us around as we dove back towards the ground.

My stomach swooped and I couldn't help but shriek in fright as I wrapped my arms around his neck, clinging to him like my life depended on it. Which it did. Even though I had good reason to suspect he was a killer. But then he'd just saved me. What the hell was I even supposed to think?

My heart was racing and my thoughts were a blur which only made space for one single thing. *I don't want to die!*

Gabriel sped towards the roof of the dorm tower without slowing and I curled against him, slamming my eyes shut, unable to bear to look as we shot towards the concrete at the speed of a hawk descending on a mouse.

He pulled up short, taking a few running steps as he landed and the swooping sensation in my stomach finally fell still.

It took me another moment before I could peel my eyes open and I looked up to find Gabriel eyeing me with concern.

"Are you hurt?" he asked, his voice gravelly.

I shook my head slowly, unable to tear my eyes away from his steely grey pupils. They were the colour of a thunder cloud tonight, full of secrets and power.

"Dante is a hothead. He'll fly off that aggression and forget about it by tomorrow. It might be better if you don't go back to the dorm tonight though," he said thoughtfully, placing me down on my feet and I stepped back out of his hold.

I nodded, unsure what I should really say to that. A part of me never wanted to go back to that room again. But if I didn't, I'd never get the answers I needed to figure out who was responsible for Gareth's death and this hole inside my heart would never heal.

Not that I really thought it could anyway.

What were you thinking in coming here? You're so far out of your depth it's untrue. Taking on Fae more powerful than you and going up against gangs so ruthless even the FIB can't stop them. You're just a stupid little girl. You can't get justice for Gareth. You didn't even realise he was in danger. You're useless. Pathetic.

I turned away from Gabriel just before the first tear fell. My heart fluttered with panic as the walls I'd built to keep me strong came tumbling down and the grief poured in, threatening to crush me.

My bare feet were cold in the puddles forming on the roof as the storm continued to build around us. Gabriel stopped the rain from hitting us but the crash of thunder and arc of lightning in the sky couldn't be contained.

More tears spilled over and I wrapped my arms around myself as I took a few steps towards the edge of the roof. I tried to hold them back but the more I did, the more they seemed to find a way through. I tightened my hold on myself as I slowly lost control.

The chill of the wind whipped around me and I shivered. I was only wearing my thin pyjamas which consisted of a tank top and a pair of shorts. Not what I would have chosen for a midnight walk in March during a thunderstorm. But the cold gave me something to focus on outside of myself, just enough to rein in the worst of the tears and hold back the sob which was threatening to tear its way out of my throat.

A hand landed on my shoulder and I stilled at the sound of rustling feathers.

"I can see how sad you are even when you aren't crying," he breathed. "You don't have to hide your tears from me."

His grip on my shoulder tightened a little and I let him turn me to face him, looking up at him as I fought to rein in the tempestuous grief that had risen to the surface in me.

Ever since Gareth's death, I'd been obsessed with the fact that he'd been murdered and the idea of catching the culprit and making them pay. I'd cried for a solid day then stopped. I hadn't really let myself feel the grief I knew I should have since then. I was driven towards this goal of vengeance and retribution but then what? He'd still be gone. I'd still be alone...

Gabriel leaned forward and pressed a kiss to my cheek, my tears washing over his lips.

I looked up at him in surprise as the heat of his mouth on my skin trickled down into my veins, awakening a completely different set of emotions in me.

"You don't have to tell me why you're so sad," he said, a faint frown creasing his forehead. "But I think the stars brought us here. I was meant to be here with you now. Before I entered our dorm I had a vision of me carrying you through the sky in my arms and less than ten minutes later it came to pass. This was meant to happen."

"You really think fate brought us here together? She clicked her fingers and made a Dragon throw me out of a window just so that you could catch me?" I shook my head in denial but the seriousness in Gabriel's gaze stopped me from outright refusing to accept it.

"I think you were meant to end up in my arms tonight," he agreed in a deep growl though I wasn't sure if he sounded happy about it.

A cool breeze gusted around us, rustling the feathers of his giant wings at his back. He'd half shifted back out of his Harpy form, the silver scales withdrawing from his flesh so just the black wings emerged while he stood before me in the jeans he'd been wearing while he perched on his bunk in our room five minutes ago. Or a thousand years ago, depending on if you asked my head or my heart.

"Thank you for rescuing me," I breathed.

"I couldn't just let you fall."

His stormy eyes captivated me and I found myself at a loss for words as I looked up at him. He was so tall, so strong and sure of himself. I should have felt small in every way beside him and yet somehow I didn't. There was strength in his solid aura of calm and I couldn't help but steal a measure of it for my own as I stood before him.

His chest was bare and his tattoos stood out on his flesh, highlighted by the flashes of lightning which scored the sky overhead. I spotted the symbol for my own star sign, Libra, etched into the skin right above his heart and reached up to touch my finger to it.

Gabriel's wings flexed and spread at my touch and my eyes widened as they opened up behind him, blocking out the vague moonlight beyond the clouds and shrouding us in darkness. They were huge, magnificent, like the wings of an angel who had fallen from the heavens just to save me.

Gabriel leaned forward to press a kiss to my other cheek, stopping those tears too.

My heart skipped a beat and I decided to take a leap of faith. He said fate had brought me here and tonight, for the first time since I'd come to this academy, I was letting myself truly *feel* something other than rage. And I didn't want it to stop too soon.

Before he could pull back, I turned my head and touched my lips to his.

Gabriel fell still. He didn't return my kiss but he didn't pull away either. I stayed there for another second then stepped back, heat filling my cheeks as I dropped my gaze.

"Sorry," I muttered, backing up again. "I don't know why I-"

Gabriel caught my face between his hands and pressed his lips to mine again before I could say anything else.

My heart tumbled over itself in surprise as my lips moulded to his. His kiss was gentle at first, unsure, like he thought I might change my mind as the salt of my tears slid between our mouths.

But with each second that passed, desire for the dark angel before me was pushing out my grief.

Gabriel pulled back and I looked up at him with my heart pounding and the moon shining through the clouds above us like it was watching.

A shiver raced along my skin and I bit my lip as goosebumps rose everywhere. Gabriel's gaze slid down my body, taking in my hardened nipples which pressed against my thin cami and my bare legs beneath my shorts.

"You're cold," he stated, offering me his hand which I accepted hesitantly. "Come on."

Gabriel tugged me along toward a canopy set up on the far side of the rooftop. It had three walls and a roof formed out of dark blue canvas and was tall enough for us to walk inside even with his wings out. He dropped his hold on the water magic protecting us and the sound of the storm thundering down on the canvas roof surrounded us.

"Do you just...hang out up here on your own?" I asked, looking around at the piles of books strewn about the place. To the back of the tent was a thick mound of blankets which probably explained why it seemed like his bed hadn't even been slept in some nights.

"I find the clamour of too many people...stifling," he admitted slowly. "Sometimes I just need to *be*."

I chewed on my lip, realising that this wasn't just some man cave he was showing me, it was personal, private, a place he called his own and I was most definitely trespassing.

"Look, Dante has gone off in his Dragon form and I've got a perfectly good bed downstairs. I don't wanna intrude on your space and you've already done more than enough for me, so-"

Gabriel cut off my babbling by pressing his lips to mine again. His long fingers slid into my hair and every particle in my body came alive for him as my breath caught in my throat.

I hardly even knew him and I had every reason to be suspicious of him but somehow the feeling of his body against mine seemed like the most natural thing in the world.

His hands moved to my waist and he started walking me backwards as the passion between us grew into something more tangible.

I slid my arms up around his neck, my fingers pushing into the hair which curled at the nape of his neck.

Gabriel slid his hands down my spine and I arched into him, a sigh escaping my lips between kisses.

My bare feet brushed against the soft blankets at the back of the space as he continued to move me backwards and I dropped down onto them, tugging him down with me.

Gabriel moved over me, his wings flexing behind him, casting us in shadow. The lightning flashed on them, making them appear like a spill of oil. I couldn't help but reach over his shoulder, running my hand along the hard ridge at the top of his left wing.

Gabriel groaned as I touched him, looking down into my eyes with such intensity that I could feel myself blushing.

He trailed his hand along the side of my face, his fingertips carving a burning path along my flesh as he studied me in the dim light.

"You're so beautiful, Elise Callisto," he said seriously, his thumb brushing over my lips.

"I didn't know you'd ever even looked at me before now," I teased, unsure how to react to his intensity.

"I haven't stopped looking at you from the moment you walked into our dorm. I've seen your pain, your sorrow, your light and your fire. And it isn't enough. You captivate me."

I blinked up at him, lost for words but his mouth captured mine again before I had to think of any to give him.

This time when he kissed me it was deeper, fiercer, the heat of it warming me right down to my core and causing desire to pool in every inch of my skin. Where we came together my whole body hummed at the contact, needing more and more of him.

Gabriel pressed down on me and I wrapped my legs around his waist as he ground against me through the barrier of our clothes.

It wasn't enough. I needed more of him. All of him. I needed to feel alive again and every touch, every kiss he placed on my flesh felt like it was waking me up. Like I'd been lost and cast adrift but he was calling me back from the edge of an endless void. Offering me hope that I could feel something more than pain and misery.

It didn't make sense. I hardly knew him. But Gabriel thought the stars had meant for us to come together and I'd never wanted to believe in fate as much as I did in that moment. And it wasn't like I'd never had a one night stand before. Maybe one of the Kings wasn't the most sensible option in the world, but tonight I felt like being anything but sensible.

His hands slid up my sides, pushing at my cami as he moved it off of me.

I arched my back, breaking our kiss as the material passed over my head and the cold air caressed my exposed flesh. Even the smallest brush of his skin against mine sent butterflies warring through me. I'd never felt desire as keenly as this, I was ready to explode and he'd barely even begun to touch me.

Gabriel's mouth started carving a line down my neck and I moaned again. "Why does this feel so good?" I gasped as a shudder ran through my body.

"I don't know," he replied breathlessly. "I've never wanted anyone this much. I could lose myself in this feeling."

I moaned as he kissed me again, the passion of it bruising as we acknowledged the strength of this connection between us and took advantage of it selfishly.

His mouth made it to my breast and his tongue ran straight over my nipple, sending a surge of need between my thighs. I ran my fingers through his dark hair, my nails scraping his scalp. He sucked and teased at my nipple, biting down just hard enough to pull a moan from my lips.

Gabriel's hand slid to the waistband of my shorts and he pushed beneath it, a groan escaping him at the wetness he found waiting for him there. He pushed a finger inside me just as he drew his teeth across my nipple again and I arched against him as I felt his touch in every single inch of my flesh.

"Shit," I gasped, my body trembling and toes curling as he moved his finger in and out a few times before adding a second.

I ran my hands up the strong swell of his biceps, my nails biting into his flesh each time he pushed his fingers into me again.

I was tightening around him already, my body giving in to the demands of his hand even though he'd only just started touching me.

Gabriel dragged his teeth over my nipple and drove his fingers in harder, his thumb pressing down on my clit in the same movement and I cried out as pleasure crashed through my body. My vision darkened and I tipped my head back as I soaked in that feeling like I'd been starving for it and hadn't even realised until this moment.

Gabriel growled in satisfaction as he returned his lips to mine, devouring the pleasure he'd just given me as the hard length of his arousal drove into my thigh.

Thunder crashed overhead again and I felt it rumbling right through my body as I lay trembling in the wake of what Gabriel had already done to me.

We were both panting with want and need, our tongues moving against each other's in a desperate dance as our movements grew faster. I wanted more of him. Every hard inch.

Gabriel reached between us and unbuckled his jeans, rearing back to push them off of him and I slid out of my shorts.

As he knelt above me, I couldn't help but stare at his tattoos which stood out along his skin even in the dim light. My gaze caught on the symbols for Libra and Scorpio which almost seemed to be glimmering against his flesh.

I opened my mouth to point it out but Gabriel lowered back down onto me in the same moment and I instantly forgot all about it.

As his mouth came down on mine again, Gabriel swept his wings out around us. Pressing the edges of them down to the blankets either side of us and completely cocooning us in darkness beneath them.

I reached out behind him, dragging my fingertips down the inside of his wings, impossibly soft feathers sliding over my skin.

Gabriel groaned against my lips, shifting his hips forward with need as he pressed against my opening for a moment. I moaned in encouragement, need gathering in me as I kissed him harder, urging him on.

He pushed into me slowly, devouring the sound I made against his mouth as he filled every single inch of me before drawing back just as slowly. It was a heady feeling, my body adjusting to accommodate him. He seemed to take delight in the way his body was possessing mine as he paused a moment, holding me in suspense.

"More," I begged against his lips as he pushed into me once more, his pace still achingly slow and making me writhe beneath him.

A dark laugh was the only response he gave as he pushed into me just as slowly again, taking my body hostage with each inch of movement. I gasped as he stilled there, owning me, filling me, possessing me. And right then I was more than happy to be his.

It felt so good that I could hardly even breathe, but I needed him to stop torturing me and move faster.

I wrapped my legs around his waist, digging my heels into his back in an effort to force him to do what I wanted.

Gabriel slid a hand beneath my lower back, tipping my hips up before thrusting into me more firmly at last. I cried out as he hit the perfect spot deep inside me and his kisses moved to my neck as I rolled my head back, lost in the sensation of what he was doing to me.

He slowly increased his rhythm, pushing me higher and higher as each thrust got a little harder, a little faster.

His mouth was on my flesh, his tongue worshiping me as he held me in torment beneath him and I cried out for it never to stop.

My skin was tingling, aching, buzzing with the promise of release again as he built me up and up, climbing to the top of a precipice with me which I was desperate to fall off of.

Each powerful thrust of his hips had my head spinning, my body bowing and my lips pouring out cries of pleasure which only seemed to encourage him to torture me more.

"Please," I begged when I finally reached my limit, unable to take any more of his torture on my flesh. "*Gabriel.*"

His name on my lips was my undoing and I tumbled into a well of pleasure, crying out as he continued to move faster and faster while I could only cling to him and ride through it.

My muscles tightened around him as he moved his mouth back to mine, kissing me hungrily. He kept moving, a growl of desire escaping him as he pounded into me, prolonging the pleasure he'd given me and sending more and more of it skittering through my body with each thrust. I couldn't take it, I'd never felt anything like it; I was going to burn up with the power of it at any moment.

With a final thrust, he slammed into me, growling as he found his release too and I groaned beneath him as he filled me completely.

My heart jackhammered against my ribs as his weight pressed me down, our slick bodies moulding together as we tried to recover from the intensity of what we'd just done.

I slowly loosened my grip on him so that I was just holding him instead of gripping onto him like the world would fall away beneath me if I let go.

I traced my fingers over his shoulder blades, skimming the line where his wings burst from his back and feeling him shudder at my touch.

"Do you like that?" I asked, unsure if his response was pleasure or discomfort.

"That feels...unbelievable. No one's ever touched me like that," he replied in a devilish tone, leaning back to kiss me once more before he rolled onto his side, untangling our bodies.

As he shifted, the moonlight spilled in on us as the storm began to burn out and I blinked at the silvery light.

Gabriel flexed his wings for a moment before withdrawing back into his Fae form as they glimmered out of existence.

He rolled onto his back, pulling me close and I let him, not wanting this moment between us to end despite how unexpected it had been.

"I never would have imagined tonight ending up this way," I breathed, biting my lip against a grin as I touched my fingers to the Scorpio mark which sat just beneath his collar bone, slowly tracing the lines of his star sign.

"Fate," he replied roughly. "She does whatever the fuck she wants." He hooked a blanket over us as I let my eyes fall shut and his hand trailed over my breast making me wonder if he was considering round two.

He kept touching me as I lay in his arms but he didn't seem inclined to disturb me again yet and I felt so damn tired that I was already starting to drift off.

I shouldn't have felt safe to sleep in his arms but something about the way he'd said that word just felt so... *right*. Fate. I was so tired of suspicion and fear, I just wanted to feel this moment while it lasted without second guessing any of it. Fated or not.

GABRIEL

CHAPTER FOURTEEN

Though it was almost dawn, I still tasted cherries in my mouth from Elise's lips, her effect lingering on me like a second skin. I pulled away as she slept, shifting to sit up and scratch at my jaw. There was something so fucking seductive about this girl. And her body had felt more divine than I'd thought possible. It was the most intense sex I'd ever experienced. Fate had sent me women before but this felt like...well shit, I didn't even have words for it. But that left me in a serious predicament.

I didn't get attached to anyone. No ties. That was my mantra. Anyone who'd ever gotten close in the past was firmly removed from my life. My adopted father had taught me that. We'd moved all over Solaria when I was a kid before finally settling in this town where the air tasted like piss and gangs owned every street you walked down. *Great choice, Marty.*

Visions hovered on the edge of my mind. The Sight often gave me a glimpse of things to come. I couldn't control what I saw. Sometimes it was just a taste, a feeling, other times a snapshot of the future. Every ink stain on my skin was something I'd seen. Something the stars had deemed to show me.

Fucking stars. They were so damn cryptic. I scrawled their messages on my body so that I didn't forget them though, because each one had either come to pass or was yet to.

I grabbed my Atlas, opening my horoscope in hopes of gleaning some answers.

Good morning Scorpio.
The stars have spoken about your day!
With great revelations comes great choices. A storm rises of your own creation but it may blow out if you take time to think before you react. With a Libra sitting firmly in alignment with you, a night of passion may give way to new problems.
Beware of taking a dark path, you might end up on a road you can't turn back from.

The sign of Libra on my chest was itching and I scored my nails across it to make it stop. Elise's sign. *Dammit, I should have seen her coming.*

Two inked manacles wrapped around my wrists and I ground my teeth as I trailed my eyes over them. *Yeah, I don't get tied to shit. Except the stars. They keep me in a jar which they like to rattle sometimes.*

"Morning," Elise said, clearing her throat.

I didn't answer, my back to her. A knot of heat tightened in my chest as her fingers brushed down my spine. I wanted her flesh again. I ached for it, the need making me hard for her already. But screw what the stars wanted. *I* didn't want a girl in my life. I didn't need the complication. Last night had been a one night thing. I'd let my guard down, fallen under her spell and the spell of the heavens. But in the cold light of day, I realised Elise wasn't just some girl who'd stumbled into my bed. Her sign was printed on my fucking skin. Why hadn't I stopped to consider that?

I eyed the left manacle on my wrist, reading the words that wrapped around it. *We fall together.* It made me think of the tattoo I'd seen on Elise's

156

ribs while I'd run my mouth over her flesh, *even angels fall...* almost like it made a damn sentence.

"I'm gonna head back to the dorm."

I said nothing.

She stood, dressing and as she moved past me, I caught her ankle on instinct. "Don't tell anyone," I snarled.

Her gaze collided with mine and my throat tightened as a vision from the stars pushed into me, demanding my attention. Her eyes were ringed with silver and fear crashed over me so hard I couldn't breathe. *Fuck fuck fuck.*

I knew I'd been in trouble with this girl, but not *this* much trouble.

My grip tightened on her leg and she tried to shake me off to escape.

"Don't move," I growled, rising to my feet. I hounded into her personal space and she leaned backwards but held her ground. I hunted her eyes, pinching her chin firmly between my finger and thumb as I searched.

"What are you doing?" she demanded, curling her hand around mine and pushing it away.

Her lips were still red from how hard I'd kissed her last night. Screwing like it was our last night alive. And that urge was rising again now. I blew out a breath of irritation. *Fuck fate.* The last thing I could ever afford was letting someone get close to me. I'd known that my entire life. The stars had rarely tested the strength of that decision. But this was the mother of all tests. And I wasn't going to fail it.

"This didn't happen. Don't come back for more." I brushed past her as her expression skewed into a sharp frown. I drew on the power of my Order form so my wings burst from my back then dove from the roof and flew into the golden light of the sunrise before she could reply. Alone. Where I belonged. Where the world made fucking sense to me. And as far away from Elise Callisto as I could get.

The stars kept showing me that vision of Elise with a silver ring around her irises. And worst than that. So much fucking worse. They showed me *my* eyes with the exact same thing. I'd been looking in the bathroom mirror one moment and the next, there it was. A sign. A promise. A life sentence.

If she was my Elysian Mate then that meant this infernal bond between us was only going to grow more powerful. So I decided to read every book I could about how to break it off before it was too late. But there was one major problem with that plan: there was a sum total of zero books on that subject. Because no one had ever done it before. Once you came into contact with your mate, the time bomb started ticking. But I wasn't some ordinary Fae. I was Gabriel Nox. And I had a heart of fucking iron. So if anyone could break this off it was me.

I was going to be cold, cruel and heartless. By the time I was done, she was going to rue the day she'd met me. It was callous, but I'd been hounded by girls I'd slept with before. And I couldn't take the risk this time. Because if she got close again, my inner compass was going to point me firmly toward her. I wasn't going to underestimate the magnetic power of Elysian Mates, so I needed to drive the point home today.

I followed her down the hallway before our first class, silent as a ghost as I crept up on her. Before she turned down the next corridor, I snagged her wrist and crowded her in against the wall with a dark look that made even the shadows run from me.

"Get out of here," I commanded the other students and they scattered like mice. "A word," I growled at Elise.

"That sounded like two words. Which is more words than you've spoken to me since last night on the roof. Thanks for living up to my expectations and being a complete asshole."

I cocked my head, mouth flat. "You have no idea." Even this close to her, I could feel the urges of our bond rising in me. Which meant she could feel them too.

"I'm guessing you're about to show me."

I shifted closer, dipping my head to look down at her. Prey in the talons of a hawk. But she didn't cower, she tilted her chin up and faced me. I tried not to like that about her. "Guess what the stars whispered in my ear earlier?"

"What?" she frowned and I eyed the v between her eyes with the slight urge to run my thumb over it.

"That we're destined. Elysian Mates. Together forever if we want it."

She laughed and I had to admit it was hot. So many girls would fall at my feet for the mere thought that I could be mated to them. This girl laughed in my face and part of me wanted to kiss her until I swallowed that sound right up. But fuck if I would.

"You're joking?" she assumed.

"No," I said hollowly. "I don't do jokes."

"I can see that." She raised a brow then shook her head at me. "Why do you even think something crazy like that?"

"I told you: the stars."

"Liar liar," she purred.

I shoved myself against her, moving my mouth to her ear, her heart drumming against my chest. "I'm not lying, Elise. And I don't tend to do what the stars tell me. So do you want to avoid fate with me?"

She frowned for a second. "I don't believe you're my Elysian Mate."

I crushed her back against the wall until a breath of discomfort rolled from her lungs. "So you don't feel this power dragging us together? You don't want to kiss me?"

Her brows dipped and her eyes scoured me. "I want you to step back, Gabriel. I'm not beyond biting you." Her fangs snapped out and I smirked, glancing down between us and she followed my gaze to where I'd bound her hands in vines, so gently she hadn't even felt it.

I stepped aside and with a flick of my hand, threw her across the floor. She rolled and I bound her tighter in vines until she was wrapped up like a Tootsie Roll in the centre of the hallway. It felt like shit. Like cutting off a chunk of my heart. But I had to drive the message home.

"Fuck you!" she snapped as my eyes locked with hers. I guided a vine up around her mouth, gagging her as I strolled forward, staring down at her and tasting the bile pushing against my throat. The urge to help her free and drag her into my arms was almost overwhelming, but I wouldn't let it win. I'd treat her so mean, she'd refuse me even if her soul burned right out of her body in search of mine.

"Let's play a game," I snarled. "It's called stay the hell away from me."

Her eyes spewed venom as I released her from the vines. Her skirt was caught up above her waist and her cheeks flushed scarlet as she shot to her feet with her Vampire speed. I was ready for her attack, throwing up a shield as a storm of air crashed into me from her outstretched hands. She was stronger than I expected and I stumbled back a step as I had to work to maintain my shield. I was more powerful though and I gritted my teeth, defending against her until she gave up.

"Asshole," she hissed. "I'll gladly stay out of your way." She stalked off down the corridor and I stood there, letting the pain of that encounter crash through me.

Had to be done.

She didn't seem tempted to look back and that didn't piss me off at all. But I did wonder why the hell I was still watching her go.

I perched on my bed, visions capturing my mind as I stared at the opposite wall. Colours and tastes, smells and feelings, all giving me hints of things to come. The most frustrating thing was, I couldn't control what I saw.

The past eluded me. I couldn't remember a single thing before my fifth birthday, but sometimes the stars showed me snippets, memories, and I clung onto them with all my might.

I knew next to nothing about my past. My adopted parents didn't know much either. What they did know, was that I'd been planted into their care with strict instructions: to keep me hidden. When I pushed them for answers about who exactly had placed me into their care, they outright refused to tell me. Maybe they didn't even know. Either way, they received a generous sum of money deposited into their bank account monthly from some anonymous source. Since I'd turned eighteen, I'd been getting the payments too. I'd spent my young life thinking they loved me, now I just wondered if I'd always been a job to them.

They'd spent years teaching me to fly under the radar. Someone was after me. Didn't know who, or what, or why. But the extent to which my adopted parents had gone to keep me hidden was proof that I was in serious danger if I was ever found. Since I'd enrolled at Aurora Academy, they were more worried than ever. And frankly, so was I.

For the first time in my life, attention was on me constantly. With two Elements making me the most powerful Fae in school, I was naturally noticeable. Because of my double Elements, the girls here all battled for my attention and talked non-stop about me on fucking FaeBook. It set me on edge. What if whoever was after me caught wind of me here at the academy? Marty said homeschooling wasn't an option anymore after I was Awakened because I needed the best education available to train me on how to defend myself. So I took my education more seriously than most. I was miles ahead of my class because my life fucking depended on it. If I dropped the ball, it could mean the difference between winning or losing in a fight. And I was determined to be prepared.

Elise kept shooting me glares like I was staring at her, but I wasn't.

Mostly. Except sometimes my eyes trailed to her as the visions faltered. The curve of her neck, her full lips which had looked so good pressed to my tattoos.

Sharing a room with her was not going to be easy. I'd no doubt be sleeping on the roof more often than not. I'd never realised the bond of Elysian Mates was so powerful. It dominated every inch of me. The guilt of what I'd done to her earlier today was eating me alive. Like fucking locusts feasting on my insides. I was strong. But was I strong enough for this?

"Say something or stop fucking looking at me," she snarled and the poison in her tone made me both seriously miserable and relieved at once. She hated me. Job done. But also...*shit I wish she didn't have to.*

"He never says anything unless it's to piss me off." Dante pulled back his sheet to glare out at me. White hot energy burned from his core since I'd rescued Elise from him but he wouldn't dare challenge me.

"For fuck's sake Dante you're making it so hot in here. What's your deal?" Laini stormed into the room, wafting her face as she headed to the window and pushed it open.

Elise flinched so imperceptibly, only my hawk-keen eyes caught it. Fear flickered in her gaze. She didn't like heights. And the Dragon had thrown her out there like an unwanted house spider. I'd been compelled to go after her. The stars had shoved her into my way and refused to let me ignore her.

Dante disappeared behind his sheet and I slid down from my bed, not drawing anyone's attention as I moved across the room, my wings brushing past Dante's bed and making the sheet fall. *Asshole*. I hated the gangs. They were pathetic, sucking more blood out of this town than all the Vampires in Alestria combined.

I shut the window and was back on my bed before Dante poked his head out again. Elise wouldn't know I'd done it for her so it didn't matter, but I was quietly pissed at myself for giving in to the urge.

"Gabriel!" he barked at me. "You do it on purpose. Admit it. Just fucking *admit* it."

"Define admit," I said, mocking him. Not rising to meet his arguments was the best tactic to piss him off. It was hilarious.

"By the stars, I hate you," Dante growled, then yanked the sheet back across his bunk so furiously that he ripped the whole thing down. "Argh!"

I lay down on my bed, sliding one hand under the pillow and my fingers met paper. I tugged it out with a frown, finding the note Elise had written me.

Define yours.

I still wasn't sure why I'd kept it.

Define mine? Everything and everyone in this school, Elise. So long as I want it. But I don't want you. Not now. Not ever.

ELISE

CHAPTER FIFTEEN

I finished my dinner in the cafaeteria quickly and headed to my counselling session with Miss Nightshade. It was damn tempting not to go at all. I didn't need counselling. It wasn't like I'd had a traumatic loss and ended up beating the shit out of a guy before watching him kill himself and then embarked on a vendetta of revenge while disguising my identity or anything crazy like that.

Okay so maybe the more accurate assessment was that I didn't *want* counselling. I didn't want anyone poking about in my head, wondering at all the fucked up things they found there which had been caused by my grief. Because, yeah, maybe I was unhinged, unstable, unbalanced… psychotic. But I was okay with that.

It was the way I'd found to cope with losing my brother. The only way that I could make myself get out of bed in the mornings. The only way that I could see to keep on doing anything at all. Nothing really mattered to me since he'd died apart from exacting revenge on the person responsible. And my mission in coming here was all I cared about now.

I'd worry about scraping together some form of a real life after I'd finished this. If I survived it. I wasn't even sure if I cared whether I did some days.

It was raining so I shot away from the cafaeteria and back to Altair Halls with my Vampire speed. The counsellor's office was down a short corridor decorated in neutral tones and I dropped onto a comfy leather couch outside her door to wait.

I was a few minutes early and as I strained my ears, I realised I could hear the counsellor talking to another student as they finished up their session.

"-working on exploring more emotions before next week," a soft feminine voice said which I presumed was Miss Nightshade. "I know you like to believe that you only feel lust and pain, but I can promise I've sensed more complexity to you than that."

"Whatever you say," Ryder Draconis's voice came disinterestedly in response and I straightened in my chair, wondering if I might hear anything interesting by snooping on them. Maybe I'd turn up even earlier next week.

The counsellor sighed and footsteps sounded across carpet before the door was pulled open.

Ryder looked at me as he stepped out, surprise registering in his gaze for a moment.

"Come in, Miss Callisto," Miss Nightshade called and I got to my feet.

Ryder stayed planted in my way as I approached him, but I refused to show any fear of him. I walked straight up to him, smiling sweetly as I slid into the small space between his body and the doorframe. His eyes lit with what I could have sworn was amusement as the length of my body pressed against his for a moment and I slipped through the doorway.

I headed straight for the cream couch opposite the counsellor and dropped onto it.

"Close the door Mr Draconis," Miss Nightshade commanded as he continued to linger there and I looked back at him as his hand curled around the door.

"See you in Astrology, Elise," he said, making my name sound like something dirty. Which I didn't totally hate.

I shrugged in response, looking away from him like he was the least interesting person I'd ever met. "Maybe."

There was a beat of silence before the door clicked shut and I looked at Miss Nightshade as she tittered a laugh.

"I wasn't sure what I'd make of you, Miss Callisto, but you just managed to draw surprise, amusement and intrigue from Ryder Draconis with a shrug and one word, so I'm already thrilled to have met you." She was pretty, middle aged with short brown hair and warm eyes, something about her was very inviting. She made me feel calm, trusting, ready to open up and my lips parted as I prepared to do just that.

Tell her about Gareth. She can help with this pain.

Before a word could escape my lips, I frowned. Why the hell would I consider telling someone I'd just met about the secret I'd sworn to keep since coming here?

"You're a Siren," I blurted, more than a little rudely.

I gritted my teeth as I worked on shoving her influence back out of my head. Sirens were tricky fuckers, they could sense your emotions and make you feel anything they wanted. But I'd grown up around Old Sal and I was more than used to fighting off Siren powers. I wouldn't be letting this one get under my skin, though I had to admit she was more powerful than Old Sal and fighting her off was harder.

"I am," she admitted. "It makes my job easier because I can sense exactly what my patients are feeling."

"Right." I folded my arms. "I'm not obliged to tell you shit about myself though, am I?"

"Do you want to hide yourself from me? Is that something you often feel with strangers or is it everyone?"

I raised an eyebrow at her. *Nosey bitch.*

"Why do I have to have these sessions? I don't see what it has to do with my education."

"Well as you may have noticed, this school is subject to a lot of social pressures with the gangs and such. We find it beneficial for all students to attend these sessions. They aren't optional." Face impassive, giving nothing away.

I sighed dramatically, giving her a dose of stroppy teenager and not bothering to add anything else.

Miss Nightshade smiled like this wasn't her first rodeo and I was struck with the urge to tell her to back the fuck off.

"Okay, we can do this my way," she said with a shrug. "I'm picking up a lot of anger from you. More than just regular teenage angst. How's your home life?"

My scowl went from resting bitch face to ice queen but she didn't even blink.

"Grief?" she asked with surprise.

"Stay out of my head," I snarled. "That's not your business."

"Well, it is, actually. You might find it helpful to try and work through your pain with me."

"I'm working through it on my own, thanks," I snapped. I'd be taking revenge for a starter, going light on the mercy as a main course and if I was still around for dessert I'd figure that out then.

"Anger is a perfectly normal symptom of grief. Why don't you tell me about the person you lost? I'm sure they wouldn't want you to suffer like this for-"

I leapt to my feet, snatching my bag and pointing one finger at her in warning. "I might have to attend these sessions, but I don't have to give you details about my private life. So I suggest you back the fuck off next time and stay out of my goddamn head or I'll give you a demonstration of *my* Order gifts." I snapped my fangs out and bared my teeth at her before speeding from the room without waiting for a reply.

I didn't care if I'd only stayed for five minutes. I wasn't hanging around a second longer while she dug into my brain.

If she didn't get the message before the next time I was forced to endure her company, then I'd happily drive the point home with my fangs. It wouldn't be the first time I'd bitten a teacher.

I headed to Astrology class after spending the evening stewing over Miss Nightshade. The idea of someone getting suspicious of me had me pacing up and down the Vega Dorms' stairs thirty times before I came up with a plan to manage her. I'd tell her my dad had died. Give her some bullshit daddy issues to contend with while I thought about my brother just enough to give her some real grief to feed on with her Siren gifts. It wasn't a foolproof plan, but it would probably work. She might catch on to some deceit, but I was a damn good liar and I'd been practicing more than ever recently. It was the best plan I had so I'd just have to try it and see what happened. I had two weeks until my next session anyway so I had time to plan my strategy before then.

I made it to the observatory at five to ten in the evening so that I could wait for Leon Night to arrive and corner him for a few questions. He was always extra sleepy during the late night lessons at The Capella Observatory and I was hoping that might mean he wouldn't catch on to me questioning him about his old roommate and think it was suspicious.

I headed inside amongst the first students to arrive and picked a seat at the back of the auditorium while I waited for Leon to appear.

Instead of the Lion Shifter I was looking for though, the next guy to walk through the doors was none other than my least favourite Dragon in Solaria, Dante.

I pursed my lips, dropping my gaze so that I didn't have to look at him as he stalked into the room like he owned the damn place.

I waited for him to pass me by but unfortunately I was in for no such luck and he dropped into the seat beside me instead, clearly done with letting me ignore him like I had been since he'd thrown me out of a fucking window.

I stiffened, wondering whether Gabriel had been right about his temper blowing itself out or not and guessing I was about to find out.

"I haven't seen much of you today, carina," he said casually, flipping his textbook open as he leaned back in his chair, his knee brushing against mine as he felt the need to spread his legs as wide as humanly possible. "And you didn't sleep on top of me last night either. Where did you run off to?"

"What difference does it make to you?" I asked dismissively, "So long as you didn't have to hear me laughing, I thought you'd be satisfied."

"You can laugh as much as you like," he said, waving a hand like it was no big deal even though he'd tossed me out of a window for it. *Fucking psycho.* "Just don't make the mistake of doing it *at* me again."

I bit my tongue on a response just as the chair on my right juddered as someone else dropped into it.

"Why was she laughing at you?" Ryder asked, slinging an arm around the back of my seat which felt a hell of a lot like being pissed on. "Did you show her your tiny cock?"

"I'm actually waiting for someone else-" I began but Dante cut me off like I wasn't even there.

"She was begging for me to show her my *massive* cock after you kept sending her your little mind pornos like a pervertito even though it makes her sick. She wanted to see what a real man looks like instead of gagging over images of you."

"The only thing she'll be gagging on is my-"

And I'm out.

I shot out of my seat with my Vampire speed before either of them could continue to score points against each other at my expense.

By the time they even noticed I'd gone, I was leaning back in a chair on the opposite side of the auditorium with my feet kicked up on the one in front of me like I'd been there the whole time.

Dante scowled at me across the space but I pretended not to notice. Neither of them seemed willing to be the first to vacate the seats they'd chosen and I almost laughed at the ridiculous power play they found themselves in now. It looked like they were going to be stuck a seat apart for the whole lesson out of pig headed stubbornness alone. I just hoped they didn't end up blaming me for it afterwards. It wasn't like I'd asked either of them to sit with me anyway. That was on them.

Just as I thought I'd escaped the most mortifying part of the lesson, Gabriel wandered into the room. He cast his eyes across the space and I instantly hardened my gaze, refusing to look down while not actually looking at him at all. I was so fucking mad at him. Who the hell did he think he was using his magic on me and knocking me over like that? It was a one night stand! He was the one talking like a fucking stalker and making out that we were Elysian Mates. As if I'd want to be bonded to an asswipe like him for life anyway. He was good in bed, but his personality was severely lacking and I couldn't think of many people I'd less want to be bound to than a jumped up asshole like him.

Heat clawed along my spine and I wondered what the hell had possessed me to sleep with him in the first place. Aside from his devastating godly looks of course. But then he'd dropped that Elysian Mate shit on me. What the hell did he want me to say to that? Had I felt that connection with him last night? Hell yeah I had, my body still ached in the most delicious way because of it. Did that mean I was ready to settle down for good, say bye bye to every other guy I might ever meet just like that because I had one night - albeit a fucking mind blowing night - with a guy I barely knew? No. Like seriously. What was his favourite colour? Or food? Did he have a middle name? Or any weird habits? Or *parents*? The guy was a stranger to me, not my soul mate. Hell, he was still a murder suspect as far as I was concerned, though I really, *really* hoped I was wrong about that now that I'd slept with him. Maybe the whole mates nonsense was just to scare me off. Make sure I didn't get any ideas about being his girlfriend or something. Whatever it was, I had no issue with staying away from him anyway. He clearly thought last night was a mistake, so I'd just put it down to that too and move on with my life.

I felt Gabriel's eyes on me but maybe he read the general aura of keep the fuck away hanging around me and it satisfied him because he moved to sit on the far side of the circular room and left me alone.

At least I didn't have to worry about any repercussions from our night together aside from awkwardness in our dorm and avoiding contact with him as much as humanly possible. When you had a mom who did the kind of work that mine did, you learned to cast a monthly contraception spell before you even had your magic Awakened.

I started twirling a pencil between my fingers to use up some of the nervous energy in my limbs. Cindy Lou strutted into the room and headed straight for the chair beside Dante but he didn't seem to notice her arrival at all.

A deep laugh drew my attention to the door again and I sagged in relief as I spotted Leon walking in surrounded by a group of girls who were all in the process of doing various things for him.

"Leo!" I called, catching his eye as he looked up with a scowl. "I need to pick your brain about Pitball," I said, pointing at the empty chair beside me in offering.

"That's not my name," he replied, hesitating as his pride lurked around him.

"I've got snacks," I added as a sweetener.

Leon's face broke into a roguish smile and he shrugged as he prowled towards me. "Looks like you've won me over then, little monster."

He fell into the seat beside mine and one of his Lionesses passed him his Atlas while another placed his books down beside him. A third unscrewed a bottle of water and actually lifted the damn thing to his lips so that he could take a swig.

"Shit Leo, you're gonna be one fat old man," I commented as I watched the weird display unfolding.

"It's my Lion charisma," he complained half-heartedly. "It makes women crazy for me, I can't help it. Call it animal magnetism. I can't switch it off, it just works."

"Not on me," I disagreed, though I had to admit that I was drawn to him. That came with zero desire to start folding his undies into neat stacks or feeding him by hand though. Maybe weaker willed women were cursed with those desires around him but not me.

"I know. I'm quite enjoying having to chase you though - it makes a change. So I'll let you off," he said with a wink.

"Good to know. You wanna talk me through the training schedule for the team then?" I prompted as I pulled a candy bar from my bag.

"Sure. Mindy, can you email Elise a copy of the training schedule?" Leon asked and the three girls all said yes, making me frown. "Good. Now piss off, you're making little monster uncomfortable."

They all hurried to do as he said and I raised an eyebrow in surprise before deciding to let it drop. They seemed perfectly happy with pride life and who was I to judge other Orders for the way they handled their shit?

I looked up and fought the urge to flinch as I found both Ryder and Dante glaring at us. If looks could kill I was pretty sure I'd be mid crucifixion by now. Or maybe Leon would. Or both of us. Like a weird, double hanging from the cross situation...

Professor Rayburn swept into the class, her grey hair twisted into a braid which ran along the back of her head. She waved her hands into the air and the lights around us extinguished. We all dropped down into our seats so that we could look up at the night sky as the lesson began and I was saved from the torture of gang leader glares.

"Today, we are going to be looking at fate. More specifically, asking the question of can we avoid it? Are certain moments of our lives pre-planned by the stars or do you perhaps think that every single second of your existence is already mapped out?"

I pursed my lips as I broke off a block of chocolate and pushed it into my mouth. The idea of fate had pissed me off rather a lot since Gareth's death. In some ways it was tempting to cling to the idea that his time had just come. He had only ever been allocated so many years to live and they were up. But then that would suggest that the monster responsible for killing him hadn't done anything wrong. It was fate. He'd always been doomed to die. And what kind of cruel fate would dictate that someone good and kind and full of life never stood a chance? All their dreams and plans had always been pointless no matter what they did...

No. The idea of fate didn't sit well with me. At least not the idea that it was all pointless and nothing we chose for ourselves even mattered or changed anything.

"Can anyone give me an example of a fated moment?" Profession Rayburn called.

"Elysian Mates," Gabriel's strong voice came back to her and almost every head in the room snapped around to stare at him in shock. He aced every class but Gabriel Nox never participated. It was unheard of. Until now. When apparently he wanted to make sure that my fate included total mortification. He was looking my way again, I knew it. But I refused to return his gaze. I couldn't.

"Perfect example. Your Elysian Mate is your true love, soul mate, happily ever after, etcetera, etcetera," Professor Rayburn said. "Meeting them is *not* a fated event as some Fae never find them, and many don't even have them. However, should you come into contact with your potential Mate, you *will* end up in a Divine Moment with them. Fact. Fate. Unavoidable. You will

174

be drawn from your bed when the stars align just right for the two of you and in that *fated* moment you will of course be given the opportunity to choose them for your own. If you do, both of you will gain the silver ring of true love around your irises to mark your union, changing your eyes forever. Or of course you could always choose *not* to pair with them, your irises will be marked with a black ring instead and you will become star-crossed - destined never to be together and to mourn that loss forever more. Not much of a choice, but a choice all the same. So fate will put you in the Divine Moment but free will allows you to make your own decision about where your destiny will go from there."

I released a breath as she moved on from the subject of Elysian Mates to listing other examples of fate and free will colliding and I zoned out a little, taking another bite of my chocolate bar. At least if I was Elysian Mates with Gabriel I could decide whether or not I wanted him when the time came. But I still wasn't convinced he wasn't just cuckoo.

Leon made an impatient noise beside me and I glanced at him, finding his chin practically on my shoulder and his mouth open demandingly as he looked at my chocolate.

"You promised snacks," he reminded me.

"I said there *were* snacks. I never said they were for you."

Leon growled playfully, eyeing my chocolate bar with intent.

"Besides," I added. "There's no way I'd be hand feeding you even if you could convince me to share."

"Oh c'mon," he whispered. "I'll suck your fingers."

"That's not appealing."

"Fine." He lunged for the chocolate but I was faster with my gifts, swiping my hand away from him and biting another piece off. I grinned at him tauntingly with it between my teeth and his smile widened too.

"I'll happily take it from your mouth, little monster," he said, leaning even closer.

With a surge of motion he twisted in his chair and pinned me in place, his hand reaching for the chocolate as I leaned back, holding it as far away from him as I could.

He growled again, the noise as playful as sin as his breath danced over my neck and I leaned further back, quickly devouring the piece in my mouth to save it from him.

Leon's eyes widened in surprise like he couldn't quite believe I'd done that then his gaze slipped to the rest of the bar in my hand as I tried to hold it away.

He lurched across me as I tried to keep it out of his reach and I laughed in surprise as I was forced to try and wrestle him off. His hand closed over the fist hiding my chocolate bar and he grinned excitedly, looking right into my eyes as he still half pinned me in my chair.

His skin was hot against mine and my pulse skittered in response to his touch.

I sighed dramatically and released it into his hold, daring a glance at the rest of the room as he slowly withdrew with his prize before falling back into his seat. Luckily, no one seemed to be paying us much attention in our shadowy spot but I caught Dante glaring at us briefly. Glaring seemed to be his signature look recently though so I tried not to take it personally.

Professor Rayburn was still discussing theories on fate with the rest of the class and pointing out that some decisions were set in stone by the stars before we were even born. For example, our star signs defining our Elemental magic. I had to admit she was right on that one. Because Libra was an air sign, I'd always known I'd have control of air magic once my power was Awakened. I guessed you could call that fate.

Leon started groaning in the seat beside me as he devoured my chocolate and I couldn't help but laugh as he kept getting louder and louder with each bite.

"Mr Night, do you care to tell the class what it is that you are finding so pleasurable?" the Professor asked suddenly, swinging around to fix a glare on him.

I bit my lip, keeping my eyes low as everyone in the auditorium turned our way.

"Elise just gave me a mouth orgasm," he explained innocently, holding up the wrapper of the chocolate bar he'd just finished.

I scoffed dismissively even though I could feel a blush lining my cheeks. "You wish."

A few sniggers came around the class and Professor Rayburn rolled her eyes dramatically. "Please try to keep the wooing for after class. Some people are trying to learn here."

Leon nodded seriously, miming locking his lips up before handing me the imaginary key which I took for some reason with a soft snort of laughter. I pretended to slip it into my blazer pocket as Leon smirked at me like we were sharing a secret.

The Professor rolled her eyes dramatically and went back to her lecture.

We stayed silent for a while and I began to wonder if I could get away with just asking what I wanted to find out from Leon. With my Vampire hearing I'd be able to pick up on any changes to his heartbeat while I questioned him about Gareth anyway so if I started to draw his suspicion I should be able to fix it. Besides, I'd already pretty much ruled Leon out as a suspect. I just couldn't marry his easy-going behaviour with that of a killer. Unless he was the best actor I'd ever met. I'd ease into it though just in case.

"I have to wonder what would happen to you if you were left on a deserted island somewhere," I whispered thoughtfully. "With no one to get you meals and pre-chew them for you, what would you do? Not to mention the fact that you'd have no one to wipe your ass for you when you took a shit either..."

Leon twitched a smile before pointing at his mouth then holding his hand out to me. I frowned in confusion and he rolled his eyes at me before leaning into my personal space and sliding his hand into my blazer pocket. I widened my eyes at him but he just drew back and mimed unlocking his lips with the imaginary key I'd stashed there and a laugh escaped me.

"Firstly," he said in a low voice. "I wipe my own ass. Mostly. Mindy did it once but it was too weird-"

"Ohmagawd eww," I said, wrinkling my nose. "Which one's Mindy?"

"All of them are," he replied. "There are too many names to remember plus they come and go, easier not to have to keep track."

"Wait...those girls all follow you around doing everything and anything you want and you don't even bother to learn their names?" I asked in shock.

"Don't sound so horrified, like I said: they come and go. I can't help that I draw them in, half of them aren't even Lionesses but they get snagged on my macho Lion charisma and they just want to do all that shit for me. It'd be meaner if I told them no, they'd be all lost and crying."

"Plus, I'm sure having a whole host of girls to screw whenever you like comes in handy," I teased.

Leon smirked but didn't reply to that.

"So I'm guessing whoever used to have that empty bed in your room was a Mindy who saw sense and left," I said slowly.

Leon cast a lazy look my way but didn't respond for a moment.

"No actually, my old roommate...died."

I strained my ears to listen carefully to Leon's heartbeat but it didn't change at all at the subject.

"I'm sorry," I breathed, looking at him as he lowered his eyes.

He sighed, straightening in his chair a little. "Yeah...it was, well it was an overdose I guess so..."

Leon frowned as an unnatural stillness seemed to come over him and I got the feeling he didn't want to talk about it. But more than that, he seemed... sad.

I reached out slowly and slid my hand into his on the armrest between us. "Sorry if I pried," I whispered. "I can see you cared about him."

Leon frowned out towards the front of the class like he wasn't listening to me but his grip tightened around my fingers.

We stayed silent as Professor Rayburn began to explain about Celestial Markers and how they could be used to try and unravel our fates if we wanted to try and do that. It sounded very complicated and there were a lot of factors that could change things at any time so I wasn't convinced there was much point to it. Besides, I didn't want to live my life believing it was all mapped out for me. I wanted to be free, wild, make wrong choices and learn from them or not. Become my own person with my own flaws and own the responsibility for whoever I was, not blame any of my failings on fate.

"Gareth was one of my best friends here for a while," Leon breathed. "Before he fell in with the Black Card anyway."

A shiver tingled along my spine at that name and I turned to look at Leon from the corner of my eyes. "What's that, another gang?" I asked gently, though my heart was pounding at this new crumb of information.

Leon shook his head. "They're just a group of students. They're like a club of some kind but people can only join by invitation. They're secretive little shits so no one really knows what they're into but it doesn't take a genius to figure out that more than half of them are hooked on Killblaze."

"And your friend joined this club?" I asked.

"Yeah...and then he just became distant, withdrawn. Maybe I should have tried to snap him out of it. But he was a grown man, he had his own mind, you know? And I was living my own life too so I guess I just put it down to us growing apart and didn't really pay much attention to whatever he'd gotten himself into."

"So you think he was an addict then?" I asked despite the fact that every inch of my body balked at the idea.

Leon shrugged. "No. I mean, he was sleeping in the bed across from me every night and Killblaze makes people act fucking crazy. He was a bit quiet but not...I never would have guessed he was taking the stuff. When they told me he'd overdosed I didn't believe it at first but I guess... I mean maybe it was his first time and he was just unlucky."

Relief spilled through me at his words. I'd been right. I knew it. And no matter what Gareth had gotten himself into with these Black Card people, I was still sure he never would have taken that shit willingly.

Leon fell quiet and I wondered how much I could keep pushing him on this.

I moved my fingers in his, painting circles along the back of his hand with my thumb and he shifted in his seat, leaning towards me.

"Do you think the people he was hanging out with might have forced him to take it?" I asked.

Leon's brows pinched and he ran his free hand through his long hair. "I dunno. Why would they? That seems like taking peer pressure a bit too far to me, but what do I know? I'm not in their creepy cult."

"Cult?" I asked, that word sending a jolt through my heart.

A smile pulled at the corner of Leon's mouth. "Could be. They keep their little club secret enough," he teased though I could tell he didn't actually know that for sure.

We fell into silence and my mind whirled with what he'd told me. I was going to have to find out more about the Black Card and what they were up to. If Gareth had any friends in this place then it sounded like they would have been there, but it also sounded like his enemies might stem from there too. I was gonna have to do some more digging. And maybe try to earn myself an invitation into their club.

GARETH

CHAPTER SIXTEEN

EIGHTEEN MONTHS BEFORE THE SOLARID METEOR SHOWER…

*M*y new roommate, Leon, bunked across the room from me. My other two roommates were called Sasha and Amy - but Leon insisted on calling them Mindy – and they did anything under the sun to please him. That was Lion Shifters for you. The males didn't lift a finger to do anything for themselves unless they absolutely had to. And this guy had the strongest aura I'd ever experienced. Hell, even I wanted to do shit for him sometimes and that male Lion bullshit was only supposed to affect girls.

I was currently laying on my bunk with my Atlas in hand, looking into Gabriel Nox in the hopes that I could dig up some dirt and blackmail the shit out of him. He had plenty of money to spare and I was fucking desperate for it. I had three more days until the deadline, meaning Ella was royally screwed if I couldn't pull through for her.

First thing I noticed about Nox? His parents didn't add up. Two low powered Fae, one a Werewolf and the other a Caucasian Eagle. Gabriel was a Scorpio, so that explained him possessing the power of Earth. But to be gifted with *Water* too and *be a Harpy with mixed parents?* That shit was rare. Possible. But rare. And from the look of his scrawny, blonde-haired father and petite, red haired mother I'd found a picture of by trawling FaeBook, I didn't see the family resemblance.

Pooling all of that information together led me to one conclusion: Gabriel Nox wasn't their son. So maybe this Falling Star guy was the real parent? But I'd found myself at a hundred dead ends when I'd tried to figure out who Falling Star was. All I really knew was that they had some vested interest in depositing huge amounts of money into Gabriel's bank account every month. So maybe it wasn't a someone. Maybe it was a company or a foundation. But I'd searched and searched for one that fit the bill and drawn a blank. So I went on a hunch that it was a pseudonym. And if that was the case, I had a few theories that spanned from conceivable to absolutely batshit.

Theory number one...Gabriel's real mother or father was famous. Perhaps he was the lovechild of a singer, actor or even a Celestial Councillor who were keeping him hidden from their real husband or wife. But that didn't explain the fake-ass parents. Unless one of them really was related to him.

Theory number two...Gabriel was taking part in a drugs test that gifted him with a powerful frame which had nothing to do with his parents and the gift of an extra Element. Yeah okay, maybe I'd come up with that one after three or four beers.

Theory number three...(my personal favourite) Gabriel was undercover. Running from the law or maybe even from an Astral Adversary who was hunting him to the ends of Solaria.

Theory number four...I was a desperate motherfucker looking for a way to blackmail Gabriel Nox that simply didn't exist.

"Hey Gordon." Leon strode into the room, walking straight towards me.

"It's Gareth."

"That's what I said." He smirked. "You're on the Pitball team, right?" He pointed to my filthy Pitball uniform in a heap on the floor.

"Yeah and?" I asked.

"I wanna try out. I've been playing Pitball with my brother since I could walk. I make a killer Fireshield. My tackle is legendary." He grinned in a way that said he meant that in both senses of the word and Sasha and Amy giggled from their beds.

"You missed try outs, they were last weekend. Professor Mars is gonna announce who made the team tomorrow. You can probably be a sub though if you can convince him to watch you play."

"Na, that doesn't really suit my needs. I wanna play Fireshield, then I want to make Team Captain."

"Well that sucks for you, because I'm gonna make Team Captain this year." I grinned tauntingly and his eyes danced with the challenge.

He ran a hand through his long, beach blonde locks, his blue t-shirt stretching over his broad form. "Listen dude, you want to have an actual chance at winning the inter-academy tournament this year, right?"

"Right," I agreed, raising a brow. "And you think you'd give us the edge to do that, do you?" I surveyed his frame, quietly accepting that he would probably make a decent addition to the team.

"I do," he said easily.

"Well like I said. You missed try outs." I shrugged one shoulder.

"Were you on the team last year?" Leon asked thoughtfully.

"Yup. I'm a star player and I'm gunning for Captain. It's basically a done deal," I said with a sideways smile.

"Then Mars will make an exception for you if you ask him." He leaned down, grabbing my wrist and hauling me out of bed.

"Hey asshole." I shoved him back with a blast of air and he stumbled away with a grin.

"Come on, dude. I'll make it up to you," Leon implored.

"How?" I folded my arms.

"I'll give you the login for my Faeflix account? You'll have access to all the best movies and shows in Solaria right on your Atlas."

"Really?" I asked, tempted by that shit. I couldn't afford the ten aura a month subscription and had to listen to my friends talk daily about a new action film called Fae Hard which sounded awesome.

Leon reached into his pocket, taking out his Atlas and a glittering white crystal was pulled free, bouncing across the floor. It was the size of my thumb and fucking beautiful. Leon didn't move to get it and Sasha jumped out of her bed to grab it for him. Before she could, I dropped down, picking it up and turning it over in my palm. It shimmered like starlight and a strange energy seemed to pour from it, bathing my heart in a pool of warmth.

"Oh thanks, dude." Leon took the crystal, tucking it back into his pocket.

"What is that?" I asked, missing the feel of it already.

"It's white jasper," he said, raising his eyes from his Atlas. "And it's mine."

"Right...isn't jasper normally red?" I was hopeless in Potions class so I couldn't remember what jasper was capable of anyway and I'd never heard of a white version. It was my least favourite subject and when Professor Titan started babbling about the power of crystals, my mind just checked out.

Leon laughed. "Yeah dude, the white ones are rare as hell and ten times as powerful as the red ones. You could feed a family of ten off this crystal for a month."

I forgot to breathe.

Or save my baby sister from parading herself on stage for a bunch of horny unwashed guys.

"Shit," I exhaled, my eyes trailing over Leon for a second. Could I screw this Lion over? It wasn't like we were friends. And that crystal was the answer to my damn prayers. I could pawn it for cash before he even knew it was gone. How would he ever trace the crime back to me if I was smart about it?

Hell, what other choice did I have? The stars were putting a solution right in front of my eyes. I'd be a fool not to take it. I hadn't made any headway with Nox and my time was running out.

"I've messaged you the login to my Faeflix account on FaeBook," Leon announced with a bright smile. "So...?"

"Let's go see Mars," I agreed, ignoring the tug in my gut as I led him out the door. "He runs detention on Thursdays in the Empyrean Fields." I had to figure out a way to get my hands on that crystal, so I might as well start by cosying up to him.

Leon fell into step beside me as we headed downstairs and out of The Vega Dormitories. He thumbed through his Atlas as he walked, moving as slow as a snail riding a tortoise which was frustrating as hell.

"Do you wanna walk a bit quicker, bro?" I glanced over my shoulder at him.

He chuckled to himself, lifting his eyes. "Sure, dude. But check this out first." He passed me the Atlas and my gaze fell onto his FaeBook newsfeed, showing a post from him.

Leon Night:

So I've thought long and hard about this and I've decided it's time for us to take things to the next level. The blowjobs you give me are sublime and fuck if I don't think about you all day and all night long. You know who you are. Wear a pink flower to show me you love me too and wait for me to come and claim your heart. #meanttobe

Susan Gwent:

Ohmystarsss Leon finally! I'll wear it every day until you come for me!

Amy Starling:

It's me, I know it's me! I've waited so long for you to admit your feelings!

Rachel Jupiter:

MY LION KING! I'M WAITING! #Icanfeelthelovetonight

Dione Apollo:

He's mine bitches!

Susan Gwent:

He's talking about ME. Don't try and get in the middle of true love, Dione.

Dione Apollo:

As if he'd go for your skinny ass, bitch. Leon likes a booty on his cutie.

#donthatemecozyouaintme

Principal G:

Now now, gals. A skinny kaboose can be just as appealing as a big booty.

#anotherproblemsolved #Gforce

Click to load 283 more comments.

I arched a brow as I turned to Leon, passing him back his Atlas. "So who's the real mystery girl?"

He leaned in closer, looking like he was about to burst out laughing. "There isn't one." He lost it, clutching his side and it was so infectious that I couldn't help but fall apart too.

He clapped a hand to my shoulder and I grinned.

"That's hilarious." Dammit, why did I have to like this guy?

We headed on, walking down the corridor side by side and I didn't really care about hurrying anymore.

Leon started telling me about the pranks he'd pulled in school so far and he'd only been here a month. He'd swapped sugar into Ryder Draconis's morning eggs instead of salt, causing Ryder to hit his minion so hard he went to the ward, he told Dante Oscura a dark-eyed woman was out to kill him so he broke up with two girlfriends and glared at any dark eyed girl until she left him the hell alone. He'd convinced Gabriel Nox he was moulting by scattering black feathers behind him wherever he went, and he set off the fire alarm more times a day than was even funny anymore.

When we arrived on the Empyrean Fields, I was feeling extra shitty about planning to rob him. But I couldn't pass up this opportunity for the sake of some guy I barely knew. I needed to help my family. It was my priority now. And I'd sworn I'd do whatever it took, so I wasn't gonna blink at this.

Mars was standing to one side of the field, making five students run laps around it. When they ran up to him, he ordered them onto the ground to do push-ups before sending them off to do another lap. I'd attended a few of Mars's detentions in the past and I knew how fucking gruelling they were. He'd have this lot out here until midnight, dripping sweat and covered in blisters. They weren't allowed to heal until Mars decided it was time and that usually lasted at least until the next day.

We headed over to him and he noticed us, placing his hands on his hips. "Evening, Mr Tempa," he nodded to me. "And Mr Night, isn't it?" He looked to Leon who nodded.

"Hey sir," I said, ready to work the charm I'd relied on my whole life. "So I was thinking....you want the best Pitball team in Solaria right? One which stands a chance at beating the other teams. Even Zodiac Academy...?" I said enticingly and Mars's eyes narrowed.

"Yeah..." he said suspiciously and I nudged Leon forward.

"Well Leon just showed me his tackle and it's fucking ace. Like Solarian Pitball League good. I think you should consider him for the position of Fireshield."

"I've already filled the spots. It's too late." Mars folded his arms and Leon pushed a hand into his hair.

"Maybe I can still change your mind?" he suggested. "Nothing is set in stone unless you say it is, right sir?"

I fought a smirk. Looked like Leon Night was as much of a charmer as I was.

Mars was a hard nut to crack but I could see his shell splitting. "Well I suppose so."

"Let him prove it," I suggested with an innocent shrug and Leon nodded keenly, eyeing the detention squad running around the edge of the field.

"How about I take down every one of those students?" Leon offered and a laugh escaped me.

Mars grinned at the idea, watching the five of them as they ran. "If you do it in under ten minutes and impress me with each tackle, I'll consider you," he announced and Leon bounced on his heels. "But," Mars said firmly. "You also have to stay for the rest of this detention so I can test your mettle."

"A-fucking-greed," Leon said brightly, tugging off his shirt and exposing muscles as golden as a sandy beach. He was already in sweatpants and sneakers so he didn't need to change. He scraped his hair up into a bun, eyeing up his prey across the field then ran off at high speed, chasing down the nearest student with a whoop of excitement.

She glanced over her shoulder, her eyes widening as she spotted Leon charging her down. She screamed as he caught her by the waist and slammed her to the ground. I laughed and Mars's lips pulled up at one corner.

Leon was already up again, powering along the edge of the field. Cries went up ahead of him as the other four students realised what was happening.

He took the next guy down like a car crash, their limbs tangling as they rolled and Leon slammed his face in the mud. Mars's smile grew wider as Leon sprang up again, chasing after the third one. She stopped, raising her hands as if to fight him, but Leon cast a fiery blaze around him which blinded her. He leapt through it, throwing her to the ground and splaying his whole body over hers to keep her in place.

The final two guys were running like an axe murderer was after them, shoving each other as they both tried to take the lead. Leon sprinted after them at full speed and I started to think we really did need him on our team.

The first guy went down with a yelp and a crack that said something was broken, while the second guy was thrown into a tree at the edge of the field by the force of the collision. Leon held him down for the five second count before jumping up and hollering excitedly in our direction.

"Good call, Tempa," Mars said to me. "That's why you're gonna make a great Pitball Captain."

I lay in bed, fucking thrilled to know I'd made Captain. I'd worked my ass off to gain that spot and nothing compared to actually attaining it. But my excitement was short-circuited knowing what I had to do tonight. I'd come up with a plan and I just hoped it worked out.

It was past midnight when Leon finally returned to the room. The lights were off and as he shut the door, the dorm was plunged back into darkness.

I kept my eyes shut, the sound of Sasha and Amy's shallow breathing filling the air.

The scent of shower gel reached me as Leon moved about then finally climbed up into the bunk above mine with an exhausted exhale.

I waited half an hour before I made my move, shifting out of bed and urging my skin to glow just enough to see by. In the dim light, I spotted his dirty sweatpants dumped on a chair. I crept toward them, pushing my hand into the pocket with my heart hammering in my ears - jackpot.

I took out the crystal then hurried to the door. I was fully dressed, shoes and all. I'd been waiting for this opportunity all night and I had to be careful not to fuck it up at the final hurdle.

I tiptoed out the door, sending a message to the strip bar's bodyguard Petri with my heart hammering like crazy. The guy knew the dodgiest dealers *in town and if anyone could pawn this crystal in the middle of the night, it was him.*

I'd be back before dawn, tucked up in bed with no evidence on me. I'd tell Leon he must have dropped the crystal in the Empyrean Fields. I'd even help him look for it if he asked.

The guilt I felt was nothing in comparison to the rush of relief that filled me. Because Elise was safe from Old Sal for another month. And that was worth everything.

RYDER

CHAPTER SEVENTEEN

Combat class was an excuse to use my earth magic to hurt every motherfucker who I was paired with. Eugene Dipper had the misfortune of being paired with me first and I smiled darkly at him as he approached me across the Empyrean Fields. His small frame lacked an ounce of muscle and his large front teeth and blonde hair gave him the appearance of the white rat of his Order form. He was shaking like a leaf in a hurricane and I smirked as he raised his hands to fight me. He also possessed the power of earth, but the pathetic quake he rocked beneath my shoes was a damn joke.

"Is that the best you can do?" I hissed, planting my feet.

"I- I um-" He screwed up his face in concentration and the ground beneath me rocked harder.

I took an abrupt step forward and he shrieked, falling down into the mud on his ass. I lifted a hand, making a vine grow beside his head and push its way into his mouth and down his throat. He started choking and I drank in his pain like fresh water. He began to turn blue and I grew bored. He'd be so easy to kill, no challenge at all.

Mars barked an order at me to stop and I released Dipper, offering him my hand to get up. The one inked with the word *pain*. He stared at it like it was a loaded gun then hesitantly reached for it. I curled my fingers into a fist and terror flashed across his features.

"Hurry rat boy or I'll start breaking teeth."

He scrambled away from me, springing to his feet and sprinting across the field. I cracked my neck, turning to face Mars as I waited for him to re-pair everyone in class.

And it was my lucky day because the professor directed Elise over to me.

She tugged at a lilac lock of hair, twisting it around her finger as she walked toward me. She was chewing gum, popping a bubble like she gave zero shits about pairing with me. After the other night in the Acrux Courtyard, I realised how unbreakable she really was. And that made me want her even more.

I'd spent a lot of time thinking about the exact way I was going to punish her for her rudeness over the orange soda. And how she'd bitten me after I'd vision-fucked her. Sure, I'd damn well liked it. But I was still Fae. And in Solaria, everything was tit for tat.

I snatched her arm, drawing her toward The Iron Wood at the edge of the field away from all the other fuckers in class. Cutting off prey from the herd was the first essential step in a hunt.

"Are you ready to take me on, new girl?" I asked, settling into a fighting stance and cracking my neck to drag a satisfying pop out of it.

She observed me with indifference, lowering into a fighting stance of her own with a simple nod.

"I'm gonna make you choke on that gum," I warned. "Then you can choke on something else after."

"Fuck you." She popped another bubble and I grinned. *Game on. This is going to be fucking hilarious. But if I actually laugh I'll have to print happy on my shitting forehead.*

She raised her hands, drawing a storm of air between them with a finely tuned skill. I conjured a thick green vine into my right palm, letting it lengthen until it was a deadly whip. Adrenaline thumped at the base of my skull and that swinging dial that lived in me flipped onto pain.

She moved to release her gust of air and I didn't even bother to shield myself. I locked her in my eyes, sending her a vision of my dick in her mouth that made her stumble back and cast her magic right over my head. A laugh built in my throat but I didn't allow it out. I let *pain* take over and slashed the whip across the backs of her tanned legs. She staggered forward with a yelp as a reddened line raised across her skin. I drew power from her pain, sighing as it filled up my magic reserves and swam like sweet honey in my chest.

She gritted her teeth. "No Order gifts," she growled. "That's cheating."

"In the real world, people don't fight by the rules, new girl. They fight filthy, bloody. They'd gut their own mother if it meant their worthless heart kept beating. But maybe you've lived in a comfy little home all your life and don't know that?"

Something flickered in her eyes and the warmth inside me built again as I tasted something else in her. Emotional pain. I sucked it in and I knew she felt my invasion because she threw up a shield beneath her skin to keep me out.

I ran my tongue across my teeth. "That was quite the appetiser, baby. Give me a little more."

"I'd rather you take pain from my flesh." She lashed out with her hand, a storm of air flipping me off my feet so I slammed onto the ground. She rushed forward, hand raised above me, holding me down with the raging force of the wind blasting from her palm. It compressed my chest but not nearly enough to give me the pain I wanted.

I swung my legs, taking her out by the knees and she crashed into the grass. Her sports skirt got caught high up on her thighs, revealing more of that untarnished flesh. It was so smooth and creamy it practically begged for bruises. I pinned her arms down with two vines that grew from the earth as I got to my feet, a third one curling around her throat and tilting her chin up so she was looking at me. And I finally gave it to her. Her punishment.

The gifts of my Order form took over, the power of hypnosis rearing up and slithering into her mind.

Her mouth skewed and her eyes widened as I showed her a torture chamber of my own design. The vines which held her now appeared as chains. She was splayed across a metal table wrapped in nothing but leather and the sight was so arousing, I jerked forward a step on instinct.

Her eyes whipped across the scene I'd conjured, the walls wet with blood, oozing, painting the word *pain* to my right and *lust* to my left as I approached her.

"Are you frightened, Elise?" I used her real name for once because a name held power. And I claimed it from her now by possessing it with my tongue.

In the vision I was stripped to the waist in jeans with a bone white mask across my face, the mess of scars on my body on show for her to see. She didn't shrink as I expected, she bloomed. Her eyes glittered with trepidation, but not fear. Maybe because she knew this was a vision. Or maybe, just fucking *maybe*, she had a part of her which was as twisted and frayed as me. And that was what I'd searched for my entire life. A mate who understood this need. Someone who could withstand what I needed from their body.

"No," she answered, though her delicate throat bobbed. "Not yet."

I removed the mask from my face with nothing but a thought. I didn't want her fear. That was a test. What I wanted was her pain.

She yanked at her chains. "A true Fae would let me fight back."

"I will. But I want my pound of flesh first. You bit me...so I'll bite you." I pushed her right thigh to one side, admiring the leather thong I'd done a damn good job of conjuring. Then I dipped my head. She inhaled deeply, but didn't flinch. I grazed my tongue piercing along the inside of her thigh, ice cold and sending goosebumps rushing outwards from my mouth.

"Don't toy with your food," she said breathlessly, her thigh muscle tightening beneath my hand as I held it in place like a rare steak I was about to devour.

I bit gently, groaning into her flesh at the taste of her. I wanted this to be real so bad I almost stopped to ask her if she wanted to sneak out of Combat Class and come to my room. The visions were good but never enough. Like I was feeling it all through a layer of plastic. If she tasted this good here, she'd taste like a cardinal sin in real life. I dug my teeth in, harder and harder. Waiting for that blissful moment when she-

"Ah!" she yelped and her pain washed into me. I bit even deeper, marking her with a red welt that would have remained there for days if I'd really done it. She didn't even thrash against her chains as I tightened my jaw and tasted blood. I ran the pad of my tongue across the wound, lifting my head and meeting her dilated gaze. Her lips parted as she exhaled, breathless and wanting.

"You like it," I stated, my voice raspy, hopeful even. When was the last time I hoped for something?

Slowly, excruciatingly, she nodded and I swear I came in my pants. "You passed with flying colours, new girl."

"I'm not new anymore," she said with an eye roll.

I stood up, leaning over her, ready to plunge my tongue into her mouth and take no prisoners.

"You're new to this," I breathed against her lips, so ready for this kiss. It was going to be anything but sweet.

She broke the chains through will of mind and I fucking loved that about her as she tangled herself around me, her back arching like a bow to press her body into mine. I was about to claim her mouth and take this vision a whole lot further when someone punched my head so hard, I was knocked out of the hypnosis.

I found myself collapsed over Elise, the two of us tangled on the ground like we had been in the vision. But that wasn't right. I never actually moved when I was casting. We must have been so deep in the hypnosis I'd lost control, and it looked like she had too.

Someone's fist connected with my temple again and I hit the ground beside her, dazed and drinking in the power their blow had offered me. I looked up to find Dante fucking Oscura standing over me and a feral beast unleashed itself in my chest. My muscles rippled, threatening to shift, my teeth sharpening to points as the process started.

"I will not have gang fights in my class!" Professor Mars roared. He was huge and of the Cerberus Order. As a guy from the streets himself and now the teacher of Combat Class, I knew fucking with him was a bad idea, but I wasn't going to let this go.

"You want a fight, Inferno?" I snarled, rising to my feet as Mars darted between us, planting a hand on each of our chests. He was about the only guy in this school who ever dared to step between the gangs.

Elise scrambled to her feet, brushing down her skirt, her eyes flitting between us. Then she turned her back and walked away, like she gave no shits in the world. *Yes you do, baby. You'll be back for more of me before the week's out.*

"She's not yours, Draconis," Dante spat at me.

"She's not yours either, scum," I hissed as Dragon Boy began to pace side to side, anxious to destroy me. But I'd bury him if he tried.

"You are both going to be in detention *together* for a week if you don't take this outside of my class," Mars warned and that was enough to end this. Because I wasn't going to spend a fucking second in that piece of shit's company unless I was crushing his skull with my bare hands.

"This isn't done," Dante warned.

"I know. It's not done until you bleed," I confirmed, spitting at his feet and marching away.

If he wanted Elise, I would make it my personal mission in life to never let her fall into his bed. Which meant I needed to lay my claim outside of visions and tricks of the mind. Dante Oscura was clearly trying to take my girl. So I needed to lock her down fast.

After dinner, I waited in the stairwell of The Vega Dormitories where Elise would have to pass me to get to her room. I had one foot kicked against the wall while I rolled a razor blade between my fingers.

Everything up from the tenth floor was Oscura Clan, everything below was Lunar Brotherhood. The unallied were scattered between us, but if they ever chose a side it was imperative they were in a dorm on the right side of the lines we'd drawn. No Oscura would dare sleep below the tenth floor. If they did, they'd wake up in ten pieces. It was our signature kill. If a body was found in the city hacked to bits, you knew the Lunar Brotherhood was responsible. We didn't just kill our enemies, we obliterated them.

I waited right on the edge of my territory on floor ten. The stairwell was no man's land. We had to cross paths from time to time, but we tended to stick to different schedules to spend the least time possible rubbing shoulders.

Rain tapped against the window behind me and I fought a flinch at the first raindrops.

"Pain is your friend. Show me how strong you are, Ryder."

I cracked my neck, forcing out that voice. That fucking voice which haunted me, wormed its way into my head no matter how hard I tried to cut it out. But nothing short of a lobotomy was gonna rid me of *her*.

That particular memory involved three days inside the box with her casting water into the single air hole every other hour. That was before I'd been Awakened. Before my blood had turned ice cold. Back when the cold actually hurt. Just before she filled the box with freezing water, she showered it over the wood above me like rainfall to let me know what was coming. Even after all these years the sound of the rain still made me flinch.

I rolled the razor blade along my thumb, letting out the pain, the crippling squeeze around my ribcage. From the outside I was an unshakeable fortress, but at that moment, on the inside I was crumbling apart in a silent earthquake.

"Ryder?"

Elise's voice jumpstarted my heart and I kicked off of the wall. Her eyes were wide as they dropped to my hand and I realised it was pissing blood. I dropped my arm and the blood pooled into a puddle at my feet.

"Heal it," she practically commanded, stepping forward as if she was going to do it herself.

"Are you worried about me, new girl?" I smirked and she snatched my hand, healing the wound in an instant.

"No, I just don't appreciate the hazard you're causing in the corridor. Someone could slip over on all of that blood." Light danced in her bright green eyes, causing something warm and airy to fill my chest that I wasn't familiar with.

"Sure could." I shrugged as she released my hand. "So here's the deal, I want you in the Brotherhood. You can skip initiation if you agree to be my girl. I'll have you moved to a dorm downstairs before tomorrow." I raised my brows, waiting and she looked at me like I'd just put on a tutu and done a pirouette.

"No."

The rejection stung. And for once it wasn't a pain I liked. "Elise," I growled. "I've never offered this to anyone. Take a long moment to think about what you're refusing. You won't ever get this offer again."

She tapped her chin, taking a long fucking time to mock pretend to think. "It's still a no. I don't want to be in your gang." She tried to move past me and I snatched her wrist, squeezing hard enough to make her wince.

"Is that because you're with them? With the Oscura filth?" The mere idea made me want to burn down this entire building with everyone in it.

"No," she said, softer this time as she leaned into me and rested a hand on my chest. She dug in her nails and I relished the dry scrape through my shirt. "I don't want to be in *any* gang. And I'm not anyone's girl. That's not how I roll."

"How can I make you mine?" I demanded.

"I can't be owned."

"How do I make you see me exclusively then?"

"I dunno, maybe you can figure that out." She twirled a lock of hair around her finger and I nodded, pressing my tongue into my cheek. "To be honest, Ryder, you're an open book. It's a short book, but definitely an open one." She took both of my hands in her small ones, brushing her thumbs across the two words painted over my knuckles. "I tend to go for a little more depth in the guys I date."

On impulse, I snared her in my gaze and showed her something I'd never shown anyone. Me before I was Awakened. Before that she-devil came into my life.

I was young, smiling, my knuckles tattoo free. My father sat beside me on a bench reading a newspaper. The street was busy in front of us. I couldn't quite get my father's face right, the memory blurred around the edges like a snowstorm blowing in. Clearer than anything was the bright red ice cream in my hand, the way the sweet strawberry taste sat so intensely on my tongue. And if I pulled the strings of that memory just right, my father lifted his arm and dropped it over my shoulders.

Then I got it, just for a second, but every time I remembered it right that memory sharpened tenfold. The stale scent of cigarette smoke mixed with the suede of his jacket. Then it was gone, lost to the darkest depths of my mind, replaced by *her*.

The vision shifted before I could stop Elise seeing this part. I didn't want *anyone* to see this. But it was too late, it was already playing out and I couldn't halt it.

Me in that box. Screaming. By the sun, how I'd fucking screamed. I didn't make noises like that anymore. My throat had been rubbed raw like I'd scraped off several layers of my oesophagus.

Every time I stepped out of line, I went in that fucking box in the garage. The smell of gas fumes rose around me as that bitch started the car and revved the engine again. Red brake lights flared against the walls of the box. I was seeing it from inside, but outside too. The vision was swallowing me, taking me so deep I couldn't get out.

I was coughing in the vision and coughing in reality. I couldn't fucking breathe. Couldn't see.

Hands were on me, soft and warm. I found two light green eyes to hold onto and it took me an age to recognise them. Her magic crashed through the barriers of my skin and melded with mine. For a moment we were one and it was bliss like nothing I'd ever known. I didn't power-share with anyone. But somehow, I'd let Elise's magic into my body, let it wash through my veins and fill me up. It was intoxicating, like a drug only better. So much fucking better.

She released me and I was free from it all, aching for that contact again. I stood before her in the stairwell panting, exposed. Humiliation crashed into me at what she'd seen followed by a torrent of rage.

Sympathy crawled across her face and my right hand curled into a tight fist.

"It's okay-" she started but I stormed away, heading downstairs to throw my knuckles into a wall until I broke every bone in my hand. I wouldn't stop until the pain inside bled outside. And then I'd shed my skin and leave it there to rot.

ELISE

CHAPTER EIGHTEEN

Once I'd asked Laini to point out the Black Card to me I wondered why I hadn't noticed them before. They hung out on the fringes of the school wearing dark clothes and darker scowls. I couldn't pick out what precisely it was about them that made them stand out, but they all had the same look about them. And they had zero interest in making friends.

I'd approached seven of them now. In class, the cafaeteria, the corridors, even in the sports hall locker rooms. My friendly greetings were met with cold, hard resting bitch faces and zero words. I'd even faced a group at once. Nothing. It was mildly humiliating. It also meant I wasn't getting anywhere. So I decided to narrow down my hunt in another way.

I knew Gareth had been dealing Killblaze before he died so maybe if I followed that back to the source I could glean some more information. At the least, he might have been friends with some of the other dealers. Because drug dealers tended to be chummy right?

By the sun I'm scraping the bottom of the barrel now.

But now I had another issue. Drug dealers didn't exactly wander about wearing a sign on their heads announcing their line of work to anyone and everyone. And I obviously didn't have that buyer look about me to mean they'd approach me.

Nope. I needed information. And there were three guys in this school who traded in just about everything so I was sure that I knew where to get it. Trouble was, I had nothing to trade. But I guessed it couldn't hurt to ask.

I squared my shoulders as I headed across the courtyard towards the corner where the Kipling Brothers were holding court. A small crowd was gathered around them, trading for snacks and drinks which weren't available in the cafaeteria while negotiating the best prices.

The crowd parted and I found myself before the oldest brother. He was bigger than the others, broader, meaner by the looks of that frown too.

"You'll have to pay for orange soda if you want it today, unless you're Ryder's girl now?" he asked, seeming interested from a business point of view.

I glanced over my shoulder to the bleachers where Ryder was sitting, surrounded by his gang. He was leaning forward, elbows on his knees as he glared off into the distance, utterly still and seemingly oblivious to everything going on around him.

"No. I'm not Ryder's anything," I said firmly. I didn't need those kinds of rumours circulating about me. Oscura Clan would be out for my blood in an instant.

"Then that'll be two auras." He held out a can of soda for me like I was a regular and he had my order pinned despite the fact that I'd only visited their little shop that one time several weeks ago.

Nice to know I made an impression.

"Umm, no thanks. That's not actually why I'm here." Though I eyed the soda longingly. I'd spent every scrap of money we'd had on getting my mom into that wellness centre and had literally come here penniless. Aurora Academy was full board so I got all of my meals, uniforms and a bed which was all I really needed anyway and I'd brought enough of my own clothes for use outside of class. But sometimes the knowledge of just how broke I was made me feel a little uncomfortable and I chewed on my lip, half wishing I could afford the damn drink. I was running low on gum too and I wouldn't be able to replace it once it was gone. That was damn depressing.

"So what can we do you for then?" Kipling Senior asked, drawing a little closer to me conspiratorially.

I glanced around a little nervously and my gaze caught on Gabriel who just happened to be right behind my shoulder.

"What are you staring at?" he snapped and my lips parted in surprise.

"I'm not entirely sure," I replied icily. "But my best guess would be the result of a turkey mating with an asshole."

Gabriel leaned close to me, his breath dancing over my neck as he whispered into my ear. "If you won't keep away from me on your own then I'll have to give you more reasons to."

My eyebrows pinched but he was already striding away, gliding between the crowd as if he hadn't been lurking at all. And maybe he hadn't. But it seemed like every other time I turned around he was there recently. Which seemed pretty weird for someone who claimed to want me to stay away from him. *Stalker Harpy.* My cheeks heated at the memory of his mouth on my flesh and I quickly turned away from him to give the Kipling my attention again.

"I'm actually looking for a Killblaze dealer," I said in a low tone.

Kipling Junior, the shortest, skinniest of the bunch perked up at that, sidling closer and cocking his head at me.

"Wouldn't peg you for a Blazer," he said analytically.

"I'm not," I scoffed.

"Killblaze is easy enough to come by," Senior cut in, clearly not caring if I looked like a user or not. "We don't keep illegals with us in the courtyard though so you'll have to wait until-"

"No, no," I interrupted. "I don't want any Killblaze. I want the names of the dealers." I folded my arms and waited as Junior released a low whistle.

"Gonna cost you," Middle Kipling added as he joined the conversation.

For the moment the rest of the crowd had dispersed so I was alone with their full attention.

"I don't have any money," I said flatly. No point in beating around the bush. "Or anything of value really. I was hoping maybe I could trade a favour."

The Kiplings all exchanged a look, though instead of the scoffing I expected, they seemed eager.

"We could keep it in the bank," Junior said. "See how the tug of war plays out between Dante and Ryder. Once she's all in with one of them she'll have their ear."

"Pfft, if we wait for that we might lose out. When she makes a choice between them the other won't let it stand. She'll end up gutted before we can call in our debt," Senior said dismissively.

I scrunched my nose up at that assessment. "I'm not going to be picking either of them," I piped up. "Gang life is absolutely not in my future."

Three sets of amber eyes swivelled on me for half a second before turning to each other again.

"She's unproven anyway. Her word could mean shit for all we know, we should get the payment before giving her the information she wants," Middle said.

"Hey!" I objected. "My word is good."

They all shrugged.

"She could help with the import tonight?" Junior suggested half-heartedly.

"That's not a terrible idea," Senior said thoughtfully. "Professor Mars almost caught us last time. She could cause a distraction and take the detention if she gets caught while we get the goods in."

"I like it," Middle agreed. Junior nodded, seeming pleased he'd come up with it.

"Alright then," Senior said, taking control of the negotiation again. "Tonight at two, we have a delivery coming in via the Empyrean Fields. You need to get down there and draw any lurking teachers away from The Iron Wood on its border. Somewhere near the Pitball pitch should be close enough for them to hear you and far enough from us to let us get our goods in. You do it and the names of every Killblaze dealer in the academy is yours. I'll throw in the name of two street dealers from the local area too."

I grinned. A distraction I could manage just fine. "You've got a deal."

Senior held his hand out and I shook it, a clang of magic echoing through my palm as I gripped his and the bargain was struck.

I looked over at Ryder as I walked back through the Acrux Courtyard and into no man's land. I couldn't approach him in his gang territory but I wanted to speak to him. I didn't really know why I cared but ever since he'd shown me that flash of his childhood, I'd found myself thinking about him more and more often. He hadn't spoken one word to me since. Hadn't come anywhere near me.

I stopped walking and looked at him on the bleachers, meeting his gaze without flinching even though I knew it left me vulnerable to his hypnosis.

I tilted my head just a little, not an order but an invitation.

His gaze trailed over my face for a long moment before a vision slammed into me. Ryder stood right in front of me, covered from head to toe in blood.

"Fuck off!" he yelled in my face and I almost flinched.

I claimed control of the fantasy version of me as he tried to make her bow her head in deference to him. Instead, I held my chin high and looked him right in the eye.

"Gladly," I replied, my tone clipped and my gaze cold. "But if you didn't want me to see inside your head then you shouldn't have shown me. Don't blame me for your own failure."

My fangs snapped out and I shattered his illusion before he could respond, narrowing my eyes at the real Ryder who still sat unmoving on the bleachers glaring my way.

I turned and strode away from him without looking back. That would teach me to try and see anything good in him. If Ryder Draconis wanted to stay on my shit list then that was fine by me. I didn't have time for his melodramatic bullshit anyway.

I walked up Devil's Hill, smiling at Laini and her friend Daniel as I headed their way but before I could reach them, a dark shadow dropped from the sky and landed right before me.

Gabriel smiled darkly as I stumbled to a halt and scrambled to throw up an air shield to defend myself. Before I could get it into place, the ground beneath my feet trembled so violently that I tipped back onto my ass half a second before a torrent of water crashed over me.

"You asshole!" I snarled as I directed air magic into the shape of a whip, slashing it at him with a jerk of my hand.

Gabriel cursed as his arm split open and blood spilled from the wound. A moment later, gloves of ice formed over my hands.

The ice kept growing as I struggled against it, immobilising my magic and getting so heavy that I could no longer hold my hands off of the ground. I snarled between my teeth like a caged animal and Gabriel scowled at me for a moment before launching himself into the sky.

I only realised that silence had fallen around us as our fight played out when the murmurs started up.

I tried to ignore my classmates as I struggled against the ice which still bound my hands. My teeth wanted to chatter from the cold and I was already losing feeling in my fingers.

"Damn girl, you sure don't know how to pick a fight. What's with you and the Kings?" Laini asked as she drew closer to me and I looked up at her hopefully.

She started melting the ice with the aid of her fire magic without me even having to ask and I smiled at her gratefully.

"I told you," I replied ruefully. "I'm just unlucky."

Laini tutted knowingly as she continued her work to free me with her

212

magic and I could only wonder why she was helping me. The answer slapped me in the face like a snowstorm in July and I looked at Laini in surprise as I realised the truth of it.

She was my friend. Somewhere amongst everything I'd come here to do I'd never really considered the idea of making any friends along the way but it had happened all the same.

For a moment I didn't know what to say. I'd never found it particularly easy to make friends. I put it down to the solitary nature of my Order form, but I knew deep down it was just the way I was too. Not many people liked my sense of humour. Even less of them appreciated the way I never held my tongue and had an answer for everything. But despite all my flaws, Laini had found reason enough to like me. And I realised I really liked her too. She was the kind of girl I could talk to easily and her laugh was infectious, but she knew how to enjoy the silence too without making it awkward. We could hang out without talking and still enjoy each other's company. Which for a creature prone to being solitary like me meant a hell of a lot.

"Thank you," I breathed and Laini rolled her eyes like the last thing she needed was thanks.

I smirked in return, relaxing as the warmth of her fire melted through the ice.

I'd made a friend without even trying to. So maybe there was hope for me yet.

My Atlas buzzed lightly beneath my pillow and I jerked awake, quickly switching it off before it disturbed my roommates.

In preparation for my late night adventure, I'd gone to sleep wearing black leggings and a tank top. I pulled a navy sweater over the top of it and slid out of bed.

My gaze snagged on Gabriel's sleeping form where he lay on the other top bunk. His sheet had slipped down to pool around his waist and his beautiful tattoos were all on show for me to study. For once I was the one looking at him instead of the other way around despite the fact that he claimed to want nothing to do with me and I took a moment just to watch him.

I'd relived the night I'd spent in his arms in my dreams multiple times. And if I was being honest, I'd relived it while I was awake too. In my fantasies he obviously hadn't gone all super asshole on me. In fact he never even spoke. Which was exactly the way I preferred him. If he hadn't gone and turned all insane on me I probably would have hooked up with him again since. Who was I kidding, I *definitely* would have hooked up with him again. But I wasn't about to start announcing my desire to be with him forever or even admit to the possibility of him being my Elysian Mate. It was too crazy. And it didn't seem like he was wasting much time pining over me either. Aside from the staring which could also be put down to hatred. Not that I'd done anything to earn that. But who was I to judge the mind of a crazy person?

It was like he really thought I'd want him as my mate for life just because I'd screwed him once. He was so obsessed with the idea of me being obsessed with *him* that he hadn't stopped to notice I straight up hated him. Fucking Gabriel.

Besides, after watching the effects of two heartbreaks on my mom's life I had no intention of giving my heart to one man alone for safekeeping. Especially one who promised me the stars. I didn't do hearts and flowers, I didn't want promises and forevers. I just wanted something real and honest and in the moment. Which was what I'd had with him. Until I hadn't anymore because he had to go and start being my own personal nightmare stalker. Like a goddamn psychopath.

I blew out a breath and turned away from the perfect temptation of his body, heading to the door to retrieve my boots.

"Sneaky, sneaky, Vampire," Dante murmured, lifting the corner of the sheet which hung around his bed.

I stilled, looking into his dark eyes which roiled with the tempestuous energy of a storm.

"What makes you say that?" I asked on a breath.

"Where are you running off to now then? And don't try and pretend you're hunting this time. Who are you gonna catch at half one in the morning?"

I pursed my lips, assessing the hungry look in his eyes. He wasn't going to let this drop.

"What if I told you I'm hooking up with someone?" I asked slowly.

"Then I'd follow you and rip their dick off," he growled.

I rolled my eyes. "Fine. I'm doing a job for the Kiplings. I said I'd cause a distraction while they get their latest stock onto the grounds."

"I want in." Dante stepped out of his bunk in one swift move, pressing his broad shoulders back as he kicked his sneakers on. He didn't bother grabbing a shirt, just prowled towards the door in his grey sweatpants which were riding low on his hips.

"I've got it under control, thanks," I said, a little bite to my tone. I didn't need an asshole tagging along for the ride.

"I wanna see what you've got, carina," Dante said, ignoring me. "So you'd better not disappoint."

I sighed as I followed him out into the corridor. I clearly wasn't going to win this debate and I couldn't afford to be late.

I jogged down the stairs, fighting against the urge to shoot away with my Vampire speed. No doubt if I did that he'd make me pay for it later.

Dante kept pace beside me, his arm brushing mine more than once in the dark stairwell and sending electricity skittering across my skin.

We stepped out into the cool night air and I shivered, drawing my arms around myself. I led the way around the back of the building to where I'd stashed the supplies I'd liberated earlier that evening.

Dante watched me with interest as I grabbed the fuel can and pocketed

215

the lighter. My plan was simple but effective. Nothing was distracting like a big ass fire and with my air magic I could stoke the flames and make them difficult to put out.

The Kiplings needed me to distract Professor Mars for ten minutes. That was it. There was no need to do anything more flashy. I knew a good little spell to make the effects of it stick around for a while too so I'd decided to have a bit of fun while I was at it.

"Arson?" Dante asked with a smirk. "I thought better of you, carina."

"Well that was a mistake," I replied. "I'm as low and dirty as any asshole in this school. It might do you a favour to remember that."

He chuckled as we started walking down the sloping path which led towards the Physical Enhancement grounds and the Pitball pitch.

The clouds were thick tonight making it dark, which suited me just fine as I used my abilities to sharpen my vision. We'd be harder to spot like this but unfortunately Dante wasn't finding it quite so easy to navigate the darkness.

The third time he cursed, catching his foot on a tree root, I reached out and snatched his hand into mine. "Just stay close," I commanded. "You're ruining a perfectly good plan with all your noise."

"If you wanted me close you didn't have to make an excuse," he replied but I ignored him.

I got him moving at a faster pace, heading past the Pitball pitch and straight for the steep hill beyond it.

The clouds parted as we reached the bottom of the hill and I released my grip on Dante's hand.

"What now, bella?"

"Now you wait here." I smirked at him as I unscrewed the fuel cap on the can I'd liberated from the maintenance shed and shot away from him up the steep hill.

I started pouring as I ran, the heady scent of gasoline overwhelming me as I drew a huge outline into the long grass.

I made it back to Dante and grinned as I dropped to my knees, touching my fingers to the edge of the outline I'd made with the fuel. The spell was slightly complicated but I'd practiced it on a small scale several times this evening and it had worked each time. There wasn't really any need for it, so if it failed it wouldn't matter anyway. But for my own personal amusement, I was really hoping the magic would work.

Once I was fairly confident the magic had taken root along the outline, I quickly pulled my Atlas from my pocket and checked the time.

01:57. Time to go.

I snatched the lighter from my pocket and flicked it once. Twice. Three times. No flame appeared and I cursed as I flicked it again and again.

"Let me," Dante muttered, a smile hooking up his lips as he called on the electrical power of his Dragon form.

Static energy rose all around us and I could feel my hair lifting on my head as a shiver danced down my spine.

Dante caught my hand in his again just before he released a shot of his magic and I gasped as I felt the energy spike through my skin, waking every nerve ending and heating my veins. The taste of his power danced across my tongue and a heady feeling sped through me as my body was filled with electricity for a bliss filled moment.

A shot of purple electricity slammed into the ground in front of us where the edge of my gasoline art began and it burst into flames instantly.

I directed a surge of air magic after it, driving oxygen into the flames to stoke them as they raced along the path I'd created.

A grin pulled at my lips as Dante started laughing.

"You drew a huge dick?" he asked just as the balls burst alight at the far end of the hill.

"I did," I agreed on a laugh. "And I cast a holding spell to block earth magic beneath it too. So they won't be able to make the grass grow back over the burned soil."

Dante's laugh was so loud that I glanced around in concern. The huge blazing cock was sure to attract Professor Mars at any moment and Dante couldn't run as fast as me.

"Come on," I urged, tugging on his hand.

Dante shook his head, tightening his grip on me but refusing to move. "Too soon," he said. "We aren't even close to getting caught yet."

"You want to get caught?" I asked incredulously, adrenaline thundering through my veins, urging me to run.

"I want it to be a close thing," he countered. "It'll make you feel alive."

I hesitated short of yanking my hand out of his grasp. He'd just said the one thing to me which was likely to give me pause and I doubted he even knew it.

"I don't want to get in trouble," I murmured, though I'd already stopped trying to run.

"You were in trouble the moment you came out here with me and you knew it," he replied. "And I think that's exactly what you want."

I looked up into his eyes where the flames of the burning field were reflected back at me.

"One month's detention!" Professor Mars bellowed from somewhere way too close and I screamed as a blast of water magic shot towards us like cannon fire.

I barely managed to throw a shield of air magic up in time and I glanced at Dante as I realised he'd done the same.

The water crashed over our combined shields like a tidal wave before running off of them again to reveal Professor Mars charging toward us up the hill, his face contorted with rage as he spun more water between his hands. He was bellowing at us to stay put but with our backs to the flames I was sure he couldn't see our faces.

Dante threw a vortex of air at our teacher and snatched my hand into his grasp as we turned and started running.

I could have gone a lot faster with my Vampire gifts but I matched his pace instead, my heart thundering adrenaline through my limbs in a delicious way as we ran.

We raced around the Pitball pitch and started uphill back towards the dorms.

I threw a wild look over my shoulder as another wave of water was thrown our way. It scattered wide though, flooding down and drenching us but not doing enough to actually slow us at all. I squealed at the onslaught of cold water but Dante barely even flinched, yanking on my hand to keep me running with him.

We made it to The Vega Dormitories and Dante pulled me inside. I tried to run for the stairs but he dragged me to the right, opening a metal door and pulling me through it. He closed it again and tugged me after him down a short flight of stairs in the pitch black. Dante threw up a tiny globe of orange light, just enough to banish the shadows so that we could see where we were placing our feet.

At the bottom of the steps he led me down a stone corridor lined with pipes and cables and we finally stopped running as he pushed me back against the cold wall, placing his hand over my mouth to keep me silent.

I looked up at him in the almost-dark, my chest rising and falling heavily as I fought to catch my breath.

A door opened and closed above us, heavy footsteps thundering straight towards the stairs for the dorms as Professor Mars stalked his prey.

Dante's hips were pinned against mine and his gaze was alight with thunderstorms as he looked down at me.

"Who knew you were such a bad influence, carina?" he purred, easing his hand from my mouth.

A smirk tugged at my lips. "Yeah, I totally corrupted you."

A dark chuckle rumbled through his chest and I could feel it where we were locked together as if it came from within my own body.

Professor Mars cursed loudly upstairs and the front door slammed again as he gave up his hunt.

"Did you feel the rush?" Dante breathed.

I nodded slowly, biting my bottom lip as I fought to keep my fangs under control. I could hear the whooshing of the blood in his veins, see the steady pulse in his throat as it drew my hungry gaze. I'd used a fair bit of magic out there and I hadn't been running on full to begin with.

Dante seemed to realise what was on my mind and he reached out and brushed his thumb over my lips. I lost control over my fangs with his flesh that close to me and they snapped out, the promise of his blood calling to me.

He eyed me for a long moment but I didn't make any move to try and bite him. We seemed to be on the same side tonight and I didn't want to do anything to change that again.

He held my eye and slowly shifted his thumb until it was pressed against my fang. My heart pounded with bloodlust but I held still through pure force of will.

A knowing smile tugged at the corner of Dante's mouth and he exerted just a little pressure, splitting the pad of his thumb open so that his blood spilled into my mouth.

A moan escaped me at the pure, electric taste of his power flooding into me and his smile widened. I moved my hands to grip his wrist and slowly pulled him closer, sucking his whole thumb into my mouth while I held his eye.

"Do you like that, carina?" Dante growled.

I moaned again, sucking harder as I drank more of his delicious blood which tasted like a hurricane and charged my veins with lightning.

Dante pressed against me, the bulge in his pants straining hard against my hips, his leg pushing between my thighs. I sucked harder and a growl of desire left him as he watched me, his eyes alight with need.

I swept my eyes over his bare chest, more than a little tempted to give in to what he wanted. His huge muscles were taut beneath his skin, the energy he exuded was purely masculine, demanding my attention in a way that was impossible to ignore.

He didn't skirt around what he wanted from me but I wasn't going to forget myself with another one of the Kings. I wanted them close because they were suspects. But I wasn't going to complicate my investigation by letting them become anything else.

When I'd finally had enough, I pushed his thumb back out of my mouth and looked up at him. "Do you like that, baby?" I teased, echoing his words back at him. Before he could respond, I wriggled out from his grasp and started backing away. "Race you back to the dorm."

"What?" he asked with a frown.

I laughed as I shot away with my Vampire speed, the sight of his shocked expression the last thing I saw before I sprinted all the way back to my bunk.

I hopped in with another soft chuckle, changing into my pyjamas and throwing the duvet over me in the dark before he even made it up the stairs.

As I rolled over, my face pressed against a piece of paper on my pillow and I squinted at it until I realised it was a list of names. At the bottom were the words, *thank you for your business, payment received in full. We hope to work with you again in the future. 3K.*

I grinned at my prize in the dark and let sleep call to me on the breeze slipping in through the window. It looked like I was finally starting to turn up some answers at last.

I'll figure this out, Gareth, I promise.

LEON

CHAPTER NINETEEN

"Well aren't you just a strawberry dipped in yoghurt?" I said to a strawberry dipped in yoghurt as Mindy placed it in my mouth.

I lazed in the morning sun on Devil's Hill. The bell had sounded a few minutes ago but I didn't wanna get up and Mindy's strawberries tasted so damn good. I parted my lips as she placed another one in my mouth, grinning at me before checking her watch. This Mindy was gonna be late to class. This Leon did not give two shits.

"Read me my horoscope, Mindy."

She picked up my Atlas, tapping in the code and clearing her throat. "Good morning Leo. The stars have spoken about your day! You're feeling great today, but then again, you always feel great." I nodded at that as she went on, "Your libido is extra high since the influence of a Libra entered your life. If you wish to find relief from your daily frustrations, you'll need to work harder than is normally natural for you. Be warned though, for the inner scales of this Libra may have been tipped, leaving them unpredictable in their behaviour. Tread carefully, or you may end up more frustrated than when you started."

Well that didn't sound too bad. And I was ready to put in a little work for my unpredictable Libra.

I yawned broadly and a soft growl escaped me as I stretched my arms above my head and my shirt rode up. Mindy eyed the line of hair that trailed beneath my waistband hopefully and I almost considered letting her go down on me before I headed to my first lesson. But it was important I actually made it to Potions Class today. Not because I gave a damn about learning – I had Mindys for assignments and Mindys for tutoring me for mid-terms – but because today I was gonna ask Elise Callisto to the spring formal. And she was gonna say yes. Well I hoped she'd say yes. Okay, I was one percent shitting myself she'd turn me down in front of the whole class, but whatever.

I stood up, waiting while Mindy gathered my things. She followed me to class in the basement of Altair Halls where I *just* made it into the classroom before Professor Titan started the lesson. *Success.*

I weaved through the chairs while Mindy followed me to my desk and I dropped down beside my lab partner – Mindy – while the other Mindy placed my bag down in front of me. She scurried out of the room to whatever class she was late for and I leaned back in my chair, looking to Mindy beside me. This was a blonde Mindy with perky tits and come-fuck-me eyes. But I was tired of Mindys. I wanted Elises. One Elise in particular.

I glanced over my shoulder to where she was sitting beside Ryder, chewing gum while he stared at Professor Titan like he was thinking up ways to kill him. I didn't imagine he actually wanted our Potions professor dead, he just had that expression permanently knitted onto his face. And I wouldn't have been half surprised if he really had stitched it into his skin with a needle and thread. That was the kind of fucked up guy he was. My little monster didn't buy into his bullshit. Which was great, except she also didn't buy into mine. And that was infuriating in the best damn way.

"Today, you're going to be brewing a healing potion for Faeulosis," Titan announced, turning to write out ingredients on the electronic board.

"Unlike many ailments, healing magic is unable to fully cure this virulent disease. That is because the virus which causes it possesses a nasty little enzyme called Faeulase which attacks magic itself, eating it away like a caterpillar." He tapped the board and a photograph appeared of a Fae in the depths of Faeulosis. Blood seeped from his pores and his veins were a horrible, vivid red colour, shining beneath his skin. "When left untreated, Faeulosis can kill within a week. So does anyone know the name of the potion we'll be making today?" He turned to the class, scratching one of his sideburns as he waited for someone to raise their hand.

He looked to Ryder who clearly fucking knew but had no interest in sharing it with us.

Silence rang out and Titan sighed. "No one...not even you, Mr Draconis?"

Ryder grunted in irritation. "Spirisine for fuck's sake."

"Yes, five rank points to you, but less of the swears please," Titan said with a cheery smile, not quite meeting Ryder's eye.

"Make me swear less, dipshit," Ryder muttered and Titan cleared his throat, carrying on like he hadn't heard him.

"If you'd like to come and gather your ingredients from the store cupboard, and for those of you who don't own your own equipment, help yourself to the supplies at the bottom too." He looked over at Elise and I glanced her way, colour blooming in her cheeks. I vaguely wondered why she didn't have her own things, but there were plenty of kids in class who chose to just borrow stuff so maybe she just didn't wanna haul equipment around school. Wasn't really an issue for me as my Mindys carried my shit.

I turned back to face the front, waiting as Professor Titan laid out the instructions to make the remedy for Faeulosis then left us to start cooking it up. Mindy took control of our potion and I swivelled in my chair, watching Elise as she headed up to the store cupboard and started getting out the ingredients and a cauldron. Ryder was right behind her, aggressively pointing out what she needed without actually saying the words. And I mean *right* behind her. Crotch to ass. *What a snake.* She nudged him away, shaking her head at him and he marched back to his seat, looking like she'd just pissed in his cornflakes.

When Elise sat down again, they didn't look at each other and I sensed they were not getting along like a house on fire. Mindy returned with our ingredients, setting about making the remedy.

"Do you want me to write two sets of notes?" she asked.

"That would be great," I said with a smile that made her blush.

"Bing bong!" Principal Greyshine's bright voice sounded over the tannoy. By the sun, he was a douche. That was pretty much the only thing in Aurora Academy every single student agreed on. "This is Principal G checking in with your morning announcements...the blood on the walls of Acrux Courtyard has now been removed, however due to the explosive nature of the incident, there may still be splatter on the sidewalk so please watch your tootsies when skipping by!" He thought he was so 'down with the kids' but really he was just an erect dick dressed into a semi-nice suit. I literally had no idea how the guy had secured the position of principal in one of Solaria's academies. Maybe he was more powerful than I realised, but he barely showed his face in the corridors and I never saw him using his magic around the place.

Greyshine went on, "Eugene Dipper is still stuck in his Tiberian Rat form in the U-bend of the men's toilet after he was accidentally flushed down there so try to tie a knot in it if you need a tinkle between classes. Never fear though - we are still sending him air regularly to keep him alive. Unfortunately he tried to shift back into his Fae form in the early hours of this morning and it went spectacularly badly so let's all send positive thoughts his way today and cross our fingers and toes that he manages to wriggle his way free lickety split."

Laughter rang out in the room. My eyes wheeled to Eugene's empty chair at the front of the class and I shook my head. Guy seriously needed to embrace his inner Fae. You didn't get anything in life without fighting for it.

I noticed Bryce high-fiving his Lunar pal, Russel Newmoon, under the table and I casually flicked my hand, igniting a small fire under Bryce's seat. It wasn't really for Eugene; he had to Fae up if he was going to survive until graduation. No, this was for me. Because Bryce Corvus was a sadistic shit who liked to torture kids for fun. So I liked to torture him back sometimes.

I watched the small fire build in strength, licking the base of his seat while Greyshine finished his announcement. "The party which will be held on the vernal equinox marking the start of Spring will be an under the sea theme! Our water Elemental staff will be providing the decorations so expect to be wowed. Don't forget to get your glad rags on and be ready to boogie the night away. That's all for now! Have a groovy day. Catch you on the flip!"

"Holy fuck!" Bryce leapt out of his chair and I extinguished the fire as he wrenched his seat aside to check beneath it. He stared down in confusion as he found nothing there.

"Problem, Mr Corvus?" Titan asked him.

"No..." Bryce frowned, rubbing his ass then kicking the chair away and grabbing a spare one from the end of the row.

I sniggered as he sat down carefully and threw a suspicious glance around the room.

I picked up a pen, swivelling it between my fingers then rising to my feet when I felt it was time to put my plan into action. I set Elise in my gaze, walking over to her and dragging my chair after me so it screeeeeeeched across the floor. Another Mindy jumped up to carry it for me, but I wafted her away. I could do stuff. And things.

Elise looked up with a confused frown as I planted the seat down on the opposite side of their table and joined them. Ryder shot me a glare, sending me a vision of him stabbing my eyeballs out with the pencil in his hand.

I fronted it out, though it was kinda difficult to forget the image of me on my knees, holding my face with a pencil sticking out of my eyeball.

I set Elise in my sights, giving her a dark smile as I placed my pen down on the table.

"Hi," I said with my most swoon-worthy grin. The pen rolled off the table as planned, dropping to the floor with a clatter.

Come on, bite little monster.

Her soft green eyes trailed from me to the floor where the pen lay, then flipped back up to me. "Are you gonna pick that up or…?"

I huffed, moving to grab it when a Mindy swooped on it and planted it in my hand. She darted away as quickly as she'd arrived and I tucked the pen into my pocket with a scowl.

"It feels good to do things for people sometimes, you know?" I said, arching a brow.

"If it feels so good, Leo, why don't you try it sometime?" Elise suggested with a playful smile.

"*Leon,*" I warned in a growl and Ryder stiffened beside her.

"You know what might feel good, fuckwit? You leaving this table and never coming back," Ryder suggested but I ignored him.

"Oh you're talking now, are you?" Elise shot at him and I glanced between them in surprise.

"I don't recall ever stopping, baby." He fixed me with a death glare. "Now fuck off back to Pride Rock, Simba."

A smile grew and grew on my face. "Oh shit, I didn't realise you were a Disney fan, Ryder. Which one is your favourite?"

"Fuck. Off," he growled, trying to grab me in one of his visions again but I was ready this time, blocking him out with a mental shield.

"Lemme guess…" I tapped my chin as I took my time mocking him and a smile danced around Elise's mouth. "You get your inspiration from The Jungle Book and sing yourself to sleep with the snake's *Trussssst in meee* song."

His gaze rammed into mine and his twisted Order gift battered against my shield. I gripped the table, trying to force his magic out and he hissed between his teeth like the serpent he was.

"You should watch your tongue," Ryder snarled when he couldn't get through. *Ha.*

"Oh I do. I watched it pretty well as it slid into Elise's mouth the other day actually." I smirked. Elise stilled. Ryder blew a blood vessel somewhere in his body. Not sure where, but I'd bet on the stars it was in his dick.

"*Leon*," Elise snapped, baring her fangs at me.

"Surely that's not actually true?" Ryder demanded of her, incredulous. I wasn't sure I'd seen that emotion on his face before. His knuckles were an idiot's guide to his mood settings. I hadn't realised he ever deviated from them. "New girl?" Ryder pressed coldly and she rolled her eyes.

"It was just a kiss, who cares?" She focused back on her work and I continued to grin.

"I care. Ryder clearly cares. That's over sixty percent of us. Majority wins." I reached into my pocket, taking out what I hoped would buy me a yes to my coming question. I placed the large chocolate bar down, sliding it across the table, a rush going through me as I did one of the first things I'd ever done for another person. *Look at me all generous.*

I smiled hopefully as I pushed it under her nose and she looked up in surprise, her lilac hair falling into her eyes. My chest swelled as I waited for her reaction, ignoring the way Ryder was trying to mentally push a bullet into my brain.

"Oh, this is for me?" she asked.

"Well I ate most of yours the other day so…" I wasn't sure what the end of that sentence was. Maybe: *So…I traded for that one off the Kipling brothers because I'm horny as hell for you.*

"Well thanks," she said brightly, pushing it to one side of her notepad and continuing on with her work.

"That's it?" I asked. "Thanks?"

"Yeah that's um…all I have to say really. Thanks a bunch?" She snorted and a warm feeling stirred in my chest.

I raised an open hand, angling it toward Ryder's face so I could no longer see him glaring at me. "Come to the Spring Formal with me," I said. "It'll be fun."

"Pah," Ryder spat behind my hand but I ignored him. "As if she's into dancing at pathetic school parties with pathetic fucking Lions."

"I love dancing actually," Elise said firmly, not looking his way. "Not that that's any of your business, Ryder."

"If I decide it's my business, it fucking is," he growled and she flipped him the finger, causing a deep rattle to emanate from him.

"So?" I asked hopefully, leaning forward in my seat.

Gabriel was walking by and he halted with a terse frown on his face. "Did you just ask Elise Callisto to the Spring Formal?" He practically glided around the table to stand between us, looking from me to her with a scowl. Elise glanced up at him, a flicker of vulnerability in her gaze.

"Yeah, what's it to you?" I snapped. Dude was cramping my moment. I lifted my other hand, angling it toward his face so I couldn't see him either. "Elise?" I asked. She'd turned bright red and kept looking between the three of us. "Eyes here, little monster."

"Why are you still here, Gabriel?" she asked sharply and he stepped forward, towering over her. "This is none of your business."

"You're right," Gabriel said in a deadly purr. "I'm not interested in your business. Or who you go to the party with."

"Then why are you *still* standing here?" She gave him a pointed look that was so heated it was almost sexual.

"Ex-fucking-scuse me," I interrupted sharply. "I'm in the middle of something here, so can you piss off now?"

Gabriel shoved my hand aside and glared down at me, his eyes seeming to swirl like ink. "Make me."

I sighed in frustration, knowing I couldn't take him on. He was too damn powerful. For fuck's sake. This was *my* moment. Why was everyone trying to ruin it?

I lifted my hand to block out Gabriel's face again, locking Elise in my gaze.

Dante appeared, looking over her shoulder. "What's going on? Did you just ask Elise to the ball Leon?"

"Oh fuck my life," Elise muttered.

I growled in annoyance, not having another hand to block him out too. *Maybe I should throw a shoe?*

Actually, better idea.

"Mindy!" I called and the blonde one appeared behind me. I took her hand, lifting it so Dante's face was covered then smiled at Elise as I returned my hand to blocking out Gabriel.

"Soooo?" I pushed.

"Wait wait wait," Dante said behind Mindy's hand. "Are you seriously asking her?""

"Yes," I snarled. Mindy's hand slipped and I caught sight of his expression. *Dammit Mindy.*

Dante eyed the chocolate on the desk then took off one of his gold rings and planted it down in front of Elise. I inhaled sharply. I'd given him that fucking ring.

"Traitor," I growled, though I kind of liked the idea of him and me taking her together. Like, just a little bit. Mostly I wanted her as mine though.

Dante laughed. "Sucks to suck, bro."

Elise huffed. "Can you all just go away?"

"Not until you decide," I demanded. I dropped my hands, my arms growing tired and I ushered Mindy away, feeling exhausted. Gabriel continued to stand there, his gaze burning into Elise like her answer was as important to him as it was to me.

Ryder glanced at the objects in front of Elise with a shake of his head. "Pathetic. I wouldn't be seen dead at the formal. I'd crawl out of hell just to destroy my body in case someone decided to take it there."

"Well no one's asking you to go," Elise said airily.

"You're right," he said, fake nice. "Here's my offer then, Elise. Please oh fucking please come to the party with me. Shit, did I forget to give you a grand gesture?" He reached into his pocket and placed a razor blade down in front of her.

"Real classy, asshole," I said, shaking my head and Elise pursed her lips.

"Tell you what, Elise. Just because I can't bear to watch this lame-ass bullshit continue, here's a worthwhile offer. Come and spend the night in my room and I'll give you the best party of your life. But remember to tell me your safe word a few times prior, I tend to forget when I'm pissed at the girl I'm nailing," Ryder said.

"Fuck you," she spat a second before I did. Because shitballs, what unholy creature crawled up his ass and died today?

"Maybe you should just not go, Elise," Gabriel said with a smirk playing around his mouth. "They're all just trying to fuck you anyway and they're probably only going to be disappointed..."

"Well maybe I want to be fucked by a real man," she said dismissively and Gabriel's eyes turned to pitch.

What's with the two of them? And also, did she just admit she wants to fuck me?

"Back. Up," I snapped at Gabriel. My spine rippled with the heat of the sun. I was gonna shift on this motherfucker in a second and tear his head off with my teeth. "Give her air so she can decide."

"I'll let you ride on me after the formal, carina," Dante offered.

"*Dude*," I balked.

"I meant as a Dragon," he said with a grin that said he hadn't *entirely* meant that.

"Come on, little monster, you know I'd give you the funnest night," I pressed. It was a joke we were even having this discussion. I was the obvious winner. "So what will it be? A night in Psycho the Snake's funhouse, a ride on a Dragon who threw you out a window, or a night with a mighty Lion who will bring you more chocolate before and after the ball." Bribery was a winner. Not something I'd actually used before, but I could see she was tempted.

"Well…Leon did ask me first," she said, shrugging one shoulder and triumph filled me.

Gabriel pinned me with a look that said I'd just made it onto his shit list. But he didn't even seem to like Elise so I didn't know what his deal was. He walked away, his shoulders tense and his hands balled into fists.

"Fuck's sake." Dante headed off, snatching up his ring before he left and Cindy Lou gazed at him hopefully.

"Maybe you could take me, sweetie?" she purred as he slumped into his chair beside her and he nodded half-heartedly. She rested a hand on his arm, shooting Elise daggers over his shoulder.

Ryder grinned darkly, leaning in to Elise's ear. "Well my option doesn't expire. If you get bored of Mufasa's kid and fancy a taste of Scar, you can come to my room. And all over my room too. I'll wait to hear about the safe word."

"Yeah, thanksssss," I hissed like a snake. "But shhhhe's not interesssted." I got up and walked away with a satisfied smile, hearing Elise's musical laugh following me.

When I finally meandered my way back to my desk, I took a nap until Mindy finished our potion. Titan gave me ten rank points for showing power by getting another Fae to do my work for me. Today was gonna be a great day.

GARETH

CHAPTER TWENTY

SEVENTEEN MONTHS BEFORE THE SOLARID METEOR
SHOWER...

*T*he Lunar Brotherhood were holding a party in The Iron Wood on the
outskirts of the academy and all of the unallied students were invited
too. Leon said they used it as an opportunity to swell their ranks, but
he also said they threw a fucking ace party so it was worth going even if you
weren't interested in joining their gang.

"The last time they had a party a couple of weeks ago, most of them
got drunk and forgot to try and recruit people anyway," Leon said as we
walked across the Empyrean Fields towards the wood under the light of the
moon. "Oh and you should definitely attend the Oscura Clan party next week
too because you don't want them thinking you've picked a side. Unless you
actually decide to join the Brotherhood tonight." He shot me a grin and I
shook my head.

"Hell no. I'm only going because Cindy's going." And because I had a plan to get my next instalment for this month. And hopefully every month after that. The crystal had secured my first payment, but I needed a steady income to fund Old Sal's debt, so I was going to go balls out tonight and ask Ryder Draconis for work. And I was definitely not shitting myself about that.

"Yeah she's hot," Leon said with a smirk, pushing a hand into his loose hair and flexing his bicep.

"If you pull your Lion bullshit on her tonight I'll knock you out. Pegasus style."

Leon chuckled, slinging an arm over my shoulders. "I wouldn't do that to you, dude. And I don't need to anyway, do you have any idea how many Mindys are going tonight? It's gonna be a fucking orgy."

"Do you ever think you might want a girl who doesn't fall at your feet the second you look at her?" I asked, genuinely curious. That shit would get old fast for me.

Leon considered it for a moment, scrubbing the stubble on his jaw. "You mean like someone I had to work for...so that she'd do stuff for me?"

"No, man," I blew out a laugh. "I mean a chick who doesn't do shit for you unless you do shit for her."

"That sounds like a lot of work," he said thoughtfully.

"The sweetest fruit is the one you pick yourself," I said and he raised an eyebrow at me.

"Did you write that poetry just for me, baby?"

I shrugged out of his hold, ramming my shoulder into his and we both laughed. "Shut the fuck up."

"Noted." He grinned.

We headed into The Iron Wood where the darkness was thicker and the air seemed stiller. The sound of the party carried from afar and I lifted my hand to create an orb of blue light, casting a glow on the dirt track beneath our feet. We were late considering Leon had changed four times before we'd left and I swear he'd taken a nap in the shower too. The guy was infuriating *any time I wanted to get somewhere fast.*

It sounded like the party was in full swing, the clamour of a thumping bass pounding through the earth. We reached a T-junction where the path split left and right and my neck prickled as the shadows pressed in around us. For a second, I could have sworn I saw white masks peering out from the trees beyond the track and my heart rate picked up. As soon as I reached for Leon to point them out, they vanished and I took a breath, mentally rolling my eyes at myself. This place was creepy as fuck so I was putting it down to my wild imagination.

"It's right to the Oscura Haunt and left to the Lunar Pit," Leon said and I had to wonder how he knew that. He'd only been in this school a month but he seemed to be friends with everyone and know everything.

The only person I didn't ever see falling for Leon's charm was Ryder. But then I never saw Ryder being particularly friendly toward anyone. It seemed like the people who hung around him worked for him. I couldn't imagine him letting loose. But maybe tonight I'd see a different side of him. I was quietly banking on him relaxing after a few drinks so I could approach him more easily. It was pretty hard to picture him without a permanent scowl etched into his face though.

We headed to the left and followed the winding path through the trees, the deep orange glow of a fire flickering in the distance. My heart rate picked up as we closed in on the party and arrived in a wide clearing.

A huge bonfire blazed in a pit at the heart of the space. Tree stumps circled it and several were grouped together at the edges of the clearing too with tables between them. It looked like some powerful earth magic had been used to create this place and I wondered if Ryder was capable of it already or if he had senior students doing his bidding. Maybe both.

I hunted for him in the crowd gathered around the fire, my eyes snagging on a dark shadow at the edge of the clearing. Ryder sat on a huge throne carved from an enormous log, the serrated crescent symbol of The Lunar

237

Brotherhood etched into every corner of it.

His second in command, Bryce Corvus, sat to his right on a smaller seat and a group of his most loyal gang members sat around them. A band of girls were hovering on the verge of Ryder's clique, throwing him hopeful glances, their bodies clad in skimpy dresses, tight shorts and some in just bikini tops. Ryder wasn't paying them any attention, his face set in an unreadable mask as Bryce spoke into his ear. It almost would have been funny if Ryder hadn't been fucking terrifying. I'd heard what happened to the people who'd crossed him and I'd seen the blood on the floor of Altair Halls to prove it.

I looked over my shoulder for Leon, realising he'd fallen behind and grinned as I took in the girls flocking around him. They handed him beer and pointed out a seat by the fire which had clearly been saved just for him.

Leon nudged his way through them, directing one of his entourage to hand me a beer too. He led me over to the seat waiting for him and the girl jumped up from the next one along, immediately offering it to me.

"You don't have to get up," I said in surprise but she shook her head, her eyes on Leon as she moved away to join the group of girls beyond him.

Leon yawned broadly, twisting the cap off his beer and taking a swig. I relished the warmth of the fire, drinking some of my own beer as I hunted for Cindy Lou across the party. I spotted her talking to some friends and took another gulp of my drink, the heat of the alcohol spreading into my chest while I drew on the courage it leant me. She looked like a country girl in a checked red and white dress with a modest neckline. She was sweeter than sugar and I wanted a taste.

I glanced at Leon to tell him I'd be back in a bit, but found a blonde girl curled on his lap, kissing him and caressing his chest.

I snorted a laugh as another girl massaged his shoulders, standing and mock saluting him as I bailed.

I wove towards Cindy, my heart ticking faster as I tried to come up with a decent opener.

Hey, remember me? – but what if she didn't?

Oh hey Cindy, I didn't see you there (real subtly bumping into her) – lame.

Sup girl? – Shit, I was screwed.

I drew in a breath, pressed my shoulders back and walked over to her with an air of fuck it.

"Hey Cindy." I tapped her on the shoulder and she turned around, her raven hair falling over one shoulder and her soft hazel eyes drinking me in. Her lips pulled up into a bright smile and the knot in my chest eased.

"Oh hey Gareth, I didn't know you were coming tonight," she said, fluttering her eyelashes and I had to hope that was a good sign.

"Yeah, I thought I'd cruise by." Cruise by?? Asshole.

"What did you say?" she called over the pounding bass of the dance music which was playing. Score. *It looked like the stars were on my side tonight.*

"Nothing. Wanna hang out for a bit?" I asked and she beamed, resting a hand on my arm.

"I sure would."

"Cindy Lou get your ass over here!" a girl with way too much pink eyeshadow called from the edge of the woods. Cindy's friends were all heading that way, dancing and laughing as they went and Cindy hesitated, biting her lip as she looked to me.

"Apparently some juniors have Killblaze," she said, shifting closer to me, her hand tightening around my arm.

"What juniors?" I frowned, but before she answered, Harvey sauntered out of the woods beside us high as a fucking kite. His bloodshot eyes, hooded gaze and cocky swagger told me he'd been blazing.

"Broooo!" he whooped as he spotted me, wrapping me in his arms and resting his entire weight on me.

I pushed him back with a frown. "You alright, man?" I asked.

"I'm so fucking alright. I am so, so alright." He grinned at me, swaying left and right so his coppery hair danced around his face. "You wanna blaze?"

"Fuck no. Haven't you seen the articles in The Alestria Gazette? That shit is killing people every week in the city."

"Well we ain't in the city we're at school," he slurred, laughing maniacally then latching onto Cindy. "You wanna come, right babe? I've got a test tube with your name on it."

A surge of irritation flooded me and I caught his collar, yanking him off of her.

She folded her arms, glaring at him. "Do not put your dirty paws on me, honey, or I'll set your pants on fire."

I barked a laugh and Harvey joined in before waving a hand and chasing after Cindy's friends into the trees.

Cindy shot me a sideways grin. "So...do you wanna hang out?"

I nodded keenly and we headed toward the fire, grabbing a couple of the logs and sitting knee to knee with each other. Leon was in a full make out session with three girls and I took the opportunity to steal a couple more beers from the pile of offerings at his feet – which included several bottles of liquor, two crates of beer and three pizzas.

I shook my head as I dropped back down beside Cindy and she giggled. "Your friend sure knows how to draw attention."

"He's a Nemean Lion," I said in explanation and she nodded in understanding as I passed her a beer. "What's your Order?"

"I'm a Centaur." She twisted off the cap and we clinked bottles before falling into conversation which flowed so easily, I almost forgot I was talking to a girl I had the hots for. Cindy wasn't just beautiful, she had a brain in her head and was funny as shit.

Time seemed to blur and the evening drifted by. I'd been enjoying her company so much I'd forgotten all about the beer I'd left down on the ground. Cindy had her hand on my knee and it continued to climb a couple of *centimetres every time she laughed – and hell I liked that laugh.*

Her lips were making me hungry and the way her eyes kept flitting to my mouth made me think she wanted the kiss I was craving. A pressure was mounting in my chest and I was so ready to give in to it. But did I have the balls?

"I've had so much fun talking to you," Cindy said, a blush lining her cheeks as the light of the fire danced over her. She inched a little closer and sparks skittered through my body.

I nodded in agreement, leaning in and brushing a loose lock of hair behind her ear. She inhaled deeply and I figured screw it *and moved in to kiss her. My heart slammed into my chest as I trailed my hand to her jaw and caressed her feather soft skin.*

She tilted her chin up and I claimed her mouth, my eyes falling closed. She tasted like beer and honey, the taste rolling onto my tongue as she parted her lips. Her fingers curled around the back of my neck, sliding beneath the edge of my shirt and brushing my shoulder blades. A deep groan left me as that divine feeling spread everywhere. The winged Orders were always sensitive right in that spot and Cindy Lou clearly knew it.

I pulled her into my lap and she moved willingly, her hand sliding deeper down my back and scoring lines with her nails, making a heady groan leave my lips.

I knew I needed to call an end to this if I didn't want the entire Brotherhood bearing witness to my raging hard-on and was a little thankful when Leon started cheering. Several others joined in as I pulled back and Cindy ducked her head into my neck, laughing as she hid behind a curtain of her hair.

Leon tossed me a wink, wrapping both arms around the girls either side of him. "Catch you later, man. Hopefully not in our dorm for at least an hour though, right?"

I shook my head at him. "Right."

He headed away with five freaking girls and Cindy crawled out of my lap, standing up with a wide smile on her face. "I better go check my friends aren't killing themselves on Killblaze."

"Pfft don't even joke about it. That stuff is lethal. I can go with you, if you like?" I offered.

She leaned down, placing a kiss on my nose. "I'll be just fine on my own, honey. Maybe I'll see you in a bit though?"

"In a bit," I agreed, watching her go as she turned and headed into the trees, her ass drawing all of my attention.

I sucked on my lower lip then dragged my eyes away from her, remembering why I'd actually come here tonight. Ryder Draconis.

His gang were dancing around him or playing drinking games at a table which grew from the ground, created out of tree roots. Ryder hadn't moved, his focus on something in his hand which looked suspiciously like a razor blade. His gaze shifted to a girl with flowing blonde hair in a tight black dress and I decided it was time to make my move. If Ryder went off with her, I was never gonna get a chance to talk to him. And though he looked stone cold sober, maybe I'd get lucky and find out he was actually tipsy enough to consider my offer.

I stood, trying to ignore the raging swarm of nerves I got as I strode over to one of the scariest motherfuckers in the school like I was on a suicide mission.

As I arrived at the outskirts of his group, I found my way blocked by a meaty prick who created a wall in front of me with his massive chest.

I side stepped to get around him but he immediately moved into my way. "I wanna talk to Ryder," I said.

"If you wanna join the gang, then you can talk to me," he boomed.

"I don't wanna join," I said simply. "I want to talk to Ryder."

"The King doesn't talk to just anybody."

"Well I have a proposition for him." I tried to look past him, but he

242

leaned into my way.

"You can talk to me about it or no one at all." The guy curled his hands into fists and I clenched my jaw.

Dammit, I was not gonna be stopped at the first hurdle by some asshat who looked like he'd been taking Faeroids since he was ten years old.

A huge hand slammed down on the guy's shoulder and Ryder fucking Draconis appeared, drawing the meathead away from me. His eyes said murder, but I stood my ground, reminding myself who I was doing this for.

For Ella. For Mom. For me.

Ryder's dark green gaze scraped over me like an X-ray. When he reached my eyes, a vision slammed into me that made my heart jerk violently. Ryder had me on the ground, his forehead slamming against mine so hard real pain burst through my skull. He released me from the Basilisk hypnosis and I shook my head, trying to shake off the lasting effects of it as fear took root in me.

Ryder's right fist clenched so the word pain *was aimed at me. "You get one minute. If I don't like what you say, that vision comes true, Pony Boy."*

I dug deep for my courage, nodding stiffly. "How do you know what Order I am?"

"I make it my business to know who attends my parties," he said in a gravelly tone then gestured for me to step past him into his private circle.

My heart beat harder as I moved forward and Ryder's hand rested on my shoulder, the threat in his tight grip clear. He shoved me down into a chair before dropping into his goddamn throne and turning his cold eyes on me. "Your minute started ten seconds ago, so I'd get talking if I were you."

I cleared my throat, aware of the way the nearby members of his gang drew in like shadows, ready to gut me if I upset their King. Bryce was playing with a blade in his hand, casting ice across it so it glinted like diamonds. My mouth was desert dry as I pulled my gaze away from him onto his even more terrifying boss.

"I need some cash," I said honestly. "So I thought I could do a few jobs for you. You know, anything under the radar. I've got some connections in the city. I could be of use to you for the right price."

Don't lose your nerve, Gareth. Hold his gaze.

"No," he said immediately, sitting back in his seat.

"That's it? No?" I said in disbelief, a flash of frustration radiating through me. I need this, dammit.

"I have people for everything, why would I need you?" he asked dismissively.

"Because I'm not in your gang. No one would suspect I was helping you."

"The answer is still no."

Someone beside us stumbled mid-dance move and bashed into the side of Ryder's throne. The guy splashed a shot of tequila all down Ryder's shoulder and my entire body tensed. He was on his feet in seconds, catching the freshman by the throat and slamming him into the ground.

Ryder knelt over him, choking him with both hands while the kid took it all without any effort to fight back. Bryce drew nearer, grinning cruelly as he watched the boy struggle beneath the Basilisk Shifter.

Ryder snarled in the kid's face, spittle flying as he unleashed his rage. Fear tangled with my blood, but he released him before the boy choked out and I took a shaky breath.

Ryder stood, snarling around at anyone close to make them back up.

"Get the fuck out of my sight," he spat at the guy on the floor and he scrambled onto his knees, whimpering as he scurried away.

Ryder dropped back into his seat, cracking his neck and sighing satisfactorily. He flexed his fingers, his breathing heavy as he looked to me again. "Why are you still here? I said no, asshole."

He leered at me and I hurried to my feet, sure he would attack me if I remained there a second longer. I headed out of the circle, my heart beating a *desperate tune as I marched back toward the fire, furious at myself for failing. But I still had another option in mind.*

If Ryder wouldn't offer me work, maybe Oscura Clan would. So tomorrow, I had a date with a Storm Dragon.

ELISE

CHAPTER TWENTY ONE

I sat on Devil's Hill during my lunch break with Laini and her friend Daniel, enjoying the benefits of our combined magic as it shielded us from the cold day. A late frost had shown its head again this morning and though the icy blue hue had left the grass now, it was still too cold to be sitting outside really. But that seemed to be how it worked at Aurora Academy. The cafeteria benches remained empty during lunch hour and students only ventured inside to collect food. Nothing more. Our solution was a stroke of genius though. Laini had cast a small blaze to burn on the ground between us and I'd created a bubble of air around us to trap the heat inside. It was so warm that I was almost tempted to have a nap.

Laini and Daniel were both Sphinxes so they liked to spend a lot of time reading which was how they replenished their power. They were Juniors and had been in Gareth's class but I didn't have any reason to think they'd known him well. I wanted to ask them what they remembered about him but it was hard to come up with a good excuse for me to be asking questions about a dead guy I wasn't supposed to have even met. I'd started spending a lot of my free time with them, studying Gareth's journal and occasionally getting some of my own work done too. We had a quiet kind of bond but it was solid. Each day I'd learn a little more about the two of them as we chatted while we ate lunch before descending into companionable silence as the books took over. Today Daniel had admitted that he was building up to ask someone to the ball but he hadn't said who. Tomorrow I'd get an answer out of him for sure. Our friendship was slow and steady but it was one of the few genuine things I felt I had in this place.

However, today my mind was on other things. Concealed within the heavy Tarot book perched on my knees was Gareth's journal and I was currently trying to decipher a sketch he'd done which looked almost like a circular maze.

I felt like I was missing some key component to make it make sense though. No matter what way I turned it or which route I followed through it, I always came up on a dead end. And that just couldn't be right. Beneath it were the words *pay for the passage in blood.* But what passage was it referring to?

I wasn't even entirely sure why this particular sketch kept drawing my attention back to it. There was just something about it that screamed *important* to me. But I was missing something here and I knew it.

"What if the wind changes while you're frowning like that?" Gabriel's voice came from right behind me and I just about managed not to shriek in alarm, slamming the book shut in my lap as I turned to glare at him.

"What's with the sneaking, Gabriel?" I demanded as my heart damn near burst out of my chest.

He was standing over me, shirtless, wings out and his back to the sun so that his face was in shadow. My heart was pounding with fright and more than a bit of nervous energy too. He didn't bother to give my question a response before he went on.

"The best of things move on swift and silent wings, look closely dear and you can have it all, but beware my love, for even angels fall..."

I stared up at him, totally confused for a moment as I craned my neck. With the sun shining behind him like that he really did look like a fallen angel but I was guessing the quote had more to do with him trying to unnerve me than it had to do with his ungodly looks. The words didn't mean anything to me though, aside from the last part which I happened to have tattooed on my ribs. Something he'd clearly noticed when he'd gotten me naked.

Heat clawed along my spine at the reminder and I opened and closed my mouth at least twice before I managed to find my words. Why did he have to have that effect on me? I could go toe to toe with the meanest of assholes but give me a guy who looked like a demigod and made me bathe in awkward silences and I became a mumbling wreck. I found my balls lurking in the back of my purse and strapped them on as I prepared to face off against him yet again. For a guy who claimed to want me out of his way, he sure made it his business to get in my face a lot.

"Is that supposed to mean something to me?" I asked eventually in a bored tone when it became clear he wasn't going to add anything else.

Laini raised an eyebrow at me then scooted away with Daniel, twisting so her back was to us like she didn't want to have any part in our conversation. I wasn't sure she'd ever spoken to Gabriel despite the fact that his bunk was above hers. It seemed his intimidation tactics worked a little too thoroughly on her.

Gabriel dropped down to crouch in front of me, a knowing smile hooking up one side of his mouth. I looked at his lips for a little too long and his smile grew. Why did I have to choose him to take to my bed? And why the hell had he seemed like a totally different person that night? Had it all been fake just to get what he wanted from me? But if that was all he wanted then why keep hounding me now? The only interest I took in him was in trying to figure out if he had any link to my brother which he knew nothing about. I didn't talk to him, sit with him, hell, I made it my mission not to *look* at him most of the time so why did it feel like he *wanted* my attention despite his warnings to stay away?

"It just came to mind while I was circling in the clouds," he said with a shrug. "And it made me think of *you*." He punctuated the final word by reaching out and touching his fingers to my ribs just below my left breast, exactly where my tattoo sat.

My heart leapt. I swallowed thickly, looking into his grey eyes as he looked right back. Waiting. But for what? He'd told me to stay away from him and I had. So why was he breaking his own rule?

"Umm, thanks?" I offered when I couldn't bear the silence a second longer. I wanted to tell him to fuck off but I was biting my tongue for Gareth's sake. I'd come to this academy with the intention of getting close to the Kings which would certainly be easier if I could make nice with them. Even if this one was a particularly dickish specimen of asshole.

Gabriel's gaze fell to my lips and my stomach cartwheeled involuntarily. I tucked my knees under myself more firmly, clenching my thighs shut as an echo of desire slid through me, my mind playing over what had happened between us on that rooftop. And I had the feeling that was exactly what he wanted me to be thinking about too. Why was he always able to do that to me? I didn't want him in my head *or* my bed so why was he making me think about that?

"You wanna tell me what made a girl with the most indecisive star sign decide on that tattoo? What makes it so special?" he asked in a low voice which made me lean closer so I could hear him.

My gaze automatically dipped to the countless tattoos lining his flesh.

"Clearly you don't have an issue deciding on yours," I muttered, swerving his question.

"I see flashes of the future. I already knew I'd end up with these tattoos before I'd even considered getting them. So I got them done in advance. Why delay fate?" The intensity of that question had me blushing all over again.

"I make my own fate," I replied instantly.

Gabriel's jaw locked, the storm in his eyes roiling for a moment and I knew I'd said the wrong thing. I also wasn't going to be taking it back. Gabriel Nox might be the most intense and intimidating guy I'd ever met but I sure as hell wasn't going to be bullied into changing my opinions.

The silence stretched for so long this time that I had to resort to chewing on my bottom lip to hold my tongue. But I refused to let him push me into changing my point of view.

Gabriel let out a soft snort of amusement and turned away from me for a moment, looking out over no man's land like it was a pleasant view instead of a war zone waiting to blow up.

"You gonna keep holding out on me about why you got that tattoo then?" he asked casually without looking back at me.

His persistence on the subject forced an answer from my lips despite myself. "I made it up. It's because my br-" I cut myself off, snapping my mouth shut before I could mention my brother. He used to call me the little angel child when we were kids and when I swore to exact vengeance on the person who had taken him from me the words had just seemed to fit. I marked my skin with them for him and for me.

It symbolised the moment I'd changed and headed down this path. And I knew in my soul that by the time I'd done everything I'd set out to achieve, I'd never be an angel in anyone's eyes ever again.

"It's personal," I ground out.

"It's kinda like mine though, isn't it?" Gabriel pressed, holding his wrist out to show me the words he had inked there. The script was eerily similar to that on my own skin and the words sent a shiver down my spine. *We fall together...*

I read it twice before blinking up at him again. "Kinda," I admitted warily.

"Almost like they match," he pushed, his voice low and sending a shiver down my spine. "Four months ago, I saw a flash of a future where I had this tattoo while holding the hand of the girl I loved. That's why I got it... Will you tell me why you got yours?"

My mouth was too dry and my heart beating too fast. I couldn't concentrate when he looked at me like that. It made my head spin.

"No," I replied on a breath. My tattoo wasn't for him. It was for me. And Gareth. It might as well have been etched into my heart. I certainly didn't know Gabriel well enough to try and explain that to him. I didn't even like him, let alone trust him and if he'd decided he was interested in me all of a sudden then that was his problem, not mine.

Gabriel twitched a smile at me which seemed to say *you will* and I dropped my gaze to the grass between us.

Before I could make any effort to explain myself, Gabriel reached out and tucked a lock of my hair behind my ear.

His touch on my skin sent heat skittering through me and I looked up at him between my lashes as I tried to figure out what he expected from me. I was so shocked by the gentle gesture that I didn't even bat him off of me, I just stared, trying to figure out what the fuck was going on.

"You can tell me when you're ready," he breathed, his hand lingering on my cheek for a moment. My skin tingled at his touch and memories of his flesh against mine surfaced like they'd been lurking there all along. "I'll be waiting."

I frowned, wanting to remind him that I didn't believe I was his mate or anything of the kind and had no intention of handing out personal information to him but he'd already risen to his feet.

I looked up at him in surprise and he reached into his bag, holding out a can of orange soda for me.

"What's that for?" I asked. No one ever just gave you something for nothing. Especially not someone who spent most of his time perfecting the art of being a dick.

"Because you shouldn't want for anything."

Gabriel tossed the can into my lap before I could say anything in response to that and was gone a moment later. I was gonna get whiplash from that guy. Why had he suddenly decided to do a one eighty on me? What happened to *stay the hell away from me* and attacking me for no goddamn reason at every opportunity? I didn't even know which version of him was more disturbing. And now I shouldn't want for anything? What the fuck did that mean?

When I looked around at Laini I found her staring at me with a questioning brow raised. "You sure have a knack for attracting the attention of the Kings of this place, girl," she said and it didn't sound like a compliment.

"I guess I'm just unlucky," I joked, picking up the can of soda.

I eyed it for a long moment as if it might just be a bomb about to explode then carefully snapped the ring-pull open. The sudden hiss was followed by an explosion of orange as the soda detonated all over me.

I shrieked in surprise, lurching backwards as it splattered me and I was left dripping and humiliated in the centre of Devil's Hill as people all around me stared and started laughing.

"Fuck you Gabriel!" I yelled as I scrambled to my feet and he reappeared with a cruel smirk on his face, the crowd parting for him. "Why won't you just leave me the fuck alone like you promised?" I demanded.

"Because, you don't seem to be getting the message," he snarled. "The moment I show a bit of interest in you, you're back to panting like a bitch in heat and I need to make sure you understand the fact that you need to *keep away*."

"You're a goddamn psychopath," I snarled. "I want absolutely nothing to do with you. I can't be clearer about that so just back the fuck off and I promise you won't ever have to deal with me because I don't want to be anywhere near you!" I threw a fistful of air at him but he'd already thrown up a shield expecting it and my magic just skittered aside, hitting Cindy Lou and blowing her skirt up around her waist. She glared at me but I couldn't spare her any attention as I kept my eyes on Gabriel, wondering if he was done or only just beginning.

"Good," he replied darkly, stalking closer to me and looking into my eyes. "Let's hope you remember to keep on hating me like that."

He turned and strode away from me through the crowd, leaving me in the centre of a ring of spectators who had nothing better to do than gawk at me. I glared in the direction Gabriel had taken as I clenched my fists at my sides and orange soda dripped down my face, running over my lips.

The scent of syrupy goodness made a little tug of déjà vu rise in my chest and I couldn't help but be reminded of home. Of Mom adding glitter to a thong while shouting out pop quiz questions over the breakfast bar and Gareth lazily getting every single one right while I lay on the couch and watched trash tv with a can of orange soda in my hand.

Tears prickled the backs of my eyes for everything I'd lost and I quickly gathered my things, saying a brief farewell to Laini and Daniel before dashing away from the students gathered on the hill. I was almost angry at the memories for surfacing now but I couldn't quite find the energy to turn my mind from them.

Although it was stirring up things that were painful to me, they were happy too and I just wanted to spend a little bit of time alone with them while I could.

I dropped my head, letting my hair hang forward to hide my face in case the tears sprung free. I couldn't afford to be seen falling apart in this place. Everyone would assume it was because of Gabriel and I refused to let anyone think he'd hurt me at all. Humiliated? Yeah, he'd done a bang up job of that. But hurt? I'd have to give a shit about him for that and I'd never offer an inch of my heart to an asshole like him, so that was out of the question. But I couldn't let anyone see me cry. I had to be strong, I had to be...

Fuck this pain.

Bottling up my grief for so long was bound to catch up on me at some point, I just hadn't expected a can of exploding goddamn orange soda to trigger me losing my shit.

I shot towards the dorms, needing the sanctuary of my bed. The one small space in this academy that I could call mine.

I wrenched open the door to the dormitory tower and barrelled inside just as someone moved to step out.

I slammed into a hard chest, dropping my bag and books spilling everywhere. And the fucking tears broke free like they'd just been waiting for that excuse.

I kept my gaze on my feet, fighting against the sob which was building in my chest as I scrambled back away from my victim.

"Shit! I'm sorry, I didn't mean to-"

A strong hand grasped my chin and forced my head up. I blinked furiously, trying to calm the tears which only poured faster in response.

Ryder frowned down at me and I squirmed back, ripping my chin out of his grip. I dropped to my knees and started shoving books back into my bag as fast as I could.

"Why are you crying?" he asked, his voice a dangerous growl. "Who hurt you?"

"What?" I shook my head as I tried to move past him, but he shifted his muscular body right back into my path.

"Tell me who hurt you, Elise," Ryder hissed.

"No one," I snapped. I wasn't going to say a word about Gabriel and I wasn't crying because of him anyway. "Normal people have normal emotions. Sometimes I just feel sad because..." I shook my head again, trying to push past him but he caught my wrist in his grasp, not letting me go.

"Wrong," Ryder said. "You're not feeling sad, you're feeling pain. I can taste it on you."

I sucked in a sharp breath at the casual way he referred to my whole fucking world burning down around me. The hole which had been punched through my chest when my brother had been stolen from me was raw and

255

bleeding. And I didn't want him poking at it.

I tried to duck around him again, but Ryder dragged me back inside the building, towing me after him down a long corridor while I tried to tug myself loose.

"Let me go," I protested. "I just want to be on my own."

He didn't stop until we headed into a room at the end of the corridor and he'd tossed me inside.

I blinked in the darkness, the sound of a key turning in a lock the only sound in the world.

"What are you doing?" I gasped, backing up until my back hit a cold stone wall.

"Calm down," Ryder muttered. "You wanted to escape and now you have."

A light flicked on and I looked around in surprise. I was in a dorm like mine but everything in here felt cold and dark. A torn school blazer had been hung over the window to block out the sunlight which was trying to get in around the edges of the closed shutters. Jars of various liquids sat on the top bunk to the left of the room. The bottom bunk was perfectly made up but there was dust on the sheets like they were never slept in.

Books were piled around a heap of cushions on the right hand bottom bunk looking like someone's personal reading cave and the top bunk had the covers thrown back as if someone had just climbed out of it.

"Where am I?" I asked though with how comfortable Ryder looked here I could hazard a fairly good guess.

"My room, new girl. Just like in your fantasies."

"I don't fantasise about you," I retorted. *Liar.* "Why does it look like you don't have dorm mates?"

"Because I don't. I like my own space and I made the suggestion they all come up with alternative arrangements. They agreed that would be for the best."

"Of course they did," I muttered.

I twisted my fingers through the material of my skirt as I fought against the tears, slowly forcing my pain back away so that I didn't have to bear it in front of him. Why had he brought me here? All I'd wanted was to be alone. To let an inch of this agony loose in the privacy of my room before I had to try and contain it again.

"You stole a dose of my pain the other day," Ryder said slowly, taking a step towards me.

"You were the one who offered it to me," I objected, raising my chin to meet his gaze. I'd never asked to see anything of what he'd shown me. Hell, I'd never asked for a single one of his hypnotic visions at all.

The pain in my chest was still pulsating sharply, making it hard to breathe, hard to focus on anything. Gareth's face swum behind my eyelids and all I wanted was to get the hell out of here and forget about this while I screamed into a pillow.

"I want to take a trade on that pain," Ryder breathed, moving so close that he pinned me against the wall.

I could have used my speed to get away from him, but I didn't.

Ryder stood before me, placing a palm against the stone beside my head as he leaned down to look into my eyes.

"Don't," I breathed, feeling him toying with his powers like he was half considering forcing my pain to the surface with his hypnosis. But I couldn't let him see it. He might recognise Gareth's face. Besides, it wasn't his, it was mine. I didn't want anyone else seeing my memories of the people I loved.

Ryder cocked his head to the side, assessing me slowly, like a predator sizing up their prey. But I was no prey.

He reached out to me, tracing his fingers in a slow line along the side of my face. My back arched as the pain in me sharpened unbearably and I sucked in a breath to try and steady myself as he drew the pain out of me.

It hurt like hell. Like standing there and hearing those words for the

257

very first time all over again. Gareth's dead. *Dead*. It was like the rug being pulled out from under me, and the foundations of my whole world crashing down around me. I could feel the rough carpet in our old hallway as it bit into my knees and the way I'd choked, gasping for a breath I couldn't get into my lungs. It was a sharp blade, slicing a hole right through me, cutting me open and leaving me to bleed and bleed but somehow keep on living too.

Ryder's touch awoke pain and suffering and misery in every inch of my body and yet somehow...it felt *good*.

Ryder shifted closer to me, leaning down until his forehead was touching mine, inhaling deeply like he could actually absorb the agony which was coursing through my limbs.

"What has a pretty little thing like you ever lost to make you feel pain like that?" he breathed and the ache in his voice made it impossible to refuse him. He needed to hear my answer as desperately as I needed to share it.

"Everything," I replied on a breath.

"*Fuck*, Elise, you're so broken," he groaned, his lips brushing against my ear. Somehow that didn't seem like an insult coming from him and half a laugh escaped me as more tears fell.

I wondered if they'd ever stop or if giving them this freedom meant I'd be bound to shed them forever.

I dragged a breath between my lips, the cold agony trailing through my limbs and sharpening into little spears of ice which cut me open from the inside out, exposing everything in me that had been ripped apart.

I *was* broken. This fucked up, broken little girl was trying to fix something that could never be mended. Even when I managed to figure out who'd killed Gareth it wouldn't bring him back. Even when I tore them limb from limb and bathed myself clean in their blood, he wouldn't be there at the end of it.

Ryder's hand stayed on my cheek, his power pushing me to face this agony, but I wasn't fighting against it anymore. I was leaning into his touch, leaning into the pain and using it to strengthen me. I coated my body in an armour made of it. This pain didn't rule me, I ruled *it* and I'd use it to make me more powerful.

Ryder's chest rose and fell deeply as he drew my pain out of me, fuelling his magic with the agony of it.

"Do you remember what it was like before this?" he asked me quietly. "What it was to live without the abyss inside you?"

My eyelashes fluttered, less tears falling from them as I embraced this side of me. The more I accepted this agony as being a part of me instead of fighting it, the easier it was becoming to cope with it. I didn't need to lock it up and hide it away. I needed to feel it, own it, drown in it.

I found Ryder's intense gaze burrowing into mine like he wanted to reach right into my soul and devour every inch of this torture.

"No," I breathed. "I don't remember what it was like before. Sometimes I think I do but... everything is tainted with this pain now."

Ryder grazed his fingers across my cheek again and his touch was an endless torment.

"To everyone else you're like this perfect little doll, but I can see how fractured and torn apart you are inside," he breathed. "I can see the cracks in the perfection. I can see the poison that's tainting your essence. And every break, every scar and burn and fissure in your soul only makes it more beautiful. Only makes you more perfect to me. This pain is strength. This agony is beauty."

"If I'm broken shouldn't I want to be fixed?" I whispered, his words echoing through me in an agonising moment of clarity and I already knew his answer before he gave it.

"No."

Ryder's fingers flexed against my jaw and I could only look up into his dark green eyes, his pain mirroring my own.

"Be mine," he growled, a demand and a plea. I hadn't forgotten what he'd asked me the other night. But my answer wasn't changing either.

"I'm not anyone's," I replied on a breath. "I don't want to be caged. I want to be free."

"I can show you true freedom, you just have to let go," he replied and for the longest moment I could feel myself teetering on the edge.

Ryder's hand slid around my throat, his fingers caressing gently. His grip didn't tighten on me at all, but I could tell he half wanted to. His eyes watched the steady movements of his hand against my flesh and I found myself lifting my chin a little higher, offering him more.

He held my life in his hands but he wasn't trying to take it. He just wanted my pain.

"Don't fight it," Ryder murmured in my ear. "Just feel it. It's yours. Own it and it can't own you."

I breathed in and out slowly, letting my eyes fall closed and finally letting myself look at Gareth in my memories. I didn't try to push him away or deny the ache he'd left in me with his absence.

It was raw and angry, an open wound bleeding from my soul that would never fully heal. It would scar me forever. But it wouldn't define me. It was loss and pain and death. But it was also love and light and laughter. It only wielded so much power to hurt me because it meant so much to me. *He* meant so much to me. Before. And now too.

I released a shuddering breath and the tears stopped falling.

Ryder's hand slid lower, his fingertips carving across the line of my collarbone before easing open the top button of my shirt.

My breathing stuttered. My eyes flickered open. And I found myself looking up into the eyes of the devil. But for some reason he didn't want to hurt me.

Ryder brushed the fabric of my shirt aside, two fingertips painting a feather light kiss against my skin until they came to rest above my pounding heart.

"We're the same, you and me," he breathed, using his free hand to capture mine. I let him guide my hand higher until he pressed it over his heart, a mirror image of how he was touching me. I could feel the tumbling beat beneath his flesh and my own pulse seemed to rise in response to meet it. "Do you feel that, Elise?" Ryder asked.

My lips parted to tell him I had no idea what he meant but before I could, I realised what it was. My pulse was utterly in sync with his. Our two hearts beating to the same pace.

I shook my head in confusion, not understanding what was going on, what trick he'd used to do this.

"Is that a Basilisk thing?" I asked shakily, somehow unable to withdraw my hand from his chest.

Ryder laughed darkly, pressing forward so that the space between our bodies was reduced to almost nothing.

"No, baby. That's an *us* thing."

I looked up at him, wondering how the hell I was supposed to respond to that. But before I had to come up with anything, a harsh bell rang in the corridor outside, announcing the next class.

I jerked away from Ryder like I'd just been caught doing something forbidden and his lips shifted into a knowing smirk.

I couldn't think of a single thing to say to him before I slid out of his arms towards the door. He'd left the key in it and I quickly unlocked it and pulled the door open.

I hesitated in the threshold, looking back at him like I was going to say something but there weren't words for what I had to say to him.

My gaze trailed over him and I couldn't help but wonder if the man who'd just helped me face my pain was the one who'd caused it in the first place. Was I looking at a murderer right now? Was I looking at a man I needed to kill?

The door closed between us and I hurried away, leaving my pain with him but keeping some of it with me too. It was time I stopped hiding from it anyway. And I had a feeling I was going to need it before this was over.

I seriously wanted to skip my Liaison session with Professor Titan that evening but after ditching out on most of my counselling session the other day, I dragged myself along to it. I couldn't risk the chance of me getting expelled for breaking stupid rules like bunking mandatory sessions. And at least a Liaison didn't involve a Siren sifting through my emotions like a goddamn breathing lie detector.

I knocked on the door to his office and it swung open to admit me. Titan was sitting behind his desk, his nose in a book and a pinched expression on his face as he concentrated. He beckoned me in so I knew he was aware of my arrival and I pushed the door shut behind me before dropping into the chair in front of his desk.

He kept reading and I tipped my head back towards the ceiling as I settled in, tracing the progress of a spider as it crawled towards the corner.

"Sorry for the delayed start," Titan said, closing the book with a solid thump. "I've been doing a little research on your kind before our session and I didn't quite finish before your arrival."

"My kind?" I asked with a frown.

"Yes. Vampires. We had a Vampire teaching here up until a few months ago and she would have been your Liaison had she not…well if she hadn't… didn't…leave." Titan cleared his throat awkwardly and I perked up a little as he totally failed to cover the fact that there was more to that story than her just getting a new job.

"Why did she leave?" I asked, not caring that I was being nosey. That was the best way to gain information anyway.

"Well, she ah-" Titan looked around as if he thought someone might be eavesdropping and I found myself genuinely wanting to hear the end of that sentence. "She was having *relations* with someone she really shouldn't have. Perhaps a few someones… Anyway, the point is she's gone and so you've got me and my knowledge of the Vampire Code was more than a little rusty so I thought I'd brush up."

"Okay." My mind was whirling with questions about this missing professor. Surely it wasn't usual for teachers to leave in the middle of a school year? And if she'd left a few months ago that could even tie in with Gareth's death.

"So. The Code," Titan said firmly, seeming disinclined to expand on the subject of the missing teacher.

"I'm aware of it," I replied. Though in all honesty I'd only given it a cursory glance a few days after my Order had emerged under the instructions of my old high school head teacher. He'd thought I should follow the stuffy set of rules and guidelines laid out by old, dead Vampires who had nothing to do with me and I'd agreed even if I hadn't bothered to really take in much of what the Code recommended.

The main points were obvious anyway. No killing. No permanent maiming. No keeping blood slaves. Where would I keep a blood slave anyway? In my dungeon? It was a fucking joke. There were countless guidelines beyond those few laws which suggested things like *don't indulge in the hunt* but I couldn't remember all of them. I didn't really care to anyway. I didn't want to be told how to live my life and as guidelines, I could totally ignore them if I wanted to.

"Good. So I've been reading over the things which will help you to feel the most secure and happy from the point of view of what your Order needs. And I've come up with a few suggestions which may help you settle better here."

"What makes you think I'm unhappy?" I asked.

"Ah, well, Miss Nightshade mentioned you didn't make it through

263

the entire session with her the other day. I convinced her not to impose any sanctions on you while you're still settling in but I'm afraid if you cut your sessions with her short again or miss them entirely it could put your position at this academy in jeopardy."

I sighed dramatically. "Can I be honest?" I asked, wondering if his friendly act was bullshit or not and figuring I may as well test it a little.

"Of course. Anything you tell me will stay between us."

"Okay. I found Miss Nightshade to be a nosey bitch. I get that she's supposed to be on the lookout for mental health issues and whatever. But she used her gifts to force information from me which she had no right to know. If I don't want to talk about my grief then that's up to me. And I think she abused her power to steal that information from me."

Titan chuckled and I found myself liking him a hell of a lot more for that alone. "Yes, I'd have to agree with a few of those points," he admitted before placing a hand over his mouth. "Don't you repeat that though!"

I laughed too and mimed crossing my heart. "I'll take it to the grave," I promised.

"Please do."

"Why don't you just do my counselling sessions as well as my liaisons?" I suggested hopefully.

"Ah, I would if I could. But I'm not a licensed mental health professional."

I blew out a disappointed breath and he chuckled again.

"How about I tell Miss Nightshade that you will come back to sessions with her under the premise that she doesn't use her gifts overtly to force you to discuss matters like your grief before you feel ready to. In your own time?" Titan eyed me hopefully and I pursed my lips. He went on, seeing that he hadn't sold me yet. "I do have some experience of grief myself." He cleared his throat. "Once upon a time I had a daughter…"

I frowned as he opened up to me about that, surprised that he would be so honest.

"I'm sorry," I said, not wanting him to feel like he had to give me any more information on the subject if he didn't want to.

Titan eyed me for a long moment before shrugging even though I could see that that pain still lived in him. "It was a long time ago. She was only eight when… Do you know, she had green eyes just like you. Perhaps that's why I've taken a liking to you so quickly," he chuckled. "Anyway. The point of me bringing it up was just to say that I have some experience of what you're going through and I know everyone deals with these things in their own way, but counselling *did* help me."

"Oh so you're heading into emotion blackmail territory?" I teased, not really sure how I should comment on his confession.

Titan smiled, raising his hands in surrender. "You caught me out. Did it work? Will you agree to go back to seeing Miss Nightshade under the terms I suggested?"

I realised this was probably the best offer I was gonna get on the subject so I nodded.

It wouldn't stop her using her powers to read my emotions but maybe it would make her back off a bit and with some self control I could fool her anyway. Besides, I'd been doing some research of my own about how to confuse a Siren. There were a few methods I could employ. I could take a calming draft before our sessions which would suppress my feelings, making them harder for her to pick up on. I could also exert myself physically so that my endorphins were up and I gave off happier vibes. Or I could expose myself to powerful emotions before sessions so that those were ruling my thoughts when I went in.

Ryder was actually onto the right trick with that one too because the best kinds of emotions for that were lust, pain, anger and sorrow. I could just overload myself on one of the four before meeting her and use it to hide my dishonesty, suspicions, grief, guilt, vengeance and anything else I didn't want her finding out about. The next time I had a session with her I'd be ready.

"Okay then," I agreed half-heartedly. "Thank you, Professor."

"You're welcome, Elise," he replied. "Now back to my research. Have you been making time for yourself to be alone? Your Order is naturally solitary and sleeping in dorms isn't necessarily beneficial to your happiness."

"Erm...I study in windowsills sometimes." In all honesty I spent most of my free time trailing around the school, following up on hunches about things I'd seen sketched in Gareth's journal or trying to figure out more about what the Kings got up to outside of lessons. Who they hung out with, what they did, when they left campus. I didn't really do alone time in the sense of actually separating myself from the throng of the academy.

"Well can I suggest you start going for walks? A few times a week, head off campus or down to Tempest Lake or into The Iron Wood, anywhere you fancy really. But it's important for you not to neglect your Order needs. And you *need* some time alone."

"That actually sounds really fucking good," I admitted with a heavy breath. The more I thought about it, the more I wanted to do it. If I took myself away from everyone then I could focus on my grief for a while, remember my brother being happy rather than just obsessing over avenging him.

"Great." Titan smiled widely. "And my other suggestion is that you find yourself a permanent blood Source. There's a lot of research into the value of a Vampire feeding from the same Source repeatedly. It gives you a chance to grow used to that Fae's power living in you and for you to wield it to the best of your ability. Of course, I'm sure you'll want to choose someone powerful what with your own exceptional level of power but even if you went for someone a little easier to subdue I think it would be worthwhile. Do you have anyone in mind?"

I ran my tongue over my teeth as my fangs snapped out at the mere suggestion of who I might like to bite. The answer was pretty straightforward but it was also impossible. I'd had a taste of both Dante and Ryder's blood and I wanted more of it. More and more. The problem was, they were both more powerful than me and better trained too. I wouldn't be able to maintain control over them to keep either as my Source. But every other Fae I'd drunk from since coming to this academy had just been a poor substitution for my true desires and I didn't want to commit to drinking bland blood. Not now I'd had a taste of thunder and pain.

"I'll give it some thought," I said simply, not wanting to worry Titan with my crazy ideas.

He smiled widely. "Perfect. Then I guess I'll see you in class tomorrow. And maybe you can work on claiming a Source before our session next week?"

"Will do." I stood and offered him a salute as I headed out of the room.

I'd give it some thought alright. No doubt I'd daydream about it every time I found my power running low for the rest of the week. But unless I figured out a way to make miracles happen, I guessed we'd both be disappointed with my progress by the time our next session rolled around.

DANTE

CHAPTER TWENTY TWO

It always started the same way. My Clan were gathered on the picnic benches at the base of Devil's Hill after school. Across no man's land was the Lunar Brotherhood pooled together on the bleachers. They kept standing up, cracking necks, pounding chests, never looking our way but the threat was clear. They were out for blood today. I could almost smell it before it was spilled, that's how certain the coming fight was.

I rapped my knuckles on the table in warning, the gold rings on my fingers making the sound carry. The other members of my Clan echoed the tap until everyone was alert, glancing my way, waiting for orders.

The unallied students who ambled through Acrux Courtyard grew quiet at the sound of the tapping. Those who'd noticed the change in both gangs had already made a quick exit, but now it was a mass exodus toward The Vega Dormitories as they realised what was about to go down.

I turned my head to look up at Devil's Hill. Some of the braver students would stay there to watch from a safe distance. But in my experience, nothing was a safe distance.

The Kipling brothers did their job and cast magic over the entranceways to the school. Anyone not inside now was here for the duration. Devil's Hill was the safest bet but it wasn't a guarantee. My gaze snagged on Elise up the hill. She folded her arms, watching the two gangs with curiosity. I wasn't surprised. That girl didn't seem capable of bowing to fear.

You should have left, carina. Now I'll have to keep my eye on you.

Ryder stood at the heart of the bleachers and everyone in his gang banged their chests and made an endless *sssssss* noise through their teeth.

"Dante," my cousin and Beta wolf, Tabitha, moved next to me, her crimson hair falling into her soft blue eyes. She was Felix's daughter but nothing of his cold-blooded nature was in her. She was a great fighter, but not a callous one. "Word is Ryder's out for your blood in payment for you attacking him the other day."

"I know. I've been waiting, cugino," I said calmly, flexing my fingers and drawing air between them. "Let him come for my blood, I'll take his first." The hatred between Ryder and I was more personal than most other gang feuds. In Oscura Clan, we called his father Wolfsbane for how many of my family he'd killed. And not just killed, *butchered*, left in ten pieces. My father had been his last victim before the Oscura Clan had finally cornered the bastard and gutted him.

Tabitha nuzzled into my arm in her wolfish way and I felt more of my cousins drawing closer, the urge to lead them as their Alpha rising in me. Those not of the Werewolf Order closed ranks, magic skittering under the tables, between palms. Weapons crossed hands. Weapons we shouldn't have had. If the faculty found them, they'd call in the FIB to have us all arrested. But they never looked too closely. Professor Mars was the only one who'd try and stop this fight but the Kipling brothers would keep that from happening for as long as possible. They knew the drill. Blood would be shed before the bell rang.

Ryder whistled and his ranks rose up on the bleachers, pounding their chests in time with each thump of their leader's fist.

My own Clan were banging on the tables again, the noise growing in urgency.

"Stay on my right flank, Tabitha," I murmured before passing out instructions to the other wolves. They needed a formation to attack efficiently. As far as I knew, I was the only Dragon in Solaria who was Alpha to a Werewolf pack. But I'd grown up surrounded by their kind and I knew their laws, spoke their language. I could lead a pack better than anyone.

"Are you going to shift, Alpha?" Tabitha asked me, her shoulder rubbing mine.

"I want to feel his skin split under my knuckles first," I growled.

Ryder shedded his blazer, lifting a razor blade into the air to the whooping cheers of the Brotherhood. It was his way of making sure he always drew first blood in battle, by drawing it from himself. He slit his thumb, painting two lines up his cheeks. And that was it. The signal for this to begin.

I stood, lifting my head to the sky and howling to the clouds. Werewolf or otherwise, my entire Clan echoed it. The Wolves tore their clothes from their bodies, leaping forward and shifting into their enormous six foot forms. Twenty in total, creating a triangle out behind me as I headed the line. Beyond them, the rest of my Clan locked into a wall. Some would shift, others would cast, the rest would shield.

Ryder's gang was unpredictable. He changed tactics like the wind so we could never guess their moves.

They spilled towards us like ants from a nest and we charged to meet them, hands raised.

Adrenaline surged as I cast a hurricane from my palms. My comrades cast their own attacks too.

Air, fire, earth, water. It all clashed together in the air at once with a sound like the sky was falling.

I set my eyes on Ryder and his eyes were locked on me. We tore up the tarmac parting us as I knocked his gang members to the ground with blasts of air. My feet dug into soft bodies. Yelps and screams filled my ears. I never slowed. I was made to fight. And I loved every second.

When Ryder and I collided, electricity rolled off of my skin. He hissed but didn't let go. He had three razor blades squeezed between his fingers, throwing a punch which slit open my arm. I growled and he drank in my pain as I delivered a blow to his head that knocked him back a step.

He cast vines in his palm, latching them around my legs, but I severed them with a whip of air, diving forward and locking my hands around his throat. I captured the air in his lungs with magic, holding it prisoner. He choked and I squeezed his throat to drive the point home with a twisted satisfaction in my gut.

He smiled all the while, punching my gut again and again. My skin tore and searing pain bloomed, but the clinking of razor blades said he'd dropped them after the first or second hit. I never let go. I gritted my teeth and went to the darkest place inside my mind.

His gaze collided with mine and with my focus entirely on withholding air from him, I couldn't keep my mental block in place. He sent me a vision of my mother bent over a chair, Ryder fucking her from behind while she cried out in delight.

"FUCK YOU!" I spat, head-butting him and knocking the vision away. My shirt was bloody and soaked. I didn't realise how woozy I was until I staggered sideways.

Have to heal.

I turned, falling back, determined to return the moment I could. I tore away the bloody material sticking to my skin, the wolves closing ranks behind me to hold Ryder off. I clasped the gaping slits in my side with one hand and released healing magic into the wounds. The sounds of battle filled the air as I waited, desperate to jump back into the fray.

I am the Dragon born of Wolves, and I will do my family proud.

A morte e ritorno.

When my wounds were healed I turned to re-join the battle, shirtless and howling to the sky. My Wolves thundered around me, pouncing on Centaurs, Manticores, Pegasuses and Minotaurs who rushed to meet them from the Lunar ranks.

Ryder had his muscular arm locked around a sandy brown wolf's neck and panic seized me. My cousin Helios whimpered as Ryder twisted, ready to break, to kill. But that was against the rules. We couldn't kill. Not in school, not here. But that hungry look in his eyes said he wasn't playing ball today. He was out for blood, pain, *death*. And I couldn't let him have it.

Helios barked as I leapt over him, using air to propel myself and taking Ryder to the ground. We rolled in a tangle of fists, claws, teeth. He ripped at my flesh like paper and I cracked his head against the ground with a roar. Electricity coiled around my spine as I pinned him in place with my knee to his stomach.

"We don't kill on academy grounds," I spat at him and his mouth twisted into a cruel smile.

"How sure are you of that vow today, Inferno?" Vines caught my throat, wrenching me off of him and slamming me into the concrete on my back. I battled them, but he had two wrapped tightly around my hands so my magic was contained. I jerked and thrashed as Ryder rose to his feet, pulling his shirt over his head and revealing an interweaving pattern of scars all over his body. I'd seen them before. I knew what they meant. And he wanted revenge on *me* for them.

"You have it all wrong, stronzo," I growled, but he slammed his foot into my side.

"Don't lie to me you piece of filth." He kicked me again and I felt my Werewolves closing in, but Ryder's gang held them off in their Order forms. There was a clamour above as Griffins and Pegasuses clashed in the sky.

Ryder reached into his pants pocket and took out a switch blade, flipping it open. Death didn't scare me, but Ryder didn't want me dead. He wanted me maimed and bloody.

He dropped down over me, eyeing my bare chest like it was a fresh canvas ready for him to paint. "She started here, so I'll do the same. She used essence of Wolfsbane to stop my wounds from healing so when I'm done, I'll pour it all over you," he breathed into my face as he pressed the tip of the knife to my heart.

I yanked against the vines, but I was immobilised, my arms tethered firmly to either side of me. Ryder's gaze locked with mine and he forced a vision into my mind. He was no longer him. A woman with raven hair, blood red lips and eyes full of hate leaned over me in his place. Her voice was a soft purr I knew well. *Mariella.* "If you embrace the pain, you'll eventually start to want it." She scored the knife across my chest then dragged it down and back up.

Electricity hummed in my veins and I battled the hold Ryder had over my mind with his hypnosis. With a bellow of effort, I forced him out of my head and the shift happened just as I saw the oozing red R he'd carved right into my chest.

I ripped free of the vines and he lurched backwards as the Dragon burst free of my skin. I rose up to my immense height, gazing down at Ryder and drawing a storm of electricity into my throat.

He cast a shield and the Brotherhood helped him, throwing a huge dome of magic around him so the electricity ricocheted off of it.

Claws dug into my spine and I roared, turning my head to find a Vampire on my back. It was Bryce, Ryder's second in command. He tried to get his fangs in me to immobilise my magic, but I caught his leg between my teeth, flinging him from me. With powerful wingbeats I launched myself into the sky, setting Ryder in my sights again. The air pulsed around him with the powerful shield he hid within, but he wouldn't hide for long. He never did.

A rogue fireball, billowed across the courtyard and Devil's Hill, taking out a line of trees climbing its side. A scream tugged my heart apart as burning branches tore through the air and my eyes zeroed in on a figure caught in the blast. Elise was on the ground and all I could see was blood. I tucked my wings, diving toward her with urgency.

I landed beside her with an almighty thud, nudging her with my nose. She whimpered, reaching for me, her hand trailing across my scales for a moment before she passed out. I roared wildly, panic seizing me as I scooped her up between my talons and took off toward the dormitory tower. This fight would have to wait for another day. A force of pure pain was guiding my actions. The need to protect her was so visceral it made me sick to think I'd let her remain on that hill at all.

I landed atop The Vega Dormitories, carefully setting her down before shifting into my Fae form and lifting her into my arms. I descended the metal staircase which clung to the side of the tower, pushing open the window to our dorm and carrying her inside. I lay her on my bunk, pressing a hand to the bloody welt on her head where a branch had knocked her out. My chest crushed like a tin can at the sight.

When her head wound was healed, I moved my hands to the burns up her legs which climbed beneath her singed skirt. I shut my eyes, giving her every ounce of magic I had to give as the soft green glow enveloped her wounds. Her lungs expanded and she breathed in deeply as she came to.

Her eyelashes fluttered as I leaned over her, my eyes darting between hers as relief tumbled through my chest. "You're okay, carina. You're safe."

"You saved me," she gasped, a frown tugging at her features like she couldn't understand why.

"Of course I did," I growled, the strength in my voice surprising me.

She brushed her fingers along my jaw and I leaned into her touch, electricity skittering across my flesh.

"What about the fight?" she breathed.

"It doesn't matter," I said firmly. "When I saw you on that hill, bella…"
I tried to come up with the right words to express the pain that had caused me.

Her hand circled around my neck and her eyes shifted lower.

The moment shattered as she realised I was butt naked and I swallowed the crazy thoughts I'd been about to let loose on her. I gave her a slanted smile then leaned sideways to grab some sweatpants from under the bunk. I lay down beside her, tugging them on and she rolled toward me.

"Thank you." Her fingers fell to the bloody R on my chest and her eyes rounded. "Ryder," she gasped and I said nothing, my jaw ticking.

Her hand pressed to the wound and healing magic tingled beneath it. When the mark was gone, she leaned forward and pressed her lips to where the letter had been carved into me and I felt that kiss in every corner of my body.

A shrill whistle told me Professor Mars had finally made it to the fight and it wouldn't be long before the battle was under control.

The sunset burned through the window, blood red and spilling across the room. Elise slid her arm around my waist as she rested her head against my shoulder.

"Do you want to stay here for a while?" I asked softly, surprised by how affectionate she was suddenly being.

Her eyes sparkled for a moment, then she nodded and I sensed there was some deep hurt in her that had nothing to do with the gang war. Something she would probably never tell me about. But I could be here for her all the same.

I leaned up, pulling down the sheet so it fell across the bunk and cocooned us in my own little world.

She brushed her fingers along my bicep and heat built beneath my skin from her touch.

"I thought I knew what hatred was," she said quietly. "But I've never seen two people despise each other like you and Ryder do."

"We have our reasons, carina," I sighed. "Though they aren't cut and dry. Our families' feud runs deeper than the gangs. Our fathers were enemies. Now they lie in graves and we continue to fight for the blood we're both owed.

But Ryder's mind is so twisted, he can't even see the truth anymore."

"What truth?" she breathed.

I almost told her, then shook my head at the last moment. I couldn't spill my family's secrets even if my heart did want to trust Elise. "La verità non è mia da dire."

Her fingers circled right where Ryder had cut me and a small frown pulled at her features. "What does that mean?"

"It means, bella, that the truth is not mine to give."

"Ryder's truth?" she guessed and I nodded. "You have some loyalty to him then?"

I clucked my tongue. "No loyalty, Elise. It is a question of honour. What my family did to his, and what his did to mine is between us. Terrible things went down in the name of avenging our kin. We don't speak of them. In the Oscura Clan, we have a saying. A morte e ritorno: to death and back. We embody it in every sense of the word. We fight to the death without fear, and our secrets go with us." I thought of my medallion which would be lying somewhere outside on the battlefield. After I'd shifted, it must have broken off, but one of my wolves would no doubt find it for me.

"I understand," she whispered and for some reason I was sure she truly did.

ELISE

CHAPTER TWENTY THREE

I blinked lazily at the grey wall beside me as I came to, trying to figure out why it didn't look right.

A moment later, I noticed the arm wrapped firmly around my waist, the chest in line with my back, the crotch right up against my ass and the really hard bulge that came with it.

I shifted a little and Dante growled against my ear in a way that sent fire coursing right through my body.

He inhaled deeply, running his nose up the back of my neck to the base of my ear before grazing his teeth along the shell of it.

I almost moaned in response, my back arching so that my ass ground against every hard inch of him.

Dante took that as all the encouragement he needed, his hand around my waist slipping down until he found the hem of my skirt. His fingers landed on my bare thigh and he started sliding them up beneath the material. I wriggled back against him again, meaning to stop him and yet somehow staying there as my breathing grew heavier and my ass rode the ridge of his dick.

A breath of laughter slid from the back of Dante's throat and he shifted his hand as it continued to climb my leg so that his fingers were between my thighs.

My heart was pattering wildly and I could only wait, hoping he'd touch me, hoping he wouldn't. Not knowing what I should crave at all.

Dante's thumb scraped a line right up the centre of me over the barrier of my panties and a breathy moan managed to escape my lips.

Dante groaned in response, his arm tightening around me as he planned his next move.

He shifted his fingers, curling them around the edge of my panties, meaning to drag them aside.

Despite the desperate ache I felt for him in that moment, I managed to catch his hand and stop his advance.

"Still playing hard to get, carina?" he asked in a deep tone which practically had me undone already.

I could feel just how hard he was for me and a twisted, wanton part of me ached for the feeling of every inch of him inside me. But despite the desires of my flesh, I knew giving my body to him would mean so much more than sex. It would mean I'd chosen a side. I'd picked him over Ryder. Oscura over the Brotherhood. And I couldn't do that.

I still needed too much information from them. I still needed to figure out how they factored into my brother's death. Or if either one of them was the man responsible.

The beast holding me in his arms might just be the man who had killed the one truest love of my life. I couldn't let this go any further. I couldn't pay the price it might cost.

Dante flexed his fingers despite the fact that I was holding his hand still and he managed to run them up the centre of me again, drawing another soft moan from my lips.

"Stop," I whispered. "We need to stop."

Dante grunted, letting me shift his hand back out from under my skirt and my heart thundered with disappointment as I clenched my thighs together in an attempt to cease the throbbing between them.

I rolled over which was made somewhat difficult by the huge Dragon Shifter boxing me in against the wall.

When I was finally facing him I found a second trap waiting for me in the pull of his dark eyes.

"When you finally give in to this waiting storm between us and agree to be mine, I'm gonna make you scream my name until you lose your voice," he breathed in my ear and I could only bite my lip in response.

"Why do I have to be yours for you to do that?" I murmured. "Why does it comes with so many strings attached?"

Dante frowned at me like I was insane and I used the moment to push myself to sit up beside him.

"Why don't you want to be bound?" he asked me, keeping his voice low so as not to disturb our roommates.

"Why do you want to cage me?" I asked in response.

Dante smirked at me in the dim light and I couldn't help but stare at him for a second. He really was gorgeous; strong features, piercing eyes, dark hair which matched the perfect shadow of stubble on his jaw. My gaze hooked on his lips and his smile widened a little. He knew I was tempted. But I still wasn't going to let him trap me. I'd never choose to be in one of the gangs.

"Maybe I just like to collect beautiful things," he said slowly, his hand brushing over my knee and starting a flood of molten lava which ran straight to my core. "Or maybe I want to see if you can be tamed."

"What if I can't?"

"Then maybe I wanna know what it's like to run free with you."

I smiled in response to that. If he really meant it then I'd take him up on that offer in a heartbeat. But I didn't think he did. He was too tightly embroiled with the Oscura Clan. I doubted he even knew what real freedom was.

I shifted a leg over his, meaning to climb out of his bed but he caught my waist and dragged me down onto his lap instead.

My breath hitched as I felt the impressive length of him between my thighs and it was all I could do not to turn to liquid right in front of him.

"I've refilled all of my power," Dante said, shifting his fingers to draw attention to his gold rings. I guessed that sleeping with that much gold pressed against his flesh was enough to replenish his reserves. "But you look like you're running low, bella."

I raised an eyebrow at him in surprise and his eyes twinkled with knowledge as he tipped his head to the side, a clear offering.

My fangs snapped out instantly and his dick twitched between my thighs.

Fuck he's putting up a good fight.

I leaned down slowly, giving him every chance to change his mind before my fangs were pressed against his neck.

I waited for several heartbeats, my short hair swinging forward to brush against his jaw.

A growl escaped him, sending a shiver racing down my spine and I moaned with need, no longer able to hold back as I drove my fangs into his neck.

Dante hissed in pain, his fingers gripping my hips as he drove me down onto him, grinding himself against me.

His blood washed over my tongue, electricity dancing through it and lighting me up from the inside in a way which was like nothing I'd ever experienced before from anyone else. His blood was like my own brand of temptation, made for me and me alone. I drank deeply, one of my hands cupping the back of his neck, pushing up into his hair while the other shamelessly trailed down the hard planes of his chest.

My head was spinning with the force of his power, my whole body lighting up with the electric energy of him in a way that made me moan with desire.

Dante's hand fisted in my hair as he pulled me closer and I could feel how much he was enjoying this as he shifted beneath me, aching for more.

I finally pulled back, running my tongue up the length of his neck to catch a stray drop of blood which spilled from the bite.

Dante groaned hungrily, his hips rocking beneath me in a demanding plea. But I couldn't let it go further. No matter how desperately my body ached for more of him.

I pressed my fingers to the wound on his neck and healed it, looking into his dark eyes for a long moment as I adjusted to the feeling of his magic inside me.

"Thanks," I breathed, hooking half a smile at him before tugging the sheet aside and stepping out of his bed.

My heart fell right out through the bottom of my stomach as I came face to face with Gabriel who had just climbed in through the window. Or at least I hoped he'd just climbed in. Because he was just standing there. Staring. And a part of me shrivelled up and died rather than face him and the possibility that he'd been listening in to...whatever we'd just done.

My lips parted like a goldfish gasping for air as Gabriel's gaze dropped to the bunk I'd just vacated, his jaw ticking angrily.

"Wait, Elise," Dante demanded, catching my hand as I lingered beside his bed, frozen by shock and mortification. "Can't we just- *oh.*" He swivelled to perch on the edge of his bed and scowled up at Gabriel as he spotted him. "What do you want, asshole?"

"Please tell me you didn't just screw the dragon?" Gabriel asked in disgust.

"No!" I gasped as Dante sniggered.

"Well we basically did," he contradicted me. "You had your mouth all over me."

"Why do you give a shit what we do anyway?" I demanded.

"I don't," Gabriel countered angrily. "It's just going to be fucking awkward for me and Laini if you two start fucking every night."

"They could just cast a silencing bubble," Laini's voice came from within her sheet. "Then we won't have to know anything about it."

"You'll probably notice the bed slamming into the wall hard enough to shatter the brickwork though," Dante said casually, tugging on my hand a little and reminding me he'd taken it.

"Fuck, Dante! Why are you trying to make this worse?" I snapped.

"They might as well know what's coming," he teased and I pulled my hand out of his grip.

Gabriel looked like he might just burst a blood vessel as he glared between me and Dante and I could feel heat crawling along my skin. But I wasn't going to apologise for the fact that I might be interested in other guys. He'd made it perfectly clear he didn't want anything to do with me since our run in on the roof and I was more than happy to forget about it too. But even if we had continued to see each other after that, I wasn't going to commit to one guy. Why should I? I could do whatever the hell I wanted and whatever felt right to me.

"Maybe we could work out a schedule then?" Laini suggested from beneath her sheet like a floating voice. "You let us know when the two of you are boinking and we'll make sure to be elsewhere."

"Boinking?" I barked a laugh but I was also done with this conversation. I wasn't screwing Dante and I didn't want a rumour to that effect getting out either. "I just bit him," I explained though that didn't really justify the dry humping.

"You overpowered him?" Gabriel asked, the tension slipping out of his posture a little.

"No," Dante snapped and I should have known he'd never let anyone believe that. "We have a little arrangement. Elise gets to bite me and I get... other things."

"Are you offering to be my Source now?" I asked in surprise.

284

Dante smirked, climbing to his feet. "Maybe," he said with a shrug. "I can't say I hate the way it feels."

Gabriel scowled at the two of us for a long moment then turned and leapt out of the window again before soaring away into the sky.

"Good riddance," Dante said. "I'm going to jerk off in the shower... unless you've changed your mind about finishing what we started?"

I shook my head mutely, still not recovered from the look in Gabriel's eyes. It wasn't that I felt guilty. I could do whatever the hell I liked with whoever the hell I liked. It was more that I was worried that doing so might mean I'd pissed him off. But that was insane. He was the one who'd told me to stay away so why should he care who I screwed or didn't? But if he was pissed at me again then I had no doubt he'd be after me with another plan of humiliation and bullying and I really didn't wanna have to deal with the drama of that.

Dante strolled from the room, whistling like this day just couldn't get any better and kicking the door shut behind him.

"Thank fuck for that," Laini's voice came from within her sheet fortress. "For a minute there I thought I really was going to have to listen to you screwing him!"

A laugh spilled from my lips as I quickly grabbed my wash stuff from the foot of my bed and a change of clothes for good measure. I didn't reply to her accusation though. Because for a minute there, I almost thought about it too.

My Atlas pinged before I could head out of the door and I grabbed it, glancing down at my daily horoscope.

Good morning Libra.
The stars have spoken about your day!
Today will be filled with challenges as Saturn moves into your chart. But take heart. Perseverance will pay off for you today and you will find yourself

privy to some information you have been seeking. But take note, answers will only lead to more questions and it will take hard work and patience for many more moons before you truly get the answer you seek.

I sighed, it didn't sound like I was in for a great day but at least I could try and be prepared for the worst.

I left my Cardinal Magic class with my mind fixed on what I wanted to achieve with my evening. My investigations were going so slowly it was painful and I was determined to figure out something concrete tonight no matter what.

As I reached the top of the stairs, the sound of my name made me pull up short and I glanced back to find Cindy Lou and her two cronies making a beeline for me. The rest of the class headed away quickly with dinner on their minds and I was tempted to follow them without bothering to speak with her. But it was quickly becoming apparent that Cindy Lou was the Queen Bee of our class and I had most certainly not been paying the proper respect to her in her position of royalty. Not that I gave two shits about it, but she clearly did.

"Do you need something?" I asked innocently as she came to stand before me at the top of the stairs.

"It's come to our attention that you're not really a girls' girl, are you?" she asked, tipping her head a little as she looked me up and down. The assessment was coupled with pursed lips and a look that said she'd just smelled something bad so I was guessing she found me lacking.

I shrugged. Was I the kind of girl to go in for hair braiding parties and pillow fights? Not a bit. But I wasn't sure why that was a bad thing.

"You're one of those girls who acts like she's one of the boys," her friend, Amira, added, twisting a lock of bushy hair around her finger. "Apart from the bit where you wear skirts that are too short and spend all of your time alone with them on your knees with your mouth wide open."

I rolled my eyes. When your mom was a stripper, slut shaming was kinda like calling me a sissy. It didn't hit the mark. Sex was sex. Everyone did it. If you were good at it then you enjoyed it. If you were great at it, even better. And though I was hardly doing the things they were accusing me of, I wouldn't be the least bit embarrassed if I was.

"Well you know what they say about blowjobs right?" I asked. "Give three a week and you won't get wrinkles." I pushed my tongue into my cheek a few times to add to my point and Cindy Lou's gaze darkened.

Her friends stared at me and the other one's lips parted. "Is that really true?" she asked, her eyes lighting with interest.

"Of course it isn't, Helga," Cindy snapped irritably.

"It is," I disagreed. "And because I'm a Vampire, I can suck magic out of them right through their dicks too."

"Really?" Helga breathed in astonishment.

"Oh yeah. In fact, they say any Fae can do that. You just have to suck real hard and *believe.*"

Helga looked so intrigued by that idea that I was fairly sure she'd be on her knees for someone within the hour to try it out. I snorted a soft laugh and Cindy planted her hands on her hips.

"I think you may need a lesson in the way things are done around here. For a start; the Kings are out of bounds to the likes of you. They may be interested in fucking the new girl this week, but you'll be old news, tossed aside and forgotten before the month's out so you should probably back off of them now, sugar. Especially Dante. He's mine."

"I didn't know you were Oscura," I said lightly, ignoring the rest of her bullshit.

"I'm not," she snapped. "I won't join up officially until we're…"

I raised an eyebrow at her. "I'm fairly sure you were about to say married there, Cindy," I said with amusement. "Does the groom know he's engaged?

Because it kinda seems like he hardly notices your existence half the time."

Cindy shrieked, throwing a fireball at me so fast that I barely got a shield up in time to deflect it.

I stumbled back a step and cursed as I fell down the stairs. I almost managed to catch myself on the bannister but the second fireball hit my shield even harder and I tripped again, falling down the stairs and hitting every damn one on the way down.

I cursed as pain seared through my ribs where I hit the stone floor at the bottom and dropped my shield so that I could heal myself.

Cindy and her friends descended on me and I tossed another shield up as they formed a close circle around me where I still sat on the floor, glaring up at them as I worked on fixing my busted rib.

"Call this a warning," Cindy Lou said lightly. "Learn your place or I'll put you in it, sugar."

I bit my tongue against the retort I wanted to give as she strolled away from me. I so wanted to throw my magic at her and call her every name under the sun, but I didn't have time to get caught up in a feud with a mean girl.

My focus needed to be on Gareth and the Kings. She was irrelevant and not worth my time. But as she strode away with a spring in her step, I couldn't help but imagine up ways to wipe the smile off of her smug face. Maybe once I was done with my mission I'd find a little time for her too. But I had to keep my priorities in order. And Cindy Lou just wasn't one of them.

I walked down the corridor after dinner with my Atlas out and my mind full of questions. Every time I thought I was getting close to something, it ended up being useless, but I refused to give up hope.

I was armed with the list of Killblaze dealers the Kipling brothers had given me and I was currently stalking the FaeBook pages of my suspects to see if there was any link between them and Gareth on their profiles. It wasn't like I could just go around asking who he'd been friends with and I imagined drug dealers wouldn't be too keen on doling out answers even if I could. No. I needed to figure out which of them had known him then try to form connections to them myself. Worm my way in.

This whole undercover investigation was taking a long time to get anywhere and I still had no real idea about what had happened in the lead up to my brother's death but I was determined to figure out what had happened.

It was cold and rainy outside and I didn't feel like sitting out on Devil's Hill even with the aid of my magic to keep me dry. It was stupid that we were expected to hang out in the socially divided outdoor space at all times just because the gangs had carved this school up like butchers.

I pursed my lips as I glanced out of a window at the pounding rain and turned away from the exit, finding a dark corner to hide in while I continued my social media stalking.

I hopped up into a wide windowsill which gave a view over the murky grounds and crossed my legs. I didn't care if I was breaking some stupid unwritten rule. If Dante or Ryder had an issue with it then I'd happily have it out with them. There was no good reason for me to go out in that storm and I challenged them to come up with one.

I scrolled through the FaeBook profile of a guy called Toby Bingham, hunting for any photos he'd been tagged in with my brother or even any sign that they might have had anything in common. I pursed my lips as my search went on. I read every comment, clicked through every photo, zoomed in on background randoms...nothing.

With a sigh I gave up on Toby Bingham and leaned back, knocking my head against the window with a dull thud.

A narrow corridor headed away from me and I frowned as I realised I wasn't the only one breaking the rules and staying inside out of the rain. In fact, the group of kids I was currently looking at seemed decidedly suspicious as they looked around nervously before taking a turn down a corridor to their right.

A prickle ran along my spine. I wasn't entirely sure, but I thought I recognised at least one of those kids as a member of the Black Card. They hadn't spotted me lurking in my perch and I was struck with the sudden urge to follow them.

I flicked my Atlas into my satchel and shot down the corridor after them using my Vampire speed. I paused as I reached the turning, listening for any sound of them before leaning out to look down into the empty space.

I frowned. It had taken me less than three seconds to shoot down that hallway. There was no way they could have made it to the far end of the corridor and disappeared that fast.

I strained my ears and I could just pick out the sound of footsteps somewhere ahead of me and to my left.

I moved closer to the spot and found an empty stretch of wall.

What the hell?

I leaned closer, pressing my ear to the wall and there was no doubt about it; the footsteps were coming from beyond it. But how had they gotten through?

I stepped back, scouring the brickwork for some clue and my gaze snagged on a symbol scrawled across the stones. It was black like the wall but once I'd spotted it, it was obvious and more than that, it was familiar.

My heart stuttered in my chest and I whipped my satchel off of my shoulder, yanking Gareth's journal from it and flicking through the pages like a woman possessed.

I sucked in a breath as I found what I was looking for and my eyes widened as I held the journal up to compare the sketch of a circular maze with the symbol on the wall. It was the same. Gareth had scribbled a note at the bottom of it which had made no sense to me before but maybe now-

Pay for the passage in blood.

I lifted my finger to my mouth, my fangs snapping out at my command before slitting into my skin. Blood pooled on my fingertip and I instantly reached for the wall, swiping my finger across the symbol and leaving a red trail behind.

Magic sizzled and suddenly I wasn't looking at a wall anymore, I was standing at the top of a flight of stairs lit by burning torches. I hurried down them, shooting forward with my Vampire speed as the footsteps grew distant and I worried I might lose my targets.

At the foot of the stairs, the space opened up and I crept forward as I looked into a room lit with burning sconces. It was filled with people wearing black robes with deep hoods that they'd pulled up to conceal their faces.

In the middle of the room was a stone altar and standing upon it, raised above the crowd was Laini's friend Daniel. My lips parted as the crowd of robed figures drew closer to him and a deep hum of magic filled the air.

It wasn't hard to figure out who they were aiming their spells at, but I had no idea what magic they were casting.

Daniel stood with his arms wide and a euphoric expression on his face, tipping his head back to look up at the ceiling as the combined magic of the chanting crowd rushed over him.

The hairs rose along the back of my neck as the magic in the room grew thicker. I didn't know a lot about the use of combined spells like this. Only that there weren't many of them that didn't involve dark magic. The kind that the Celestial Council had outlawed. So what were a bunch of students doing casting it in the basement of the academy?

Daniel started trembling, a little at first then more and more until he was practically convulsing. The creepy as fuck smile on his face didn't shift one inch. Not even when he pissed himself.

My mouth fell open as I stared on, afraid to keep watching but desperate to learn more all at once.

The crowd were fully occupied with what they were doing, never so much as glancing back my way so I was able to stay and watch in morbid fascination.

Daniel cried out once then collapsed to the altar in a heap. The magic disbanded and the robed figures fell still, a hushed silence falling amongst them.

Slowly, Daniel pushed himself up onto his knees, his gaze falling on someone at the centre of the crowd in front of him.

"I heard the call," he breathed.

"And the Black Card answered," every other whacko in the room replied as one.

"And now I shall answer too," he sighed, seeming to release a breath filled with all the worries of the world until he was left standing tall and free of them.

Someone handed him a black robe and he pulled it on with an expression of pure joy.

"I'll follow the path the Card Master deals," he said solemnly. "Until my Card is cut."

"Let the hand of fate deal true," they all replied.

Daniel stepped down from the altar and my heart beat a frenzied rhythm in my chest as some of the cult turned towards the door. And *me*.

Luckily my gifts helped me shoot away before any of them spotted me and I raced up the stairs, through the hidden doorway and kept going all the way back to my bed.

I leapt up into my bunk and turned my back on the room as I tried to figure out what the hell I'd just witnessed.

One thing was for sure, Leon had been right about the Black Card being a cult. Which meant my brother had somehow gotten himself tangled up with them too.

I couldn't tally the brother I'd known with someone who would join a group like that but I was beginning to think there were a lot of things that

Gareth had kept a secret from me. And I was just seeing the tip of the iceberg in finding out what the hell they all were.

One thing was for sure though. I wasn't going to stop. If the Black Card were involved with my brother's death then they might wanna deal their decks sharpish. Because an angel of vengeance was coming for them. And I wouldn't rest until I was bathing in the blood of the guilty.

GARETH

CHAPTER TWENTY FOUR

SEVENTEEN MONTHS BEFORE THE SOLARID METEOR SHOWER…

I sat in the cafaeteria drumming my fingers on the wooden table top as I tried to psyche myself up to approach Dante Oscura.

Somehow, Ryder Draconis had been easier; he was often alone and at the party everyone had been milling about. I'd had a few drinks, I just went for it. This was going to be a whole other level of difficult. The Oscuras didn't talk to many people outside of their clan. Although, I'd noticed Leon cosying up to Dante more than once. He was even talking about getting him on the PitBall team and one look at the huge Dragon Shifter made me think Leon could be onto something with that idea. And maybe if we were teammates I'd find it easier to have this conversation with him. But I was nearing the end of the month again and I couldn't afford to wait.

I could have asked Leon to help me out with this but as often happened when the weather sucked, he was nowhere to be seen. No doubt one of his Mindys had brought his lunch to our room so that he didn't have to bother his ass with walking down the stairs. The only time he appeared before the start of class was if the sun happened to be shining so that he could head out and sunbathe to replenish his power. And today was a decidedly grey day so there was no chance of that.

Cindy Lou was drinking a coffee beside me while chatting to a few of her friends. I had one arm around the back of her chair and she shot me little smiles whenever the gossip paused but most of her attention was on their conversation. I'd zoned out of it when they started discussing dresses for the Halloween Ball but I made a mental note to ask her to be my date for it the next time we were alone.

Harvey sat opposite me, nursing a plate of fried food which he was really just pushing around his plate. He'd had way too much to drink last night and I was beginning to realise he never knew when to say no. He was one of those guys who just had to push the limits, never satisfied with one drink or two...or twelve. He had more and more until he was paralytic and left to suffer the after effects the next day. I guessed he was out of power too because he obviously hadn't healed himself and I was running fairly low myself so I couldn't offer to help him either.

"You wanna go for a fly in the clouds after we eat?" I asked as I took another sip of my coffee. We could recharge our power together and I could stretch my wings which I hadn't managed for a few days.

"Yeah man," Harvey agreed. "Just let me force some of this food down and I'll be up for shifting. I feel like if I do it at the moment I'll puke."

I laughed as he fell back into his hangover mood and my gaze drifted back to Dante Oscura. Five tables surrounded him filled with more members of his gang than I could easily count. I noticed a lone figure sat at the far end of the Oscura side of the room and my gaze lingered on him as I recognised him. Faebook had been full of the rumours about Lorenzo Oscura and I guessed they were true.

Apparently he'd taken a liking to snorting Killblaze in his spare time *and Dante had shunned him for it. It wasn't quite as extreme as kicking him out of the gang but the rest of the Clan were wholeheartedly ignoring him. It was all over school. No one was to acknowledge him until he kicked the habit. I had to admire Dante for his commitment to keeping his gang clean of drugs but Lorenzo looked so miserable that I wondered if it was really the best way. Not that I had any interest in mentioning it to the gang leader.*

My gaze slid to Dante again and I steeled myself to approach him.

It has to be done.

I let out a long breath, half rising out of my chair just as my Atlas pinged in my pocket. I dropped back into my seat again and pulled it out, smiling as I spotted the message from Ella.

Ella:

How's life at the academy? I got detention for biting my Professor...again. Apparently I can't keep on using the excuse of Vampire urges. But she's so damn powerful and slow as a brick so it's just too tempting. Surely I'm just doing what Fae do, right? Feel free to call her many creative names in your reply. My classmates think I swear too much and I can't fucking cope with their shitty tastes in music and pathetic attempts at being cool. Maybe I should join the Oscuras to alleviate my boredom?

I couldn't help but laugh out loud as I read her message. I wished she'd been able to come to Aurora Academy this year but she'd argued against abandoning Mom and I'd had to admit she had a point. Our mom couldn't cope with being alone. She had serious abandonment issues after both of our fathers had left her and if we both came to the academy she'd end up clinically depressed.

I hated feeling like I was the reason Ella couldn't have a better education even though she'd insisted that I be the one to come to the Academy. And I couldn't deny the fact that I'd always dreamed of coming somewhere like this.

I was going to learn everything I could here and really make something of myself. I'd teach Elise all of it too and I'd get her out of here. We would move out of this shitty city and escape the gang crap and Mom could stop stripping for money. It was all going to come together for us.

Gareth:

Fuck no, don't do that. I'm looking at the future leader of the Oscura Clan as we speak and he's an ugly bastard. You wouldn't want to be stuck following his orders for the rest of your life.

P.S.

Your professor sounds like a total assclown and you should definitely keep biting her.

Ella:

Assclown? Hahaha. Send me a photo of the Oscura dude so I can see how ugly he is for myself. I'm in Cardinal Magic and I'm dying of boredom while we learn about Pegasuses - as if they can teach me anything on this subject that I don't already know from hanging out with you and Mom my whole life. I still don't think I've ever gone a day without finding glitter in my hair...

I rolled my eyes at the tired complaints. I'd always known Ella wouldn't emerge as a Pegasus; she was nowhere near cheery enough to be one of us. Vampire was always more likely. Her father, Mom's second great love who up and vanished before Ella was even born, was a powerful Vampire according to Mom so that was obviously who she took after.

I glanced up at Dante Oscura, trying to be subtle as I took the photo Ella requested. He was sitting on the end of his table, his wolf pack flocking around him as he told some story about beating up a Lunar kid in a loud voice. The eating schedule laid out by the gangs meant that there were no Lunar

Brotherhood members about to take offence to his story and his followers were lapping it up.

I sent the photo and waited for Ella's response.

Ella:

Liar. You said he was ugly. Now I'm definitely signing up. Go get his number for me.

I snorted a laugh, imagining what she'd say if I really did that. Not that I'd even consider it for half a second. Dante Oscura was about the worst person I could imagine for my little sister. And with the way he was screwing his way through most of the girls in the academy already, maybe I should have been glad she wasn't going to come here.

Gareth:

Sorry Little Angel, he said he doesn't date Vampires...because you suck ;)

Ella:

Wow, you'd think that joke wouldn't get any funnier after the hundredth time but it really comes back around.

Ella:

Dipshit x

I smirked to myself and pushed my Atlas back into my pocket. I may have been intimidated by the idea of talking to Dante Oscura but my sister sure as shit wouldn't be. That girl had never learned the concept of self preservation and her mouth got her into trouble every other day. Either with what she said or who she bit. And I was going to channel a little of her confidence in the name of protecting her.

I got to my feet and crossed the room, heading straight for Dante Oscura.

His Werewolf pack noticed me first. They straightened their spines, eyeing me up, circling out to surround me. It was pretty fucking intimidating but I kept my spine straight and my gaze fixed on Dante as he shuffled a Tarot deck in his palms. His fingers were lined with chunky gold rings and I'd seen the imprints of them beaten into the faces of more than a few Fae since he'd arrived at the academy.

He'd wasted no time in asserting his dominance and with his high level of power, Storm Dragon Order, massive physical presence and family name there weren't many people willing to take him on. Aside from Ryder Draconis of course.

Dante's dark eyes lifted to me. His gaze travelled over me slowly then he looked back down at his deck, dismissing me as a threat. I balked at that but as I had no reason to want to get into an argument with Dante Oscura I tried to see it as a good thing.

"What do you want?" his cousin, Tabitha Oscura, asked as I came to stand before him. Dante's Beta was perched on the chair beside him, eyeing me with more interest than her Alpha had given me as she twisted a finger through her wild red hair.

"I was hoping for a moment of your time, Dante," I said firmly, ignoring Tabitha. If I let her draw my attention from him, he'd gladly palm me off on her. I'd spent enough time observing the way he worked to figure that much out.

"Is that so?" he asked, shuffling the deck slowly, still not bothering to look at me.

"Yeah. I was thinking...there must be things that are difficult for your followers to do. Jobs that would go unnoticed if someone unaffiliated was carrying them out for you but might draw attention if an Oscura was seen doing them."

"So you wanna offer your services to the Clan out of the goodness of your heart?" he asked, brushing a thumb across the deck as he fanned it out before him.

"Obviously not for nothing," I replied, my voice level and certain. I couldn't show an inch of weakness now.

A couple of the wolves at my back growled but I forced myself not to react. A wolf pack was harmless all the time their Alpha was calm. And if Dante Oscura lost his patience with me then I'd be more concerned about him than them.

"Hmm..." Dante teased a card out of the pack and held it out to me without turning it over.

I reached for it, not really having any choice but to do so. I flipped it over and the Wheel of Fortune looked back up at me, various magical creatures coiled around it while sitting on clouds in a blue sky.

Dante clicked his fingers at Tabitha and she piped up instantly. "Good fortune's coming your way. Things are turning in your favour," she supplied.

I knew what the card meant, Mom had been obsessed with reading the damn things our whole life, always looking for a sign her luck would change. Gambling because of things she read in the cards. Sometimes she interpreted their messages correctly and won, other times...not so much. I didn't care for Tarot thanks to that.

"Do you think that's referring to you or me?" Dante asked, finally raising his eyes to meet mine. And I had to admit it was pretty damn hard to hold his gaze. The guy had nearly a foot on me and I wasn't short and his power crackled in the air around him. I could actually feel the hairs on my arms rising in response to the static he exuded without even trying. "I drew the card but you turned it. So?"

"Either. Both, hopefully," I added. "Maybe my idea would work out well for both of us."

Dante started shuffling the cards again, seeming amused by my response. His gaze slid over my shoulder to the table I'd been sitting at before I'd approached him. I could feel Harvey and Cindy Lou looking this way but I didn't turn to look at them.

"I didn't catch your name," Dante said.

"Gareth Tempa," I supplied.

"Is that your girl...Gareth?" he asked slowly.

I turned and followed his gaze to Cindy Lou who started blushing as she realised we were looking her way.

"No. Well, I mean...we're kinda starting something," I said, unsure what he wanted me to say. "She could be," I finished lamely.

Dante's gaze lingered on her longer than I would have liked and he thumbed another card from the deck, offering it to me again. As I took it, he finally looked back at me and I had to hope that his interest in Cindy Lou would end there.

The Fool looked up at me this time, wearing a flowery dress as he stood beneath the sun at the edge of a cliff.

Dante snorted a laugh despite the fact that we both knew The Fool wasn't a card meant to ridicule anyone.

He snapped his fingers for Tabitha again and she pushed a hand through her frizzy, crimson hair as she explained its meaning for us.

"New beginnings and experiences. Taking a leap of faith," she said, her eyes wandering over me with more interest now.

"There you have it then. I'll be in touch with your first assignment, Gary." Dante pushed himself to his feet and the wolf pack stood too, following him as he strode from the room.

"It's Gareth," I called, refusing to let that stand and Dante's dark chuckle called back to me as the wolves circled close to him again.

I watched as they walked away with a smile playing around my lips. I'd just managed to land myself work from the Oscura Clan without having to declare myself one of them. It looked like Old Sal's second payment would *be ready too.*

If I could just figure out what the hell Gabriel Nox was up to too then maybe I'd even be able to put some money aside for our new start as well. Things were starting to come together. I was going to get my family the life they deserved if it was the last thing I did.

RYDER

CHAPTER TWENTY FIVE

I woke like glass breaking in reverse. The shards jagged and slicing, drawing back together piece by piece. But they never fit together the same way. Crumbled dust lay between them like diamonds; the parts of me which were lost forever.

The nightmares still lingered and my mouth was desperately parched as I drew in a ragged breath.

"Can you be brave for me today, Ryder?"

"Always, Father."

"You will have to be braver than you have ever been this time."

I forced the memory away through sheer will, dragging myself out of bed and falling to the floor to complete my morning routine. Push ups till the pain burned me from the inside out. Sits up until my gut was so tight it felt like I was about to bust an organ. Pull-ups until my arms were numb and pain was nothing but an old friend I missed the caress of.

I stood, naked, dripping with sweat, the memories long gone. Pain devoured them. It was the one thing *she* had taught me which had ever been worthwhile. Pain was my ally. It gave me freedom from the cage of my mind.

But most of all, it gave me power.

I didn't have to be stronger than anyone in Solaria, I just had to outlast them in a fight. And that was something no one could beat me at. It was what made me the most frightening motherfucker in this place. Because you can't break a man who has no breaking point.

My Atlas buzzed again and again, demanding I read my horoscope. I growled under my breath, snatching it from my bed and tapping the screen. I only read the damn things to try and decipher whether Dante was plotting against me. But the stars were never too clear so they often set me on edge for no reason.

Good morning Capricorn.

The stars have spoken about your day!

Even the strongest walls have cracks and you may find today it is a good day to embrace those weaknesses. A Libra may slip under your defences with or without your permission so it is the perfect time to open your heart and show your romantic side. With Venus moving into your chart, you may find your body tingling around the object of your affections.

Beware of giving in to the stubborn urges of Uranus and sabotaging yourself today.

I shook my head in dismissal, tossing the Atlas back onto my bed. *My body does not fucking tingle.*

I headed to the bathroom at the end of the hall and everyone in there ran out like rats down a drain. Didn't matter if they were mid-shit. If I was in there, they weren't.

I showered in one of the private units then returned to my room without a towel, giving zero fucks if anyone saw me.

Back in my room, I tugged on my uniform and stuffed my Atlas in my pocket before heading out the door.

As I strode through the halls of the academy, students shrank from me

306

as if the air I exhaled was poisonous. I didn't have friends in this place. I had recruits. Soldiers who bled for me on command. Friendship was weakness. People were commodities to serve my purposes. They either fought for me, facilitated me or fucked me. And if they did none of those things, they tended to be my enemies. Elise was the first Fae to hold out this long to pick which one of the three Fs she wanted to make camp in. But my patience was wearing thin.

I pushed through the mahogany door into the cafaeteria, scouring the room as I always did, taking a moment to check no Oscura scum were in sight during Lunar hours. They were gone by eight, we arrived at five past.

My gaze snagged on the colour lilac and raked down Elise's back. She sat beside her Sphinx friend and I triple checked there was no sign of Inferno. Satisfied, I moved to an empty table at the back of the hall. The Brotherhood sat in their ranks to remind them where they stood within the gang, so as their leader, I ate alone.

The second my ass hit the seat, two freshmen appeared, planting down a mug of black coffee and a giant bowl of scrambled eggs with a spoon tucked into it.

They scampered away and Bryce appeared before I started my meal. I sipped my too-hot coffee, the mellow, bitter taste rolling over my tongue and making my mouth burn. I sighed as pain mixed with caffeine and I gestured for Bryce to sit.

He dropped down beside me to give me his daily report. "Word is Inferno's got new eyes and ears working for him."

"Unallied?" I confirmed.

"Not anymore." He pushed a list of names across the table to me and I memorised them.

"Get a full report on them. Star signs, Elements, Orders. I wanna know what they're capable of."

"Will do, boss." Bryce snapped his fingers at one of the freshmen who'd brought my breakfast. "Hey, I have a job for you."

My hand came down on Bryce's shoulder and he flinched, turning to me with his fangs popping out.

"I didn't say him. I said *you*, Corvus. Do your fucking job or step aside and I'll find a new second."

His eyes trailed over me and I glared at him, readying a hypnosis to drive the point home when he didn't automatically bow his head to me. Before I sent him a vision of me ripping his limbs off, he dipped his head. But the challenge had fucking been there. I wasn't blind.

"Sorry, boss. I'll get on it now."

A deep rattle rolled from me as he hurried away and I made a mental note to keep a closer eye on him. No one hesitated like that with me and I decided to break a few of his bones later today to remind him of his place.

I picked up the spoon to eat my eggs just as a slender shadow fell over my table. I lifted my gaze to find Elise standing there with her head tilted to one side as she eyed my breakfast. "That is the saddest breakfast I've ever seen."

"Well it ain't crying, new girl." I stuffed a spoonful of eggs into my mouth. Protein for muscle. Muscle which made me strong. And with strength I could destroy the Oscuras. Every action I took in life brought me closer to that goal. Eating included.

She released a breath of laughter like I was amusing the fuck out of her then dropped into the seat opposite me. The Sphinx was staring over at her like she'd just pulled up a chair with a hungry shark.

For one long second, I took in her bright green eyes, the way she pressed her tongue against her fangs, her index finger painting a circle on the table then I dropped my gaze to my food and ate savagely, eating my meal like I wanted to eat her.

"What do you want?" I asked when it was clear she wasn't going anywhere.

"Just to hang out." She shrugged and my eyes narrowed to slits.

"I don't hang out, and Fae certainly don't want to fucking hang out with me either."

"I'm not like other Fae, I think you know that Ryder," she said airily and I swear my dick hit the table from the sound of my name on her lips.

"I do fucking know it," I growled, placing my spoon down. "Have you come over here to tell me you're mine now?" I concealed the hope in my voice but her eyes told me she knew how much I wanted that. And shit, I wanted it so bad. I couldn't remember the last time I'd wanted anything beyond the Oscura Clan dead at my feet.

"No," she said simply and anger rocked my chest. "Are you his?" I'd seen that scumbag Inferno carry her off the battlefield. Playing the fucking hero, stealing my girl. It was all bullshit. It was his fucking Clan who'd cast the rogue fireball. He was *responsible*.

"No," she said just as simply and a knot of barbed wire unravelled in my gut.

"So you just want to...hang out," I stated and she nodded brightly. I lifted my spoon to continue eating and she shot around the table with her Vampire speed, snatching it from my hand.

"Wait here," she commanded then shot away again before I could ask what the fuck she was doing and why I now had no fucking utensils.

I stared down at my eggs, trying to work her out but I came up short. She sped back to the table, sitting up on it beside me, her long leg brushing against my arm. She placed down a bottle of ketchup, salt and pepper, toying with my spoon in her other hand.

I gazed up at her, pressing my tongue piercing between my teeth. "What are you playing at?"

She answered by snatching up the ketchup and squeezing a dollop onto my eggs followed by a sprinkle of salt and pepper. She used my spoon to mix it all then dangled it before my eyes. "Tuck in."

"Why would you add that shit?" I frowned, quietly enjoying the attention she was showering on me. I could feel the looks we were getting from all around the room, hear the disbelief in the voices who spoke about us. About her. My little she-devil. But fuck if I cared.

"By the stars, Ryder," she sighed dramatically. "Just try it." She scooped up a spoonful and lifted it to my lips.

I stared at her like she'd gone mad and a dare entered her eyes.

Was I going to let this girl feed me like a fucking baby in a high chair? I hesitated on that thought, pursing my lips.

"Hurry up, Ryder, or I start making aeroplane noises," Elise teased and a single breath of laughter escaped me.

This went against everything I was. Every. Fucking. Thing. Down to my pissing DNA. But for some reason known only to the stars themselves, I opened my damn mouth.

She slipped the spoon in with a bark of laughter and fuck if that didn't taste like the best thing ever. I couldn't remember the last time I'd eaten food for pleasure. *Definitely not since Father died.*

Muttering broke out around the cafaeteria and I shot my people a look to make sure they weren't fucking laughing. Anyone who so much as twitched a smile was gonna get two broken legs for it.

I snatched the spoon from her as the muttering grew louder from the unallied students. I was fairly sure someone had fallen off their chair when she'd fed me. That was confirmed as Eugene Dipper scrambled to his feet, apologising profusely to everyone around him. *Dickwit.*

"Food is fuel," I spouted my own bullshit at her, not able to admit how much I actually enjoyed the change. I continued to eat and she watched me with a satisfied smile.

I devoured every last mind-blowing bite then she leaned in and wiped ketchup from the corner of my mouth. She sucked it off her finger and I grunted in desire, my frozen blood heating up a few degrees. Something happened in my gut. It was like an instinctive sort of prickle only…better. I frowned, wondering if I was getting sick. *Better up my vitamins.*

"Do you wanna skip Potions Class? I'll treat you." I snagged her gaze, throwing a vision at her with her legs wrapped around my neck on this very table, my tongue dragging up the middle of her while she screamed with delight. I could almost taste her, but it was all of my conjuring. I had no idea what she'd really taste like but I reckoned it was even better than my upgraded breakfast.

She blinked hard, throwing off the hypnosis and I smirked at her flushed cheeks and the way she shifted on the table.

"You're so fucking wet for me, Elise. Just give it up and I promise I won't bruise you too hard." I grinned widely.

She clucked her tongue. "You're all talk, snake boy." She hopped to the floor, shaking her head at me as she walked away.

Anger pulsed in my veins, all of it aimed at myself.

Well done, asshole. You've really got a way with fucking words.

When it came to sex, I couldn't experience pleasure without pain. On some level, I knew that was fucked up. And on another, it maybe bothered me. It wasn't like I'd chosen to be this way. And much as everyone just assumed my Order form made me like this, I knew otherwise.

Being a Basilisk didn't actually mean I had to hurt anyone, including myself. I could feed on emotional pain as easily as I could physical. And in doing so, I could take that pain away from Fae. Just like I had with Elise.

If my Order was less rare, maybe they'd know that. But I was the standard by which they judged my kind. So I let them think we were all this way, let them blame my psychotic nature on the snake that resided beneath my skin. But I knew the truth; I was fundamentally broken and a lot of my pieces were completely missing. I had the feeling Elise was starting to figure it out too. Which was the first thing that had scared me in half a fucking decade.

By the time I finished my meal, Elise was heading out the door with her friend and I stood, leaving my shit for other people to clean up as I marched after her.

When I arrived at Potions Class, she was already in the seat next to mine and I relaxed as I knew I had her for the next hour. And I was determined to face out this fear in me. If she wanted me to drop the bullshit, maybe I could for her. I'd seriously fucking try anyway. The three Fs were becoming four. Because I needed Elise to *feel* for me.

I dropped into my seat, slinging my arm around the back of hers and leaning in close as the rest of the class continued to chat. Professor Titan wasn't here yet so I had a few minutes to get her agree to something I had never, ever offered anyone. A date.

She turned into my body, a smile playing around her mouth that could either mean she was bordering on pissed off, or she was genuinely enjoying herself.

Dante stepped into the room, his shoulders pushed back as he headed to his chair, throwing us a not-so-subtle glare. Ice drove through my veins like a glacier had taken the place of my heart. So maybe Elise Castillo didn't have to be mine, she just had to not be his. Fucking Inferno's.

"Do you like dinner?" I blurted and she frowned as if she was trying to work me out.

"Who doesn't like dinner?"

Right yeah. Fuckwit.

I drew my arm tighter around her so she was pulled into body, breathing in the elderflower scent of her hair. The scent of cherries was suspiciously missing. "What do you like to eat?"

She laughed, pressing a hand to my chest to stop me from reeling her any closer but her touch set off a fucking volcano in my chest – which was saying something for a coldblooded reptile like me. "Are you screwing with me?"

"Take out the *with* and we're getting nearer to where I wanna be," I taunted.

She rolled her eyes. "Is there a point to this conversation? Because it feels like we're circling one."

"Yeah…" I shifted. "Maybe tonight you'd wanna-"

Dante whistled and we both glanced his way, a growl rumbling from my throat.

"Elise, now or never." He tilted his head, exposing his neck and she sucked in a breath. She was out of her seat in a heartbeat, pushing my arm aside and shooting into Dante's arms like a fucking lap dog as her ass met his knee. Her fangs dug into his throat and he slid his hand up the back of her shirt. She moaned loud enough for the whole class to hear and something in me snapped.

Fucking – what?! She was Dante's? Did she lie to my damn face?

She'd chosen. She'd fucking chosen. And she hadn't picked me.

She released another moan and I lost my fucking head. I stood, upturning the entire desk as my Order form slithered beneath my skin. My jaw ached for Dante's throat and I was determined to have it. Fuck the consequences. Fuck it *all*.

I tugged my blazer off and every student in the class lurched backwards as they realised I was gonna shift.

Elise extracted her fangs while Dante continued to smile like he'd won the fucking lottery. And he had. *My* lottery. She was mine to win. No one else's. Least of all that Oscura *vermin*.

Elise was suddenly right up in my face, his blood on her lips. His fucking pain.

I reared away from her, ready to lose my mind, but she wrapped her hand around mine, her eyes begging.

"He's just my Source," she said hurriedly and Dante barked a laugh like that was far from fucking true.

I locked eyes with him and drilled a vision into his head he'd never forget. He lay in ten pieces on the ground while I pounded every one of them with a hammer.

Elise tiptoed to get in my way and block the vision. My gaze slammed into hers instead and I snared her in hypnosis. My hand locked around her throat, her feet lifting off the ground as I held her against the wall. "If you're with them, you're my enemy. And if you're my enemy, you're fucking dead."

She clawed at my arm and I released her from the vision, finding her face pale as she stared at me. "He's my Source!" she shouted again and her palm crashed into my cheek. Pain stung keenly, locking me back in the present and finally making me hear what she'd said.

I searched her eyes for the truth and found it shining back me. My mind worked over that nugget of information as I tried to figure out what to do with it.

The answer came to me like a lit-up bulb and a dark smile pulled at my mouth.

"Then *I'm* your Source too."

ELISE

CHAPTER TWENTY SIX

"Y ou want to be my Source too?" I asked with a frown. It wasn't exactly unheard of for Fae to offer themselves up as a Vampire's Source but they were always weaker Fae, looking for the protection of said Vampire. And yet somehow I now had two of the most powerful Fae in the school offering to be mine.

"Not happening," Dante snapped from his chair behind me. "She can only have one Source and I'm already more than filling the position."

Ryder's eyes flared dangerously and all the accusation in them was aimed at me.

"That's not true," I blurted before he turned to violence. "The Vampire Code says that claiming multiple Sources is perfectly acceptable. It means I don't have to drain so much from one person consistently so it'd be doing you a favour."

"See, Inferno," Ryder taunted. "It's perfectly fucking acceptable. So I'm hers now too."

I snorted a laugh. All the talk of me being his and now suddenly he was mine?

"Fine by me," I said before either of them could keep bickering over it. I wasn't sure in what world they thought they were getting one up by agreeing to be my personal blood donors. As far as I could tell I was the only winner in the equation and I had zero issues with it. Every Vampire knew the more powerful the Fae you drank from, the better it tasted, the more exhilarating the buzz. I'd have to be fucking insane to argue against this situation for one second.

"No," Dante snapped, getting to his feet. "I don't want you putting your mouth anywhere near *him*."

"Well sadly for you, you don't get to tell me what to do," I replied firmly. "And I've already made it clear I'm not going to pick between Oscura Clan and The Brotherhood so this seems like a pretty good way to show I'm remaining neutral."

"Unless you want to resign and leave the position to me?" Ryder taunted his rival.

Static electricity rolled through the classroom as Dante's eyes flared with rage. My scalp tingled as my hair lifted a little under the influence of his magic. Most of the students got up and scurried away to the sides of the room and Ryder cracked his knuckles, stepping closer too.

Gabriel leaned back in his chair at the back of the classroom, not seeming inclined to move an inch though I'd bet there was a strong ass shield sitting around him right about now.

I shifted between the two of them and a gasp came from several of the onlookers as if they thought I was suicidal or at least unhinged. Which I probably was for stepping between the gang Kings as they faced off. But this was about me and I refused to be used as a chess piece in their ongoing game.

"Or maybe I should just ditch both of you and find a Source with less drama attached?" I suggested, though I was really hoping they wouldn't take me up on that because the mere thought of their blood had tingles running along my skin and saliva pooling in my mouth.

That stopped them. Which was fucking insane because being my Source shouldn't have meant anything to either of them. It was beneath them. They didn't need to bow to the whims of a Vampire with less power than them. It wasn't how Fae worked. But for some reason their desire to win me for their respective gangs seemed to mean more to them than that because they both shifted their gazes to me and stopped their advance towards each other.

"Settle down everyone! I'm here now!" Professor Titan called cheerily like he hadn't just walked in on the brink of a battle. There was no way he could have missed it though so I guessed he was hoping that by pretending it wasn't happening he might get his wish and find out it wasn't.

Dante dropped back into his chair with a smirk, brushing a thumb over the bite I'd left on his neck. "It hurts so good," he said, his eyes on Ryder who stilled beside me. "Feel free to climb into my bunk if you need a top up in the night again, Elise."

I rolled my eyes and headed back across the room, nudging Ryder to make him walk too. He did so a little reluctantly, throwing an arm around my back as we went and very nearly skimming my ass.

I shrugged out of his grip and darted forward to pick up my books from the floor where they'd fallen when Ryder had upended our desk, but a member of the Lunar Brotherhood beat me to it.

I recognised him as Bryce something, Ryder's second in command. He was tall and slender like a wraith and his dark eyes swept over me, assessing me from head to toe and seeming to find me wanting. I resisted the urge to hiss at him as I recognised another member of my own Order. Vampires didn't tend to socialise together much unless they mated. It was a pecking order thing. We were pre programmed to secure the most powerful blood source available which always put us in direct competition with each other.

I was fairly sure his power was an even match to mine from what I could sense and I imagined he was more than a little tempted to challenge me for access to the blood I'd just laid claim to. And in any usual circumstance he'd be well within his rights to do just that. If a Vampire claimed a Source then no other Vampire could bite them but they could challenge for it if they wanted to. In theory if Bryce challenged and beat me he could lay claim to both Ryder and Dante's blood for his own. But as I hadn't claimed them in the traditional way of overpowering them, I knew he wouldn't. For some reason they'd offered themselves to me but the look in Bryce's eye said he was more than a little envious.

Two other brotherhood members flipped our desk back into its original position and placed Ryder's things down again.

Bryce stepped closer, the scent of too much aftershave assaulting me as he moved into my personal space and offered me my books. I reached for them but he didn't let go, dark eyes looking past me to Ryder like I didn't even matter.

"Boss, are you sure about this?" he asked in a low voice. "Letting an unsworn Vampire use you for-"

Bryce flinched as Ryder threw a hallucination at him and I pursed my lips as I continued to wait for my stuff.

"Do you still want to question me, number two?" Ryder hissed and Bryce shook his head, dropping his eyes submissively.

I tried pulling on my books again but he still wouldn't release them.

"Is she one of us?" Bryce asked, seeming unsure.

"No," I snapped before Ryder could reply.

"Okay then." The asshole yanked my books back out of my grip and tossed them on the floor before sauntering back to his own desk.

"Are you freaking kidding me?" I snarled as I moved to gather them again.

"If you want The Brotherhood's help then you only have to say the word," Ryder growled as he dropped into his chair. "Just one word. Yes."

"No," I replied instantly, tossing my books onto the desk and moving to my seat. "I'm never going to belong to any gang. Or any*one* for that matter.

So stop asking."

Ryder hissed between his teeth but didn't respond as Professor Titan started explaining our task for today. We were making Essence of Moonshine which was a strong healing tonic, particularly effective against poisons.

"Bing bong!" Principal Greyshine's voice came over the tannoy and everyone fell quiet to listen to him. "Just a quickie this morning gang! I wanted to remind everyone that having humpy pumpy in the classrooms is a no no. We've had to have strong words with six couples this week for defiling the desks and no one wants a tooshy print on their workspace now do they?"

A girl on the far side of the room was burying her head in her hands while the guy sitting beside her high fived his friend in the next row. Titan was conveniently looking down at his desk like he hadn't noticed and I wondered if he just didn't want to deal with handing out a detention.

"In other news, the FIB are asking for any information that anyone might have on a missing squad car which was seen heading onto academy grounds. They're willing to put it all down to high jinx if it's just left out by the road with the keys so why not give it back, eh fellas? That's all for now. Toodle pip and I'll catch you on the flip!"

"Unfortunately, I heard that cop car took a dip in the lake," Leon said loudly as he sauntered into the room ten minutes late, buttoning his shirt up as he moved towards his desk. He flashed me a smile and I couldn't help but grin back.

"Did you do that?" I whispered as he passed my desk.

"You wanna come with me next time, little monster?" he offered, looking down at me with excitement lighting his eyes.

"Only if you let me drive," I replied instantly.

"You can sit on my lap," he promised and my smile widened as I snorted in amusement.

Ryder hissed beside me and Leon rolled his eyes before heading on to his own desk.

Professor Titan paused as he found his seat then started taking speaking again as if nothing had interrupted him.

I started taking notes, letting my hair fall down to create a curtain between me and Ryder.

Ryder didn't feel the need to break the silence so I continued to ignore him as I copied down the ingredients.

A loud screeeeech made me look up as Leon started dragging his chair across the floor until he set himself up opposite me again.

"Hey, little monster, you looking forward to playing with my balls later?" he asked and I laughed out loud in surprise.

"What?" I asked, pushing my hair out of my face as I looked up at him.

"At Pitball practice," he said innocently, leaning back in his chair.

His toe nudged against mine under the table and I shifted my foot, knocking his back.

"Oh you mean when I wipe that smirk off your face and make you consider handing over the captain's spot to me?" I taunted.

Leon laughed and leaned further back in his chair, his foot nudging mine again and drawing a little smile to my lips as I realised it wasn't accidental.

Apparently Ryder was still ignoring me and he extended that courtesy to Leon too as he stalked away from us to gather supplies from the cupboard.

"I was thinking we should spend tonight working on our tackles," Leon said, pushing a hand through his long, blonde hair and drawing my gaze to the press of his bicep against his shirt. "You wanna be my partner?"

I tapped a finger to my chin, pretending to consider it for a long moment then shook my head. "I think I'd just embarrass you when I pin your ass to the dirt."

Leon nudged my foot beneath the table for the third time and I hooked the toe of my shoe around the back of his ankle to stop him from doing it again. My lips twitched with amusement as his toe shifted against the back of my calf and a little skitter of energy ran through me.

"I think I can take the embarrassment if it means being locked between your thighs," he replied, twisting his foot away from mine suddenly then nudging my toes again. A laugh fell from my lips and he smiled knowingly. "Although, I'm a bit bored of women doing all the work for me, so maybe I'll end up on top for a change."

"You must be terrible in bed if you just let the women do all the work," I said, rolling my eyes at him.

"Only one way to find out, little monster," he challenged, kicking me again. I probably should have just drawn my feet back beneath my chair but I couldn't help but nudge his foot with mine in response.

"I'll pass, thanks," I said airily, though I let my gaze wander to the patch of bronzed skin on show where he'd left the top three buttons of his shirt undone.

Ryder returned to the table and slammed the ingredients down while scowling at Leon. "That's your cue to fuck off," he snarled.

"I'm not done talking to Elise yet, thanks," Leon said dismissively, keeping his gaze fixed on me.

Leon reached into his pocket with a wide smile, his eyes twinkling excitedly.

"If you give her any more chocolate you're going to give her diabetes," Ryder snarled.

"This is better than chocolate. I noticed you haven't been chewing gum this week, so..." Leon placed a six pack of cherry gum down on the table between us and I couldn't help but squeal excitedly. I reached for it, pulling one of the packets out right away so that I could have a piece while Leon smiled so widely I could have counted every one of his teeth.

"Thank you," I said earnestly. The chocolate had been nice but with me having zero funds I'd been depressingly lacking in gum for way too long now and I'd come to the realisation that my habit was more of an addiction. I'd been in serious withdrawal all week and he'd just given me my own personal heroin.

"If you wanted gum so badly why didn't you just buy some from the

Kiplings yourself?" Ryder asked irritably.

I glanced at him and my cheeks flushed with embarrassment. I wasn't going to admit that I couldn't even afford some fucking chewing gum. It was mortifying and depressing and none of his goddamn business.

I shrugged, refusing to answer as I pushed a stick of gum into my mouth and turned back to Leon with a smile as sweet as the cherry taste which danced over my tongue.

I could feel Ryder's eyes still on me and I shifted uncomfortably as I scrambled for something else to say. "What made you think of the gum?" I asked Leon.

"I can't get the taste of your cherry kisses out of my head, little monster," he purred, nudging my foot again beneath the table. "And I wanted to make sure you still tasted the same when I kissed you next time."

Ryder's foot slammed between ours and he smacked a hand down onto the desk as he leaned forward with a snarl. "I'm not going to ask nicely again, Simba. Stop playing footsie with my girl and fuck off."

Leon yawned like Ryder was boring him and I bit my lip to stop myself from laughing.

"I'll see you at practice, Elise," Leon said, pushing himself to his feet. "Then maybe we can get dinner after and discuss our plays?"

"Oh." I glanced at Ryder who leaned back in his chair with his arms folded and a scowl etched so deeply into his features I wasn't sure it would ever wipe off. "Ryder, didn't you say something about dinner-"

"No," he snapped. "I eat alone. Everyone knows that."

I pursed my lips at him, leaning away as I forced aside the little stab of hurt which came with that rejection. *Okay asshole, be like that.*

"It's a date then, Leon," I said before blowing a bubble with my gum and letting it pop loudly.

He smirked at me then tossed a smug look at Ryder before dragging his chair away again.

Silence descended on us and I decided to give my focus to the task at hand, lighting the Bunsen burner and sorting through the ingredients that Ryder had gathered. I could feel his gaze boring a hole in the side of my face but I pointedly ignored his death stare.

"Seriously?" he asked eventually and I turned my eyes his way.

"What?" I questioned when he failed to explain that question.

"Leon the lion?"

I sniggered. That still cracked me up.

"He's nice," I replied. "And funny. And hot. Why do you care?"

"I don't. I just would have thought you'd go for more than *funny,*" Ryder said it like the word was dirty.

"You don't really know anything about me. And you always could have asked me to have dinner with you if that's what you wanted?" I raised an eyebrow at him.

"I didn't. I don't."

"Good."

"Fine."

Ryder snatched the moonbeam from me before I could add it to the potion and proceeded to correct every minor mistake I'd made.

By the time the lesson was over, I had one perfectly brewed Essence of Moonshine potion, a piece of gum that had lost its flavour and an air of tension you could cut with a knife.

Great.

"Come at me harder!" Dante demanded, holding his arms wide as he baited me.

My Pitball shirt was riding up again and I tugged at the material irritably, wondering when the hell Leon was gonna get me a better fitting kit. He said that there was a funding issue and it had gotten held up, but I was more than fed up of bursting out of this one. I was gonna ask Coach Mars about it at the end of the training session.

"You'll regret that," I snarled as I leaned forward, readying to rush Dante.

Pitball practice was well underway and I was enjoying the chance to vent a little bit of my frustrations while we practiced our tackles as Leon had promised. We were rotating partners and I was eagerly awaiting the next change when I'd be partnered with Harvey Bloom. There was one really good reason for me to want some one on one time with Harvey; I'd spent a bit of time on my Atlas looking into him before practice. He was the last name on the list of Killblaze dealers the Kiplings had given me and I'd finally hit the jackpot.

Harvey Bloom had multiple pictures on his FaeBook page with my brother. Apparently he didn't go in for tagging people which would have made it a hell of a lot easier for me to track down their connection sooner. But once I started looking through his photos from the last two years, I found shot after shot of him and Gareth hanging out. I also had several other faces which I needed to put names to because it looked like I'd caught onto Gareth's social group at last.

Leon blew his whistle and I leapt forward, racing towards Dante with my teeth gritted and determination driving me on. He had well over a foot on me and about a hundred pounds, but I wasn't going to let that deter me. Pitball was all about using whatever advantage you could take and though my position was offensive not defensive and I wouldn't usually need to tackle like this in a match, I wasn't going to shirk my training.

With a cry of determination, I leaned forward and slammed my shoulder straight into Dante's stomach. He instantly wrapped his arms around my waist, trying to lift me from my feet but I wasn't going down without a fight.

I threw my fist into his kidney one, two, three times until he flinched back just a little. With a growl, I twisted in his arms and swept my leg around, catching him in the backs of his knees.

It wasn't quite enough to take him down, but it unbalanced him and I sprang forward, grabbing his shoulders and throwing my weight into his chest.

Dante fell back and I went with him. I slammed my knees down on his biceps as I pressed my weight onto his chest and smirked at him.

"One, two, three-"

Dante snatched his arms out from beneath my knees, grabbed my waist and flipped me beneath him in the blink of an eye.

He laughed as he pressed me down into the sand, catching my wrists and pinning them above my head so that I couldn't use my magic against him. I didn't even bother trying to fight my way free as Mars counted down from five to zero.

Dante's huge body pressed me to the ground and I sighed, blowing a strand of lilac hair out of my eyes.

"We can practice more in my bunk later if you want to see if you can make it on top," he teased, his dark eyes glimmering with excitement. I'd quickly come to realise that Pitball was one of the few places where Dante let his mask slip entirely and just let himself have fun. Most of the players were unallied aside from him and one other Oscura gang member and it was like he just let himself forget about all that bullshit whenever he stepped onto the pitch. And I had to admit I liked it.

"Thanks," I said. "But I've had enough blood today."

"That wasn't what I was offering. What I have in mind requires us to ditch these kits and-"

"I said *five*!" Coach Mars snapped above us. "You can let her up now!"

Dante grinned as he took his sweet time climbing off of me before offering me his hand. I let him pull me to my feet then moved away from him to join Harvey Bloom.

"Hey," I said, smiling sweetly as I approached.

"Hey," he replied. We'd been training together for weeks now but between the various team members and subs and the fact that I'd been giving most of my attention to sussing out Leon and Dante during these sessions, I hadn't spoken to him much before. But now that I knew he was interesting that was all about to change.

He was tall and his copper hair fell in front of his eyes in a way that made me want to just push it back for him or demand he get a hair cut. I bet he had a mother somewhere who was blue in the face from nagging him about it. He was well built, though slimmer than the other guys and his position as Fireside meant he was in an attack position like me. Better built for speed than brute force. I actually had a shot at pinning him down if I was lucky.

"You're a Pegasus, right?" I asked as we moved to stand opposite each other.

"Yeah. What gave me away?" he teased, letting his skin sparkle for a moment with a faint blue hue.

I smiled at him. "My mom and the rest of the family are Pegasuses," I said. "I'm kinda missing the whole vibe of your kind."

"A Vampire who hungers for the warm feelies, huh?" Harvey mocked.

Coach Mars blew his whistle and I sped forward. Harvey was a much easier target than Dante had been and I managed to throw him to the ground with my first hit. I didn't intend to give him the chance to uproot me like Dante had and before he could fight back, I directed a blast of air at him, pinning him in place.

"Good job, Callisto!" Coach called as he finished the countdown and I remained on top.

I withdrew my power and offered Harvey a hand up.

"Well you've certainly got the cutthroat nature of your kind even if you're secretly craving warm hugs," he joked.

"You have no idea," I agreed, meaning the cutthroat bit though he assumed I meant the hug cravings.

"Well, there's a group of us who tend to hang out most nights. We're not all Pegasuses but my herd are the main attenders so you could get your fix of our stunning personalities if you join us," he offered casually.

"Hang out doing what?" I asked, not wanting to sound too keen.

"This and that. We chill, have a few drinks...sometimes take some other recreational mood enhancers too..." Harvey was watching me in a way that said this was a test. He was wondering if I'd blink at the suggestion of drugs, but I was a girl who'd grown up with a stripper for a mom and had lived through her brother being murdered. I wasn't going to flinch at the mention of getting high. Not that I'd be joining them in that particular pastime; I'd never felt a pull to risk my life chasing some illusionary high when I could just go out and experience something real instead.

"Sounds good," I said. "Where do you meet?"

"It varies. I'll send you a message the next time we have a gathering though. You can come down, get to know a few people aside from the Kings, find out what the normal kids do for fun around here." He smiled and it seemed pretty damn genuine. Was I currently talking to someone who had meant a lot to my brother? Had his death carved a mark on Harvey's heart too? I wished I could just ask him, tell him who I was and question him on all the things I wanted to instead of playing this damn game, but I couldn't risk it.

Instead, I thanked him for the invitation and made myself move away from him to face my next opponent as Mars blew his whistle. Harvey Bloom may have been the next piece in my puzzle but if I wanted to find out where he fit, then I was going to have to be patient. And in the meantime, I planned on digging deeper into the Black Card.

Leon moved to face me with a smirk playing around his lips and I couldn't help but smile in response.

"You're going down, Callisto," he taunted.

"You'll have to catch me first," I teased.

A slow smile spread across Leon's face as he dropped into position, ready to pounce at me. A low growl left his lips and my heart beat a little faster.

"Are you going to teach me what it's like to be hunted by a Lion?" I asked.

Leon's eyes flashed but the whistle blew before he could reply.

He sprang at me and I turned and sprinted away as fast as I could without using my gifts.

Leon's footsteps were hot on my heels as he gave chase and a spike of adrenaline flooded my limbs as I fought to escape him.

His fingers brushed the back of my shirt and I squealed as I used the tiniest touch of my Vampire speed to escape him. It didn't count as cheating so long as no one noticed. Leon laughed excitedly from way too close behind me for my liking and I threw myself away from him at speed.

I did a whole circuit of the pitch, sprinting between the other players as they stopped to watch us.

"See if you can catch her Oscura!" Mars called and I shrieked as Dante leapt after me too.

I switched direction fast and shot across the pitch towards the Pit. I didn't slow as I raced towards the edge but kept running, planting my foot on the edge of it and leaping into the air. I used a hint of my enhanced strength to make sure I got a good kick off and flew over the ten foot Pit with a whoop of triumph.

I hit the ground on the other side and rolled across the sand, shoving myself to my feet as Leon and Dante raced towards me from either side of it.

"Thirty seconds and you've won it Callisto!" Coach bellowed and I sprang to my feet as I took off again.

They were closing on me, two sets of feet thundering way too close behind me as I sprinted on. My breath was coming in harsh pants, my arms and legs were pumping but I sure as shit wasn't gonna let them catch me.

Mars blew his whistle to mark the end of the time and I whopped in triumph, twisting back to look at them and rub my win in their faces.

My eyes widened as I realised they hadn't slowed one bit and a scream escaped me half a second before they collided with me.

I hit the ground hard, rolling between a mountain of muscle as we tumbled across the sand before coming to halt in a tangle of limbs.

Leon snatched both of my wrists and pressed them into the sand on either side of me while Dante sat over my hips, immobilising me.

The breath was driven from my lungs in the collision but as soon as I caught it again, a laugh burst from my lips.

Leon grinned widely as he leaned down over me, half of his long hair spilling free of his top knot. For a moment his eyes shone with all the intensity of the sun and I couldn't help but stare as his Order form swam beneath his skin.

Dante was laughing too and he shifted forward, tackling Leon so that the two of them fell off of me as they started wrestling on the ground.

I got to my feet as Coach Mars waved us back over to the rest of the team and waited for the two of them to finish their play fight.

The dust began to rise off of the ground as Dante released a wave of static energy as he tussled with Leon and a shiver raced down my spine in response.

Mars blew his whistle impatiently and they finally stopped, getting back to their feet with wide smiles on their faces.

Leon moved straight towards me and pulled me under his arm as he turned back towards Mars. Dante growled as he moved to my other side and shoved Leon off of me before wrapping his arm around my waist.

"Get your paws off my girl," Dante joked and I rolled my eyes.

"I'm not yours," I said, feeling like a broken record.

"Yeah, asshole," Leon agreed as he moved to my other side and threw his arm around me as well. "She's mine too."

"I'm really not," I said but they both ignored me, drawing me back across the pitch to the rest of the team while both keeping hold of me.

And if I was being totally honest there were worse places in the world that a girl could find herself than caught in the arms of Leon Night and Dante Oscura.

GARETH

CHAPTER TWENTY SEVEN

SIXTEEN MONTHS BEFORE THE SOLARID METEOR SHOWER…

*T*he bell rang and I was up and out of my seat before anyone else in my class. I had one free period to do what I had to to discover Gabriel Nox's secret. He would be spending that time in Potions class and I'd be heading up to his not so secret hideaway on the roof of The Vega Dormitories.

Pretty much everyone knew that he'd claimed the roof as his own personal retreat so that he could replenish his magic with the rising sun whenever he wanted.

No one else went up there.

Ever.

Until now.

My heart thundered a panicked tune as I ran back to the Vega Dorms but I couldn't back out. Dante Oscura could give me enough money to pay off Old Sal. But Gabriel Nox was a goldmine which could change my family's lives forever if I could just tap into it. He had more money in his bank account than I might earn in my entire life.

If ever there was a chance for a new start for us, then maybe its name was Gabriel.

I made it to the dorms and ran up the stairs, taking them two at a time as I felt my hour slipping by already. I had to get up there, search his hideout and get the hell away again before the bell rang for the end of his class. Gabriel ended almost every day by shedding his shirt and blazer, freeing his wings and flying straight up there. And Harpies moved so swiftly and silently that I wouldn't even see him coming before he was on top of me, no doubt beating the shit out of me a little more thoroughly than the last time too. So I had to be long gone before then. Because if he caught me snooping into his shit for a second time then I was seriously screwed.

I made it to the top floor and ran straight to my room. Leon and my other dorm mates were in class for the next hour too so I could use the fire escape straight out of my window to get to the roof.

I opened the window and a breeze swept in around me.

My fingers trembled where I clutched the frame and I closed my eyes briefly, picturing Ella's green eyes to remind myself of why I was doing all of this insane shit. She was the risk taker in our family. I bet she'd already have run rings around this whole academy if she was here. But I was the one who had to step up when she needed me. And she needed me now more than ever. Even if I hadn't told her that. I'd thought about it. I'd thought long and hard about telling her what Old Sal wanted from her, but I hadn't done it. For two reasons. One; I didn't want her to know that Mom had actually considered selling her into that life to clear her debts. It was bad enough growing up knowing that your parent couldn't actually parent you properly without having to wonder whether she loved you at all. What kind of mom would consider pimping out her own daughter's flesh to pay her debts?

And two; a part of me which I didn't like to look at too closely was

336

afraid that Ella would just do it. Take the job for Old Sal and auction herself off to the highest bidder. Not for Mom. But for me. Because she wouldn't want me taking these risks. She wouldn't want me distracted from my studies or to allow the possibility of me making the kinds of enemies who made people pay debts in blood.

So I'd decided to lie to my sister for the first time in my life. And I felt like a sack of shit for it. But I also knew I was doing the right thing.

The metal fire escape stairs clanged a hollow tune beneath my feet as I powered my way up to the roof. One thing that had definitely paid off when Ryder Draconis stole my dorm from me was the fact that I only had to ascend one flight of stairs to the top of the building. I'd be sure to send him a thank you card and a box of dead mice once I was rich.

At the top of the stairs, I stepped out onto the flat concrete roof which Gabriel had claimed for his own personal patch of turf.

The space was wide and flat, with nothing on it barring Gabriel's tent which he'd set up on the far side. From here it looked dark and uninviting, the shadows within it promising secrets and terrors as well.

Silence reigned up here, only punctuated by the wind. A shiver raced down my spine. My heart rocked a heady tune in my chest. I took half a step back towards the fire escape.

This is insane. Gabriel has three times as much power as me on a bad day. If he catches me he'll grow a tree from the ground beneath my feet and entomb me in it for all of time, leaving only my face poking out through the bark, a look of horrified failure etched into my dead features as a warning to anyone else who might be tempted to be as stupid as me and take him on.

The wind picked up around me and I flinched as a small black shape shifted across the roof, coming straight for me. Before I could quite manage to piss my pants, the large, black feather flipped over and I harnessed the air around me as I brought it to my hand.

I twisted the Harpy feather between my fingers. It was bigger than any bird's feather, the spine thick and near unbreakable, like a rod of steel in my grip. The soft down was black but it shimmered with a rainbow of colours like a spill of oil as the sun caught it. I'd always kind of thought of Harpies as fallen angels even though I knew it was absurd. But there was something about seeing them with those giant wings that always planted that image in my mind. My little angel wouldn't have run from this challenge. And I wouldn't either.

I cast the feather away from me and strode across the rooftop to the tent Gabriel had erected for himself. It had three blue canvas walls and a roof. A fluttering noise sounding as the wind buffeted one side.

The place which should have held a fourth wall stood open, facing east so that the rays of the sunrise would spill inside it every morning and he could replenish his power just by laying there and bathing in it.

My heart was pounding so hard that the whoosh, whoosh, whoosh of it was all I could hear in my ears.

I paused just outside the tent, debating with myself one final time. But I was already here. So the arguments I wanted to present were pointless.

Most of the space inside the tent was taken up by a mound of blankets and pillows which Gabriel obviously used as a bed when he slept up here. By the head of it sat a pile of books so I moved closer to them first.

My gaze slid over the spines as I read titles on Tarot, Numerology, sooth saying, earth magic, water magic and everything else in between. It seemed Gabriel didn't just sit around up here for the sunrise. He liked to study hard too. So maybe we had one thing in common.

I closed my eyes and pulled a green crystal from my pocket which I'd liberated from the potions store cupboard. I'd have to return it before Professor Titan realised it was missing but I'd needed it to make this search easier.

A green crystal, a lock of manticore fur and a four leafed clover combined with the right spell created a powerful energy sensor. And I needed to find something that Gabriel had been holding while feeling strong emotions. It didn't matter what they were, the crystal would point me in the right direction. I just hoped I wasn't going to be drawn towards a stash of Harpy porn if the crystal got hooked on the trail of lust.

I pressed my magic into the crystal and the tuft of manticore fur I'd wrapped around it caught alight suddenly, sizzling away in an instant before the four leafed clover exploded with a small pop. A tendril of thick, green smoke rose from the crystal and instantly headed towards the stash of Gabriel's things.

As it reached the bed, the smoke split into three distinct lines, each of them heading off of their own accord. One slid beneath the blankets by the foot of the bed. The second twisted around the heaped books before forming a cloud around a small book beside his pillows. And the final tendril headed straight for the back of the tent where it gathered along the seam of the canvas in the middle of the wall.

I put the crystal back in my pocket and the smoke dispersed as if it had never been there at all.

I reached for the closest thing first, pushing my hand beneath the blankets at the foot of the bed and lifting them to get a look at what was there.

I arched an eyebrow at the half-expected dirty magazine, refraining from flipping through it. I may have wanted to learn Gabriel Nox's secrets but I didn't need a mental picture of what got him off.

I placed the blankets back down carefully, making sure I didn't disturb anything before heading for the book by his pillow next.

I licked my dry lips as a shiver of fear ran down my spine and quickly looked over my shoulder almost feeling like there were eyes on me. But I was just being paranoid; if Gabriel caught me, the first I'd know about it would be the pain of his retribution.

I whipped my Atlas from my pocket and took a quick photo of the book's position so that I could be sure to return it to its place then I picked it up.

I opened the first page and frowned at the strange words there, not making any sense of what I was reading.

The void.

"Don't look back!"

Mars under the influence of the stars.

Golden crossroads.

Three pennies.

A hand guiding me free.

Chamber in the walls.

"I love you - run!"

Death rattle.

The eyes of the devil.

"Even your memories aren't safe."

Dark eyes filled with love and sorrow.

A baby crying.

He didn't help.

Lies.

I flicked over the page and saw more and more lines of the same kind of things. Some of them were repeated multiple times. There were crude drawings too, notations and arrows linking one thing to another. As I struggled to understand what I was looking at, one line stood out to me.

I woke up screaming again. And I still don't know why.

The last word was underlined six times, the pen almost breaking through the page like he'd been infuriated when he'd scored the lines. I suddenly realised that I must have been holding Gabriel's dream diary. It was well known that he had a touch of The Sight and was gifted with visions of the future and perhaps the past as well. It was one of many reasons why what I was doing was a terrible idea. What if he saw what I was trying to do to him in a vision?

I shuddered at the thought but dismissed it again as I looked down at the ramblings in his diary. He clearly couldn't make much sense of whatever his dreams were showing him. And if his waking visions were this confusing too then I doubted he'd be able to figure out much from any of them. And I'd keep telling myself that every time I doubted this insane plan until I was safely tucked up in my dorm again.

I carefully replaced the dream diary and shifted around his bed to search the final spot.

The back wall of the tent looked completely innocent to me but as I reached towards it with my hand outstretched, a faint pressure pushed back against me, almost like it wanted me to leave.

I smirked as I detected Gabriel's magic and pushed my hand forward, ignoring the concealment spell without disarming it. It didn't contain any kind of warning system that I could sense so I just reached through it until my fingers brushed against a pocket I couldn't see.

I dipped my hand inside and a thick cardboard file grazed against my fingers.

I tugged it out quickly and flipped it open, my pulse rising.

The top page held a picture of Gabriel beside the name Gabriel Strongarm. *Beneath it was a social security number, an address somewhere in the east of Solaria and a birthday which made him a Cancer even though I was sure he was a Scorpio.*

I frowned and flipped the page to find another bio. It was almost exactly the same information again except this time Gabriel was named as Sanchez Vontora *and he was a Pisces who lived in north Solaria. A smile pulled at my lips as I realised that this was what I'd been looking for. I started taking pictures, counting off seven identities aside from Gabriel Nox.*

Who the hell is this guy?

I glanced at the time on my Atlas and my gut lurched as I realised I only had fifteen minutes to finish up and get the hell out of here before I could find myself at the hands of a seriously pissed off Harpy with ten times my power and an attitude to rival the devil on a bad day.

I stopped reading and started taking pictures faster and faster, making sure I caught a snap of every single page in the folder before hastily stuffing everything back inside.

I pushed through the illusion and found the pocket again, hiding the folder where I'd found it then scrambling upright and sprinting back across the roof.

The bell sounded to mark the end of classes for the day and my heart almost leapt out of my mouth as I tore down the fire escape.

I threw myself inside through my window and slammed it for good measure, slumping down on my bunk as my racing heart finally began to settle.

I kept my eyes on the sky through the pane and sucked in a breath as I caught a glimpse of Gabriel soaring by.

I held my breath for longer than I would have thought possible, half expecting to hear him screaming bloody murder at any moment from the rooftop, but nothing happened.

When I could finally breathe normally again, I dug under my mattress for the burner phone I'd bought on my last trip to town and powered it up. I quickly sent the pictures of Gabriel's identity to the burner and found the number for Gabriel's Atlas on the school contacts list.

My tongue was sticking to the roof of my mouth as I composed the first message I was going to send to him under the code name Faeker and let my thumb hover over the send button for a solid minute.

Once I started this, there was no backing out. But I'd already done the hard part. So now it was time for the pay-off.

Faeker:

Looks like someone's having a bout of schizophrenia.

Maybe you should see the nurse about that, Gabriel.

Now all I had to do was wait to reel him in.

Hold on little angel, I'm gonna buy you a better life.

GABRIEL

CHAPTER TWENTY EIGHT

Gabriel:

I want answers. I'm done waiting.

A predictably evasive message came in response and I grunted in fury, tempted to slam my damn Atlas into the wall.

Falling Star:

When the stars are ready, you'll get your answers.

I marched down the dark alley I'd landed in on the outskirts of Alestria. The stench of piss and rotting food hit the back of my throat and I swallowed thickly as I circled out of it to the front of the shitty bar where I was meeting Mr Fortune. Not his fucking real name, obviously.

I pulled a shirt out of my bag, tugging it on and slinging the pack over my shoulder. The Dirty Wand wasn't somewhere I wanted to spend any time. It was the sort of place dreams went to die, and every time I stepped through the doors, I felt like I needed a scalding shower to wash off the experience.

I entered through the bloodstained door and headed past worn red velvet chairs full of half-cut punters. I was tempted to hold my breath as I stalked through a maze of hookers in tight dresses and too much make-up, the smell in this place like a hobo's wet dream.

"You here for a good time, big boy?" one of them purred at me and I ignored her, moving deeper into the cesspit.

I was right in Lunar territory and their half-moon symbol with a serrated edge around the outside was stamped everywhere possible. Behind the bar, on the bar, on some fucking guy's forehead. My sleeves were rolled up, tats on show and muscles too. No one would question whether I was one of them or not which made me invisible. Besides, this place was full of has-beens and won't-haves. No one of importance.

When I'd grabbed a bottle of beer - fuck if I was gonna put my mouth on one of their glasses - I headed to a black leather booth in the far corner, finding Mr Fortune waiting for me. He was a stocky guy with a thick moustache and cold eyes. Bill Fortune was the best damn private investigator in this corner of Solaria. He was a Cyclops which meant he could draw memories right out of people's heads. And on top of that, he knew this shitty town better than most. Every shadow, every shithole, every hooker nest, and all the people who frequented each of them too.

"Mr Nox," he said with something of a smile, his voice gravelly from the fifty-a-day cigarettes he sucked on. "How are you?"

"I'll be better when I hear some good news." I dropped into the booth, casting a silencing bubble around us to ensure no one overheard us. But apart from the drunk hooker leaning on the bar ten feet away, no one else was even close. "So? Have you found out anything about her?"

Bill took out a cigarette, planting it in the corner of his mouth and lighting it with a flame he cast on the tip of his index finger. He took a long drag and released the smoke, the acrid cloud making my eyes burn. "Thing is, kid, it looks like someone worked real hard covering up the connections so-"

346

"So what you're saying is you have fuck all information for me. Again," I snarled, ice forming around the beer bottle in my grasp.

"I didn't say that," Bill mused, puffing on his smoke and letting me agonise over that while he kept me in suspense. "But I've been busy. In fact, I've been spending all of my time covering for the bullshit you pulled a few months ago."

My heart jerked uncomfortably.

"You said that was dealt with," I growled. "What am I paying you for if you can't manage the jobs I give you?"

"It is fucking sorted," Bill snapped. "But some asshole wrote another article about it last week, dragging up the past." He painted a headline banner with his hands in the air before him and said, "Aurora student who died horrifically on Killblaze said to have been in school cult."

I shifted awkwardly in my seat, guilt pinching my heart. "What did you do about it?"

"I sparked a gang war out in east Alestria. It took up everyone's attention the next day so that article was forgotten and the class picture on the front page went with it."

I blew out a breath of relief. "Good."

"You don't pay me to sit on my ass, kid. I do my job. And I do it better than anyone. Maybe if you'd controlled your temper better that day..." He puffed on his cigarette and anger burned in my chest.

"I know, alright? I just got so fucking angry. But I didn't mean for things to go that far." Hell, I really hadn't. I regretted it every day. But that night would haunt me forever.

"Well it did. So here we are," Bill said, but not judgmentally. I imagined my problems were nothing compared to the shit he dealt with on a regular basis. "Best to just leave it in the past," he added as he eyed my expression.

I wish I fucking could, but it eats me alive every day.

"So what information have you got on her?" I asked, wanting to move

347

the hell on from that particular subject. "Tell me you've got something substantial at last."

"I wouldn't say substantial. But I've got a lead."

A loud thud sounded behind me followed by a gut-wrenching scream then another and another. I twisted around in my seat, my pulse elevating as my eyes swept across the bar. The crowd was suspiciously relaxed and I realised a second too late the sound had been sent to me through The Sight.

"Fuck, get down!" I caught the back of Bill's shirt, yanking him under the table just as the door to the bar was kicked open and a flood of Oscura Clan poured in. Three of them were in Werewolf form, the first grey wolf diving on one of the men standing by the bar and ripping his throat out before anyone realised what was happening. The screams from my vision rang in my ears as a full on gang war broke out.

My heart hit a rapid pace as I tried to figure out what the fuck to do.

I knelt on the sticky floor, crawling forward. A loud bang sounded above us as a guy was thrown down onto the table and a wail rang out. His legs stopped kicking and blood oozed onto the seats. It dripped to the floor between us as his attacker darted away and I felt the heat of it soaking into my pants.

Shit shit shit.

"Here," Bill hissed, reaching into his bag and taking out a file, his cigarette somehow still lodged in the corner of his mouth. He handed it to me and I stuffed it into the back pocket of my jeans. I was tempted to fight my way out of the bar but we both knew I couldn't bring focus on myself.

"Don't be a hero, kid. Those are fully trained Fae out there, you haven't even graduated school," Bill growled, his tone making me think he gave a damn about me for a second. But that wasn't Bill. He cared about two things. Money and himself.

"Fine, I won't show my face, but what's *your* excuse asshole?" I shot at him and he gave me a dark look as another scream tore the air apart.

"I don't have a death wish, Mr Nox."

A hooker slipped in the blood right in front of us, crashing to the floor on her knees. Her eyes locked with mine just before she was hauled backwards with a shriek and my gut spiralled. I lurched out far enough to try and cast vines to help her but a spear of ice was already lodged in her chest by the man standing over her. Bill yanked me out of sight, his cigarette falling from his mouth, hissing as the cherry dropped into the puddle of blood.

The guy who'd killed her was branded on my retinas. I knew him from the papers, his reputation seriously preceding him. Felix Oscura. Dante's uncle and one of the most cutthroat Fae in the city. His body was sinewy and his eyes were empty like an abandoned house, the occupants long checked out. Psycho was the only word that sprang to mind when looking at him.

"There's a back door," Bill whispered as Felix marched past our table, stepping behind the bar.

"We can't move," I hissed back, disbanding my silencing bubble in case any of the Clan felt it. If they found us here, they'd assume we were aligned with The Brotherhood and we'd be deader than dead. I might have been a double Elemental, but I wasn't a fucking idiot. If I went out there, I'd be dripping blood before I could even try to explain I wasn't part of The Lunar Brotherhood.

"Free booze, boys!" Felix crowed and the rest of his pack howled in return, sending a bead of anxiety down my spine. "All the better to burn this place to the ground with." The sound of smashing bottles rang in my ears and a shard of glass skittered beneath the table, the scent of whiskey and blood rising under my nose.

Bill jabbed me in the leg and I glanced at him. "*Run for it,*" he mouthed.

I gritted my teeth as alcohol splashed across the floor a few paces away, screams still calling out from The Brotherhood as they died in the hands of their enemies. These were old guys and a few whores, they hadn't stood a chance against the Clan.

"Fire," I whispered to Bill and he nodded in understanding.

He threw out a hand and sparks exploded from his skin, igniting the alcohol in a blaze near the bar. Felix shouted out and that was our moment to run.

I ducked my head and darted out from under the table. Bill was hot on my heels, casting a wall of fire behind us as we ran for the back door, shouts of fury sounding as the Oscuras gave chase. The clamour of pursuit followed as we broke out into the alleyway behind the bar. We threw the door shut and I cast vines across it, sealing it as tightly as I could just before a heavy weight collided with it from the other side.

"See you next week," Bill croaked, tipping his head to me before he raced off toward the road.

I shed my shirt, clutching it in my hand as I released my wings from the barrier of my skin. The door flew open behind me but I was already in the sky, climbing and climbing as I raced for the cover of the clouds. They'd cost me my conversation with Bill. But I had the file. So as soon as I got back to the Academy, I was going to find out what information he'd dug up. And hopefully, my wait would be over.

The sounds of sirens filled the air, but I knew they'd circle the block before they stopped here. Even the cops in this town didn't get between the gangs. If they did, they ended up in pieces too.

Pain burst through my wings as shards of ice punctured my body and I cried out.

"Chicken is on the menu tonight, boys!" Felix cried as I cast a shield behind me, an idiot for not doing it sooner. The second it was in place, a torrent of ice collided with it, enough to have killed me.

Adrenaline poured through me in a heated wave and magic flooded my limbs as I tore away from the blazing bar, my wings shredded and blood oozing from multiple wounds as agony tore through my skin. But I wasn't dead, and when it came to Felix Oscura, that was nothing short of a miracle. It seemed the stars were on my side tonight, I just prayed it stayed that way because it was a long way back to the academy on broken wings.

ELISE

CHAPTER TWENTY NINE

"So." Professor Titan leaned back in his chair, rocking from side to side a little as it rotated. He surveyed me with a smile playing around his lips. Which seemed to be his permanent expression. Fuck knew what he had to be so happy about teaching a bunch of assholes like us but there it was. Maybe he was a glutton for punishment. Or maybe he really just liked educating people, even if that did mean he was caught in the middle of a gang war every other day and had to put up with little dipshits mouthing off left, right and centre.

"So?" I asked, reclining in my own chair.

Titan's almost smile became a full smile and I tried not to feel the little surge of warmth towards him. The guy was a bit of a sucker but he actually seemed to give a shit about me and I couldn't even say I hated my Liaison sessions with him. It was kinda nice to let the mask drop for a bit. I didn't have to pretend with him. I mean, I was hardly going to start talking to him about my brother or my home life or anything of any real relevance, but I never caught any judgment from him. He didn't need me to put up a front or fight to maintain my position. He was happy for me to just *be*. And this office might have been the only place in this school where I could claim that. Sharing dorms with two of my potential suspects meant I couldn't even relax fully while I slept and there was certainly no chance of it once I was wandering the corridors of the academy.

"A little birdie tells me there are bets being placed on you," Titan said, seeming a little amused, a little concerned.

"What?" I asked with a frown.

"The Kiplings are running odds on which gang you'll choose," he explained.

I sighed dramatically. "Neither. Obviously." We'd discussed the school gangs enough times that I was fairly sure he knew my stance on the idea of joining up.

"I didn't think so. There are damn good odds on you not choosing either side. Maybe I should place a bet. Do you think it would be immoral of me to use my inside information like that?"

I laughed, leaning further back in my chair. "Go for it. Do the Kiplings usually take bets from the faculty though?"

"I'm sure they could be persuaded," he replied with a grin.

"If you're gonna start offering out As to them for allowing you to place a bet, then I should get one for giving you the inside scoop," I said.

"Hmm. Maybe you're right. I probably shouldn't use my position to my advantage."

"Heaven forbid," I agreed. Though I really wouldn't mind a free pass in his class. I guessed that was a little over ambitious though even for me.

"Life as the new kid has obviously attracted a fair bit of attention your way," Titan said. "It can't be easy having the two gang leaders hawking after your attention like that all the time. You will let me know if you start to feel under threat in any way, won't you?"

Like if I start to think toying with the four guys I suspect murdered my brother might be getting too dangerous?

"I honestly think they'll get bored soon," I replied, shrugging off the risky tug of war I'd placed myself in.

Titan frowned like he didn't believe that any more than I did.

"Elise... I know that you grew up in this city and you have some understanding of the way the gangs work but..." Titan frowned like he wasn't really sure if he should go on. Or like he was afraid to. The idea of that sent a prickle down my spine. Even the teachers here didn't want to cross the gangs. He feared speaking out against them even in private just to me.

"I won't tell them you said anything," I said with a shrug. I was hardly about to run blabbing to the first gang member I met that a teacher had been a bit rude about them and get him in trouble.

Titan offered me a faint smile. "I'm only concerned at how this could end for you. Dante Oscura and Ryder Draconis are accustomed to getting anything they want. *Everything* they want. And even if this is just some power play or game to see who can bed the new girl first, you have to see that there's a chance that this could really come down hard on you."

"How so?"

"Well...let's say that you were to start falling for one of them and ended up sleeping with them. Or even kissing them. The other one would be publicly humiliated by that decision. And do you suppose either of them are the kinds of men to take humiliation well?"

I didn't miss the way he called two of his students men like he was actually intimidated by them himself. Or the way his gaze kept flicking to the door like he was afraid we might be overheard.

"Obviously not," I sighed. "But I really don't intend on picking between them anyway. Like I said, they'll probably just get bored eventually."

"Let's hope they do," Titan said. "Because it would be a real tragedy if you fell prey to their revenge tactics."

He held my eye and worry swam in his gaze for a long moment before he blinked and it was gone, banished by a benign smile.

I shifted uncomfortably. I'd never really had many people who looked out for me in my life. Gareth had been the only one I could truly rely on. My mom did her best, but it wasn't really good enough. She was only ever semi-present; one half of her mind on the men she'd once loved or the bets she wanted to place next. She dipped in and out of depression which wasn't really her fault but still kinda sucked for me. And since Gareth's death, she'd been worse than ever. I called the retreat every few days for an update on her progress, but they didn't have much to tell me. She wasn't up for talking to me yet. She wasn't really talking at all. They told her I called. They told her I loved her. And I could only hope she knew that that was true.

To find out that Professor Titan actually gave a shit about me was weirdly...nice. He didn't want anything from me or ask for anything in return. He just cared.

I gave him a genuine smile as I let myself accept that fact.

"In more exciting news..." Titan grinned as he tapped his fingers against the table like a drum roll and I found myself leaning forward to find out what he had to say. "I have your class rank ready..."

"Oh really?" I asked a little anxiously. In a class of two hundred students who had all had an academy education since their Awakening I really wasn't sure where the hell I'd rank. I didn't want it to be too low but I wasn't holding my breath. I just had to hope I wouldn't end up at the bottom with Eugene Dipper.

"We had a faculty meeting last night and Principal Greyshine signed off on this, so it's official and your new score is already on the board for everyone to see."

"For fuck's sake just tell me already!" I demanded with a grin as he drew out this torture for as long as humanly possible.

"You are currently ranking at...fourteenth!"

"What?" I asked, not even managing to conceal my disbelief at all. I mean, yeah I'd actually been doing fairly well in my classes considering how behind I was and I was definitely finding it easier to cast magic and conduct proper spell work than I had been before coming here. But fourteenth in the whole class? It didn't make sense.

"We all agreed that securing Ryder Draconis and Dante Oscura as your Sources merited a substantial boost in points. As did the fact that you've somehow found a way to dance between the two of them without falling prey to their ire. You're proving yourself to be a very powerful young Fae. And your behaviour has been an exceptional example of power claiming. It's very Fae of you."

I couldn't help but laugh at the turn of events. But he did have a point. Leon ranked well despite the fact that he didn't even do any of his work himself because his power meant others were doing it for him. And as a Vampire, the truest form of power you could display was in who you drank from. I had two of the biggest, baddest, most powerful Fae on the tap. It didn't matter if I hadn't gotten them there in the traditional way. I still held that power over them one way or another.

"Congratulations," Titan said warmly before turning to pull a book from the shelf behind his desk. "So. On to more educational matters," he said ruefully. "Let's catch you up on some of the Cardinal Magic lessons your high school skimmed."

I leaned forward eagerly as I looked down at the book he presented. The last thing I'd had on my mind when I'd hacked my way into claiming Gareth's scholarship at this school was my education, but I had to admit that I was drinking in everything I could learn in this place.

Aurora Academy may have been the lowest ranking academy in Solaria, but it felt like going from drinking piss to champagne to me. In the short time I'd been here I'd already gained more control over my Element and Cardinal powers than I had in the year and a half I'd spent at my high school. I was learning new things every day about Tarot and star alignments, auras and Orders. This place was better than I'd ever really comprehended from

Gareth's stories. And I couldn't help but lose myself in the call of it from time to time.

My mission here wasn't changing. But Gareth had always wanted a better life for me. If I managed to find whoever had killed my brother and exacted my vengeance, then maybe there was a chance that I could get away with it. No one looked into Gareth's murder properly after all. What was one more death at this academy? And if I got away with that then maybe I could leave this place with proper control over my power and a shot at claiming a better position in Solaria for myself far, far away from here.

I headed back to my room with my mind full of the lesson Titan had just given me on mental shields. I'd already had a pretty strong grasp on them before coming here, but he'd helped me tighten up my defences in a way that was specifically aimed at keeping out visions. It hadn't taken me long to realise that it had been a thinly veiled lesson on protecting myself from Basilisk hypnosis and I was glad that he'd given me a few new tricks to use even though I'd already been doing pretty well at kicking Ryder out of my head. Professor Titan might have been a bit indirect in his approach, but I couldn't help but appreciate the help.

The dorms were fairly quiet as I headed up the stairs to the top floor. It was Friday night and a lot of the students had headed out to enjoy the local bars as usual. And as usual I wouldn't be joining them. I had no money for drinks and no one I could really call a friend as such to go drinking with even if I did. Aside from Laini who didn't drink and spent her Friday nights alone in the library where she could enjoy the silence. So I had no one. That fact was actually a bit depressing. I'd given so much attention to figuring out what the hell had happened to my brother in this place that I hadn't let myself form many real bonds with any of the other students here. I guessed in a way I blamed all of them for Gareth's death. For none of them seeing something, saying something, *doing* something which might have resulted in him surviving.

I let out a breath as I tried to let some of my anger go, but I couldn't. It lived in me with every waking breath. Consuming, devouring. There wouldn't be an end to it until there was an end to the one who'd killed him. And even then I wasn't sure I'd ever be able to claim my heart was at peace again. Because a part of it would always be missing. And nothing I could do here would change that.

I pushed open the door to our dorm and found the place empty for once. It was such a novelty to have the room to myself that I quickly kicked off my shoes and loosened the top buttons of my shirt, preparing to...well I guessed to just sit on my bunk and scroll through shit on my Atlas. But I'd be doing it *alone* for once so that made all the difference.

I pushed a hand through my hair and made a move towards my bunk when a grunt of pain caught my attention.

I frowned, turning towards the window as I focused my enhanced senses on the sound and a pounding heartbeat came to my ears followed by a growled curse.

"Gabriel?" I gasped, shooting towards the window and pulling it wide.

My lips fell open as I spotted him clinging to the fire escape, his bare skin smeared with blood and his chest rising and falling heavily. He looked like he might pass out and I reached for him as panic bled through me, my own heart racing as I took in the state of him.

"What happened to you?" I breathed as I caught his hand.

He let me drag him forward into our room then almost fell on top of me as he dropped down from the windowsill.

I gripped his shoulder, using my gifted strength to support his weight as his grey eyes looked into mine.

"Don't tell anyone," he breathed, his voice a plea instead of a demand

and that alone had me nodding in agreement.

His blood slid between my fingers as I gripped his bare shoulders and I swept my eyes over him. His skin was covered in slits which oozed blood and his beautiful wings were half shredded, gaping holes stabbed through the black feathers. They glimmered wetly and when I reached out to touch the top of one of them my fingers were stained a deep red.

Gabriel hissed in pain at the contact but I didn't pull back, I pressed my hand down more firmly and directed healing magic into my palm. The spells I knew were a bit of a catch-all so I was using more power than I would have if I had more training, but I didn't care. I just needed to take this pain away from him.

Gabriel dropped his forehead to my shoulder and groaned slightly. It seemed like he might pass out on me and I forced my magic to work faster, the tug of it leaving an empty place in my chest.

I listened to the pounding of Gabriel's heartbeat as it slowed. When the wounds on his wings had healed over, I slid my hand over his shoulder and down his back, seeking out the lacerations which marred the rest of his skin so that my power could find them faster.

Gabriel's breathing evened out and he shifted his hand around my waist, drawing me closer while his head remained on my shoulder.

The well of power in me was steadily draining out until a hollow, echoing sensation resounded within me but I didn't stop until every wound on his body was healed.

My fingers started trembling as I finished, the last of my power slipping from them and into his skin.

Gabriel's breath was dancing over my collarbone and he hadn't released me despite the fact that he was healed now.

I swallowed a lump in my throat, remembering the last time I'd gotten this close to him with a surge of heat that ran through my body.

I didn't know what to make of Gabriel. Most of the time he was so cold and distant. It was impossible to feel like I knew him even at all. But in that moment it felt like our souls were reaching out to each other. Both of us stood there, stripped of our power, silence echoing around us, not making a single move to back away.

"You just used all of your power to help me," Gabriel breathed, his lips brushing against my neck.

"I couldn't leave you in pain like that."

His arm tightened around my waist and I arched my back in response.

"Why not?" he asked.

"I..." I frowned at that because I didn't really have an answer for him. Maybe I should have just let him suffer. He certainly hadn't done anything to earn my loyalty, let alone my help. But seeing him like that had hurt me too and I didn't know why, but helping him hadn't felt like an option. It was just something I'd had to do. Maybe that made me an idiot because I still couldn't be entirely sure that he hadn't been involved in Gareth's death but in the moment that idea hadn't even occurred to me.

"What happened to you?" I asked again instead of replying.

Gabriel was silent a long time and I pulled back an inch, presuming I wasn't going to get any answers but his grip on me tightened, keeping me in place.

"I was out in the city having a drink with a friend in Lunar Territory," he said slowly. "Felix Oscura came in with his pack-"

I inhaled sharply. Felix Oscura was the most infamous member of their Clan. He was their leader ever since his brother Micah, Dante's father, had been killed. His reputation was brutal. I'd read more stories about the horrors he and his pack had been responsible for than I could even count. He was a butcher. A tyrant. A maniac. And there was only one reason why he would show up in Lunar Territory.

"How did you escape?" I asked, fear flickering through me.

"I had a vision. I managed to hide and then I ran for it. They spotted me before I could get far enough away but I doubt they'd recognise me. Besides, I'm not going to be talking to the FIB and I'm not a member of The Brotherhood so hopefully they'll just forget about me."

"That's a lot of hope to put on the actions of a psychopath," I said, drawing back so that he was forced to lift his head and look down at me. "What if they come for you to cover their tracks?"

Gabriel's lips twitched like he found me amusing. "Well then maybe you can offer me an alibi if Dante asks where I was."

"You want me to tell him you were here?" I asked, a faint frown pulling at my brow. Would I do that for him? If the Oscuras found out I'd lied to protect him they'd come for me too. But if he really had just been unlucky, caught out in the wrong place at the wrong time then could I really let them come after him if I could offer a simple lie to protect him?

Gabriel rolled his shoulders back and his wings retreated, glimmering out of existence as he shifted back into his Fae form.

"No," he said slowly. "I wouldn't really ask you to lie to the gangs for me."

I looked up into his stormy eyes and my heart began to beat faster for a whole other reason. We hadn't been alone together since that night on the roof and suddenly it was all I could think about. Heat prickled along my skin and I bit my lip as I tried to shift my mind onto something else.

"Thank you," Gabriel said as I failed to come up with anything else to say. "For helping me."

"You owe me one," I teased.

Gabriel smiled darkly as he looked down at me and I couldn't help but imagine a few ways that he could show his appreciation.

As if his mind was heading in the same direction, his gaze slipped to my mouth and my breathing hitched in response.

"I'm sorry," he breathed. "For all the things I've done to try and keep you away from me."

"You've been an asshole," I agreed.

"Can you forgive me?"

"No," I replied though I was pretty sure that was a lie.

"We should stop," he said, drawing closer.

"Okay," I agreed, not moving an inch.

He reached out and caught my jaw in his grip, tilting my chin up as his mouth sought mine out.

I melted against him, every sensible thought tumbling from my skull and blowing away into a corner of the room as my body took full control of my actions. I should have hated him for the way he'd treated me. I did hate him. I *hated* him. But somehow I wanted him too. Just for now, not forever. But for a little while maybe I could just forget and let my body have what it wanted…

I fell into his kiss, his tongue teasing my lips apart and pressing against mine as I gasped in desire.

Gabriel's other hand skimmed the hem of my skirt, his fingers roaming across the bare skin of my thigh and making heat pool in my core.

My heart was pounding to a relentless pace, my lips tingling as he kissed me harder and my fingers twisted into his midnight hair.

Gabriel's hand shifted higher beneath my skirt and I moved back a step, pulling him with me towards my bunk.

His kisses lit a fire within me that wouldn't be put out. I needed more of him. All of him. I didn't understand this pull I felt towards him and I didn't want to believe his crazy theory about him being my mate, but with his hands on my skin it was impossible to deny the power he held over me.

"You told me to stay away from you," I breathed against his lips.

"I was wrong," he replied. "I wanted to keep you safe from me. Away from me…"

"And now?" I demanded. His hand was moving higher and higher with every passing heartbeat, carving a line of sin beneath my skirt and up my thigh.

"Now I want you closer," he admitted. "Even though I know I'm being selfish."

Gabriel pressed himself against me and my heart thundered as I felt the keen bulge beneath his jeans.

My insides were drowning in a torrent of pure need and I wouldn't be able to come up for air until I'd claimed him for my own entirely.

Raucous laughter sounded from the corridor and a spike of fear darted down my spine as I recognised the voice drawing closer to our door.

"Dante," I breathed, breaking our kiss.

"What?" Gabriel growled, a frown spilling through the lust on his features.

"In the corridor," I explained, heat finding my cheeks as I realised he'd thought I was saying Dante's name out of desire.

"Oh," he said, his gaze flipping to the door then back to me.

A growl escaped him and he pressed forward, kissing me again and making my pulse race.

My hands slid down the hard planes of his bare chest and a faint tingling buzzed beneath my palm as I swept it over the Libra tattoo which was etched above his heart.

Gabriel drew back, looking down at his chest like he could feel it too. He met my eye and a question hung between us as my star sign continued to throb on his skin. Was there any chance his vision had been true? Was I looking at the man the stars had chosen for me?

Dante's voice sounded loudly right outside the door and Gabriel shot away from me with the swift speed of his Order.

"I need to sleep on the roof to claim the power of the sunrise in the morning," he said in a low voice as he made it to the window. I vaguely remembered learning that Harpies replenished their power from the rays of the rising sun, so I guessed that was what he needed to get his magic back.

Gabriel hesitated with his hand on the window frame and I wondered if he was going to ask me to come with him. And why the hell I wanted that so much.

"Gabriel," I breathed, not even sure what I was going to say.

His gaze pinned me in place but before I could get any more words out, the door swung open and Dante strolled into the room.

Gabriel cast a glower his way then leapt out of the window.

Dante raised his eyebrows and his gaze swerved to me. He took in the flushed appearance of my cheeks, my messy hair and swollen lips and his eyes narrowed slightly.

"What did I just walk in on?" he asked slowly, his voice dark.

"I'm out of power," I replied, my gaze dropping from his eyes to his throat.

"And you tried your luck with Gabriel?" Dante laughed and stalked towards me.

"My Sources were nowhere to be seen," I said innocently as my heart beat faster again.

Some wild part of me was aching for him too and I couldn't help but wonder if I was playing with fire by shifting my attention back and forth between all four Kings of this school. I wasn't sure if my obsession with them stemmed from my desire to seek justice for Gareth or if I was just falling under their spells. No amount of attraction or chemistry would divert me from my goal though. I refused to be blinded by them no matter what happened. They were cruel and wicked beasts and I wasn't going to lose my head over them. But I could look. And maybe touch...just a little.

Dante kept coming for me, a smile playing around his lips as he bared his throat.

My power was so empty that I didn't even hesitate before shooting forward and biting into his neck.

The power of a thunderstorm roared into my core and static energy raced across my flesh, lining my skin with goosebumps.

I moaned in satisfaction as I drew his power into me and Dante pulled me closer, his strong arms encircling me.

The door opened and closed again as Laini appeared and she tutted loudly, waiting for us to move out of the middle of the room so that she could get to her bed.

I forced myself to draw back, my fangs retracting as I swallowed the last mouthful of Dante's blood.

His eyes were hooded, his hands lingering on my waist, but I forced myself to back up.

I leapt up onto my bunk and turned my back on the room without saying a word.

My heart was racing and I was more than a little drunk on Dante's power.

I wasn't sure what the hell was going on with me. I needed to get close to the Kings, but I was beginning to worry that I was letting them get too close to me in return. And I couldn't let that happen. Because if they started to see too much of me, they might figure out who I really was and why I was really here. And I could find myself at the mercy of my brother's killer before I'd even figured out who he was.

LEON

CHAPTER THIRTY

I trailed toward the Empyrean Fields for Combat Class, stretching my arms above my head as I made it to Voyant Sports Hall to get changed. I headed through to the men's locker room, slinging my kit bag onto a bench at the heart of the space. There was no one there because I was late. Duh.

I opened my locker, stripping down and changing into my Combat kit; black sweatpants and a shirt with the Aurora Academy crest on the breast. I stuffed my bag into the locker then reached into the pocket with a smile pulling at my lips.

While the cat's away...

I pulled out my skeleton key which could unlock any door in this entire school, lockers included. It was made from actual bone and was enchanted with the kind of dark magic I'd be locked up in prison for if it was ever discovered. It had been passed down to me from my great grandpa and was the most prized possession I owned.

I moved strategically along the aisles, opening lockers and checking coat pockets, skimming off a few aura notes here and there. The best thieves didn't draw attention to themselves. And in this school, I couldn't rock the boat. So I took a little, never enough to get noticed. That wasn't the only reason I was searching bags though. There was something specific I was looking for. Something that would get me in serious shit if it ever got linked back to me. And I knew for a fact someone in my class had taken it. But so far, I was yet to find it.

When I'd hunted every locker and come up empty handed – apart from the wedge of cash now stashed in my bag - I headed to Dante's locker and smirked as I pulled it open. I wouldn't steal from my friend, but I *did* like to fuck with him.

I rummaged through his bag, finding his Atlas and chuckling as I opened up FaeBook. I left him a status with a grin on my face. He'd know I'd done it, but we always ribbed on each other. He'd go full Storm Dragon when he saw it then be laughing about it by dinner. That was how we rolled.

Dante Oscura:

The stars are not in my favour today. First I shit my pants in front of Professor Mars (like legit down the leg) and THEN while cleaning it up, I managed to flick it into my eye – and mouth! Cures for pink eye needed.

I barked a laugh, stuffing his Atlas away as the pings of comments came ringing in like music to my ears. I shut the locker and turned back to mine on the opposite side of the room to put my key back away, but my gaze snagged on a piece of paper on the floor. I frowned, cursing as I headed over to it, realising I must have knocked it out of someone's locker. It was fucking amateur. My parents would be pissed as hell.

I scooped it up with a sigh, turning it over and stilling as I gazed across it. In the top corner the initials *E.C* had been scrawled and a weird ass list followed beneath it.

Alternates between Lunar/Oscura breakfast times. Route: Vega Dorms >
Devil's Hill > Acrux Courtyard > Cafaeteria
Girl's bathroom. Altair Halls before lunch.
L/T Devil's Hill.
Kipling Emporium. Orange soda.
W/E stays on campus. Library pm (Sundays after dark)

What the hell was this? I was half tempted to leave it on the floor but my eyes trailed over those initials again. *E.C.*

I reread the list and my heart beat harder as I put two and two together. I heard someone coming and hurried to my locker, opening it and shoving the page into my bag.

"Night!" Professor Mars barked as he strode into the locker room. "Detention! You've missed nearly half my lesson you little shit."

"It's my Order, sir," I said, shutting my locker and turning to him with a shrug. "I can't be blamed."

"Yeah, well *my* Order makes me wanna rip your head off with my bare hands, but actions have consequences. Detention. Thursday. If you're late I'll extend it to the end of the month. Now get to class."

I sighed, heading past him onto the field. I glanced over my shoulder but he wasn't following me so I upped my pace to a jog, diving on Dante. He'd been paired with Eugene Dipper who'd been knocked on his ass so hard that it didn't look like he was getting up any time soon.

Dante clapped my shoulder and I steered him away from the possibly dead Dipper on the floor. He groaned as we went so my conscience was clear. "How's it going, man? Get that shit out of your eye?" I taunted and he frowned at me like I'd lost my mind.

"What?"

"Ah nothing." I hid a grin.

Dante was staring at something and I lifted my chin to figure out what.

Elise was battling with a Mindy, looking like a warrior as she flipped through the air with her Vampire speed and blasted Mindy to the ground. I grinned stupidly, moving forward but found Dante doing the same.

We caught each other's eye and both frowned.

"You still taking her to the ball?" Dante asked, not bothering to hide his irritation about that.

"Yep," I said simply. "She's mine, dude. Let it go. There's plenty more hot chicks in the sea."

"Not like her," he grunted and I silently agreed with that. Elise was so beyond Mindy status she was practically an anti-Mindy. And it reminded me of what Gareth had said to me once.

"Do you ever think you might want a girl who doesn't fall at your feet the second you look at her?"

I hadn't understood that before, I was kinda getting it now though.

The thought of Gareth sent my gut spiralling and I turned to Dante, raising my hands to fight him and distract myself at the same time. The night of the Solarid Meteor Shower still haunted me. I'd thought I could handle it. But it clung to me every day.

I cast fire in my palms just as Professor Mars reappeared from the locker rooms probably post shit. He knelt down beside Eugene, healing him with an impatient look on his face.

"St-storm...Dragon," Eugene groaned.

"Yes yes, he's quite a bit stronger than you, kiddo." Mars clapped him on the shoulder. "Up you get."

Electrical energy crackled along Dante's body, a grin playing around his mouth. I was just about to blast my friend to the ground when, Mars called, "SWAP PAIRS!"

"But we *just* paired, sir," I complained, fire burning in my palms ready to unleash on Dante.

Mars shot me a glare that warned of those extra detentions and I turned to Dante to share my rage, but found him gone. He was striding toward Elise with intention and I spotted Ryder marching toward her from the other side. Mars clearly wasn't bothering to decide who we were going to match with today and fuck if I was going to get stuck with Eugene.

I glared after Dante, knowing I wouldn't catch him, instead cupping my hands around my mouth and shouting. "Elise! Wanna pair with me?"

She glanced my way, seeming relieved as she hurried out of the gap Ryder and Dante had been closing, zipping to my side in a blur. Dante looked back over his shoulder in outrage and Elise saluted him. My brows pinched together at the sight, fiercely reminded of Gareth.

She turned to me with a smile which fell away as soon as she saw my expression. "What?"

"You just…reminded me of someone for a sec." I ran a hand down the back of my neck, suddenly too hot.

She looked at me for a long moment then shrugged. "Who?"

"Just an old friend," I muttered. "Come on let's fight, little monster."

"What no stupid pun? No 'you're gonna go down hard and fast, Elise'." She did a stupid impression of my voice, drawing a small smile from me, but I schooled it again, shaking my head.

She nudged my foot with her toe, tilting her head to one side and giving me the cutest damn expression I'd ever seen on a girl. Or maybe I was just a little bit smitten.

"Nope," I persisted, happy that I was finally getting a reaction out of her for once.

She prodded me in the chest next and I battled my grin, keeping my face flat which she seemed to take as a challenge. She threw out her palms, uprooting me with a whip of air which I didn't even bother to try and shield myself from. I landed on my back at her feet, my lips firmly pressed together.

She dropped down to her knees, pushing her hands under my arms and starting to tickle me. I burst out laughing, losing my cool entirely as she continued her assault. I didn't fight her off though. This was the most attention she'd given me since we'd kissed. Even when she took her tickly damn fingers to my sides and I convulsed beneath her, I didn't cave and touch her back.

She knelt over me, pinning my wrists into the grass and I had to admit I really liked being at her mercy.

"Fight back," she purred and I shook my head with a teasing grin.

"If this is what losing to you is like, I might have to do it more often." She lay flat on me and her tits pressed into my chest, making my grin widen. A veil of lilac hair fell around us and I was so tempted to grab hold of her that it nearly gave me an eye twitch. Elise clearly liked doing things on her terms though and all the while I wasn't touching her, she was still here.

"Are you looking forward to the ball next week, little monster?" I whispered just for her ears.

She shrugged and I chuckled.

"Do you have a dress yet?" I asked and something cracked in her gaze.

"Oh um…no." She chewed her lip.

"Tick tock." I grinned. "If you don't hurry you'll have to go naked."

"Or in my sweats," she teased.

"Mmm tell me more," I played along.

"They're gonna be *so* baggy."

"Fuuuck," I groaned, pretending to get off on it. "More."

"They'll be grey…stained with ketchup and so, so-" She dipped her head, her mouth mere centimetres from mine. "*Threadbare*."

"Mr Night, Miss Callisto, are we at a sex party?" Mars roared and Elise rolled her eyes, rising to her feet and offering me a hand. I let her pull me up and she realised a second too late she'd done something for me.

"Thanks Mindy," I said under my breath and she punched my arm.

Ryder and Dante were giving us glares which could have burned the school to the ground. And I gave how many shits? Not one.

"Fight properly or I will re-pair you!" Mars demanded and we both

374

nodded, stepping away from each other and sharing an eye-fuck which resounded right through to my dick.

"Okay, little monster, I'm gonna go easy on-"

She blasted me with a shot of air which sent me flying across the field and I took out three of our classmates. I started laughing as two Mindys ran to help me up and I pressed my knee to a guy's chest beneath me, causing him to squeak in pain.

"Oh, hi Eugene," I said brightly and he groaned as I jumped off of him.

I charged away, casting fire in my hands and creating a huge wall before her as a distraction.

While she battled to suck the air from the fire flaring from the ground, I charged around the side of it and hooked my arm around her waist. She laughed as I dragged her back against me, shifting toward the wall of fire so she had nowhere to run.

"I win," I growled.

"We're mid-game, Leo." She rammed her elbow into my gut and I wheezed as she darted away from me with her Vampire speed. She kicked me in the ass and I lurched toward my own fire, extinguishing it before I burnt my eyebrows off.

I turned to her with a wide smile, opening my arms and feigning surrender. "Let's call it a truce. We can seal it with a kiss?"

She walked closer, batting her lashes and I smiled as she approached, her hips swaying and her hair blowing in the breeze. She looked like the result of an assassin mating with a bunny rabbit. It was so fucking hot.

She reached up, tangling her hand in my hair, but I was just baiting her, waiting for my chance to strike. I was too irresistible for my own damn good, and Elise was finally giving in to my Lion aura.

I grabbed her wrist, hooking my leg around the back of hers to drop her to the ground, but her knee came up between my legs so fast, I wasn't fucking prepared.

"Mon-ster," I croaked as I dropped to the ground, cupping my manhood as tears pinched my eyes.

"Very good, Miss Callisto," Mars called to her as Dante's laughter crashed against my ears. "Ten rank points to you."

Elise dropped to her knees before me, her hand slipping down under mine to rub my junk. It was the bitterest, sweetest thing I'd ever experienced and made me choke on my own tongue.

"Poor baby," she purred, mischief in her eyes. With the way we were angled toward each other, I didn't think anyone could see what she was doing, but fuck if I cared anyway.

She laughed cheekily, standing up and I stared after her, lost for words. *What the fuck just happened? Did I just enjoy getting kicked in the nuts?*

It was so on between us. Sure, maybe I was gonna be beaten to a pulp by that chick, but I reckoned I was gonna get laid soon too. So I was definitely game.

I couldn't wait for the night of the ball. Me and her. One on one. Without Dante and Ryder trying to make my head explode with their glares. Yep. It was gonna be the best night ever for more reasons than one. Because I had something planned which Elise was never gonna see coming.

ELISE

CHAPTER THIRTY ONE

I headed out of my dorm and down to Devil's Hill with my mind on the Black Card. It was infuriating. I couldn't get close to any of them and I'd had to stop trying because it was obvious my attempts hadn't gone unnoticed.

I'd gone back down to check out the room with the altar where I'd watched Daniel being initiated and searched it thoroughly, but there was nothing there. Just an empty stone chamber with dust in the corners. It looked like there wasn't anything special about it when it wasn't in use. I hadn't sensed any lingering magic or found any more marks scrawled on the walls. Nothing that related to anything in Gareth's journal. It was just another dead end.

Daniel himself was another mystery. He'd retreated completely, saying little or nothing if I saw him around school, having zero interest in continuing the small friendship we'd begun to strike up. He wasn't even hanging out with Laini anymore. It was damn weird. Like he had no time for anyone outside of the cult now.

He started sitting with a girl called Astrid who I'd long since marked as a Black Card member during breaks and in the cafaeteria and though I never saw the two of them talking to each other, they didn't talk to anyone else either.

I wanted to know if it was something to do with the cult rules or more to do with whatever the hell that magic was he'd been exposed to. Was it brain washing of the magical variety? Or just plain old fashioned cult insanity?

I couldn't imagine my carefree brother behaving like that. I couldn't imagine him joining the cult full stop. But I knew he had. And I just couldn't figure out why. There had to be something about them. Some draw or magic or promise they made which lured people in. But so far, I was coming up with a whole lot of nothing and it pissed me off something chronic.

I pushed a piece of cherry gum between my lips and started chewing just before I arrived at the sweeping lawn of Devil's Hill.

Spring was having its way today and the sky was a clear, bright blue despite the chill to the air. I closed my eyes for a moment, turning my face to the sun and drinking it in. Summer was coming. And I couldn't wait to enjoy the warmer weather. I just hoped I could figure out some of Gareth's secrets before the academy broke up for the season. Though I still had plenty of time yet.

I looked out over the courtyard and noticed Ryder talking to Kipling Senior a little way from their emporium where the other two brothers continued to serve the masses. Senior was nodding in agreement to something and his eyes shifted over Ryder's shoulder, landing on me in a way that seemed deliberate. He inclined his head my way and Ryder turned his dark green eyes on me too.

I held his gaze and blew a bubble, letting it pop with a loud snap. I got the impression the action irritated the hell out of him and for some reason it only made me do it more often. Maybe I had a death wish. Or maybe something had shattered inside me when Gareth had been killed and I was left with a void in my chest where fear should have lived.

Ryder stalked away from Kipling Senior and headed back towards his usual spot on the bleachers. He held a protein shake in his hand which he opened and drained in one go before crushing the can in his fist. He tossed the can into the trash several feet away, making the shot look as easy as breathing. I was about to turn away from him when he raised a hand and beckoned me over.

I pursed my lips, objecting to being summoned like a dog and the corner of his mouth twitched with something which seemed a hell of a lot like amusement. Which shouldn't have been possible for Ryder Draconis unless someone was bleeding at his feet. But there it was.

I rolled my eyes dramatically to let him know what I thought of being beckoned then wandered closer. I didn't hurry; I certainly wasn't going to go running.

When I made it to the centre of no man's land where the unallied students were allowed to pass, I stopped, waiting for him to close the rest of the distance between us.

Ryder's eyes glimmered with dark promises and he beckoned again.

I frowned, looking over my shoulder to where Dante held court with the Oscura Clan on the picnic benches. He hadn't noticed me yet, his attention held by the clamouring of his wolf pack as they fooled around but he'd sure as shit notice if I crossed over onto Lunar Turf.

I looked back at Ryder, shaking my head and he caught my gaze, tugging me into one of his visions.

I was straddling him on the bleachers, his fingers biting into my waist as he dragged me closer and I bit into his neck, the bliss of his blood sliding over my tongue and filling my magic with his dark power.

"Now or never, new girl," his voice was a command and a challenge all in one.

I blinked and the vision was gone but my fangs snapped out as the desire remained.

That almost smile was back on his face and he tipped his head to the side, giving me a clear view of exactly what I needed as he bared his throat to me.

Fuck it.

I spat my gum out as I shot forward and was on him in less than a second. I wasn't going to fulfil his little fantasy though and as I reached him, I used my Vampire strength to yank him out of his seat. In the blink of an eye, I threw him around the end of the bleachers and shoved him against the wooden side of the raised seats, not bothering to be gentle. He was always looking for pain anyway.

I caught his jaw in my grip and shoved his head aside before biting the opposite side of his neck to the one he'd offered me as I drove him back against the bleachers.

I had to stand on my tiptoes to reach but it was worth it. I was a predator and my food wasn't going to tell me how to eat.

My teeth pierced his skin and he groaned in a way that made me think he might even be enjoying this as much as I was.

I snarled at him and sucked harder, being rougher with him than I usually would have been but he only caught my waist and dragged me closer, urging me to do my worst.

His blood was thick with a power so dark and tempting that I was sure I could lose myself in it without even trying. It was icy cold and tasted like the best frozen yoghurt I'd ever had.

A moan of ecstasy escaped me and Ryder's hand slid around my back, gripping my ass. I caught his wrist with a snarl and slammed it against the wall by his head. If he was going to be my Source then he'd do it on my terms which meant no pawing at me while I ate. At least not in public...

When I finally pulled back, Ryder was looking at me triumphantly. Fire burning in his gaze as his heart thumped hard against my chest where it was pressed to his.

I took a steadying breath and licked the blood from my lips. He followed the motion hungrily and I stepped back despite the ache I felt to stay there.

"You still think I taste sweet?" he teased.

"Like cherry pie," I agreed, smirking just a little.

"Elise!" Dante barked and I looked around suddenly. The whole of Oscura Clan were on their feet, their eyes on me standing on Lunar Turf with Ryder's hand lingering on my waist.

I bit my lip as I felt the tension coiling in the air. Why the hell did the two of them put so much importance on me? And why the fuck did I like it so much?

My skin heated as danger coiled through the air and I flipped my gaze back up to Ryder's.

"Thanks for the snack," I teased, smiling at him for a moment before I shot away.

I wasn't sure if I was insane or if this was going to work but it was the only idea I had.

I came to a halt, perched on the picnic bench right in front of Dante's usual spot. He'd brought his meal out here to eat and I reached out and snagged his fancy ass golden chalice. He turned around to look at me, adjusting to the fact that I was now sitting firmly in his territory instead of his enemy's.

"What the fuck are you playing at?" Dante growled, electricity crackling in the air. His wolf pack circled closer and I didn't miss the fact that I was being penned in.

Tabitha actually snarled at me, leaning around Dante to get a better look at me.

My heart beat a little faster but I kept my gaze locked on Dante's as I took a long drink from his chalice, the sharp tang of beer rolling over my tongue.

Several pack members actually gasped like I'd just done something completely outrageous but I didn't spare them any attention, swirling the drink in my hand as I watched a storm brewing in Dante's gaze.

I licked my lips slowly and he frowned like he couldn't quite decide what to do with me.

"Now you've both fed me on your pretty little turfs," I said. "So it's even. Right?"

Dante watched me take another sip of his drink then released half a laugh which instantly made the wolves back off. He dropped into his chair and looked up at me as I sat above him on the table, swinging my legs.

"And now that you can see Oscura have it better, you can feel free to stay. Permanently," he said in a deep voice.

"Tempting..." I said, pretending to consider it though we both knew I wasn't. I drank the last of the beer in his fancy cup and started spinning it between my fingers.

"Do you need more convincing?" Dante caught my knee in his grip and tugged me closer to his side of the table, making my skirt ride up as he moved me.

I looked down at his hand on my leg, heat driving its way beneath my skin for a moment before I laughed.

"No thanks." I tossed the empty chalice to him and was gone before he caught it.

I made it to the tree at the centre of Devil's Hill and looked around to find both Ryder and Dante staring at me. I was playing one hell of a dangerous game with the two of them and I couldn't help but question my sanity. But I had to do it. I had to keep finding ways to get closer to them. And if that meant I had to let them keep up this power play over me too then so be it.

No matter how hard they tried to draw me in, I wouldn't forget what they were. Or what they might be.

My Atlas pinged and I pulled it from my pocket, eyeing the message with a smirk.

Harvey:

A bunch of us are going to hang out in The Iron Wood later. I'm gonna get blazed now though, if you wanna join?

I did not wanna join. I'd sooner cut my own heart out than take a hit of the drug which had killed my brother, but I sure as shit didn't mind hanging out with Harvey while he was jacked up on it. Killblaze made people hallucinate and blather all kinds of things they might not divulge under normal circumstances. With the right amount of prodding, I might just be able to get some information out of him.

Elise:

I'll join you. Where?

The moment his reply popped up, I shot away to meet him, leaving the gang Kings to themselves on the courtyard.

Using my Vampire gifts could be tiring so I didn't do it all the time but sometimes I just loved to run with the speed of the wind. I sped around the side of the dorm building and came to a halt by the same old storage shed where I'd found the gas can for my flaming penis trick on the Empyrean Fields. They called this place The Dead Shed and I hoped that was just because it was a quirky name and not because someone had actually died here.

The teachers still hadn't managed to make the grass grow back up on the fields yet and my masterpiece remained on show for the whole school. Rumours were flying all over FaeBook as people speculated about who had done it, though so far my infamy hadn't been exposed. I wouldn't be telling people either; Professor Mars was still out for blood and if there was one scary fucker on the faculty then it was him. His detentions were legendarily awful and I had no intention of joining one of them.

I leaned against the shed and smiled as Harvey blinked at me in surprise from his perch on the steps at the back of the building.

"Shiiit. One second you weren't there and then poof. Like a goddamn ghost you appear!" He started laughing hysterically and I cast my eyes over the empty test tube beside him. It looked like he'd already had his hit of Killblaze and was feeling the effects.

"Like a goddamn ghost," I agreed, my smile darkening.

"You wanna take a hit, babe?" Harvey asked, sagging back against the steps as he tipped his head to the sky and exhaled slowly.

Babe? That little nickname didn't slip out pre high.

"Not really my scene," I said slowly. "But we can still hang out while you're buzzing. Why don't you tell me about yourself?"

"Myself? You wanna know how high I can jump?" he asked excitedly, springing up.

His eyes were full blown and he stumbled before righting himself with a lazy smile on his face. I smiled too, encouraging him to do whatever he wanted.

Harvey bent his knees and started pumping his arms back and forth before leaping forward off of the step. To give him credit, he jumped pretty damn far. It just went to shit when he fell flat on his face and a sickening crunch came from his nose.

Harvey was laughing uncontrollably as he lay face down in a puddle of his own blood and I cursed as I moved forward, rolling him over with the toe of my shoe.

He flopped onto his back and groaned in pain from his shattered nose then started laughing again.

"Did you see me go splat? I bet you're less interested in boning me now."

"I couldn't really have been any less interested in that than I was to start off with," I muttered.

"Huh?"

"Let me fix your face." I bent down and caught his fingers between mine, pressing healing magic into his skin. It would have been quicker if I just touched his nose but I didn't want a drop of his tainted blood on me. I'd never been a messy eater when I drank from my victims and I didn't want bloodstains on my clothes from an addict either.

Harvey grinned broadly, his skin sparkling as his Pegasus Order form hummed beneath his skin and his nose realigned itself.

I drew back once he was healed and he sat up, pulling another test tube from his pocket. This one was still filled with the vibrant blue Killblaze crystals and I eyed it warily. Who'd think such an innocent looking thing could have stolen my brother from me?

"Sure you don't want a hit?" he asked as he started shaking it, aggravating the crystals locked inside until they started breaking apart, becoming nothing more than sapphire smoke locked within the glass chamber.

"Not really my thing," I said, backing up a few steps before he popped the lid. I did *not* wanna inhale any of that poison.

Harvey smiled widely as he brought the test tube up to his nose and flicked the top off before jamming it into his nostril. He inhaled deeply and I stepped back again, my skin prickling uncomfortably as a shudder ran through me.

Harvey's face split into a mask of utter ecstasy and he dropped back onto the concrete, smiling up at the clouds as he groaned in pleasure.

His shoulders started twitching followed by his arms and legs. I gasped as the convulsions tore through his body, backing up again as I half considered running for the school nurse. Had he just taken too much? Was I about to watch him die just like my brother had?

He was still smiling. Did he even know his body was struggling? Was he even aware of any pain?

The hole in my heart throbbed violently as I stood transfixed while Harvey grinned at the sky, his eyes alight with joy.

Had Gareth felt like that? Was he happy in the end? Had the drug stolen his ability to understand what was happening to him? Or had he been afraid? Had some part of him known what was happening? That he was leaving me and Mom and everyone he'd ever known, never to fulfil any of the dreams he'd always had.

I couldn't breathe. There was air caught in my chest and I couldn't let it go as tears burned the backs of my eyes.

For a moment I wasn't even looking at Harvey lying on the ground. It was Gareth. And he wasn't smiling, he was screaming, begging me to save him. But I couldn't. I wasn't there. I hadn't even known he was in trouble-

Harvey's laughter cut through my waking nightmare and I exhaled in a rush. This pain wasn't going to rule me. Ryder might have been one screwed up son of a bitch, but he had one thing right about this pain. It was a part of me. I owned it. It didn't own me. And I was going to use it to do whatever the hell I had to to avenge my brother.

"Aren't you afraid that stuff will kill you?" I asked, any pretence of friendship flooding from my voice and leaving it cold and hard. But I didn't care. Harvey was shit-faced and his mind held the answers I wanted.

He only laughed in response.

"Hey!" I snapped my fingers at him to make his bloodshot eyes swivel my way. "I'm asking you a question. Aren't you worried you'll die like your friend did?"

"Gareth?" he asked slowly, licking his lips like they were parched. "How do you know about him?"

"People talk," I said, not bothering with a better explanation.

"And what do they say?" Harvey pushed himself up onto his knees and blinked at me. He was surprisingly lucid for someone who had taken two hits of that shit and I could only imagine that he was a seasoned addict. Maybe he wasn't as pliable as I'd thought.

"Where do you even get it from?" I asked, changing tact. "How do you know it's not laced with all kinds of crap?"

"This shit is pure," Harvey said adamantly, throwing his arms out to his sides. "Are you too hot? I'm too hot."

He stood and started pulling at his shirt, unhooking the buttons but I wasn't in the mood to watch him prance about naked on a high.

I shot towards him, catching his shirt in my fist and slamming him back against the shed. "I asked where you get it from," I growled.

Harvey's eyes widened and he just stared at me for a long moment.

"You got a death wish asking questions like that?" he breathed and the bitter tang of the drug washed from his breath over my nose.

I recoiled a little but didn't loosen my grip.

"I'm already dead anyway," I snarled because since I'd lost Gareth I'd felt like that more than once. "So I've got nothing to lose."

"You don't ask questions about who cooks it or who sells it unless you wanna end up in pieces," Harvey said, a manic grin pulling at his lips.

I growled at him, pulling my arm back to punch him but before I could swing my fist, a huge hand caught my arm and tore me away from him.

I inhaled sharply as Ryder whirled me around, his eyes black with anger as he looked down at me.

"I didn't say anything," Harvey gasped. "I didn't tell her a goddamn thing!"

"Fuck off," Ryder snarled, not even looking at him.

Harvey didn't need telling twice and he turned and raced away from me, not offering a second glance in my direction as he left me at the mercy of the Lunar King.

"Let go of me," I demanded, my heart spiking as Ryder tightened his grip on me.

"Why are you asking questions about Killblaze?" he snarled.

I didn't reply, scrambling backwards as I tried to claw his fingers off of me. "Ryder, let me go," I said again but he didn't. Instead he spun me around and pushed my back against the shed exactly where I'd pinned Harvey.

With a flick of his fingers, vines sprang into existence and he forced my hands together until they were encased before me and my own magic was stilled.

"Tell me why you're snooping into things that will get you killed," he snapped.

"Fuck you," I spat in response, anger burning a trail down my throat. I wouldn't get another shot at interrogating Harvey now and I hadn't even gotten any answers. I also had no idea how much Ryder had heard of what I'd asked him, so I wasn't going to give myself away by admitting to anything. Harvey was off his face, with a bit of luck he'd hardly be able to remember this anyway.

"Tell me why you want to know what's in Killblaze and I'll give you the recipe," Ryder offered, though his voice was still all threat.

I stopped struggling for a moment as I looked up at him. How did he know what was in it? The drug had been taking off more and more over the last few years, but the FIB had told me they still weren't even sure how it was created. They believed the stuff all came from one source somewhere in the east of the city but they hadn't been able to track it down yet. So if the recipe was that fucking secret then how the hell did Ryder have it?

"How could you possibly know what's in it?" I asked as he leaned over me.

"I'm gonna hazard a guess that I know a lot of dark shit which you could never even dream up. So let's not waste time trying to list it. I asked you a question." Ryder brushed the knuckles of his right hand over my cheek, the word pain touching my flesh and drawing a tremor from my skin. It wasn't a caress. It was a threat.

"Maybe I want to take some," I said defiantly. "But I don't wanna risk inhaling poison and killing myself for the sake of a high."

Ryder's gaze dragged over me slowly. "Liar," he breathed. "You're not looking to get high."

"You don't know anything about what I want."

"Yes I do. And you're not after something to blot out that pain in you, Elise. You're looking for something to make you feel alive."

My heart pounded harder at his words and the pure undeniable truth of them. But I wasn't going to admit that he'd seen through my bullshit. I wasn't going to admit that he'd caught a glimpse of me.

I held his eye and stared him down, waiting for him to do his worst. Because I wasn't offering up my secrets to him. Especially when the evidence was starting to point me in his direction. There was only one way he could know the recipe for Killblaze. And if he and his gang were the ones making it then it wasn't much of a stretch to think they'd kill with it too.

Ryder seemed to realise I wasn't backing down and he pushed himself off of the wall with a low growl.

"You should watch yourself, new girl," he warned. "Poking your nose into things like this will only end badly for you."

I didn't respond as he walked away from me, the vines immobilising my wrists falling away as he left me standing there, my heart pounding and my mind whirling.

Had I just uncovered the roots of the Killblaze distribution throughout the city? And if I had, did that mean Ryder had had something to do with Gareth's death?

GARETH

CHAPTER THIRTY TWO

SIXTEEN MONTHS BEFORE THE SOLARID METEOR SHOWER...

Gabriel Nox:
I'm going to find out who you are. If you think I can be threatened, you are so fucking wrong.
I'll rip your damn spine out through the back of your neck when I catch you. But not before I beat you within an inch of your worthless life. Message me again and there'll be no mercy when the time comes.

Well there goes my fucking balls, walking out the damn door. By the stars, what kind of psychotic asshole says they're gonna rip someone's spine out?

I took a steadying breath, tucking the burner phone back into my bag as I walked out of the Cafaeteria and headed for the dorms. I'd grabbed a late dinner so night had well and truly fallen as I trailed across campus, definitely not glancing at the sky repeatedly, vividly picturing Gabriel descending on me and fulfilling the promise he'd made in that message.

Though it terrified me to my core and made my heart feel like it was about to combust, I had to search for the positives. If Gabriel was threatening me, that meant he was scared. And if he was scared, maybe this was just an attempt to make me back off. Perhaps all I needed to do was go and hunt down my balls and throw another message at him to make him crack.

I took the phone out again, fear staying my hand. But then I pictured Ella on that stage, pulling her clothes off and I tapped out a reply before I could chicken out.

Faeker:

The price of my silence is the entire contents of your bank account. You know which one I mean.

Threaten me again and those fake IDs hit FaeBook hard.

I stuffed the phone away, not liking who I was becoming under these circumstances. But I'd sell every scrap of morality I had if it saved my family. I just hoped it wouldn't come to that.

Come on Gabriel, bite the fucking bullet.

I headed into the Vega Dorms, hurrying up to the top floor and planning on watching Faeflix for the remainder of the night. I paused as I found Dante waiting outside my door, his arms folded and one foot kicked back against the wall. He smiled as he spotted me, seeming genuinely approachable as he walked toward me. He was dressed in suit pants and a nice shirt, his gold medallion on display as it hung from his neck. It was a Friday night and like most of the students on campus, he probably had somewhere to be.

"Hey Gareth, I've got a job for you."

My stomach lurched, but I nodded, slapping a smile onto my face. "What is it?"

"Not here." *He headed into his room, leaving the door open for me and*

I walked in behind him. He twisted around, eyeing up my chest. "You're not really my size, but some of Gabriel's shirts might fit you."

"Gabriel Nox?" I demanded, shaking my head. "No man. I've got a shirt I can wear, I'll go change." I was not gonna give that guy any reason to be pissed off at me.

"Well if you're sure you've got something nice enough, cavallo."

"Cavallo?" I frowned.

"Horse." He smirked then checked his watch. "Hurry up. We're leaving in three minutes. If you're not ready, I'll replace your ass."

I shot out of the room, hurrying into my dorm and pulling my clothes off as I went.

"Did I order a strip show and forget?" Leon snorted as I tossed my shirt onto my bed. "Slow down, dude, I don't have time to enjoy it." He was lounging on his bunk, his hand draped over the side as Amy gave it a massage.

"I'm going out," I said, heading to the closet and grabbing out the best shirt I owned. It was white and clean, so that was something. I left my school pants and shoes on with it, figuring it was the best I could do.

"Me too. Just as soon as Mindy's finished here. Where are you going?"

I gave him a look of disbelief. He was half dressed and I sensed a nap was dawning on him from the sleepy look in his eyes. If he was going out he was gonna be late as hell. "I'm going to town."

"Maybe I'll catch you later then?"

I left my bag on my bed, subtly switching off the burner and tucking it into my pillowcase before casting a concealment spell over it. I pushed my Atlas into my pocket then headed to the door.

"Yeah maybe." I exited, jogging down the corridor. Dante was heading onto the stairs already and I sped to his side as he shot me a glance.

"Don't walk with me, asshole, I'll text you where to go." He headed off down the staircase and I slowed my pace, my head spinning as I trailed after him, waiting for his message.

When I reached the bottom and he still hadn't texted me, I lingered in the atrium, leaning against the wall and pretending to check my FaeBook feed. My eyes blurred it all out as my pounding heart and fearful thoughts took up all of my focus.

What's he gonna make me do?

What if it's illegal?

What if it's dangerous?

I sighed, knowing that it didn't matter if it was either of those things. I was gonna do it. Because not doing it and losing out on the money Dante was going to pay me wasn't an option.

The door opened and I realised my mistake for standing here as Ryder stepped through it. I moved forward in an attempt to hide the fact I'd been loitering in the Lunar half of the Vega Dorms, but his frosty gaze fell on me. He caught my arm, yanking me to a halt.

My throat tightened and my Order form reared up beneath my skin.

"I've got a job for you," he growled and my heart bashed against my ribcage.

"What? You said-"

"I know what I fucking said, dipshit. I'm capable of forming functioning memories. I changed my mind."

"Right," I said. "Well the thing is-"

A vision slammed into me and I found myself with a wad of cash in my hand. I could feel the crisp notes, smell the money almost sharply enough to be real.

Ryder released me from the vision, hissing between his teeth like a snake. "You asked for work. I'm giving it to you. Are you in or not?" His jaw was tight, his posture rigid, like if I said no to him he might just batter my skull in.

I swallowed the lump rising in my throat. I couldn't work for both gangs, that was suicide. If they found out I was helping their mortal enemies,

I'd be so fucking dead.

But then again...if I pulled it off, I could pay off Old Sal's debt faster. Gabriel still hadn't fallen for the bait I was dangling over him and if he wasn't gonna cave, I needed a solid back up plan.

Besides, who knew exactly how much work either of them were going to offer me?

"Are you slow, Pony Boy?" Ryder snarled. "I don't need help from dead weight." He moved to walk away but I caught hold of his blazer. He snapped around, throwing me a vision of me lying on the floor at his feet soaked in blood, gasping for air through a punctured lung. He threw me back out of it and I stumbled away, my breathing rapid.

Note to self: don't touch his damn blazer.

"I'll do it," I said firmly, holding his gaze.

"I'll message you." He strode through the double doors across the hall and the tension ran out of my shoulders.

Positives? I now had two employers. Negatives? One was a psychotic snake with a tendency for drawing blood. And the other was a Storm Dragon who could cook me whilst simultaneously eating me alive.

My Atlas pinged at last and I took it out, finding a message from the Dragon himself.

Dante:

Leave through the main gate.

Head east and don't stop walking until you're at the corner of Griffin Street.

I walked out the door, heading across campus past Altair Halls and along the wide path which led to the front gate. Other students were heading out, catching the shuttle bus at the entrance and I ducked my head, slipping past them as I turned east.

I walked half a mile before I reached Griffin Street. Parked cars lined the road and tall trees intersected the pavement either side of me. I grew cold as I waited, checking my Atlas for messages, but no more came through. I wondered if I should change Dante's name on my phone to a code name. If I started working for both gangs, it wasn't worth the risk of either of them seeing their enemy's name popping up on my Atlas. I had to be smart about it.

Eventually, Headlights turned on across the road and flashed to catch my attention. I jogged over to the dark blue SUV, opening the passenger door and jumping in beside Dante.

"You've been here the whole time, man, why didn't you call me over?" I asked, shivering against the chill in my bones.

"I was checking to see if you were followed, cavallo."

"Oh right," I said. Being in one of the gangs probably meant constantly looking over your shoulder. Especially if you were its leader. I didn't like the idea of leading a life like that. It sounded too damn stressful.

Dante took off down the road and nerves pricked my gut. "So what is it you want me to do tonight?"

"You just gotta do exactly as I tell you, alright?"

"Which is?" I pressed.

He clapped me on the thigh, smiling at me in a way that somehow came off threatening. "You're gonna help me get a little collateral on someone that's all."

"Right." I nodded, gazing out of the window as Dante turned into Oscura Territory and moved deeper into the south of the city.

We soon pulled down an alley between two dark walled buildings and my heart rate began to rise.

He pulled the parking brake and jumped out and I followed him into the shadows beyond the car. A doorway was illuminated in a deep blue glow and a huge guy stood beside it with his arms folded.

"Fabio!" Dante said brightly and the guy cracked a smile full of silver teeth.

When he spoke, his voice was a deep, rumbling tenor. "Hey boss, what brings you down to The Black Hole?" Fabio embraced Dante, kissing the air either side of his face before he turned to beckon me closer.

"Work. This is Gareth, he's helping me out with a job tonight," Dante said.

I was suddenly crushed into a hug by the huge guy and the scent of spicy aftershave assaulted my senses. He pushed me back, gripping my shoulders tightly as he air kissed either side of my face, smiling broadly. "Benvenuto, Gareth. Don't work too hard, huh?" He held out something black and sparkly and Dante grabbed whatever it was, turning to me.

"Put this on. Don't take it off unless I tell you to." He passed me it and my brows arched as I realised it was a mask. It covered the top half of my face and Dante put his own one on too, winking at me before turning away.

Fabio opened the door for us and Dante headed inside. I trailed after him into a narrow corridor lit up by neon lights. "What is this place?"

"Just one of the clubs run by the Oscura Clan," he said lightly.

We headed down a stairway, the sound of pulsing music thumping in my ears as we emerged in an underground bar. The lights were low and a huge rectangular stage ran down the heart of the room. I knew we were in a strip bar before I even spotted any dancers. This place smelled the same as Old Sal's. Like money, sex and dirty secrets. Except whereas Old Sal's bar whispered it, this place screamed it.

Ringing the room were leather booths draped in red velvet curtains, some of which were closed over. A girl took centre stage wearing nothing but a shiny pink thong and a horse bridle to match. Her skin shimmered with her Pegasus Order and a lump formed in my throat as I realised this wasn't just a strip club. It was a damn fetish club.

Dante had walked ahead of me and he turned back when he realised I wasn't following. He jerked his head to make me move and I jogged after him up to the bar. He ordered us a couple of beers while I stared at the Vampire waitress serving us who had blood smeared over her face and all across her bare chest. I couldn't help but wonder what Ella would make of this place. She'd probably take it all in her stride and spend the night cheering on the stage acts.

Dammit, I miss her. I must remember to call her soon.

Dante handed me my beer and I took a long swig of it. He preceded to take a golden chalice from inside his jacket before pouring the entire contents into it.

"What is that?" I snorted and he smirked.

"Anti-poison chalice. Stops fuckers trying to assassinate me."

"You really need that?" I breathed, knowing it was true the second the words left my mouth.

"I'm number one on the Brotherhood's kill list, cavallo. If I didn't have this, I'd be dead fifty times over."

By the stars…

My eye was drawn to a masked girl in stilettos leading a collared Werewolf into a booth and closing the curtain.

This place is fucked up.

Dante leaned back against the bar, gazing across the room and I had the feeling he was looking for someone. I was distracted again as the girl on stage shifted into a bright pink Pegasus, her bridle and thong still in place.

The crowd cheered and one guy in particular went wild, throwing aura notes onto the stage at her hooves. She trotted up and down and I realised my beer was paused half way up to my lips as I watched. This was just too damn weird.

The clientele all wore the same masks as ours to conceal their identities so I didn't know how Dante was going to recognise anyone. Apparently he did though as he elbowed me, subtly nodding over to a booth on the far side of the room. "See that guy?"

I nodded.

"He comes here every week. Same day, same time, same booth. And do you wanna know what the best part about that is?"

"What?"

"That's Principal Greyshine."

"No way," I breathed, a grin pulling at my mouth. He wore a shirt and slacks and was leaning back in his chair, nursing a cocktail. He didn't seem too interested in the Pegasus on stage and I wrinkled my nose, not wanting to find out what his fetish was.

Dante slammed his hand down on my shoulder, turning to me with a manic grin. "I need you to go over there soon and offer him something for me."

"Why do you need me for that?" I narrowed my eyes.

"Because I'm too recognisable even in this mask. Especially if I was wearing skin tight lycra."

"Wait - what?" I balked.

His smile widened and he kicked away from the bar. "Come on, cavallo. You're not backing out on me now are you?" He raised a brow and I sighed, shaking my head.

He continued to smile as he led me across the bar toward a glittering curtain at the back of the room. I followed him through it and loud moans sounded from behind a row of doors as we marched past them. Dante led me into a private dressing room and I pushed the door closed behind me.

A long mirror ran along one wall highlighted by pink fairy lights and a rack of costumes hung opposite. Dante strolled over to it, plucking out a bright green lycra suit and a wig full of snakes.

"You're gonna be the prettiest Medusa in the club." Dante started laughing as he handed them to me and I scowled as I took them. But hell, I'd already made my bed. It was time to lie in it.

I pulled off my shirt and pants, folding them on the chair with my Atlas. Dante seemed mildly impressed by my willingness, his brows raised as he handed me the suit. I tugged it on and he moved to zip up the back for me with another chuckle. I pulled off my mask and put on the Medusa wig so plastic snakes fell around my shoulders. Dante approached me with some bright green make up that glittered.

"Dude." I frowned. "Is that really necessary?"

"Greyshine might recognise you. It's gotta be done." He started painting it onto my face with more skill than I'd expected, finishing off the look with some snake eye contact lenses. I looked in the mirror and groaned; the suit showed every fucking bit of my junk and ass crack.

Oh man, the lengths I go to…

"Do you not have any real Medusas in this place?" I asked, frowning down at my costume.

Dante moved to search for something beyond the rack of clothes. "Yeah there is, but some people just like the illusion. They're building up to the real deal I guess- what's your shoe size?"

"Eleven," I called.

"Here we go." He reappeared holding a pair of rhinestone encrusted high heels apparently made for men.

I frowned, shaking my head. "How the hell am I gonna walk in those?" He's gonna make me wear them even if I can't, I just fucking know it.

He shrugged, tossing them in front of me. I pushed my feet into them with my pride flying away on the wind. When I lifted my head, I found Dante holding a massive blue strap on dick.

"No fucking way." I shook my head. "That is not necessary."

"Sure it is." He moved closer, his eyes dancing with amusement.

"Dante I swear on the stars-"

He lunged at me and I yelped as he spun me around with brute force, wrapping that freaking massive cock around my waist.

The door opened and we both looked around. A cyclops with fake spinning eyes on her nipples and a real one in the centre of her face gazed at *us in alarm. Her eyes landed on where Dante's hands were locked around the shaft of the huge plastic dick now protruding between my legs and she backed up with a giggle. "Oh sorry!"*

Dante's crotch was pressed to my ass and I huffed angrily as the woman shut the door and hurried away.

"Great now she thinks we were screwing."

"You need to chill, cavallo. Who cares what some girl thinks?" Dante barked a laugh, releasing me as he stepped away, the strap-on firmly strapped on. Life.

"So what now? I am not coming onto our fucking Principal." Though a horrible part of me knew I would if it came to it. For the money. Which was just plain rock bottom. Or maybe I'd already hit that with the massive plastic dick hanging between my legs. Or maybe it was when I'd put the lycra suit on...

"Na, you're just gonna invite him to one of the back rooms."

Sweet relief filled me.

He reached into his pocket and took something out. "Then you're gonna go in the room with him and his date and plant this camera somewhere that will get a good view of him getting fucked." He passed me the small device and a chill ran through me.

"Why would you want a sex tape of the Principal?" I asked in confusion and horror.

"Because it's good sense to get dirt on your peers, cavallo. Once he finds out I have this, I'll have him wrapped around my little finger. No more detentions or faculty members snooping into my shit. It'll keep him on side too. The Brotherhood can't use him against me if he's scared shitless that I'll out the video."

"That's...pretty clever," I remarked and his chest swelled. Clearly stroking Dante's ego was a solid way to keep in his good books and I made a mental note of it. If he did this to people who weren't his enemies, I did not

wanna find out what he did to people who were.

I sighed, thinking over how I was gonna pull this off, feeling overly hot in this damn suit. "Do I need to get the camera back?"

"Nope. It feeds directly to my Atlas and I've cast a charm on it so it will combust after two hours." He smiled proudly.

"Right. Remind me why I'm needed for this and you didn't just pay off one of your staff here?"

Dante grinned broadly, but didn't answer my question as he went on, "The next act on stage is what Greyshine's waiting for. When it's over, approach him and say he can have the dancer for an hour, complimentary of the club for being a good customer."

"But won't the staff question that?"

"No, I've paid for the dancer already under a fake name. When you beckon him off the stage, tell him Shiner is ready for him."

I nodded, memorising everything he said as I tried not to focus on how crazy this was.

He steered me toward the door and leaned close to my ear before we exited, his breath sweeping across my neck. "Oh and if you fuck this up, cavallo, I'll have your glittery Pegasus balls cut off."

Oh shit.

"I won't," I said thickly, my heart thrashing in my chest.

"Good," Dante said brightly, the threat passing from his tone. "Wait here for one minute before heading back to the bar. When you've planted the camera, I'll be waiting out front in my car."

"Got it," I said, my mouth overly dry as I reached up to tuck the camera under my wig.

He looked me over, snorting a laugh. "Hey if you ever need a job, you've got one here as a Medusa. Or maybe you wanna get that sparkly tail of yours on stage?"

"No," I snarled, the ferocity in my tone making his brows arch. I was fighting so hard to stop Elise from falling prey to this life, that I simply wasn't gonna sign up for it myself unless I was down to my last scrap of dignity. Which was pretty hard to say dressed the way I was.

He shrugged and headed out the door. I released a breath, practising walking in my heels as I waited for a minute to pass. It was surprisingly easy which might have been due to the graceful nature of my Order.

When the time was up, I slipped out the door, heading back into the bar and slinking into the shadows as my eyes fell on the stage. The Pegasus was making her exit, glitter falling from her coat as she headed off stage and into the hands of a muscular guy who stroked her mane and led her toward one of the booths. She shifted back into her Fae form and he led her inside by her bridle, his other hand squeezing her ass.

I fought a shudder as he pulled the curtain and I looked back to the stage. The lights had switched to a dark green glow and smoke poured out of vents in the stage floor to a round of cheers. Principal Greyshine sat up straighter and I wondered what the hell this guy was into.

A powerful voice filled the room, "Please welcome to the stage, a man who likes Fae to kneel at his feet, who bites as hard as he fucks and who will make you scream for mercy all night long. It's the one and only Dragon Commander and dirtiest High Councillor of them all. Lionel Afucks!"

Ho-ly shit. A Lionel Acrux impersonator stepped onto the stage, wearing a massive scaly strap-on dick that was bright fucking green. He had scales painted onto his skin to match, coating his entire body which was all muscle. He wore high heels which were twice the height of mine and a spiky tail that dragged out behind him. The crowd called to him, throwing cash onto the stage as he started dancing on the poles, casting huge showers of sparks with his fire Element.

Surely this wasn't what Greyshine was into? But as I looked his way and found his fucking hand down his pants, I was proved sorely wrong.

To his credit, Lionel Afucks was a damn good dancer. His hips sashayed to the beat of the music and his swings on the pole were top notch. When he was finally done and his tiny green briefs were stuffed with auras, he started gathering up the rest of the tips from the floor.

I made my move, digging for my courage as I made a beeline toward my principal. He didn't even have the courtesy to extract his hand from his pants as I arrived in front of him. His eyes slid over me then he leaned sideways to try and see past me.

"Is he doing any more dances tonight?" he asked hopefully.

I slapped on my most charming smile and played the role I had in Old Sal's bar. "Actually, sir, the club would like to offer you an hour with Mr Afucks on the house for being such a loyal customer." Did those words really just come out of my mouth?

Greyshine sat up straighter, taking his hand out of his pants at last. "Oh really?"

"Yes, he's all yours. I'll be glad to fetch him for you if you'd like to accept our offer?"

He nodded keenly, running a hand over his bald patch and shifting nervously. "Oh yes, that would be delightful'."

I'd always wondered if he dropped the fake ass 'cool principal' act outside of school. And apparently, he did. I wondered why he bothered at all. It wasn't winning him points with anyone.

I beamed, turning away and heading to the stage where Lionel was still gathering up tips. "Hey, Mr Shiner is ready for you."

He looked up and I realised he had reptilian contact lenses in. His face split into a smile which revealed a set of fake sharp teeth. "Oh yeah? Well I'm gonna make sure I show him a good time. Do you know he paid me double my asking price?"

"Wow, I wish I could get a night with him." I feigned a smile.

"I'll put in a good word for you, sugardick. Bring him to room three out back."

"Got it." *I saluted him as he headed off stage and walked back to Greyshine, beckoning him out of his seat. He linked his arm with mine and I tugged him toward the back rooms.*

"Is he excited to see me?" Greyshine asked.

"Yes, sir. He's overjoyed." Cringe. *I guided him through the door and headed to room three, opening it and walking inside.*

The lights were dimmed to a red glow and Lionel was spread out on the black sheets already, lubing up his strap on. I died inside. Like literally some part of me withered up and fucking died.

"Hello, Shiner," Lionel purred and I released Greyshine.

"Hi Lionel," he said shyly.

I side-stepped my principal, glancing around in search of somewhere I could stash this damn camera and high-tail it out of there. I pretended to fiddle with my snake wig as I tugged out the device and clasped it between my fingers, pressing the little button on the side to set it recording.

"Are you joining us, snake eyes?" Lionel asked, eyeing me hopefully and Greyshine looked over, seeming intrigued by that idea too.

"No, my contact lens just fell out. Don't mind me." They didn't mind me at all, immediately starting to kiss each other's faces off and I took the opportunity to place the camera next to a vase on a small table. Oh whoops that's not a vase it's another massive dildo.

I headed for the door and moans followed me. I wished I'd made it out of the room quicker as Greyshine groaned, "I've been a baaaad little Sphinx, Lionel. You'll have to punish me for breaking the Council laws."

I shut the door firmly, fighting a shudder as I strode away and headed back to the dressing room. Inside, I wiped the makeup from my face and quickly changed back into my clothes, putting my mask back on too.

Adrenaline pumped through my veins as I hurried back out into the bar and made my way to the exit. I jogged upstairs, pushed through the door and waved goodbye to Fabio with relief humming through my veins.

I jumped into Dante's car and laughter bubbled out of my chest unexpectedly.

Dante joined in, the two of us falling apart as he showed me the screen of his Atlas. "You did it."

I lifted a hand to hide the image of my Principal being screwed up the ass by a pretend Dragon, grimacing.

"You made me do this as a test, didn't you?" I guessed.

"Yep," Dante said with a bright smile.

"Did it really have to be that extreme?"

"Yep." He started laughing.

"You know you're an asshole, right?" I broke a grin.

"Yep." Dante tossed the Atlas into the back seat, kicking the engine into gear as laughter tumbled from his throat. "You know what? I think you just became my new friend, cavallo."

DANTE

CHAPTER THIRTY THREE

I t had been a few weeks since I'd visited Principal Greyshine so I headed to his office on the ground floor of Altair Halls, smiling to myself as I approached his door and rapped my knuckles against the wood.

"Sorry kiddo, I'm quite busy right now!" his cheery voice came in return. Unlike most people in this school, I knew a lot about Randal Greyshine. I made it my damn business to know because someone in his position of power could too easily fuck up my education' if he snooped into what I got up to on a daily basis.

Greyshine was moderately powerful. As a Cancer he had the Element of water, he was also a Sphinx which meant he was highly intelligent and was not to be underestimated. The 'down with the kids yet entirely unapproachable' act he put on in front of the students was actually a tactic. He flew under the radar, never drew too much attention and therefore no issues from either of the gangs. And that meant he could spend most of his days doing whatever he liked.

"Too busy to see *me*, Randal?" I asked, a smirk pulling at my features.
Several locks were hurriedly unbolted on the other side of the door

along with a magical forcefield withdrawing. A beat of silence passed then Greyshine yanked the door open. He looked hot and bothered at the sight of me. His collar was loose as if he'd been tugging at it and the bald patch atop his head was shining with sweat.

"Oh, Mr Oscura, what can I help you with?" His eyes flipped up and down the empty corridor as if he were looking for a lifeline. His back was to the door as if he was gonna stop me from coming in but fuck if he was. I shoved my way past him, entering his office which was basically a small and untidy library. Books filled every spare space on shelves, his desk, in piles on the floor. The only part of the wall which wasn't hidden behind a huge stack of them was where his certificates of excellence hung from his time as a student at Aurora Academy.

Greyshine shut the door, locking it and immediately casting a silencing bubble around us.

I shoved the pile of books out of the chair in front of his desk and dropped into it. He gasped, hurrying forward to collect them from the space around my feet before carefully re-stacking them in a corner of the room. He was shaking. And he had damn good reason to be.

"Is there something I can do for you?" he asked, all the bullshit slang utterly dropped in my presence. He knew I saw right through him, right down to his tighty whities and beyond. I kicked my feet up on the desk, my shining leather shoes resting on top of an Astrology tome.

Greyshine eyed it, looking uncomfortable but he wouldn't dare tell me not to. He sidled behind his desk between the stacks and dropped into his own chair, clearing his throat several times.

"I'm just checking in, Randal. Making sure you're not up to anything that might make me publish a certain video on FaeBook." A certain video Gareth had gotten for me. *Fuck...Gareth.*

Greyshine turned deathly pale, wetting his mouth as he stared at me. "I wouldn't do anything against you, Mr Oscura." He threaded and unthreaded his fingers, a bead of sweat rolling down his brow. "Please don't publish it," he hissed, a note of desperation in his tone.

I pretended to consider his words. "Alright. But…"

"But?" he breathed.

"I need you to get me out of detention with Professor Mars for the gang fight the other day."

"Of course," he said immediately. "Anything else?"

"There's been a noticeable decline in chocolate poptarts in the breakfast buffet," I mused, picking up one of his books and flicking through it.

"Oh well…you see, the thing is…we've had some cutbacks and-"

"And?" I growled, electricity dancing along my skin.

"A-and I'll be sure to order in plenty more chocolate p-p-poptarts."

"Good," I said brightly, flashing him a smile. I didn't even like chocolate poptarts. My eyes snagged on a picture of a navy blue dragon in his book which looked kinda like me. "Can I keep this?" I asked as I ripped the page out and Greyshine winced full bodily.

"O-of course," he stuttered.

"Great." I rose to my feet, jamming the picture into my pocket and walking around his desk. He shrank into his chair, cowering beneath me as I leaned down toward him.

"What are you doing?" he gasped.

I air kissed either side of his cheeks and leant in to speak in his ear. "Un amico che diventa nemico è il nemico più crudele di tutti."

"W-what does that mean?" he breathed, his blue eyes round with fear.

"It means, a friend who becomes an enemy is the cruellest enemy of all." I clapped him on the shoulder, beaming before walking to the door. "Ciao Principale."

I stepped into the corridor with energy humming through my veins. Now, with that dealt with, it was time to go for a fly.

I soared low over The Iron Wood, flexing my navy wings as electricity crackled across my scales and made them flash like a tempestuous sky. I roared to the moon and my pack howled in response, crying out to their Alpha who rode the wind above them. Pride tugged at my chest and I released another bellow, drinking in the sound of the Werewolves howling below me in the forest. Mia famiglia. My friends. My Clan.

I caught glimpses of their fur between the trees, their heads lifted, howling to the massive beast who swooped above. My wings brushed the treetops as I banked hard, leading them toward Tempest Lake in the north west corner of campus. I reached the water's edge before they did and dropped low, my wings skimming the still surface and sending ripples across it for miles.

I circled the dark body of water at high speed, ringing back around to where my pack were pouring out of the trees onto the pebble beach. They drank in the light of the moon, its power refilling their magic reserves as they raced along the shore.

Two powerful wingbeats had me soaring ahead of them and I flew as low as possible above the shoreline, my fanned tail whipping out behind me. Tabitha barked happily as she drew level with my flank, her grey coat seeming almost silver in the moonshine.

I released another roar which had a note of laughter to it, drinking in the high of flying in my Order form. I led the wolves around the lake four times before they grew tired and slowed to a halt. Some of them waded into the water while others played and nuzzled each other on the beach. I dropped down beside them and Tabitha rubbed her wet nose to mine before heading off to chase Nikita.

This was the only time I really felt the difference between us. Shit, I loved being a damn Storm Dragon. Alpha of the most terrifying fucking wolf pack in Solaria. It sounded seriously badass too. The only problem was, sometimes I was reminded of just how different I was to them.

When I was a kid, my siblings had all emerged early as was common for Werewolves. I'd ridden on their backs, shared baths, played in the woods with them. But when my Order had emerged, my mamma had encouraged me to take charge, to shift when the wolves shifted and lead them as a Dragon Alpha. But the longer that went on, the less easy it was to join in with them like this. And sometimes I didn't want to.

As much as I loved them, Dragons were naturally more solitary. Now and then, I just needed to slip away into the clouds and spread my wings alone. And when we came down to the lake, they knew I'd fly away eventually. It was my favourite area to fly on campus and beyond that, there was a place here I loved to go when I needed to gather my thoughts.

I flexed my wings and my pack howled their goodbyes as I took off with a powerful leap, climbing higher and higher into the sky. I raced for the clouds, twisting through them and relishing the wet kiss of the moisture across my wings. Power radiated through me, my excitement growing as I rose even higher into the heavens.

Energy was building and building in my body, begging to be released and I finally let it out. I opened my huge jaws and a tremendous bolt of white hot electricity burst from the very pit of my chest like lightning. The sound that left me was akin to a thunderclap and the clouds darkened around me, pulsing with my storm powers. Rain poured far below and I heard it hitting the lake like a tumult of applause.

The wolves howled once more as I raced through the clouds, emotions burning right out of me in the form of electricity.

When I was finally feeling depleted, I flattened my wings to my sides, letting myself freefall toward the lake, tumbling down through the clouds in a spiral. This was freedom. There was nothing in the world that equalled it. The rush, the wind, the rain, the storm. I was a living breathing part of it. It was what I was born to be.

I pulled up before I hit the lake, rain cascading over my back as I set my sights on the boathouse at the water's edge. I came to land on the pier, the wooden slats groaning beneath my weight. I shifted out of my Dragon form, heading up the pier with exhilaration burning through my blood.

The boathouse was the size of a barn with flaking white paint coating it and a huge old willow tree leaning against one side. The fronds hung all the way down over the opening at the front, creating a cocoon within it. The vessels Aurora Academy had at its disposal included three simple fishing boats a couple of rowing boats and a bunch of canoes. I couldn't remember the last time students had used any of them. That was why this place was my haven. No one came here so I'd claimed it as mine.

I swept the willow branches aside and the scent of damp wood and old lacquer tingled my senses, making the tension run smoothly out of my body. It was familiar and almost homely; the one place on campus where I could truly have privacy.

I headed inside, flexing my limbs as I lazily made my way toward the back of the boat house, passing by the fishing boats in the water at the heart of the space. Ropes and nets hung along the walls alongside a bunch of rusted tools which looked a century old.

"I wasn't sure how long to wait to tell you I'm here, but in case you came here to jerk off, I figured I'd better speak up."

My heart lurched as I found Elise perched high up on a wooden platform at the back of the boat house, her legs swinging casually off of it. She was chewing gum and had an open book on her knee.

Trust her to find my secret place. I didn't even feel angry; it was a strange kind of relief to find her there. As if this place was meant for us both. *Great, now I'm losing my fucking mind.*

"If you wanted to see me naked, you only had to ask, carina."

"Oh yes my long-winded plan of waiting out here in some busted up

416

boat shed in the hopes that you might appear in your birthday suit has finally paid off," she said dryly, a hint of amusement to her tone. And I didn't miss the way her eyes fell to my dick and widened.

I smirked as I headed to the crate at the back of the shed where I kept spare clothes and a bunch of gold to replenish my magic, pulling on a pair of sweatpants and a t-shirt. No one ever came here, but if they did, they sure as shit wouldn't dare to steal from me.

When I was done, I walked to the ladder which led up to the small platform and climbed up to join her. Although she was technically joining me because this was *my* spot.

I dropped down beside her and swiped the book from her knee, my thigh pressing up against hers. I felt her watching me from the corner of my eye as I flipped the book over to read the title.

Wuthering Heights.

I passed it back to her, cocking a brow. "Didn't peg you as a romantic."

"I'm not. I'm in it for the revenge and seeing why nice people are driven to do bad things." She pushed the book into her bag, drawing her legs up to hug them to her chest. Her uniform was bone dry so either she'd been here since before the storm or she could cast a decent air shield. The rain was drumming against the roof, making my favourite sound in the world.

"What about bad people being driven to do nice things?" I asked, leaning my shoulder against hers.

She didn't move away, looking at me as if she was capable of picking apart my soul. But I kept that shit on lockdown. I didn't need the complication of a girl claiming my heart. I liked Elise, damn well hungered for her. But Mamma had taught me to tieni il tuo cuore vicino alla tua famiglia – keep your heart with the family. The moment I gave it away, I was in trouble. I could be manipulated, deceived, tricked. And as the future leader of the Oscura Clan, I had to do everything I could to protect myself. Didn't mean I couldn't fool around though...

"Maybe there's no good and bad. There's just people." Elise shrugged and I nodded as I considered that.

"What about enemies and friends?" I looked to her and saw something splitting apart in her gaze. She didn't answer and I reached for her hand on instinct. Her fingers weaved with mine and my guarded heart twitched. "Why did you come here, carina?"

Her soft green eyes bored into mine. "I needed to be alone. I went for a walk and stumbled across this place. It sounded like a storm was coming so…" She shrugged and the rush of rain sounded between us, crashing against the roof as my power still burned through the sky.

"*My* storm," I said with a smug kind of smile.

Her brows lifted a little, but I wouldn't exactly say she looked impressed. I wondered what in this world could actually impress a girl like her.

"Must be fun up there in the clouds," she said thoughtfully.

"I'll take you sometime," I offered.

"What?" she said in surprise. "You can't. Dragons don't let people ride them. Isn't it part of your Order laws?"

I shrugged. "I don't abide by many laws, bella."

A playful smile danced around her mouth and she squeezed my hand, sending an injection of heat into my damn soul. "I'm still not seeing a scary mob boss sitting beside me, Dante. It just doesn't add up."

"I smile at people until they cross me," I said seriously. "One strike is all it takes."

"Ooo scary," she teased and I cocked my head to look at her.

"Seems like you want to see my dark side. But I wouldn't encourage that. Once you've seen it, you can't un-see it."

"Like your dick?" she smirked and I bit down on a grin.

"Yeah, carina. And once you feel it, you can't un-feel it."

"Well I wouldn't get much done with my day if that was the case."

I laughed and she blew a bubble with her gum, the scent of cherries

418

popping under my nose.

"So what do you do in here?" she asked. "I'm guessing from the clothes stash you come here a lot?"

"Well it involves copious amounts of Vampire porn and several tubes of lube."

She burst out laughing and I grinned at her, warmth spreading through my chest as I finally cracked her mask.

Her gaze caught on mine and I sensed she was waiting for a real answer to her question.

I sighed, pushing a hand into my hair. "I come here to think."

"About?" she breathed, no judgment in her voice.

"The Clan, life…" *You.*

"The Clan?" she questioned.

"The Clan hit The Brotherhood hard last week. We killed thirteen of their members. Or…my uncle did." A tightness grew in my chest as I thought of Felix. I needed to get on top of his bullshit before it got even more out of hand.

Elise had fallen quiet and I glanced her way, eyeing the lines on her brow.

"Thirteen people?" she echoed.

"Yeah and…" I stopped, reminding myself of Mamma's words. I shouldn't open up to anyone about the Clan. Shouldn't even want to. But with Elise, my tongue felt loose.

"And?" she questioned, her fingers squeezing mine again.

There was one thing I could do which bought me a free pass with this. So I lifted our hands between us, raising my brows at her. "I can't have these words leave these walls, carina. Will you take a bond of silence with me? It will only apply to this boat house. You won't be able to speak about what I tell you beyond this place."

Her lips parted. "By the fucking sun, Dante. That's senior year magic."

"It was one of the first spells I ever learned." I shrugged. "There's a lot of shit I can do that seniors can do. And there's a lot I can do that they can't too."

She swallowed, her fingers locking tighter with mine. "Do it."

"You have to let our magic blend, just for a minute." I gave her a sideways smile. Power sharing was a rush. It required a lot of trust or willpower to manage it. It wasn't natural to let someone beneath the surface of your skin. And I could see the hesitation in Elise's eyes.

"Trust me, carina. I won't hurt you," I encouraged.

Her eyes locked with mine and for some reason it was the easiest thing in the world to let my own barriers down. Hers washed away just as quickly and her power flowed into my body like a river.

Fuck me.

It wasn't just a rush, with her it was a fucking orgasm. I groaned the same time she did, the two of us pressing closer, more flesh touching, allowing the magic to flow faster between us.

"Holy shit," I gasped.

Her power ebbed and flowed under my skin like pure ecstasy and static energy crackled all over my flesh.

"Dante," she said breathlessly, almost begging and the sound sent another wave of pleasure through me.

I pressed my cheek to hers, falling into the spell of her magic as it blended with mine, filling me up and making me want to get every inch of her exposed flesh against me. It would cause a fucking volcanic eruption for sure and I sure as hell wanted to burn up in it.

She clawed at my shirt, pushing it up to get her free hand onto my stomach, her magic flooding into me at so many points of contact I was heady.

The spell, asshole!

I shut my eyes to focus, forming my magic into a bond which wrapped around every place our skin met. It expanded from our bodies and encased the walls in a shimmering silver light. I held onto Elise a few seconds longer than was necessary, drowning in the feel of her power inside me, then I broke the contact, pressing her back.

We were breathless as we stared at each other, my heart thumping hard and fast, her expression telling me she could hear it.

"That was insane," I growled.

She nodded, her pupils fully dilated and her lips open, inviting. I leaned in to kiss her on instinct, but she caught me by the throat and shoved me back. *Argh.*

"Sorry," I grunted, turning away and she caught my hand again, confusing the fuck out of me.

"You were saying...about your Clan?" she encouraged, amusement flashing across her features.

I sighed as I wrapped her hand up in mine.

"Well...my uncle attacked some shitty rundown bar in Lunar Territory. The people he killed were a bunch of hookers and old men." I drew in a slow breath and felt Elise staring at me.

"You feel bad," she said in surprise and I shrugged one shoulder in answer.

"It just isn't the way I'd conduct my fucking Clan. Felix is standing in for me until I graduate, but he can't go around killing people without a damn tactic behind it. So now we're just waiting for The Brotherhood to retaliate, and do you think they're gonna go for the men who did it? Fuck no. They're gonna target our weaker people like we did to them."

Rage spewed through my gut. I felt so helpless to it. It was a damn time bomb. And when it went off, blood was gonna splatter the wall and paint my name on it. Everything Felix did reflected on me. He was supposed to be checking in with me, running his plans by me. But was he fuck.

Elise leaned her head against my shoulder and my anger simmered. "Do you ever think the gangs could find some way to come together? To make amends?"

I stiffened as hatred pulsed under my skin. "Never," I snarled.

"With you and Ryder…it seems more personal than rivalry."

I pressed my lips together, wondering if I should tell her everything. But I didn't want to think about Mariella and what she'd done to Ryder Draconis. So I decided on a piece of the truth. Something that was printed in the news, that she could have found out anyway if she really wanted to know. "Ryder's father killed my father."

She sucked in a breath, but remained quiet as she waited for me to elaborate.

A scab picked off the old wound in my chest as I remembered the day I'd gotten the news. "Vesper Draconis didn't just kill him either. He cut him into ten pieces like their sick motherfucking gang always does. Him and my dad were Astral Adversaries. The stars had bound them to clash forever until it ended in blood. Ryder and I have inherited their star bond." We'd never confirmed that for sure, but it was pretty damn obvious to me.

"I'm sorry," she breathed.

I pressed my tongue into my cheek, fighting back the emotion at losing my father five years ago. "We got him back for it," I said in a dark tone which sent goosebumps rising across Elise's arms.

"How?" she whispered but I shook my head.

The rain had slowed to a drizzle and the clouds were beginning to part, allowing the moonlight down on the pier. A heavy weight descended on me and I decided I didn't want to talk about this anymore. "Another day, carina."

I moved to get up, but she tugged on my hand to make me look at her. "Thank you for telling me. I never had a father – he skipped out on me before I was able to form a memory of him so I can't imagine what it would be like to lose one like that."

I frowned, reaching out to trail a thumb across her cheek. "Well your father was a fucking idiot to give you up. If you were ever mine to protect, I'd keep you close and never let go."

"You know I don't need that," she whispered and I leaned in to press a gentle kiss to her forehead.

"I know, carina. But the earth would still turn whether the moon was watching or not. Maybe she likes the company though." I cleared my throat, gazing down at our intertwined hands. "You know…if you want to use this place to get away from the world, you can. It's good to be alone sometimes."

"Yeah," she agreed. "It really is. It can be suffocating in our dorm."

"That's why I have a sheet," I said with a grin. We fell quiet and I watched her out of the corner of my eye, realising something strange. "It feels like being alone even with you here."

"Am I that boring?" she teased, but her expression was serious.

"No I just meant-"

"I know what you meant," she whispered, like she was scared to admit it. She lifted her eyes and her soul seemed to call to mine from the depths of her eyes, spinning an unbreakable web between us. "Maybe we can come here and be alone together sometimes."

"Alone together," I echoed with a smile pulling at my mouth. "I like the sound of that, bella."

ELISE

CHAPTER THIRTY FOUR

It was two days until the Spring party and I flicked through my pathetically limited wardrobe with my lips twisting in distaste. I'd come to Aurora Academy with one fairly small bag of clothes and they were all I owned in the world. None of which was suitable for a fancy party. Or even a shitty party really. I had a few pairs of jeans and leggings, some semi appealing shirts and a leather jacket which had seen better days. There was a reason why I didn't bother changing out of my uniform after class during the week and why I tended to wear my sports kit sweats if I was hanging around the dorm on the weekends.

For a moment my gaze trailed over Laini's section of the closet which was a hell of a lot fuller than mine and I wondered if she might let me borrow something. But even as I considered it, I dismissed the idea. Laini was a lot shorter than me and my chest was a lot fuller. Nothing of hers was going to fit.

I sighed. The party had sounded like fun but I was going to have to pull out of it. Maybe I'd just wait until the day and fake a home emergency. I'd have to head off campus for the evening, but I could just go sit in a park or something...

Wow my life outside of vengeance really is pathetic.

I shook off my disappointment over the party. I wasn't here for social events anyway. I was here for Gareth.

I snagged my wash bag from the shelf, glad that the academy had provided me with it so that I didn't have to worry about running out of shampoo too. Although lilac hair dye might be an issue within another few weeks.

I walked to the end of the corridor and took a left into the girls' bathroom, heading straight for a shower.

I hung my clothes and towel outside the stall and stepped inside. I twisted the knob, waiting for the water to heat up and feeling vaguely jealous of Fae with that Element for not having to rely on the school's temperamental boiler.

When it was finally hot enough, I moved beneath the flow and started washing.

Muffled giggles carried to me from beyond my stall and I stilled as I recognised Cindy Lou's voice.

"Oh no! Silly me!" she called overly dramatically and the scent of smoke assaulted my senses.

I started rinsing conditioner from my hair with a sense of foreboding writhing in my gut. I really didn't have time for her petty bullshit, but that girl seemed determined to haunt me no matter how hard I tried to avoid her.

I was seriously beginning to consider the idea of beating the shit out of her, but I was concerned about letting my inner monster out too soon. So far, I'd managed to avoid enough trouble to be sure that the Kings wouldn't know what to expect from me when it came time for me to strike back at them and I wanted to keep it that way if I could. But Cindy Lou seemed determined to push me until I broke and I wasn't sure how much more of her shit I could take before I snapped.

I shut off the water and stepped out of my stall, reaching for my towel only to grasp at empty air.

Cindy Lou's laughter rang out and I turned to face her across the magnolia tiles as she slapped a hand across her mouth.

"I'm so sorry, Elise," she gasped falsely as her friends Amira and Helga tittered. "I lost control of my fire magic and burned your things. I guess you'll just have to shoot back to your room before anyone sees you!"

I pursed my lips. She was right; I *could* shoot back to my room with my Vampire speed like a whipped little bitch and let her see me run from her with flaming cheeks. But there were a lot of things Cindy Lou didn't know about me and one of them was where I came from. When your mom was a stripper you grew up without a fear of naked flesh. I'd spent my evenings and weekends hanging out with people wearing nothing but their birthday suits for as long as I could remember. I wasn't going to give her the satisfaction of flinching away from showing mine.

"Don't worry about it, sweetie," I replied. "I've got more clothes back in my room. I just hope you manage to learn how to contain your Element before graduation. It's pretty embarrassing that you still haven't got it pegged down yet."

I gave her and her friends a wide smile and turned to walk for the exit with my chin high and pace deliberately slow.

My confidence held until I made it to the doorway but I refused to balk as I stepped out into the corridor. The boys showers were through the door opposite and predictably a guy stepped out at the same moment as I did.

I turned down the corridor without looking his way and started walking towards my room which suddenly seemed like it was a fucking long way away. A prickle ran along my spine but I couldn't let my nerves show, I just had to front this out.

"Elise?" the guy asked from a step behind me and I turned my head before I could stop myself to find Kipling Senior looking back at me.

"Yes?" I asked lightly, aware that Cindy Lou and her friends were lurking close, waiting for me to crack.

"I've been meaning to have a word with you, have you got a sec?"

I turned towards him, fighting off the urge to cross my arms over my chest as the chill in the corridor made my nipples pebble.

"Well, I was just-" I began but he cut me off. To his credit his gaze was on my face, not once dropping to take in my dripping wet body. And even weirder than that, it didn't even seem like he was interested in the fact that I was naked. Or even like he'd noticed it.

"It'll only take a second," Senior assured me. He raised his hand to cast a silencing bubble before I could object and the magic washed over me, ensuring the rest of our conversation remained private.

I frowned a little as he stepped to the side of the corridor so that people could pass us and wondered why the hell he didn't think it was weird to be having this conversation with me while I was naked and he had nothing on but a towel around his waist. I cursed myself as I realised that I'd looked below his face and met his eye again, finding his gaze still hadn't strayed from mine.

Weird.

I wasn't sure whether I should be insulted by his complete lack of interest in my body, but I guessed I'd just focus on relief that he wasn't perving. Besides, all the Orders who had to shift got naked all the damn time so I guessed it wasn't *that* weird for me to be seen like this. Apart from the fact that I wasn't of a shifter Order.

"We've been thinking about the job you did for us the other day, causing that distraction," he said.

"Oh yeah?" I asked, presuming the *we* meant him and his brothers.

"Yeah. We were impressed. Even more so by the fact that you haven't gone around boasting about that flaming penis you burned into the Empyrean Fields. It takes a certain kind of person to remain discreet and under the radar while still pulling off a stunt like that," he added with a nod.

"Thanks," I replied, though I still wasn't sure why we were having this conversation while I was naked. People were passing us on their way to the showers and unlike Kipling Senior, they were definitely noticing the nude girl standing in their midst. I was just glad that I hadn't been spotted by anyone I knew well yet.

"So we thought you might like some more regular work? We can pay you in credit at the emporium or auras, or a mixture of both if you prefer?"

"Seriously?" I asked, excitement driving away my self consciousness at that idea. What he was offering was perfect, if I had some money then I could buy clothes and soda and *gum!*

"Are you in then?" he asked seriously, not returning my smile. In fact I wasn't sure he did smiling. I certainly hadn't witnessed one.

"Fuck yeah."

"Good." He held out a hand and I slapped mine straight into it, a clap of magic resounding between us as we struck the deal.

"We'll be in touch about your first job shortly." He released me and strode away down the corridor, waving a hand to dissipate the silencing bubble as he went.

I was rewarded with a view of Cindy Lou gawping at me from just outside the bathroom as she saw me hanging around for a chat butt naked. I offered her a taunting salute then headed on towards my room at a leisurely pace.

When I opened the door I found Gabriel sitting on his bunk and suddenly realised that I had more reason to feel self conscious in here than I had out there with the masses.

He was no Kipling Senior and his eyes instantly dropped to drink in every inch of me with a hunger that set my skin alight.

I focused on enhancing my hearing and found that Laini wasn't here but I detected Dante's heartbeat within the sheet he had hooked around his bed. I was just relieved that he wasn't looking at me too. At least Gabriel had seen it all before.

"Hey," I said as casually as I could manage as I padded through the centre of the room to the closet at the back while Gabriel's eyes hounded me the whole way. He didn't reply but that wasn't that strange for him.

A part of me couldn't help but drink in the attention of his eyes on my flesh and I couldn't resist the urge to look his way again.

He seemed caught between the desire to approach me and stay away and I bit down on my lip, my heart pounding as I enjoyed the feeling of him looking at me like that.

I looked straight into his grey eyes as I slowly pulled on a pair of black panties and he watched my movements like he was starving for them. I pulled out a matching bra and slipped it on next. Gabriel's gaze was full of fire and his throat bobbed as he swallowed hard.

I turned away slowly and took a shirt from a hanger, turning back to look at him as I drew it on, buttoning it over my chest and causing his fist to clench tightly as he watched me. I'd seen my mom put on this show in reverse so many times that it was kinda funny to see him lapping it up as I put my clothes *on.*

I pulled my pleated plum skirt on next, my gaze fixed on Gabriel who flexed his huge wings behind him so that they brushed against the wall. The movement of them made my heart patter excitedly as I remembered the way he'd hidden us beneath them while he took possession of my body on the roof.

I rolled my socks up to my knees last then pushed my feet into my shoes. I let my eyes linger on the myriad of tattoos which covered his bare chest before slowly turning away to the mirror to apply my makeup.

Gabriel dropped silently out of his bunk behind me and my gaze snagged on him approaching in the reflection as I applied my pink lipstick.

He still hadn't spoken one word to me so I had no way of knowing if he was going to touch or torment me today. His mood swings gave me whiplash, but in that moment I was definitely hoping for option A.

He passed within an inch of me before taking a shirt from his section of the closet. His wings shimmered out of existence as he retreated fully into his Fae form and he pulled the shirt over his arms as I turned to look at him.

I glanced towards the sheet tent that Dante had created and stepped forward to close the distance between me and Gabriel, my heart pounding a dangerous rhythm. A part of me didn't want Dante to see us. Another, insanely imaginative part wanted him to come out and join us.

I reached out to Gabriel and silently started buttoning his shirt for him. My fingers skimmed the hard planes of his tattooed chest and his breathing grew heavier at the slight contact.

The lower my buttoning got, the wilder the look in his eyes as he watched me, his pupils dilating dangerously, begging me to keep going.

As I reached the final button, my fingers remained against his waistband and I dragged my eyes up from my hands to meet his.

There was a dare hanging between us. We weren't doing anything at all. And yet we were at the same time. I just wasn't sure which of us would have to admit it first.

Dante shifted in his bunk and I released my grip on Gabriel's shirt, turning back to the mirror as if we hadn't been doing anything. Which we hadn't. Mostly.

Dante pulled the sheet aside and climbed out of his bed. He was already dressed for class and he switched his Atlas off as he stood.

"Do you wanna walk to breakfast with me, carina?" he asked, his gaze sliding over me.

"Sure," I replied easily, moving away from Gabriel as if we hadn't just been...well I didn't even know what we'd just been doing but I hadn't really wanted it to stop.

"See you in class, Elise," Gabriel called after me as I made it to the door with Dante.

I looked back at him in surprise and Dante scowled, never seeming to like it when Gabriel chose to speak.

"I'll save you a seat," I promised and Gabriel's lips curled into a smile just before the door closed between us.

"Why would you want to sit with that stronzo?" Dante asked me as we started walking.

"Well I'm walking with you aren't I?" I teased. "So maybe assholes are my thing."

Dante snorted a laugh and threw an arm around my waist, drawing me in. "You have no idea, bella. I'm the biggest asshole you've ever met."

I considered shrugging out of his grip but I couldn't say I hated the feeling of his muscular arm holding me close and it was a cold day so I was stealing some body heat from him too.

"I'm not sure about that," I said casually. "You don't really know anything about me or where I come from."

Dante laughed darkly. "If you think you've met a bigger badder asshole than me then by all means introduce me to him so that I can prove you wrong."

"I dunno, Dante. I mean sure, you're scary and all. Big and strong and mean and super intimidating," I smirked as my tone didn't come off intimidated at all. "But what have you really done that's so *bad*?"

Dante looked down at me and for a moment the darkness in his eyes made my heart skitter. His grip around my waist loosened and he lifted his arm, twisting a finger through my short hair like he was considering whether or not to tell me. I held his eyes, biting my lip as I silently urged him to spill his secrets to me. Maybe there was a chance that he would admit to being involved with what had happened to my brother. Or maybe I just wanted to know what made him tick.

"I was born into this life, carina. Being an Oscura isn't just something you can claim by name alone. I was forged into the man I am with blood and steel. My father trained me in everything I'd need to survive in my role as the leader of my people. The things I've done aren't the kinds of things nice girls want to hear about."

I looked up at him in surprise, wondering if he was really so blind that

that was all he saw when he looked at me.

"Look a little closer, Dante, I'm not a nice girl. And being a Callisto was never a walk in the park either. Your father may have forged you into the man you are, but I built *myself* up into the woman *I* am. Each cut and every scar only toughened my skin. Every break and fracture only steeled my determination. And *everything* I've lost has only strengthened my soul. I won't flinch at the worst of you because there is no best of me anymore."

Dante pulled me to a halt just outside the Cafaeteria and turned to face me. His gaze scraped over my features and I looked back steadily.

"If you were mine, I'd protect you from everything the world ever had to throw at you," he said. "No one would ever dare to hurt you or take something from you again." He reached out and pushed my lilac hair behind my ear as he looked deep into my eyes.

And for a heartbeat I almost wanted to say yes. How nice it would be to let someone else look after me and right all the wrongs that came against me. But that just wasn't who I was.

I placed my hand over his against my cheek and looked up at him, wanting him to see more of me than the picture he'd painted in his mind.

"That's not what I want though," I said firmly. "I don't need someone to look after me or protect me or own me. I'm perfectly capable of doing that for myself. And I have nothing left to lose now anyway."

I offered him a hard smile then walked inside to get my breakfast, leaving him to join his Clan on the far side of the room. From where I was standing I was freer than him anyway. Being in one of the gangs seemed a lot like shackling yourself to a certain kind of life and relinquishing any freedom over your own decisions. I didn't care how much power they promised or what protection they claimed to offer, I had no interest in ever joining one of them.

I made my way along the counter and grabbed a bagel and a mug of coffee before taking a seat towards the back of the room. I gave my attention to my food and only looked up when I heard someone calling my name.

"There you are!" Leon said enthusiastically as he strode right through the room towards me.

A Mindy was following close behind him holding a large black box tied with a white ribbon.

Leon dropped down opposite me with a grin and I eyed his long, messy hair with a smile. It didn't look like he'd made any attempt to tame it this morning and I was really just surprised to see him out of bed before class started at all. The Mindy placed the box down before me, offering me a tight-lipped assessment before he dismissed her with a flick of his fingers like she was a speck of dirt on his glove and she scurried away.

I frowned after her for a moment before giving him my attention again.

"Can't you just turn that shit off?" I asked before he could say whatever the hell he was bursting to say. He was literally bouncing in his seat and I could tell he wanted me to ask about the box so I decided to pretend it wasn't there.

"What shit?" Leon asked with a faint frown, clearly thrown by the fact that I hadn't asked about the box.

"The Lion charisma or whatever it is. It's weird watching a bunch of girls fall over themselves for you like a horde of wind up barbies. Surely you could just set them free from it if you want to?"

"You jealous, little monster?" he asked hopefully.

"You wish."

"Do you wanna be exclusive then?" he teased.

"Never," I replied easily. That shit had never done my mom any favours. The only way I'd ever give myself to one man completely would be if he turned out to be my Elysian Mate. Which Gabriel seemed to think he was. But I wouldn't be believing that nonsense until I was stood beneath the stars looking him in the eyes and answering the question of fate. And even then, I'd be asking to see the contract before I signed on the dotted line. I was sure even fate could be open to negotiations.

434

Leon scrubbed a hand across the blonde stubble lining his jaw and looked at me like he was trying to spot a lie, but there wasn't one to find so he had to let it drop.

"So..." Leon leaned forward and drummed his fingers on the box, an excited smile on his face.

"Aren't you eating?" I asked casually.

"I- aren't you going to ask about-"

"There are lots of studies into the detrimental effects of missing breakfast." I took another bite of my own meal to hide my smile.

"A Mindy will get me something after you-"

"And a growing boy like you really needs to make sure he looks after himself."

"If you wanna take this somewhere private, I'm sure you can watch a piece of me grow real quick," he joked and I barked a laugh as he caught me off guard. I wasn't really sure how Leon managed to spark joy in me like that so easily. When he wasn't around, I didn't really feel like there was anything like that left in me at all. Like I wasn't capable of feeling anything but grief and pain and loss. But every now and then, Leon dug right through it all without even seeming to try. He made me feel joy and light and laughter and I just wanted to drink it all in and never let it go.

"You might be able to tempt me into that," I admitted and his smile widened from teasing to smug as fuck. "But don't go getting cocky."

"Me? As if. Now if you don't ask me about this box I'm gonna lose my mind." Leon pushed the box a few inches closer to me.

"What box?" I smiled innocently, batting my eyelashes like I had no fucking idea what he was talking about even though the thing was taking up half the table.

"*Elise,*" Leon growled and I was struck with the desire to make him beg a little more as his voice went all rough and demanding on me.

"Oh *this* box!" I exclaimed pretending to be surprised by it.

"Open. It," he demanded.

"Why?" I asked, pushing my empty plate aside as I let my gaze trail over the box then back to him.

"Because it's for you."

"But it's not my birthday," I countered.

Leon growled again and a shiver rolled down my spine. I *really* liked it when he made that noise.

"What do I have to do to get you to stop toying with me and open it?" he asked, his gaze raking over me like he didn't know what the hell to do with me. I guessed for a man used to clicking his fingers and having women fall all over themselves to do every little thing for him, this was pretty damn infuriating. I wondered when was the last time he'd struggled to get his own way in anything.

I leaned over the box and dropped my voice conspiratorially. "Growl for me again, Leo," I purred.

He obliged instantly, his eyes flashing with a hint of danger as I taunted him with that nickname. For a moment I couldn't help but wonder what happened when the sleeping beast within him awoke. I suddenly really wanted to see him in his Lion form and I wondered if I could convince him to shift for me one time.

My smile widened as the sound of his growl ripped through my core and I reached out to tug at the ribbon on the box.

Leon watched me hungrily as I took my sweet time opening his latest gift. Curiosity was stinging me, but I fought against the urge to speed up, savouring the frustration in his gaze as I acted like I couldn't care less what this box contained.

When I finally slipped the lid off it, I looked down to find a black dress wrapped in rose scented tissue paper within it. It looked expensive. Like, the kind of expensive which meant the likes of me should never run their grubby paws all over it.

With a feeling like I was breaking some rule, I reached out and traced my fingers along the soft material.

Leon was drinking in my reaction as I slowly lifted it from the box and my heart pounded harder as I realised what it was for. He'd bought me a dress for the party. And not just any dress. A piece of art which seemed to call out to me in every way from the tight bodice which laced up the back to the floor length skirt which moved like water between my fingers.

"Leon," I breathed, unable to keep up my unaffected pretence a moment longer. "It's..." There weren't really words for what it was so I just shook my head, at a loss for them.

"I'm fucking nailing this generous shit," he said proudly. "And it gets better." He lifted a pair of shoes from the bottom of the box where I hadn't even noticed them.

I folded the dress back carefully and smiled at the killer heels which were the exact same shade of lilac as my hair.

"Now I won't have to bend so low to reach your mouth," Leon whispered conspiratorially and I was struck with the urge to kiss him now.

My heart beat a little too fast and I placed the shoes back in the box as I looked up at him. Had he realised that I hadn't been joking about turning up in my sweatpants? Had he realised I had zero funds to my name? Or was this just some lucky coincidence which had saved me from bailing on the first night I'd been truly looking forward to since coming to this academy? Whatever the reason for his act of kindness was, it seemed like fate was smiling on me today. Well...it was if I ignored the whole Cindy Lou incident but then that hadn't turned out too terribly either.

Leon pushed himself to his feet, clearly intending to leave and I replaced the lid on the box.

"I'll see you in class?" he confirmed, his gaze sliding to the window where the sun was shining in. He began to loosen his tie, clearly intending to head out for a power top up sunbathing style.

I shot to my feet before he could leave, stopping before him and pushing up onto my tiptoes as I pressed a kiss to the corner of his mouth.

"Thank you," I breathed and his eyes widened in surprise as the length of my body brushed against his for a moment and a shiver of longing darted through me.

Leon reached out to snare me in his arms, tilting his chin like he was going to steal a proper kiss and I laughed as I sped away from him before he could catch me.

"You'll have to be quicker than that if you want to win a kiss, Leo," I teased as I grabbed the box from the table and he turned towards me with a frown.

"No fair," he protested, reaching towards me again.

"All's fair in love and war," I taunted, shooting away again before he could reply.

I kept going all the way up to my room where I laid the box down on my bunk.

I bit my lip as I thought about the way Leon's stubble had grazed against it, wondering what it would be like to feel the bite of it against more of my flesh. As fantasies went, Leon Night was a pretty good one to have. And Friday night at the ball, I might just let myself indulge in it a little.

RYDER

CHAPTER THIRTY FIVE

Second chances didn't hang around Alestria too often. Maybe the stars didn't shine so brightly on this city. But I'd learned a long time ago that even the heavens could be bribed. So I didn't bow to horoscopes, fate or predictions. I made my own luck. Which was why I headed to the bleachers just before the Spring Party started and shot Elise a private message on FaeBook – a site I spent zero fucking time on, but which actually served me right now.

Ryder:
Is Cinderella planning on giving me a twirl on the bleachers before the ball?

I wore sweatpants and a creased t-shirt, making the least effort possible as I listened to the masses of partying idiots heading to Voyant Sports Hall. Why people wanted to dress up like morons and *socialise* was beyond me.

The minutes ticked by and I bit down on the inside of my cheek until blood soaked my tongue. I was growing impatient and even the sweet kiss of pain didn't compare to the one I wanted to take from Elise's mouth. I wasn't gonna back down this time. No more visions. This needed to happen for real. If she really thought any other man could give her what I could, she was fucking delusional. Once we took this step, she'd figure that out. We were cut from the same cloth. She was just afraid she'd drown in me if she gave in to her urges. But it was time for her to let go of the lifebuoy and sink to the bottom of the ocean with me.

My Atlas vibrated on silent mode and my eyes fell to the screen in time with the dull thump of my heart.

Elise:
I'm no princess. And I don't twirl for anybody.

A low laugh left my throat as I wrote out a reply.

Ryder:
Blame that last message on autocorrect. It meant to say: Is the shit-hot vampire planning on sinking her teeth into my veins before the ball?

A blur in my periphery made me tense on instinct, but my gaze fell on Elise as she drew to a halt in front of me, having run from the dorms to see me.

She looked like an evil queen spread onto a layer of fucking beautiful. Her black corseted dress made me hard as hell and the way it pushed up her tits helped too. It fell to the ground but I could tell she was wearing heels due to the extra four inches she'd grown – either that or she was standing on Inferno's tiny dick.

She lifted a brow as my gaze dropped to her pink lipstick which I wanted to smear thoroughly with my mouth.

"Aren't you supposed to say something about how pretty I look?" She coiled a lock of lilac hair around her finger, swinging her hips as she put on an overly girlish expression.

"You don't look pretty," I growled and her expression slammed into bitch gear, but I didn't give a shit. "You look like the most lethal poison I've ever seen. It's fucking divine."

"That's a weird ass compliment, Ryder." She stepped closer, her eyes tracing over my throat then shifting to my lips, a hint of longing in them. *What I could do to you with my mouth, new girl. You only need to say the words.*

"Do you want the normal kind instead then?" I took a step forward with every word I said next. "Beautiful. Stunning. Breath-taking." I stopped in her personal space, inhaling her. Cherries. Did she know the pits contained cyanide? Everyone savoured the sweet exterior, ignoring the deadly concoction at its heart. The piece that got cut out and thrown away. But I'd never want to get rid of the pit that lived in her. To me, that was the sweetest part of all.

Her pupils dilated and though her disinterested mask didn't slip, her body language told me just how much I was affecting her.

"I don't think you feel those words as deeply as my first ones, do you?" I growled and she slowly shook her head.

She laid a hand on my shoulder and leaned in to take a bite of me. I dipped my chin so her mouth was aligned with mine instead and she glanced up through her lashes, a flicker of lust filling them.

Her fingers knotted in my shirt and I could feel her resistance everywhere, the pressure of it building between us.

"Lust or pain," I breathed against her lips. "Your choice, new girl. But make the right one."

The heat of her body radiated from her and it took everything I had not to drag her against me. But this was her decision. And I had to let her make it. Surely she felt this between us, did she really give a damn about pissing off Inferno? She could move into my room and he could go to hell.

She pressed her fingers to her own lips, leaving a lipstick kiss on them before touching them to my mouth. I groaned with a mixture of disappointment and delight as she pushed my head aside and sank her teeth into my throat. I pulled her against me, running my tongue across my lips and tasting her.

Why can't she bow to these feelings? Why does Dante Oscura have to matter?

The sting in my neck grew sharper as she buried her fangs deeper and a growl left my lips as desire coursed through me. This was torture. Pure and simple. And not because of the pain – that was bliss – but because she'd denied me once more. Shut me down. Told me no. I'd laid out my black and wasted heart for her and she'd rejected it. Again. In hindsight, that should have been fucking predictable. But I'd made my choice. I'd told her where I'd be tonight. So she had approximately six more hours to change her mind.

She extracted her fangs and swallowed my ice cold blood like it was her favourite milkshake.

"Tonight's your chance, Elise. I'll be in my room waiting for you." It wasn't entirely true. I had somewhere to go first, but I knew Elise wasn't going to bail on this party until she stubbornly spent at least a few hours resisting the urge to come to me. I shifted closer to her and her pupils dilated. I dipped my head to her ear, my breath drawing goosebumps along her flesh. "I'll make it hurt so good."

She pressed a hand to my chest to hold me back. "It's not gonna happen."

I nodded, teasing my tongue piercing between my teeth. "But you're tempted though, aren't you? Don't bullshit me."

She tucked a lock of hair behind her ear, glancing away and I waited for her to decide to tell me. She would, because she couldn't face the alternative of bottling to the dare in my voice. "Temptation is irrelevant if your will is strong enough, Ryder. And mine's made of iron. So no matter how tempted I am…" Her hand sailed down my chest and over my waistband to press against my hard-on which was straining against my pants. I released a breathy groan as she squeezed once then stepped away with a teasing grin. "I won't cave."

I grunted in response to that then she shot away from me, leaving me standing there on full fucking display to the world. It hurt to watch her leave.

444

And maybe that was why I was so fucking obsessed with her. Everything about her made me suffer. And I was a glutton for it. But I'd vowed to myself tonight would be her last chance. I hadn't screwed anyone since she'd stormed into my life, and I wasn't gonna deny myself any longer if she was never going to be with me.

My Atlas buzzed and I took it out of my pocket, finding a message from Scarlett. Since my entire fucking family were lying in bloody graves, The Brotherhood were waiting for me to graduate Aurora Academy before I took my rightful place as King. Scarlett was filling in for me until then. She'd been my father's second in command and I trusted her implicitly. Since Felix Oscura had attacked us in our territory, killing thirteen of my people, she was anxious for me to go home and discuss tactics with her and the rest of the inner circle.

But I hadn't rushed home like a baby to its mama, I'd spent the days thinking over tactics and was heading home for a couple of hours tonight like I did every other Friday. Dante had eyes on me at all times, so there was no chance in hell I'd have let him see me run home the second the news had reached my ears.

I checked the time, figuring I'd be back on campus by ten at the latest.

I headed behind the bleachers and pulled off my shirt and pants, my focus switching to my one true calling in life. Destroying the Oscuras. And if there was one solid way to kill a boner, it was them.

The Kiplings kept a stash of spare clothes for me on the edge of campus along with a whole host of other useful shit. I stuffed my shirt and pants into a bag with my Altas, hiding it in the shadows as the laughter of other students carried to me. I shook my head at them then shifted into my snake form, choosing to shrink down to the size of a python. Another perk of my Order. I could be monstrous as all hell or sneaky as fuck.

I slid into the grass beyond the bleachers, winding my way around Devil's Hill, passing by the Vega Dorms and across campus. When I eventually passed through the Empyrean Fields and slid into the woods, I let my form grow until I was the length of a school bus and as thick as a cow.

I wound through the trees, tasting a thousand scents on the air from the crispness of pine trees to the earthiness of moss. I sensed the heat of a deer herd before they stampeded away from me and I slithered deeper into the forest. The mossy ground made my scales slide smoothly along the ground, leaving no trail at all as I headed toward the most north eastern corner of campus.

I slid through a small stream and up a steep bank, coming to a halt beside the entrance to the Kipling Cache with a deep rattle in the depths of my body.

I shifted back into my Fae form, standing up in the mud and walking to the concealed hatch which was enchanted to look like a large boulder. As I approached it, I pressed my hand against the cold rock and the magic gave me access, recognising me.

A wide hatch was revealed at my feet, the vision of the boulder evaporating before my eyes. I knelt down, taking hold of the edge and yanking it up to reveal a steep ramp that headed away into the dark. I descended into it and the Faeworms crawling through the muddy tunnel roof gave enough light to see by.

I reached the bottom, arriving in a cave which split off in several directions. Only the Kiplings knew their way around this place. It spread for miles under the entire forest, but there was just one part designated for me and my gang.

I headed past the wooden chests stacked around the cavern, taking the tunnel to my left which was marked with the symbol of The Brotherhood on the wall. Oscuras had their own stores on the opposite side and the Kiplings had cast a powerful spell on each passage to ensure we could only access our own supplies.

An eternal fire blazed at the heart of The Brotherhood's cavern. It was a circular chamber created by earth magic, the walls moulded into deep shelves and holes big enough to hold everything we'd ever asked for from the Kiplings. Beside the fire was a dark green Yamaharpie dirt bike which made a grin pull at my mouth, its gleaming paintwork resembling the scales of a snake.

I headed past it to the chest against the wall, wrenching it open and taking out a bundle of clothes. I pulled on the jeans, shirt and hoody, all of which were black to give me cover when darkness fell.

I put on some boots then tugged on a leather jacket with the Brotherhood insignia on the back. I moved to one of the shelves, pressing my hand to a metal box which unlocked with my touch alone. Inside, was a phone and my keys. I grabbed them out and shut the box, heading to the bike and pulling on my helmet before swinging my leg over my favourite piece of machinery in the world.

I kicked up the stand and twisted the key in the ignition. The engine blazed to life and the humming power of the beast beneath me sent adrenaline into my blood. I released the throttle and tore down the passage toward the exit, veering through the main cavern and speeding up the ramp that led back into the woods. Gas fumes filled my senses and brought on a buzz in my chest.

I cast a vine in my left hand as the bike surged into the forest, catching hold of the hatch and slamming it shut behind me. I released the magic and shot through the trees, speeding toward the outer fence which surrounded the academy with a rush of energy pouring through my veins.

I soon arrived before the huge metal fence which stretched in either direction and I turned the bike to sail alongside it, hunting for the red X the Kiplings had painted onto it. When I spotted it, I turned the bike sharply toward it and rode through the wall as easily as passing through water, the engine droning loudly. The effects of the magic brushed over my skin, running away again as I raced into the forest beyond it.

The Iron Wood stretched on for hundreds of miles, bordering the city of Alestria before meeting with Fable Mountain in the North. I could take a direct route all the way to Lunar Territory from here and the faculty would be none the fucking wiser.

I took the well-worn track I followed every couple of weeks, racing through the woodland as dusk descended. The lasting light was deepest red and painted the ground in bloody hues.

I closed in on the edge of town and turned the bike toward the copse where I'd leave it and walk the rest of the way to Scarlett's house.

As I rushed into the clearing, something slammed into the front wheel and the bike flipped. My gut soared as I cast earth magic at the ground to soften my fall. But before I impacted with the mud, I was snared in air magic and twisted upside down. With a yell of anger, I shot vines from my hands to counter the attack but someone froze them mid air, the ice sliding up and wrapping around my bare hands to stall my power too.

"Show yourselves!" I bellowed, my voice muffled by my helmet. I was furious as I battled the air holding me six feet above the ground, the magic overwhelmingly powerful. I wasn't trained well enough to fight it off and I cursed that school for taking so long with my fucking education.

A man stepped out of the shadows who made my insides coil with hatred. Felix Oscura. Dante's piece of shit uncle, the current leader of the Clan. And the man who'd buried thirteen members of my gang less than a week ago.

"Fuck you!" I spat as he closed the gap between us, his hollow eyes sliding over me. Three more of the Oscura Clan appeared from the trees, their faces set in sneers as they took in the son of their mortal enemy. My father had killed so many members of their family, it would have taken a century to piece back together all of the body parts.

"Ryder Draconis." Felix took hold of my helmet, yanking it off and tossing it onto the ground. The visor cracked on a rock and I snarled through my teeth. "It's not like The Brotherhood to stick to routines. You got sloppy."

Acid seeped through my blood at his words. What a fucking idiot I'd been taking this same route on the same day every two weeks. I'd gotten too damn comfortable and now that mistake was gonna cost me my life.

Felix clicked his fingers and the woman behind him waved her hand, the air magic releasing me so I shot toward the ground.

I crashed into it headfirst, my magic still useless as the ice pressed to my palms. Blood poured down my forehead but if they thought hurting me was worthwhile, they were going to be severely disappointed.

"I live for pain," I growled, rising onto my knees and the woman's air magic pressed down on my shoulders to keep me there.

Felix coated his fingers in ice, creating razor sharp nails from his water magic. His weathered features were half in light, half in shadow.

"Yeah, so I hear," he rasped, his tone common and his voice dry. "But the question we Oscuras always bet on is whether that's because of your Order or because Mariella Oscura fucked up that little Lunar brain of yours too good." His boot swung for my face and I didn't even flinch as the steel cap slammed into my jaw. Pain burst through my mouth, swelling my magic reserves. One of my back teeth was knocked out and I spat it onto the ground with a wad of blood, smiling up at him.

"I'm unbreakable," I growled. "You won't get information from me. So kill me quick or slow. I'll enjoy it either way."

Felix sneered at me, the darkness in his eyes mirroring my own. He reached down to grip my chin, his frozen nails biting into my skin and drawing blood. "I'd love to see you dead, snake. But I need something from you."

"I'd die before I'd help Oscura Clan," I snarled, rage swirling through me like a hurricane.

"You might wanna hear me out first," Felix mused. "You've got a lot to gain from this deal."

I ground my teeth, refusing to fall for his bait. I would not be fucking bribed by Felix Oscura.

He stepped closer, releasing my chin and running his tongue across his teeth. "I want you to kill someone for me. Oscura Clan can't get involved in this, but it won't affect The Brotherhood."

"Do your own dirty work." My upper lip curled back as blood sailed down my jaw. "Or can your mutts not even manage that now?"

His Clan members howled and stalked closer, baying for my blood.

Felix held up a hand to hold them off, surveying me through his lifeless eyes. "I'll give you something you can't refuse, Draconis. I'll give you Mariella's location."

I stilled, staring up at him as those words rang in my head over and over. *Mariella.* I'd longed to find her for years, to finish her for what she'd done to me. I'd cut out my own tongue for it. But why would Felix give her up?

"Liar," I snarled. "You wouldn't sacrifice one of your own."

"She's less than an Omega nowadays," he said with disdain. "What use is she to the Clan while she hides in the shadows? She won't show her face after what you did to her. I couldn't care less if you have her."

"I'll never trust you." I shook my head, my shoulders tensing as Felix stepped aside, allowing a man to move between us.

"Here's my proof," Felix said and the man's face morphed. His two eyes slid together until they were just one, large feature at the centre of his face. The Cyclops rested a hand on Felix's forehead then placed his other on mine.

Felix's memory was channelled into my brain and I saw myself on the ground, kneeling at his feet as he spoke to me. *"I couldn't care less if you have her."* I felt the truth of those words in my chest the same way he had when he'd voiced them.

The Cyclops released us and I gazed at Felix in shock, my resolve fading away. He really was offering me Mariella. And there were few things in this world I wouldn't do to get my hands on her.

"I won't hurt anyone in The Brotherhood," I said, lifting my chin in defiance.

"It's not The Brotherhood I want," Felix said with a dark smile. "There's a student in your school I need gone. Dead. Buried. With no fucking traces back to me."

"And you'll give up Mariella once it's done?"

He nodded. "So what do you say, Draconis…do we have a deal?"

I set my jaw, my mind on vengeance and nothing else. I could take a life for Mariella. And I fucking would. "Deal. Who is it you want dead?"

ELISE

CHAPTER THIRTY SIX

I twisted my fingers through my hair where it hung beside my chin as I waited outside the dorms for Leon. He had been planning to pick me up from my room but when Ryder had messaged me, I changed the plan. My Atlas was still upstairs, but I chose not to go back for it. I had no bag so I couldn't really keep it on me tonight anyway and it wasn't like I had any money to put in a purse. I was hoping the drinks were free tonight or I'd be spending the evening sober...unless I could convince Leon to buy me a few.

I ran my tongue over my lips again, tasting the lingering drops of Ryder's blood with a smile dancing around my mouth.

His power filled me to the brim, dancing beneath my skin and whispering dark promises in my ear. I was more than a little tempted to take him up on his offer tonight. But no matter how much I was drawn to him, I wasn't going to forget the reason I'd come to this academy. There was a damn good chance that Ryder Draconis had murdered my brother. And if that were the truth then the only thing I'd be taking from him was his life.

My gut twisted uncomfortably at that thought and I frowned at myself. Why was I feeling uncomfortable? I'd never once doubted the idea of seeking vengeance on the piece of shit who'd killed my brother before. And I definitely wasn't going to let my fucking hormones make me feel guilty either. Just because the guys who had most likely been responsible for his death were stupidly attractive, it didn't mean I was going to blink.

I wouldn't be going to Ryder's room tonight.

And not just because I was worried that sleeping with him would make it harder to kill him if I had to. But because it meant picking too. Lunar or Oscura. Ryder or Dante. I refused to pick either. But in the darkest corner of my heart, I wished I could have both.

I snorted at the ridiculousness of that idea. If I let myself fall into fantasies involving the two gang leaders being okay with that kind of situation, I was delusional. And I guessed that was a part of what held me back too. They were both telling me what I had to do. Both telling me what I couldn't do either. Picking one meant saying no to the other and I didn't want that any more than I wanted to join a gang. Besides, I didn't want or need any man who thought he could place rules upon me.

The door to the Vega Dorms opened and Leon stepped out, his eyes falling on me in an instant, the heat in them sending a trickle of desire running through me.

I pushed myself to my feet as he prowled towards me, his movements all masculine and animal, his eyes locked on me like I was his prey. And I found I quite liked being the hunted instead of the hunter for once.

He'd tamed his long, dirty blonde hair back into a topknot and had dressed in a deep blue suit with a white shirt beneath it. He wasn't wearing a tie and there were enough buttons left undone to give me a glimpse of his tanned chest.

Leon didn't slow as he came straight for me, a deep growl escaping him as his eyes raked over me in the dress he'd bought.

He caught my waist and I inhaled sharply half a second before his lips captured mine.

454

My lips parted for his tongue as he pressed forward, dragging me against him so that every line and curve of our bodies were pressed against each other.

I caught his lapel in my fist, pulling him closer still as his kiss devoured me whole.

My heart was pounding an erratic tune in my chest, my thoughts scattering and an aching desire riding through me like a storm. I wanted him. Needed him. More than I'd even let myself realise until that moment when he'd finally decided to stop letting me run.

Leon's grip on me tightened and I could feel the keen press of his arousal grinding against me as the heat of our kiss burned through us like a wildfire.

My fangs snapped out as I lost control despite the fact that I'd had more than enough of Ryder's blood to sate me. But I wanted more of Leon, every part of him.

He drew back a little and I caught his bottom lip between my teeth, my fangs scratching against the inside of it and offering me the faintest taste of his blood. I moaned aloud as the blazing power of him called to me like sunshine on a winter's day. He was an oasis in the middle of a desert, a diamond in a pile of coal. I ached for more but he broke our kiss before I could drive my fangs deeper.

"Calm down, little monster," he teased, leaning close to speak in my ear, his stubble scraping against my skin in a way that had my toes curling. "There's only one way I'll let you bite me."

"And how's that?" I asked, tipping my head so that I could look into his golden eyes which were blazing with the same desire I felt coursing through my veins.

"When I've got you pinned beneath me and you're screaming my name," he growled, the tone of his voice sending a shiver down my spine. "You can bite me when I make your body tremble with pleasure and you can't take it anymore."

"Well that's something to look forward to later," I teased, inching back as I fought to regain control of myself.

"Is that a promise?" he begged, holding me close for a final moment.

"No," I replied with a smirk before twisting out of his grip.

He caught my hand and I let him have it. He smiled like he'd just won a point then tugged me closer so that he could sling his arm around my shoulders instead and I let him do that too.

"I think I'm starting to get a taste for this taking the lead stuff," Leon said, dipping his mouth to my ear again.

"Don't push your luck," I teased, looking up at him from beneath my lashes.

"I'll try to control myself," he promised though it felt like a lie.

I smiled as I leaned into his hold and we started walking toward the huge Voyant Sports Hall where the party was being held.

More and more students appeared along the path as we headed closer to the party where Taylor Swift was belting out her best rendition of I Knew You Were Trouble. Leon laughed as he led me through the double doors.

"They're playing your song," he joked but my attention had slipped from him to the unrecognisable sports hall before me.

The party committee had done an amazing job and my lips parted as I looked up at the pool of water which had been conjured to hang above our heads. Schools of glimmering silver fish swam past as I watched and I couldn't help but grin at the impressive display of magic.

I dropped my eyes to the walls where waterfalls ran endlessly down them and the sound of running water undercut the music which was pounding out from speakers at the far end of the room. There were circular tables laid out around the edges of the space, each holding a beautiful ice sculpture at the heart of them depicting various Order forms. I didn't spot any Vampires but I guessed an ice girl with pointy teeth didn't look quite as impressive as a Manticore with the body of a lion, wings of a bat and a scorpion stinger for a tail.

Someone bumped into me and I flinched back just before a drink sloshed to the ground by my feet, narrowly missing my new shoes.

"Oh, I'm *so* sorry," Cindy Lou gushed falsely as I looked up to find her standing way too close to me, her arm coiled around Dante's possessively.

I didn't even bother to respond to her as I looked up at the Storm Dragon whose dark eyes were currently drinking me in like I was the only flower in the meadow. He was wearing a black suit which brought out all the darkness in his features and made him seem so much older than nineteen.

"Hi," I breathed as he pinned me in his gaze.

"You...splendi più luminosa di tutte le stelle del cielo, bella," he said with a smile that made my stomach do a backflip even though I didn't know what it meant.

"Stop eye-fucking my date, man," Leon teased, thumping Dante squarely in the bicep and drawing his attention away from me. "And don't use that foreign pantie dropping crap on her either."

I couldn't help but laugh as Leon pulled me against his chest and the warmth of him enveloped me.

"Are you worried because it might work?" Dante teased him and I rolled my eyes in response.

Cindy Lou clucked her tongue and glowered at me but the guys ignored her.

"I dunno, little monster, are you tempted to ditch me for this asshole?" Leon asked, looking down at me with a playful smile.

I looked back up at him and reached out to run my fingers across his rough jaw. "No," I replied honestly. I had no desire to ditch Leon for Dante. Though if they were willing to share then I wouldn't have objected to that idea at all.

A look passed between the two of them for a moment which almost made me wonder if they'd just been thinking the same thing but Cindy Lou interrupted, reminding us all that she was still there too. Unfortunately.

"Come on, baby," she said, fluttering her eyelashes at Dante as she coiled her arm around his more tightly. Her voice dropped suggestively as she reached out with her other hand to brush her fingers along his belt and I stilled as I was struck with the desire to smack her roaming hands off of him. "I want to show you something outside..."

Dante hesitated a moment before letting her guide him away and I watched them leave with a scream of frustration sticking in my throat. Which was totally insane because I held no claim over Dante and that was entirely by choice. But the idea of that stupid cow putting her hands all over him made me wanna spit. Which was crazy. Not to mention totally hypocritical because I was here with Leon and I had zero desire to change that fact.

"Pfft, that girl," Leon growled and I looked up at him in surprise as he narrowed his eyes at Cindy Lou's back.

"What about her?" I asked. I thought I was the only one who knew she was a total sack of shit but if Leon wanted to have a bitching sesh at her expense then I was all in.

He shook his head dismissively. "She just used to date a friend of mine and it ended...badly."

"Oh?"

Leon gave me a rueful smile and caught my waist between his hands as he dismissed the subject of Cindy Lou.

"You wanna show me how you like to party, little monster?" he purred and I smiled as I looked around the room, trying to figure out what I wanted to do first.

My eyes fell on the dance floor which seemed to be made out of a block of pale blue ice and I grinned as I started heading straight for it, tugging Leon after me by his hand.

"Don't you wanna get a drink first?" Leon asked, trying to tug me back but I only pulled harder.

"No. I want to dance. You're not gonna bail on me already are you?"

His lips twitched with amusement at the dare and he shook his head.

The music changed as we reached the dance floor and I grinned as Hot in Herre by Nelly started playing. Songs about taking your clothes off tended to get a lot of plays back in The Sparkling Uranus and I was pretty sure I could have performed a whole routine to it if the mood took me.

Instead of stripping for the entire school, I stepped into Leon's arms and fell into the rhythm of the music as our bodies moved together and the heat between us began to build again.

My breaths came quicker and my heart beat faster for every second he held me in his arms. As one song bled into two then three, four, five, I realised I was smiling. Like full on smiling with real joy in his company. Which wouldn't have been strange for anyone else. But since I'd lost my brother, I'd begun to think I'd never feel that way again.

And all the while that Leon was making me feel like that, I knew I wouldn't want to be anywhere but in his arms. Which was exactly where I intended to stay tonight.

He was like joy personified. I'd stopped even thinking of him as a potential suspect. There was just no way that someone as happy and warm as him could be a killer. So I let myself fall under his spell just a little. Because I was so tired of all the lies I'd been telling since coming here. The smile Leon put on my face was one of the most honest things I'd experienced in far too long. And I intended to spend as much time smiling with him as I could.

GARETH

CHAPTER THIRTY SEVEN

FIFTEEN MONTHS BEFORE THE SOLARID METEOR SHOWER…

*P*ing. Ping. Ping, ping, ping.

   "What the hell, man, who's blowing up your Atlas?" I groaned as I tried to pull a pillow over my face to block out the continued sound of messages flooding Leon's Atlas. It was the middle of the night and I was way too tired to cope with the ongoing sound.

   "Sorry, dude," Leon muttered and the sound of him rummaging about followed as he tried to hunt down the offending piece of technology within his bed. "It's probably just a Mindy who can't sleep because she's dreaming of sucking my- well shit."

   The serious tone of his voice made me ditch the pillow and turn to face him. I squinted in the darkness and a low growl came from him, sending a shiver of fear along my spine. I didn't think I'd ever been so sharply aware of the fact that I was sleeping a few meters away from a goddamn Lion before.

   "What is it?" I asked, pushing myself to sit up so that my duvet fell to

pool around my waist.

"Are you okay, baby?" Sasha asked as she woke too.

A growl tore from Leon's lips as she tried to reach for him and she leapt backwards, tripping over a pile of his clothes that he'd dumped in the middle of the room before she fell onto my bed. I steadied her, noticing the tremor running through her flesh as she recoiled from her King in fright.

"Leon, dude, that wasn't cool," I said warily.

His head snapped up to look at me and the moonlight spilling in from the window caught in his eyes, making me flinch. I bit down on my tongue and got to my feet, determined not to fall back in response to the dangerous energy he was exuding like Sasha had.

"Tell me what's wrong," I demanded.

Another low growl sounded from him and he leapt out of bed, yanking on a pair of sweatpants and pushing his feet into his sneakers before heading for the door. "There's something I've gotta do," he snarled. "If you wanna help then keep up."

He ripped the door open and I swore beneath my breath as I snatched a pair of jeans and a rumpled t-shirt from the end of my bed a pulled them on. I grabbed my sneakers, not wasting time putting them on as I chased after Leon into the corridor. He was already taking the stairs and was almost out of sight. I had to run to catch him and even then I could hardly keep up.

I managed to jam my sneakers on my feet one at a time as we descended flight after flight of stairs in silence.

Leon's frame was tight with a posture so unfamiliar to me that I hardly recognised him.

"What the hell's going on?" I asked as he growled beneath his breath again.

"Some asshole is about to find out what happens when you steal from the Nights."

I frowned in response to that. His family were thieves but they had a rule against anyone stealing from them*? Seriously? And it sounded like it must have been a pretty important rule at that because Leon was angrier than I'd ever seen him. In fact, I wasn't sure I'd ever seen him angry at all. But now that I had, I realised that I'd been letting his easy going facade blind me to the beast that lay beneath his flesh. He was a Nemean Lion, king of the jungle, one of the most ferocious Orders in existence. To forget about that was bordering on insanity. Not to mention the fact that I'd stolen from him once too. The guilt I felt over that still ate at me but there was nothing I could do about it. I had vague intentions to get the crystal back from the pawn shop once I hit up Gabriel Nox for all he was worth, but until that came together I just had to focus on paying Old Sal every month and protecting Ella. The money I was earning from Dante and Ryder was covering the payments, but it wasn't reliable. Some weeks they had several jobs for me, other weeks nothing at all. And I couldn't be late with even one payment. I knew she'd be true to her word about putting Ella straight on the stage the moment I did.*

"What did they steal?" I asked.

"The Heart of Memoriae. It's been in my family for three generations. And some fucker stole it and pawned it. Who the hell in Alestria is stupid enough to pawn something belonging to the Nights? They didn't even take it to some other city to sell! We're gonna pay the asshole who bought it a visit and fix this."

"Okay..." I still didn't know what we were after but Leon seemed to have lost patience with walking.

He started running and I sped after him, wondering why the hell I was going at all but feeling like I had to. His behaviour was so out of character that I didn't even know what to make of it and I had to be sure he was alright. Despite the fact that I'd screwed him over when we first met, Leon Night was one of my best friends in this place and if there was a chance that he needed my help then I was gonna be there for him.

We ran across campus and headed straight for the parking lot which was to the left of Altair Halls.

Leon led the way to a flashy orange sports car and I let out a low whistle as he hit the button on his key fob and the Faeseratti unlocked with a bleep and a flash of its headlights.

"This is your car?" I asked in astonishment.

"It is now," he replied. "I dunno who the asshole was who paid for it originally, but his loss is my gain." There was none of Leon's usual jokey attitude, he just presented me with the facts before dropping into the driver's seat.

I hurried around to the passenger side and barely felt my ass hit the expensive as shit leather before he tore out of the parking lot. The gates at the front of the school were open and he shot out onto the highway so fast that I was pressed back into my seat.

My heart pounded and I quickly clipped my seatbelt on as he pressed his foot to the floor and we flew away from Aurora Academy at nearly three times the speed limit.

"Ah, Leon, do you think that maybe-"

I screamed like a fucking girl as a horn blared and Leon swerved an eighteen wheeler, overtaking it on the wrong side of the road before swerving back into lane again.

I stopped talking, gripping either side of my chair instead as I just concentrated on praying to the stars that we didn't die. Headlights flashed by in a blur and Leon didn't slow one bit.

He took an exit and started speeding down the back streets, taking lefts and rights so quickly that I hardly saw them but I slowly realised that I recognised this part of the city. We weren't far from Mom's crappy apartment where her and Elise would be curled up in bed right about now. Old Sal's strip club was beyond the next set of lights and the entire contents of the world I'd grown up in was all within walking distance.

Leon bumped the car up onto the curb, a horrible screech sounding as the sports car bottomed out on the concrete. He either didn't notice or didn't care.

He leapt out of the car and prowled straight towards the twenty-four hour pawn shop whose red lights were creating a warm glow on the sidewalk. His hair was wild about his shoulders and his chest was still bare. I didn't know who we were going to find in this place, but I hoped they just gave Leon back whatever the hell they'd taken from him because it seemed like he'd completely lost his shit over it.

Leon threw the door open and a little bell rang a moment before the glass door hit the wall so hard that it shattered into a thousand pieces.

I leapt back, cringing as Leon released a roar loud enough to send fear spiralling through me. I'd never seen him like this. Not even close and I was suddenly worried about the guy he was looking for.

"I want to talk to you about a piece of my family's property that you purchased!" he bellowed as he headed further into the store and I followed cautiously, unsure if I was insane to do so or not.

Glass crunched beneath my sneakers as I moved into the darkened store. Shelves lined the walls, stacked to the roof with all sorts of pawned items.

My gaze was drawn straight to the Fae behind the counter as he got to his feet and raised a handful of fire in his palms.

"I don't know anything about that, Mr Night," he said and I was surprised that he recognised Leon so easily. Had I been stupid to ignore the fact that his family was one of the most powerful names in Alestria? Maybe I should have thought more about what that really meant before now. "But if you think there's anything in my store that belongs to your family then I'm sure-"

Leon slammed his finger down on the glass counter and growled in warning. "That, belongs to me."

I couldn't see what he was pointing at, but the shopkeeper quickly reached beneath the counter and tossed it to him.

"I wasn't here when that came in. I think one of the weekend boys or-"

Leon roared again and the guy's fire stuttered out. He stumbled backwards and a floppy brown toupee fell from his head. I almost laughed but the taste of Leon's rage in the air held me silent.

"Hold this for me, Gareth." Leon looked over his shoulder at me and tossed me a small white object. I caught it but I couldn't tear my eyes away from him to look at what it was.

"You've got what you wanted, Leon," I said quickly as fire ten times more powerful than the pawnbroker's had been sprang to life in his hands. "Why don't we just-"

"You will tell me who brought this in here," Leon demanded and the shopkeeper backed up fearfully.

With a burst of energy, the pawnbroker turned and fled through a door behind the counter.

Leon released a roar so loud and terrifying that I dropped into a crouch, throwing my arms over my head defensively before I could stop myself.

A scream sounded beyond the counter and I looked up again just in time to see an enormous Lion bound over it before disappearing through the door as Leon took chase.

I scrambled after him, almost tripping on his abandoned sweatpants and sneakers before I vaulted the counter and shoved my way through the door.

A terrified scream sounded ahead of me and I raced out into a stone courtyard where Leon had pounced on the pawnbroker and had his entire torso clamped in his powerful jaws. I'd never seen Leon in his Lion form before and my lips parted as I stared at him. He was gigantic, bigger than a shire horse and powerful enough to rival a Dragon.

I froze in place, my fist locked around the thing he'd tossed me and a strange sensation seeping from it into my skin.

"He was a big guy!" the pawnbroker was screaming, pain lending his words a pitchy tone. "Bald head! I think he works nearby but I didn't get his name!"

My fingers uncurled slowly as dread flooded through my chest. I was shaking, afraid of what I'd find when I looked at what Leon had retrieved from the store. Because if he would go this far to punish the person who had bought it, what would he do to the one who'd stolen it in the first place?

I opened my hand and my worst nightmare was confirmed as I recognised the crystal I'd stolen from him. The one Petri had pawned for me so I could pay Old Sal.

Leon roared again and I recoiled as he threw the shopkeeper to the ground before pouncing on him once more.

His screams were shrill and desperate and the most horrifying sound of breaking bones followed as I stared down at the crystal in my hand, wondering if I was about to find myself at the mercy of a Lion at any moment.

I should run. I should just fucking run and-

The next scream was so loud and filled with agony that I couldn't help but look back up. It cut off abruptly and Leon shook his head to the side before tossing a severed arm against the wall with a sickening thump.

My mouth fell open and I could only stare, frozen to the spot in horror as Leon reared back into his Fae form. He was covered in blood, his naked flesh slick with it and it ran through his mane of hair, staining it a deep red.

He leaned over the pawnbroker who seemed to have passed out and reached forward to heal the stump where his arm should have been before he bled out

I could only stare on, wondering if he was going to turn on me next, my mind blank and panic gripping me.

"That asshole won't cross the Nights again," Leon said darkly as he strode towards me, plucking the crystal from my grip and holding it up to the light of the moon for a moment. "Thanks for your help."

467

I nodded mutely, not knowing how I'd helped at all and wondering what the fuck had just happened. He didn't seem to be aiming a shred of anger at me though and his usual demeanour appeared to be sliding back into place as if he hadn't just mutilated that guy for buying something that had been stolen from him.

Leon started humming as he headed back into the storefront and I followed him, not knowing what else I should do.

He pulled his sweatpants back on then headed out of the shop with me trotting along behind him.

Leon turned back to the store and called on his fire Element again. My eyes widened as he threw two huge fireballs into the store and he raised his hands as he commanded the fire to burn thicker, faster, hotter. After a few moments, Leon snapped his fist shut and the raging fire went out. All that was left of the store was a charcoal husk of nothing. No CCTV, no DNA, no fingerprints...no nothing. It was just gone.

When Leon Night snapped, he snapped hard.

Leon hopped back into his car and I dropped into the passenger seat as he started the engine. He tossed the crystal into my lap like he didn't give two shits about it despite the insanity I'd just witnessed.

"Keep hold of that for me, will you?" he asked casually like we were chatting about the weather. "Just for a few months or so. In case the FIB come asking questions about it. If I don't have it there isn't any evidence."

"Okay," I agreed, not seeming to have a choice. I slid the crystal into my pocket and Leon flashed me a bright smile. I wondered if he knew how much blood was coating his skin.

"Thanks, dude. You're a good friend," he said as he reached out to turn on the radio.

"You too," I replied because Leon had to be my friend. Now and always. I'd seen what happened to people who got on his bad side and that sure as shit wasn't going to be me.

A song came on that he seemed to like and he started singing at the top of his voice while I tried to get my erratic heartbeat back under control.

I just had to hope that he never managed to track down Petri. Because if he ever found out that I was the one who had stolen from him, I was pretty sure Leon Night would kill me.

LEON

CHAPTER THIRTY EIGHT

"Are you ready for your surprise, little monster?" I whispered in Elise's ear as she ground her ass against me on the dance floor. I was rock hard. She knew it. I knew it. Even the band knew it. And I was definitely down with that. We'd had several drinks and I'd fetched them all. Like a damn saint.

"If it's your dick, it's not much of a surprise," Elise said, sliding her hand around the back of my neck as her ass ground into me again. Fuck. Me. Sideways. I didn't think I'd ever been this hot for a girl before. I was doing stuff for her. Actual nice gestures. It didn't make any sense, but it felt like a freaking rollercoaster ride I didn't wanna get off of.

"Damn, I tied a ribbon around it and everything," I joked and she laughed, her tits rising and falling with every note of the song that was playing. I gripped her waist and flipped her around, grinning mischievously.

"Hm, well if there *is* a ribbon…" She bit her lip, her eyes dancing with the game.

"Finish your sentence," I commanded and she laughed again, pressing a hand to my chest and tip-toeing up to speak into my ear.

"Maybe I want to untie it with my teeth."

Dammit, why didn't I go with the dick ribbon idea?

My manhood twitched happily and I groaned into her neck, tugging her closer. I was tipsy, so was she. We were both hot for each other, so why did it feel like I still wasn't gonna get laid tonight?

Elise stepped away, catching my hand and twirling herself beneath it. I smirked, reaching into my back pocket and taking out the surprise I had for her. Which was a far cry from a dick ribbon. I handed her the small box which I'd wrapped in red paper my damn self.

"No Mindys were involved in the purchasing of this gift," I told her with a smile which was slightly more nervous than my last.

What if she hates it?

Elise's brows lifted as she tore the paper off and I handed it to a Mindy who was walking by. The velvet blue box set my pulse racing and Elise lifted her eyes to me with a question in them.

"You didn't buy me jewellery, did you?" she asked and I could not fucking tell if she wanted jewellery or not. Either way, it wasn't what was in that box.

"Just open it," I sighed impatiently and she flipped it open, her eyes landing on the gift inside.

A fat silver coin sat in it engraved with a drawing of a furry little monster with her nickname etched into the top of it. I hooked my own one out of my pocket, showing her the engraving I'd had done of a Lion with the words *Leo the Lion* arching over the top.

It was childish and stupid and *us*. I just hoped she liked it.

She grinned at the coin, twisting it between her fingers. "You had this made for me?"

"Yeah." I ran a hand down the back of my neck, fighting away my nerves at the next part. "Will you come with me? I wanna show you where these go." I stepped away, holding out my hand for her to take and she hesitated.

"Where to?" she asked, a flash of distrust in her eyes.

I frowned. Hadn't I done enough to make her trust me yet?

"Are you really gonna make me ruin the surprise?" I gave her my biggest eyes and she chewed her lip, sliding her hand into mine.

"Well I suppose we wouldn't want that."

I towed her along, feeling stupidly happy as we headed outside and circled around to the back of the sports hall. I led her along the path to Rigel Library then pulled her up short in front of the old stone wishing well that sat out front. A wooden roof covered it but the chain and bucket had been missing before I'd started at Aurora.

I perched on the wall and Elise pressed her hands to it, leaning over the edge.

"Careful, Elise, you wouldn't wanna fall down there," I said in a dark tone. "Legend has it…a freshman was pushed in nearly a hundred years ago. The bullies who did it poured Faesine on top of him then cast a silencing bubble around the well." I leaned in closer, her lips parted as she fell captive to the story. "The kid was a fire Elemental and the moment he cast a flame to see by, he burned himself alive in the flammable liquid." I paused for dramatic effect and Elise's eyes sparkled at the wild story.

"Is that true?" She narrowed her gaze.

I shrugged. "Everyone says it is."

"That doesn't make it true."

"Fair point." I dropped down from the wall, sliding an arm over her shoulders and drawing her forward to look into the depths with me. She stiffened as if she expected me to throw her in and I chuckled. "They say if you listen *real* carefully, you can hear his moans, begging to bring justice on the bullies who killed him. And every now and then you can hear-" As if on cue a faint clack clack clack sounded from below and Elise lurched away from the edge. I turned to her with a devilish grin. "They say its him banging a rock against the wall, desperate to be heard."

Elise wrapped her arms around herself. "Alright, you're officially creeping me out."

"Na, come on, it's probably not true anyway."

"*Probably*," she deadpanned and I snorted.

"Maybe I shouldn't have led with the creepy ass story. Come back over here and make a wish with me."

"No way in hell am I making a wish in some murder hole."

"They call it The Weeping Well actually, but I think I like murder hole better." I gave her a slanted smile, beckoning her nearer.

Elise lifted her coin to look at it then frowned. "Maybe I don't want to throw it away."

"Well you can't have a wish if you don't," I pointed out.

She stepped closer with a hollow look in her eyes.

"Maybe I don't have any wishes to ask for anymore," she said and a frown pulled at my brow.

"That's pretty sad, little monster. Even the dead kid in that well has wishes."

She broke a smile which sent heat directly to my dick. *Damn.*

She took her sweet time closing the distance between us, but when she did, she brushed her fingers across my jaw and the sensation was a slice of heaven.

"I have a better idea for the coins." She reached into my jacket pocket, taking out my coin and placing her one back in its place. "Now we have a piece of each other to carry around."

She pushed the Leo coin into her cleavage and I could not stop staring as it disappeared. *Fuuuuck.*

"Do you want a few more pieces of me, Elise?" I growled as she pressed her body into mine, her curves moulding to my muscles.

"Actually, Leo, I think I do."

Her breath met my skin, her lips parted and her hooded eyes burned a line of fire right through to my soul. Her mouth met mine and her tongue swept across my lips, making me groan with wanting. I yanked her against me so she could feel what she did to me with only the faintest of touches, wishing I could have more of her.

More more more.

She twisted her fingers between mine then ground herself into my hard on with so much intention I just knew she was trying to drive me to insanity.

I kissed her with nothing of the laziness I gave other women. My hand was wrapped in her hair, I was fully fucking engaged, dominating her mouth with my tongue and wondering how it might feel to please *her* instead of myself. "I want to do more for you," I groaned against her mouth. "Let's go somewhere private. Or fuck it, I'll make you come right here on the murder hole."

Elise laughed, deepening our kiss and scraping her nails down the back of my neck. "Maybe I want to do something for you, Leo." She kissed me harder so I couldn't answer and I realised I'd been about to refuse that offer in favour of pleasuring her. *What the fuck is happening to me?*

She drew away long before I was ready for her go, sucking on her lips which were raw from our kiss like she was savouring the taste of me.

"Let's go back to the hall," she said, grinning darkly then promptly turning away and heading off down the path.

I looked up at the stars before I followed, shaking my head at them. *How long are my blue balls on the cards for, assholes? That wasn't in my daily horoscope this morning.*

With a long breath and a good effort at picturing Professor Mars's bare ass to sink my boner, I followed Elise along the path.

When we arrived back at the hall, I followed her into the entranceway, but she caught my hand and dragged me toward the locker rooms instead of heading back to the party.

"Elise?" I questioned in confusion and her laughter rang back to me.

She released my hand, darting into the girl's locker room using her Vampire speed.

I frowned, jogging after her and pushing through the door.

The lights were off and I hunted the wall, searching for the switch, knowing she could see me with her freaking Vampire eyes.

"Dammit, at least give me a clue, little monster, I'm blind in here."

"Here's a clue." Her hand pressed to my crotch and holy mother of the stars, it was on. She unzipped my pants and I reached out for her, finding nothing but air in front of me. *What?*

She tugged my boxers down and wrapped her mouth around my dick, making me swear in a hundred fucking languages I hadn't realised I could speak. I fisted my hand in her hair while searching for the light switch with the other.

Fuck, I wanna see her.

She made a torturous journey down my shaft, taking me all the way in and making every muscle in my body tighten. It was the best blow job I'd ever had and she'd barely started yet. She drew me in and out, her tongue flicking and her lips tightening at all the right moments. It. Was. Life.

I groaned louder, growling her name and yanking her hair. Her mouth was so hot and perfect and the soft moans she made drove me crazy. She sounded like she was enjoying this as much as I was but there was no way in Solaria that was true.

She moved faster, taking me in and out, pleasure chasing her skilful tongue. I was so surprised about this actually happening that I wasn't remotely fucking prepared for it ending.

"Shit shit shit." I tried to hold back but she was too damn good and I was so high on this girl I was surprised my dick hadn't detonated the second she'd touched it.

I slammed my hand onto the wall for the millionth time, needing that damn light switch while Elise laughed, the sound shooting a vibration down my length and making me explode.

I leaned back against the wall as ecstasy ripped me apart. Or maybe it was her doing it. Either way I was in shreds, fucking ruined by this girl. I rode out the wave and she released me from her mouth with a light laugh. She tucked me away, zipped up my pants and pressed a kiss to my mouth as I breathed heavily. Though she'd given me something fucking mind-blowing, she'd done it all in total control of me. And somehow, it still felt like she'd won.

"Let's go back to the party." She flicked on the light switch which was right by my damn head and I winced from the change.

Her beautiful eyes met mine, light skipping through them like a fucking rainbow.

"Yeah. Sure. Anything you want," I panted and she giggled, catching my hand and pulling me toward the door.

I headed after her, dazed and maybe a bit fucking whipped. But hell if I cared. She was the most mouth-watering prey I'd ever encountered and if I had to hunt her to the ends of the world to catch her, I would. I'd chase her tail until she gave me all of her. Every last, delicious bite. And by the end of tonight, I was going to have consumed her.

ELISE

CHAPTER THIRTY NINE

"Elise!" Leon called as he gave chase and I laughed, hurrying away from him down the corridor. "Wait!"

"Didn't you get what you wanted from me?" I teased as I kept going, turning around so that I could walk backwards and grin at him as I went.

"I'm not sure I'll ever be done with you," he joked. At least I assumed it was a joke, but my cheeks flared at the same time. "I'd like to return the favour now."

I laughed again as I kept backing up, heading into the sports hall where the party was still well underway.

I opened my mouth to respond to him but before I could, a wave of strong smelling drink was dumped over my head. I gasped in shock as I wheeled around to find Cindy Lou standing way too fucking close to me with an empty cup in her hand.

"Whoops," she said, her eyes fixed in a hard scowl which was the clearest challenge I'd ever seen.

The red drink coated me, the sticky feel of it seeping right through my hair and sliding down my back, soaking me through.

For a long, long moment I could only stare at her, feeling a hundred sets of eyes on me as I stood there, dripping all over the floor.

My lips twitched. My jaw clenched. My fingers snapped into a fist.

My patience with Cindy Lou and her mean girl crap had come to a spectacular end. And I lost my shit.

I shot towards her with my Vampire speed before she even had a chance to realise what was happening.

My fist collided with her face and I barrelled straight into her chest as I knocked her clean off of her feet and her pale pink dress flew up over her head revealing her orange thong to the room at large.

"Fight!" Leon yelled excitedly behind me and the students all around us backed up to watch.

"You stupid whore!" Cindy Lou screamed and she lurched forward, snaring my legs in her grip as she tried to take me down too. But what kind of idiot doesn't realise that if you catch a Vampire it's because they fucking let you?

My knee slammed into her chin and she screamed as blood poured from her mouth where she'd bitten her tongue but she didn't let go.

I fell on her, slamming my fists into her again and again as I took the same amount of blows from her in return.

With a grunt of effort, she shoved me off of her and I tumbled beneath the legs of the crowd before I could right myself.

People knocked into me, something spilled over my shoulder, someone else reached out and brushed a hand across my face. The sharp scent of almonds sailed under my nose and I jerked up quickly, forcing my way free of the crowd.

The ground seemed to lurch beneath me for a moment and I shook my head as my vision swam. When everything came back into focus again, Cindy Lou was running at me with her fist drawn back and a scream spilling from her lips.

I ducked her blow with my speed, wrapped my arms around her waist and slammed her back down onto the ground.

Pink taffeta exploded everywhere as she lost control of her Order form and I found myself looking up at her in her Centaur form. The lower half of her body was a grey horse while the upper half remained an undeniably pissed off Fae in a push-up bra. She shrieked as she galloped straight for me and the crowd that had gathered to watch stumbled back.

I leapt aside and strong hands steadied me before nudging me back into the ring. I looked around to find Dante watching with a smirk on his face. "Let's see what you've got, bella."

I narrowed my eyes on him and whirled around just as Cindy Lou charged me down again.

This time I held my ground, drawing air into my fist and coiling it into the shape of a football before tossing it at Cindy's face as hard as I could.

Her head snapped back as she took the hit, her body twisting awkwardly and horsey legs flailing as she was overbalanced.

Someone whooped in the crowd and she retreated back into her Fae form as she hit the ground hard.

I moved forward to finish this fight but the wooden floor bucked and shifted beneath my feet. Which couldn't be right because I was pretty sure Cindy Lou had the Element of fire.

She does, see, she's casting a pretty flame right now.

Cindy's fireball hit me in the legs and my alcohol soaked skirt went up in flames like a pile of tinder.

I looked down at the fire, a laugh bubbling in my throat as the pretty colours danced around my legs. I spun in a circle, doing a pirouette of flames as a few people nearby screamed. It was so pretty, so, so pretty and-

"Motherfucker!" I shouted in alarm as the fire brushed against my skin and it *burned.*

481

I stole the oxygen from the flames with a snap of my fingers and they disappeared, leaving me with fucking Cindy Poo again.

"Did your mother name you after a turd on purpose, Cindy Poo?" I taunted as I strode towards her, more laughter bubbling from my lips.

The ground was rocky, bumpy, bubbly and my feet trippy tripped a little as I went.

I pointed at Cindy but she wasn't Cindy, she was Gabriel who was frowning at me from the crowd like I'd gone fucking insane.

"You're the one who changes his mind every five seconds!" I shouted at him. "You give me whiplash. WHIP LASH!"

People were muttering, murmuring, saying strange and silly things. I caught the word *Blazer* more than once and wondered who they meant.

Cindy slammed into me from behind and I crashed to the ground hard. I twisted beneath her and she punched me in the face.

Laughter bubbled from my lips.

"You're naked," I pointed out like she wasn't aware that her big horse ass had snapped her thong like a cheese string and popped her dress like a...a...

Cindy Poo punched me again which was really fucking rude because I still hadn't come up with an accurate description for what her big horse ass had done to her dress.

The third time she hit me I stopped laughing and reared up to meet her, slamming my forehead into the bridge of her nose.

She fell back and I was up like a flash of light.

I was still laughing but then this *was* pretty fucking funny.

With a twist of my fingers I stole the air from her lungs and stalked closer, only stumbling on the land bubbles twice.

Cindy started panicking, clutching at her chest as she stared up at me in horror.

"I want you to say something for me," I whispered to her.

Her eyes widened and I waited for her to reply but she didn't which was really fucking rude. I waited. And waited. And someone was tittering in the crowd which was *so* fucking rude because Cindy still hadn't said what I wanted her to and she was turning blue-

"Oh!" I laughed and let her take a breath which she did, gasping like a fish. "I want you to say 'I'm Cindy Poo and my big horse ass busted out of my dress like a...'"

Her eyes flared with defiance but I stole her air again because I didn't wanna hear it. Not one bit.

I still didn't have an end for that sentence and it was driving me goddamn insane but I gave up on it with a huff.

"Fine," I snapped. "Just say 'I'm Cindy Poo'."

I waited and waited and she started nodding just as a bluebird landed on her head and did a dance. That was pretty fucking weird but she didn't seem to mind it.

I let her breathe again and gave her a psycho smile as I waited for her to say it.

"I'm Cindy...poo," she breathed and I couldn't help but laugh again.

"Damn fucking straight you are!" I turned and walked away from her naked ass, throwing my hands into the air as the dancing came for me.

The crowd erupted into calls of laughter and people congratulated me, slapping me on the back and the ass. Which was a bit weird but then there was a cheetah playing the guitar in the corner of the room and no one minded him.

Strong arms circled me and I twisted in them, finding Dante Oscura holding onto me.

"Are you high, carina?" he asked me with a faint frown.

I laughed, reaching up to touch his face because I'd always wanted to just touch his fucking face and there it was like he wanted it too so why the hell not?

"I don't take drugs, silly," I replied.

My fingers swept across the line of his jaw and I released a breathy moan as I brushed my thumb across his lips.

Dante tilted his head as he inspected me then suddenly I was flying. Well, not flying so much as cuddle-walking as he carried me away, away, away...

I leaned against his chest and the scent of him wrapped around me like a warm embrace. I breathed in deep, closing my eyes and just being with him for a long moment.

The cold bit at me and I opened my eyes again to find us outside.

Dante shifted his hand until his fingers were touching the burn on my leg and I hissed between my teeth before his healing magic slid into me and took the pain away.

"I'm sorry about Cindy," he said with half a smile on his face. "That was kinda my fault."

"God you're so conceited, I wasn't fighting her for *you*," I replied with a snort of disbelief.

Dante chuckled and a shiver ran through me. I really liked that sound.

"I mean, she attacked you because of something I said," he explained.

"What?" I asked suspiciously. Because I was a detective. So I'd detect this too.

"Well, she was on her knees, about to show me a good time," he explained and I wrinkled my nose in disgust at that but he hadn't stopped trying to scar me mentally because he kept talking. "And I might have realised I really wanted someone else...and I might have told Cindy to stop because of her."

"Who?" I asked, wondering if I was going to have to punch that bitch too.

Dante raised an eyebrow like I was the one being dumb and I folded my arms, waiting him out.

"You," he said eventually and I couldn't help but smile a big fat smug smile at that. At least until I remembered what he'd been doing while he thought about me and then I was scowling again. And maybe going to puke.

"Do you want to tell me what you took?" Dante asked as he sat me down on a low wall.

"Nothing!" I protested, getting annoyed at him for asking again. "I don't take drugs. Drugs kill people. They kill the best, best people..."

I flinched as Dante swept a thumb across my cheek, catching a tear I never meant to let fall and dropping to his knees before me. His eyes found mine and for an endless moment I could only stare into the depths of them.

"You're so beautiful," I breathed to him and he laughed, the sound waking me up a little.

"Beautiful? Now I know you're wasted," Dante said.

"I'm not," I snapped. He was annoying me now. Why did he have to talk? I liked looking at his face when there wasn't any noise coming out of it.

"You can tell me. It looks like you're on Killblaze if I was going to guess," he added.

My lips parted and I shook my head, shook it so damn hard that my thoughts fell out and everything looked black for a moment then red then a kind of pastel blue...

I was blink, blink, blinking and I wasn't sure it was helping. And if blinking couldn't help then what? Then *what*??

I was breathing too fast or too slow, definitely not at the regular speed and I didn't know how to stop it.

"Wait here for me, carina," Dante said, rising to his feet.

I wanted to call him back but my voice had up and died. I wrapped my arms around myself as I lost sight of the path and sports hall and all of it and I tipped my head back to look at the stars. The stars which were always mocking me. And they were laughing now because I was going to die.

My heart was beating too fast. The edges of everything seemed blurry. And I was alone. All alone ever since Gareth had left me. And I was so, so mad at him for leaving me. Leaving me all alone. All alone forever.

I was crying. *No.* It hurt so fucking much that I didn't think I'd ever stop. Tears just poured and poured from me in a never ending torrent.

I was flying in strong arms again but I couldn't open my eyes to look at him this time. Maybe he was taking me back to our room and I could curl up with him again like the last time I wasn't well.

But this time it wasn't the same. And I was forgetting all the important bits anyway so all I could do was float away until I was gone, gone, gone...

GABRIEL

CHAPTER FORTY

I stood in the crowd, hunting for Elise, confused about the strange fucking drama show she'd just put on. But my gut told me something was wrong. And that was confirmed tenfold as a vision slammed into me, one of the sharpest I'd ever been gifted. It rang in my head like a gong and grabbed hold of me body and soul.

A dark and winding tunnel. Elise in the woods. Voices chanting. Then an endless scream which burned a hole in my heart.

"Fuck!" I scared everyone around me as I stumbled forward, the vision clearing as I forced students aside with a wall of vines conjured from my palms. Some of them fell, but I didn't give a shit, my heart hitting a frantic beat as I threw my jacket to the ground, ripped my shirt off and let my wings burst from my shoulder blades.

I ran for the doors, pushing them open and taking off into the sky without a single glance back.

Hold the fuck on, Elise. I'm coming for you.

I raced across campus on silent wings, drawing on The Sight, begging it to do my bidding for once. It was always so volatile, just within my grasp but never coming to me when I needed it most.

Show me her, dammit.

I sped over The Iron Wood, swooping low, listening, searching.

She's here somewhere, I know it.

"Elise!" I called into the shadows, praying for them to reply.

My eyes whipped back and forth, but the darkness was thick and the forest stretched on for miles and miles. My skin was itching, the Libra tattoo on my chest on fire like it knew she was in trouble. Hell, if I hadn't wanted to accept we were Elysian Mates before, I was really getting the message now.

"Help me!" I called upon the stars, gazing up at them and asking for their mercy.

Their light fell over me and a vision swam before my eyes. Elise laughing, then crying, I could almost feel her mind in a haze and I knew for a fact she was drugged. For a second the connection was so powerful that my own mind became fuzzy. I'd never felt someone else's forecast before but I could feel hers like she was an extension of me. And maybe she fucking was.

She was blind, but I could feel hard stone as she crashed to her knees. Strong hands gripped her shoulders and pure rage found me, burning right into the depths of my soul.

I will kill whoever those hands belong to.

"Elise!" I bellowed again before a searing sensation in my Libra tattoo jolted me out of the reverie.

I lost focus, crashing into the canopy and hitting my shins against the branches. I curled my wings around me to soften the blows, my heart in my throat as I tumbled lower and lower. I wielded the power of earth and the trees reached out to me, cushioning my fall in a net of leafy branches before I hit the ground

I groaned, righting myself and healing the wounds I'd sustained, blood coating my fingers as I did so. Before I was done, an idea struck me and I dropped down to the forest floor, digging my hands into the damp soil.

I closed my eyes and pushed my will into the dirt. I became detached from my body, using powerful magic to feel out into the world around me. Tunnels spread out like a spider's web deep underground. I felt the passages splitting and forking a hundred times and I searched for a warm body, for Elise amongst the cold, wet earth that stretched for miles around me.

Finally, I latched onto something burning hot. A fire. The soil alight with heat beneath it. I lifted my head and sprang upright, spreading my wings and launching myself into the trees.

I landed on a branch high up in the canopy and started to run, controlling the trees around me as I raced across their limbs, springing from one to the next. I bent the branches to my will, meeting every one of my footfalls so I never faltered, racing on and on.

Voices carried to my ears and I slowed my pace, coming to a halt in the arms of an oak tree and lowering to a crouch. I waited a long moment before they appeared then three figures arrived on the path dissecting the woodland beneath me. Two of them wore hooded robes and I knew on instinct they were part of the Black Card. Between them was a boy with yellow hair and reddened eyes. They each held one of his arms, guiding him along as he gazed up at the trees, laughing to himself like he was having the time of his life.

"There's so much wood out here," he mused, seeming high. "How many books could they make from all this wood? A thousand at least. At *least* a thousand."

The members of the Black Card ignored him, towing him through the trees beneath me and I stilled as the stoned guy looked up. "Ohhhh flappy wings. Look how flappy they are! *Haaa.* A bird with a man's head."

I shrank deeper into the shadows, but the Black Card weren't paying his nonsense any attention luckily for me.

As they moved deeper into the woods, I followed them through the canopy, my jaw tight as I feared what I might find at the end of this trail. It wasn't exactly my style to go chasing after Fae to help them. But Elise wasn't just any Fae. She was bonded to me so deeply that abandoning her now simply wasn't an option. The bond between us was impossible to ignore, it possessed me heart and soul. All my work at breaking it was coming undone and I was a slave to it, bound in shackles like the ones inked onto my wrists.

I'm close. I sense you. I hope you sense me too and you know just how much pain I'm gonna rain down on the assholes who took you.

The chanting from my vision reached me from afar and panic tore through my limbs as I moved even faster. I didn't know what awaited me up ahead, but I was prepared to face it. For her.

ELISE

CHAPTER FORTY ONE

The warm arms which carried me didn't do enough to combat the cold and my teeth chattered as we moved through the dark.

We were underground, deep, deep below the earth where the worms would eat me up if I got lost. I giggled at the thought of that and a growl sounded from the man who was carrying me. He was so strong, so big and strong. I felt like I knew him but it was too dark to see anything so I wasn't sure.

Suddenly the moon was shining down on me and I gasped as I looked up at its pale face. It seemed sad and that made me sad too. I took a deep breath which burrowed down into the core of me where all my grief and pain lay waiting like an open wound. Always looking for a way to claim me. Never letting me forget for long.

I was dropped to the floor and I didn't flinch in time, hitting the ground hard and tasting blood as my lip busted open. I hissed in pain and licked my lip, the call of my own power like a strange kind of temptation. Could I drink my own blood? What would it taste like? Cherry gum and lies probably. That was all I was these days.

Someone grabbed my wrist and yanked me upright before I could think on it any more and I looked up at them to find their face hidden within a deep hood.

I blinked at them but they didn't give me a chance to look any closer before tugging me along.

"Are we going to a party?" I asked.

"Something like that," they responded and I was sure I knew their voice. Or did I? Had it been a man or a woman? Now that I thought on it more closely I wasn't entirely sure.

An owl hooted in the trees and I swivelled as I hooted a response, trying to spot the creature in the branches overhead. He was my friend. And he wanted me to join him in the deep dark wood.

"Hurry up, the King doesn't like to be kept waiting."

"I've been looking for a King," I murmured and for a moment I was sure I could see a crown hanging between the trees ahead of us. But when I looked closer it was a cabin. Not a crown at all.

I laughed as I realised how stupid I'd been to think it was a crown, laughing and laughing until I could hardly breathe. I doubled over, clutching my waist and my helper yanked me back into their arms.

There was a crowd of dancers wearing black cloaks which covered their bodies and hid their faces, all waiting for us before the cabin with a huge fire burning between them.

I was dropped on the wooden porch and the crowd started chanting forcefully. I frowned at them as their words started to chip away at my mask.

They were pulling me apart, making me look at my grief again and holding my head in place so that I couldn't turn away from it.

There was nothing and no one apart from the abyss echoing endlessly inside me.

I saw my brother, the last time I'd ever seen him when he left me to come back to the academy after Christmas. He pulled me in for a hug and I didn't hold on long enough, pushing him back and telling him not to get glitter in my hair.

Oh how I missed finding glitter in my hair.

I'd cried alone in my bunk for an hour the first time I'd brushed it and found nothing glimmering in my hairbrush. I'd missed Cardinal Magic and told the professor I'd gotten sick. And I had. In my heart. And my soul.

I was so sick that I knew it would kill me. This grief was a cancer, slowly eating away at everything I used to be.

Sometimes it seemed like I forgot about it but that wasn't so. Because every move I made, every action I took came back to him. To this lie I was telling by pretending not to know him. To this injustice that had taken place when someone had killed him. Forced him to take that fucking drug. Just like they'd forced me to take it now too.

My heart was still beating too fast and I knew it was the Killblaze soaking through my limbs. There was no cure for it. Fae drugs were made to be immune to healing magic. So when my heart finally reached the climax of this desperate race it was running, I knew it could only end one way for me.

Death.

And maybe that wasn't so bad. Gareth would be there waiting for me in the stars. I'd have him back and maybe I'd be whole again in the afterlife. Maybe, maybe, maybe.

A thump sounded beside me and I turned my head as a sandy haired boy stumbled to his feet on the porch to my right. Beyond him was a girl with raven hair who was laughing so hard she could barely breathe. She reminded me of Cindy Poo and in an instant I was laughing too.

She'd said it. Fucking said her name was Cindy Poo in front of everyone!

I didn't even know how I'd managed to make that happen, but it would go down in history as one of the greatest accomplishments of my life. Maybe one of the last ones too...

The chanting stopped suddenly and I looked up as footsteps approached me. The cabin door opened in front of me and the trees billowed in a wind I couldn't feel as a loud creak sounded the arrival of the person we'd been waiting for.

A robed figure drew nearer, pausing before the boy on my right and running their gaze over all three of us.

It was definitely a woman, though I couldn't see anything of the face beneath the hood which was drawn up to conceal them. But everything about their bulky frame and broad shoulders told me it was a man...or had I thought it was a woman? I frowned as I tried to figure it out again but the more I looked at them the less sure I was; they were curvy then tall, thin then short, broad then slight. Everything and nothing all at once. I didn't know if it was the Killblaze or some magic they'd cast to conceal themselves but each time I tried to figure it out I only felt more confused.

"Do any of you poor, lost souls wish to offer your power up to the light?" he asked, his voice soft and lilting, utterly feminine.

For a moment I caught sight of the face beneath the hood and gasped as I recognised Gabriel.

"Your sacrifice must be given freely. You must choose death and give your powers to me as you pass for the magic to cleanse you. And if you do, it will banish all of your pain, erase your heartache, consume your grief...and leave you pure and free of it in the afterlife," he said. I blinked and realised it wasn't Gabriel at all; it was Ryder.

His hand reached out towards me and I almost took it as the pain in me welled up sharply. But I hesitated as I searched for the tattoos which should have been on his knuckles, shaking my head in confusion as I realised it wasn't Ryder either. It was Laini...or Cindy Poo...Principal Greyshine... Leon...Gareth-

My heart squeezed as my brother looked down at me and the tears I'd been fighting fell free, running down my cheeks in an endless flow.

"I'm sorry," I choked out. "I should have seen that you were in trouble.

I should have done more-"

I reached for him but he was moving away from me to the sandy haired boy beside me who was murmuring something over and over again.

My heart thundered in my ears but I managed to tune it out for a moment to listen to him.

"Make it stop, I'm ready, I'm ready, I'm ready-"

My lips parted as I took in his broken expression and the hooded figure leaned closer eagerly.

"You must make the sacrifice yourself," she breathed, egging him on, encouraging him to take his life.

"Don't," I gasped, wondering if I was imagining this or if it was real. Because so much seemed so strange to me right now that I just didn't know. And with that poison in my veins it could be a long time before I found out. If I ever did at all - I was still almost certain I was going to die once the drug ran its course.

"Thank you," the boy breathed, opening his palm and growing a coil of vines with his earth magic which reached up and wrapped themselves around his throat.

I stared on as they began to squeeze, his own magic choking him while he did nothing to stop it. A euphoric smile lit his face and the cloaked figure groaned as the rest of the crowd started chanting again.

Their words were spoken in no language I knew, but they made the hairs stand to attention along my flesh, fear coursing through me in a wave.

"Stop it!" I demanded, lurching towards the sandy haired boy, meaning to make him stop if he wouldn't listen, but I somehow managed to throw myself backwards instead of towards him.

I fell off of the porch and down to the ground on my back. The breath was driven from my lungs as pain speared along my spine.

I wheezed and laughed and thrashed about, unsure what the hell to even do with my body.

Hands clutched at me, one after another, more and more of them trying to force me to my feet. I screamed, smacking and kicking and biting as I fought to get their scaly claws off of me.

They stumbled aside as I managed to use my Vampire strength and more than a few of them cursed and howled as I broke bones and drew blood.

The crowd parted and I was suddenly looking right into the eyes of the sandy haired boy. He lay on the porch, eyes wide and unseeing as death stole him away on swift wings.

My eyes widened in shock and I looked beyond him, finding the robed figure there, moaning in pleasure as a soft green light seemed to spill from the corpse and into him. There was something about the way the light moved that stirred up recognition in me. When unformed, Earth magic was that colour, the colour of nature and life. I'd seen it conjured by earth students in class. Somehow, that monster was stealing his magic in the moment of his death.

This was more than just some crazy cult. It was the darkest of black magic. The kind that was only ever whispered about in shadowy corners before being hastily hushed and forgotten. The kind that shouldn't have existed at all. Because the root of it was so evil that no one who touched it could survive with their soul intact.

My mind spun to Gareth and my hammering heart sped up further still.

I cried out, a savage snarl leaving my lips as I leapt at the figure, fully intending to rip them limb from limb. Because suddenly I knew. I *knew*. That this was the King who'd killed my brother. And I was going to tear him into pieces with my bare hands or die trying.

Before I could get close, a missile of fire crashed into me, knocking me back down into the crowd. Someone else cast vines to hold me and a shower of frozen daggers shot at me next.

I threw an arm up, scattering the ice blades with a whip of wind and whooping in triumph. But still more of the cult threw magic at me to keep me down.

This wasn't right. Fae fought one on one for their position, never like this. All of them stood against me as I battled the fog of Killblaze which clouded my mind.

More fire flew my way and I screamed as it came crashing right for my head.

Before it could reach me, a torrent of water slammed down over my body, dousing the flames and making my skin come alive. It was like the wetness I could feel was the result of a thousand kisses against my flesh instead of water.

I tipped my head back to the moon as the cool wind blew over me and for a moment, clarity prevailed and I tried to shake my head to clear it of the drug once and for all.

I looked around just as black wings sailed overhead and my hammering heart reached a terrifying crescendo. It didn't matter that I was fighting. Because I couldn't win against the Killblaze. It had me in its grasp and I could tell I wasn't going to survive it.

I threw my hands out as more magic was aimed my way and cast a shockwave of air to slam out from me, launching the full weight of my power into the blow.

The hooded figures fell back, the chanting ceased and the King retreated into his cabin at a fierce pace.

Before I could think about how to fight back next, arms closed around me and I was lifted off of the ground.

A shriek left my lips as I twisted in my captor's grip but he only tightened his hold, hoisting me up until I was pressed against his chest and his arm was hooked beneath my legs.

"Gabriel?" I breathed, blinking several times to see if his face was going to change or not.

"I've got you," he replied, his tone dark as we swept higher, leaving the cult behind and bursting through the canopy until we were heading straight for the moon which hung low and fat in the sky.

Gabriel beat his wings powerfully and we sped away over the woods, gaining height with each passing second.

The wind whipped around me and it felt like I was breathing clean air for the first time all night.

My pounding heart finally started to slow and the shaking in my fingers eased off.

Maybe I was going to survive this after all.

I leaned closer to Gabriel, stealing strength from the warmth of his arms around me and the fierce expression on his face.

I reached up to touch his cheek, a shiver running through me as his gaze shifted to meet mine.

"You rescued me," I breathed.

Gabriel frowned like he was going to disagree but he released a growl instead.

"They were going to kill you," he said grimly. "I saw it through the stars. And for a moment I thought I was going to be too late. I wanted to rip them all apart but every way that played out ended in your death. Your only chance was to get you away from them."

I shook my head, unable to get a grasp on what had happened.

I drew closer to Gabriel, tightening my hold on him as I laid my ear against his chest and listened to the steady thrum of his heart, willing mine to match the pace of his.

My memories were a tangled web of confusion and fog, but some things stood out and I wasn't going to forget them.

I'd seen the King tonight and he'd seen me too. I just had to try and figure out which face belonged to him. Or if any of them had.

And more than that; someone had gone to great lengths to get me in front of him.

I didn't know if it meant they'd figured out my connection to Gareth, or if I'd just asked one too many questions and drawn too much attention to myself.

But it didn't matter.

Because now I knew I was getting close.

I'd looked into the Devil's eyes and lived to tell the tale. I wouldn't be caught out the next time. And there would be a next time. Because I was closing in on the answers I sought. And I wouldn't stop digging until I unveiled them and their guilty blood was spilled.

ALSO BY

CAROLINE PECKHAM

&

SUSANNE VALENTI

Brutal Boys of Everlake Prep

(Complete Reverse Harem Bully Romance Contemporary Series)

Kings of Quarantine

Kings of Lockdown

Kings of Anarchy

Queen of Quarentine

Dead Men Walking

(Reverse Harem Dark Romance Contemporary Series)

The Death Club

Society of Psychos

**

The Harlequin Crew

(Reverse Harem Mafia Romance Contemporary Series)

Sinners Playground

Dead Man's Isle

Carnival Hill

Paradise Lagoon

Harlequinn Crew Novellas

Devil's Pass

**

Dark Empire

(Dark Mafia Contemporary Standalones)

Beautiful Carnage

Beautiful Savage

**

The Ruthless Boys of the Zodiac

(Reverse Harem Paranormal Romance Series - Set in the world of Solaria)

Dark Fae

Savage Fae

Vicious Fae

Broken Fae

Warrior Fae

Zodiac Academy

(M/F Bully Romance Series- Set in the world of Solaria, five years after Dark Fae)

The Awakening

Ruthless Fae

The Reckoning

Shadow Princess

Cursed Fates

Fated Thrones

Heartless Sky

The Awakening - As told by the Boys

Zodiac Academy Novellas

Origins of an Academy Bully

The Big A.S.S. Party

Darkmore Penitentiary

(Reverse Harem Paranormal Romance Series - Set in the world of Solaria,
ten years after Dark Fae)

Caged Wolf

Alpha Wolf

Feral Wolf

**

The Age of Vampires

(Complete M/F Paranormal Romance/Dystopian Series)

Eternal Reign

Eternal Shade

Eternal Curse

Eternal Vow

Eternal Night

Eternal Love

**

Cage of Lies

(M/F Dystopian Series)

Rebel Rising

**

Tainted Earth

(M/F Dystopian Series)

Afflicted

Altered

Adapted

Advanced

**

The Vampire Games

(Complete M/F Paranormal Romance Trilogy)

V Games

V Games: Fresh From The Grave

V Games: Dead Before Dawn

*

The Vampire Games: Season Two

(Complete M/F Paranormal Romance Trilogy)

Wolf Games

Wolf Games: Island of Shade

Wolf Games: Severed Fates

*

The Vampire Games: Season Three

Hunter Trials

*

The Vampire Games Novellas

A Game of Vampires

**

The Rise of Issac

(Complete YA Fantasy Series)

Creeping Shadow

Bleeding Snow

Turning Tide

Weeping Sky

Failing Light

Printed in the USA
CPSIA information can be obtained
at www.ICGtesting.com
CBHW030920140724
11443CB00027B/31